A WHOLE LOT

Copyright © 2015 Bradley Wind

All rights reserved.

ISBN: 978-0-9972805-0-0

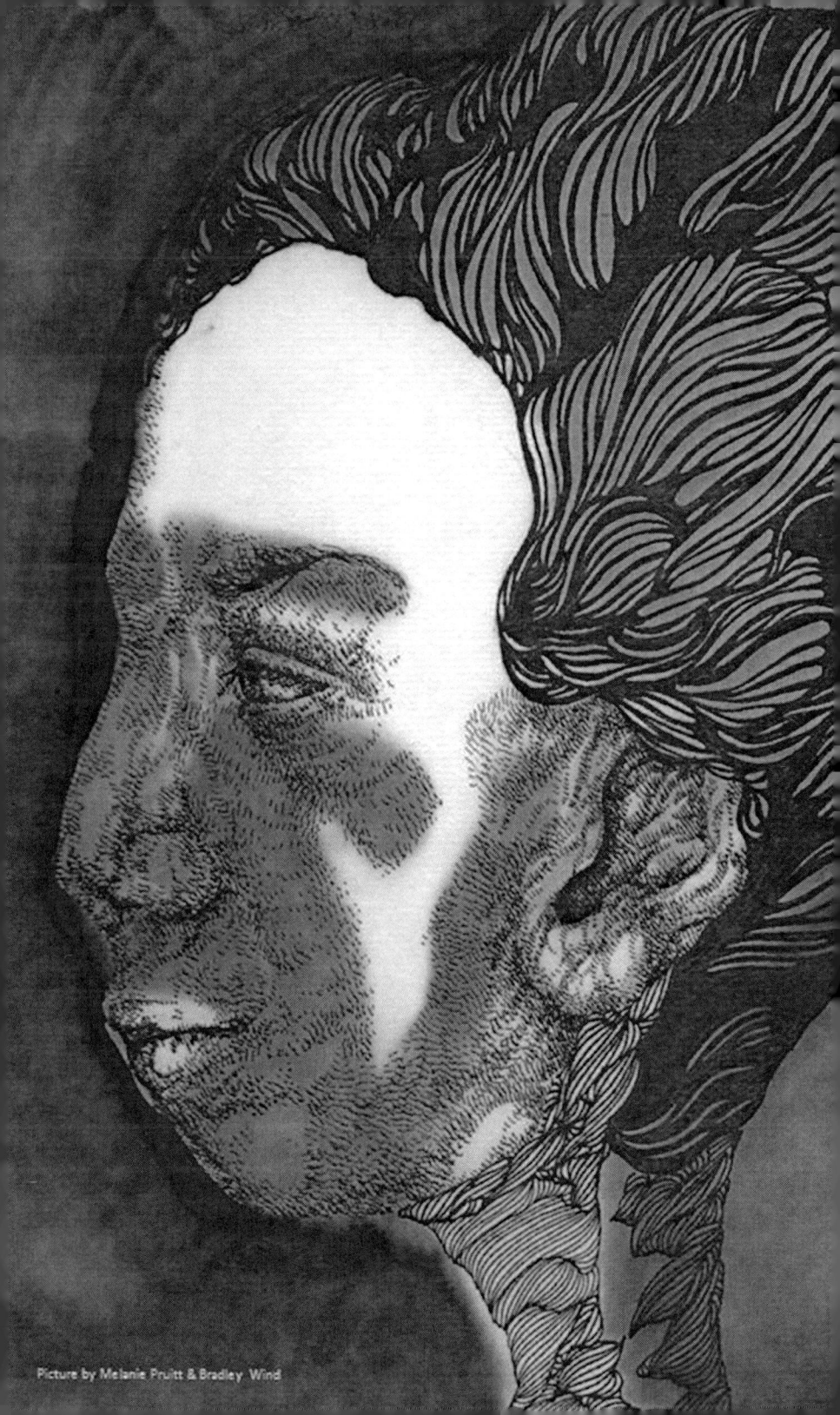
Picture by Melanie Pruitt & Bradley Wind

This is for you, Mom.

E-book
available
from

CONTENTS

Acknowledgments   i

1. I sense something divine in you. Yes, I do.
2. Bobos, they make ya feet feel fine. Bobos, they cost a dollar ninety-nine!
3. Unlikely Friends
4. Liggett Se, Dog Doo, The Infinity Killer
5. L'Ecole des Filles and the Allure of Abandoned Dwellings
6. The Dreams of St. Martin and Descartes
7. Records Broken and Spun
8. Douche Bag vs Scum Bag
9. Rod Hull's Legacy
10. Crimson Gold
11. A Strabismus Tiger Clears Up The Miracle Boy Blues
12. Barking About The Firestone Library
13. An Erection of the Mind
14. Feaguing for a Good Ride
15. Drink Budweiser Beer = 666
16. Cheeseburger Babel
17. Phi and a Scoop of Long Division
18. Six Million Dollar Men
19. Ivan Nikolayevitsh Panin Wasted 50 Years
20. Hamburglars
21. A Breath of Fresh Air
22. The Price of Babylonian Blood
23. The Milk Dud Defense
24. You're Number Two
25. It's All Right – I Think We're Gonna Make It
26. Human Faucet Sonata
27. Ponce De Leon Never Beat Up a Fat Woman
28. How To Kill A Shadow
29. Jesus, John Lennon and Norman Vincent Peale
30. Miscalculated Certainty
31. Paul Erdős's Shoes

About the Author

Note from Author

Acknowledgements:

During the research for this book I was very generously invited to attend a Math Tea by Prof. Robert Gunning of Princeton University. I spoke with mostly no one, but enjoyed my eavesdropping on Prof. Conway and other unnamed students. Without Prof. Gunning's invitation I'd never have found the names of students such as Jon Lenchner on that class photo, or gotten a real feel for the Firestone library and landscape of P.U.. I also enjoyed visiting Prof. John Nash's office, even if his door was closed.

It is my privilege to thank Prof. Ken Ribet (Berkeley U.) who came up with his contribution to the resolution of Fermat's Last Theorem all on his own. No doubt he's been as nurturing to his many students as he is to Abel herein.

Michael Drosin deserves my appreciation as well. I don't know if he has a nephew that attended Berkeley in the 80s, but if he did, he was highly unlikely to have influenced Michael's book *The Bible Code*.

Mr. Laurence Kim Peek (RIP), you were and are a great inspiration. If it weren't for Dr Oliver Sacks (RIP), Dr Darold Treffert and Barry Levinson I may have never known about Savants or thought so much about what we could be.

I wish to express sincere gratitude to my sister, Amanda, and friends like Lee Mundell, Rena Rossner, Alexis Washam, Gerry Dailey, and the team at Kindle Scout - and the many acquaintances I made on Authonomy.com.

To my wife Charlotte Cloe, and my daughters Lucia and Roselaine – thanks for the joy, for the rice-N-beans, and the love-filled reverberations.

CHAPTER ONE

I sense something divine in you. Yes, I do.

23-47.34.3-106.17.34-106.134.38.24.3-10.4.1645.38.1.10.4-38.57

In December 1666, the Chevalier de Terlon plucked a finger from the skeletal hand of the great mathematician René Descartes. When caught, de Terlon defended his theft as being worthy for, after all, it was the "instrument of the defunct's immortal writings." As documented in several of my favorite encyclopedias, Descartes was the father of modern philosophy and a key figure in the Scientific Revolution. No doubt he deserves respect, but I believe the finger theft a fitting tribute.

Descartes was a real a-hole. He called animals *automata*, basically flesh robots, and thought them without souls. How horrid to think of him dissecting living dogs, doing so only to learn how their hearts beat. A finger bone taken postmortem appears minor when one considers all those lives he stole, but still, he is my greatest hero and possibly, when I turn thirteen next year, I'll care less for dogs. Most adults seem uninterested in animals.

I wish my neighbor, Mr. Sutkin, merely felt apathy toward his dog. He appears to hate Mister Scratch. Why own a dog you hate? Each time I see him hit Mister Scratch, I wish someone would steal Mr. Sutkin's, premortem.

From my back porch, I watched Mister Scratch sniffing for a discreet bowel-relief location. Mr. Sutkin would beat him if he crapped in his own yard, or if he found him on the obsolete train tracks that ran behind our houses. The options left were our property or on the banks leading down to the tracks. Crapping on a slope was no easy feat, so he preferred our yard. I tried to signal him to go next to the clothesline—neither Mr. Sutkin nor Pigpie (my aunt) could see him there, and I could take care of his pile—but he was too busy sniffing to notice me.

I dodged between the drying sheets to retreat from the breeze, pausing to smell the flowery detergent and experience the secret-passageway feeling that standing between sheets can give. Leaves flittered above, and the sheets started to whip against me. I considered sneaking a quick trip to the tree before mowing the lawn. The weather felt perfect for tree climbing.

Mister Scratch finished up his business and came over to sniff me as I started toward the tracks. His scent reached me first. If you eat what you smell, which we all do, and you are what you eat, then part of me is Mister Scratch - while most would find that a disquieting fact, I breathe deeply when he's near. He's a bent-tailed mutt who's mostly beagle with conceivably some German shepherd, and he follows me all over the yard whenever we're outside. He stopped at the slope, as he always does, and I waved good-bye as I climbed down.

A dirt trail detoured off the main path and wound through dense weeds and brushwood. Few could navigate it, especially not heavyset individuals. One had to keep alert to each root, rock, and thorny twig, but the path ended at a worthy destination: a giant old sycamore with a slat ladder nailed to the trunk.

At the seventh slat, I knew *AC/DC Rocks* and followed the directions to *Keep Going!!* At the eleventh, my heart doubted the truth that *Alan ♥ Lisa* and they had *True Luv Always*. At the seventeenth slat, the writing on the board unnecessarily tipped me to being *high in the sky* with a little marijuana leaf drawn next to it. It was somewhat frightening to climb this far above the ground into such an old tree, but I always focused on the ladder's words until I rested in her huge limbs. The gold and still-greenish leaves enveloped me as I dug my fingernails into the bark. After five minutes of careful climbing, the branches went rubbery, a stoplight signaling to go no farther. I did a quick scan for anyone who might see me.

Last May 19, 1981, when I first climbed the tree, Mr. Sutkin with his overgrown mustache and gray, greasy hair roared at me, "Get down here, that's too high!" I listened, of course. A couple of limbs hung over part of his property, but since the tree didn't actually grow on it, I knew he didn't have final say. I could take a shortcut across Mr. Sutkin's property to get to the tree, but Mr. Sutkin is a bit of a neighborhood busybody, and I don't like having to answer his questions if I don't have to. What he does for a living remains a mystery, as does why he knows so much about trees. If the information he shared wasn't neighborhood gossip, it was often about trees. I've meant to research its veracity. He told me how tree roots mirror the tree's crown, that is, the roots grow down as deep as trees grow tall. It doubles the monumental quality of their size when you think of them that way and created tree fractions for me, the earth dividing numerator limbs from denominator roots. Occasionally, I torture myself imagining what it'd feel like standing in my mirrored position, breathing in cold earth and worms on those denominators far below the forest floor.

In the blustery fall wind high above it all, you can feel the earth pulling and the blue sky pulling and you are free. I counted yellow leaves for a while before I began forcefully hurling breezes with my eyelashes, propelling clouds to slide shadows on top of Pigpie's roof. I drove small flocks of starlings from a telephone line to mess with Mister Scratch's nap, and without any effort, unintentionally summoned Russell.

Russell Ghety wove down Overbrook Road on his three-speed Huffy, dumped it at our secret spot, and ran to the sycamore. The leaves and wind were creating so much noise, I couldn't make out what he repeatedly sang until he arrived at the branches beneath me.

"flip it right, flip it baby, flip it rye-right!"

"Uh, you sang, you sang the wrong words," I said.

"Hey, Apple, what?"

Russell has never used the name my mother gifted me, which is Abel. I wasn't bothered because it reminded me of how she used to say I was the Abel of her eye, a clever twist on the Deuteronomy derived phrase. "It's, ah, it's *whip* not *flip* and *all night*, not, uh, *rye-right*."

"It's in my head going round and round." Russell looked at me with slight annoyance and continued singing, "Oh-hoo-hoo!"

He could maybe compete with ravens in the mellifluous-voice department.

Maybe.

Russell is so dumb, he'd probably try to put M&M's in alphabetical order, but he could sniff me out even if I only had a couple of hours to spend. I'm not being an a-hole, honestly. His stupidity is all genetics, nothing to blame him for. Russell flunked the fifth grade and took a late bus home from his school because he got extra tutoring. It was the first thing he told me about himself when we met. He also mentioned his propensity for producing spittle. The latter he attributed to having an incredibly powerful tongue, which I considered commendable, a positive twist on the substantial derision I'd witnessed him absorb for the globs that formed on the corners of his mouth. I've since found the spittle occurs mainly but not only when he's nervous or upset.

"Feel that breeze, man. Oh, we might get knocked down, don'cha think?" Russell hugged the branch, his thin frame hardly bent, and looked out over the trees.

No, I didn't think, but I nodded, anyway.

"You could lay a gasser up here and no one would know! Hey, didja see it?" Russell asked, referring to the fort we'd been searching for since the Fourth of July. We'd overheard Kevin Groter's sister Gwen mention it at the fairgrounds.

"Nope."

"Next week for the mansion, right?"

He's been talking about going to the abandoned Pierson mansion "next week" since I met him, but we never have. You could see part of the roof from our current and regular spot at the top of the sycamore. The neighborhood mythology surrounding the mansion, and the murders that took place there, is quite compelling, and I will likely explore it one day, with or without him.

"OK, you ready? I'm ready. Go!" Russell shouted without prompting—the start to our normal game. His fingers went to his temples, and he stared intently at me. Russell was a dreadful-looking individual with a pinched face made even worse by his almost-black Russian-politician eyebrows, massive and hairy. He's likely doomed to inherit his father's full-blown brow shrubs before his twenties.

The game's rules were simple: We had to stay quiet and try to read each other's minds. One of us would say, "Done," wait for the other to agree, and exchange what we'd mystically extracted, which ended the game. Usually, it lasted closer to three minutes, but Russell immediately started swaying the branches, impatient to tell me whatever it was he wanted me to read.

"Done!" Russell shouted.

He always said "Done" first.

"Done."

"You were thinking about Mr. Suckin, right?" Russell enjoyed the altered pronunciation.

I shook my head no.

"Your turn. What am I thinkin'?"

I looked at his Adam's apple, "Food?"

"Shit no. Try again."

"Uhhh, okay, okay TV. Mork and Mindy, Mork and Mindy, Robin Williams, Pam Dawber."

"No, time's up. I was thinking about how I heard they're putting in an arcade where the old Laundromat used to be."

I glanced at the leaves that suddenly started whooshing next to us again.

"You wanna go see if it's true?" Russell asked.

I wished we could be better friends, but mostly he's just another person my age to spend time with. I listen to him talk, and he listens to me, but it's like the time I told him, "To you, 5,329 is just a five, a three, a two, and a nine, but I say, 'Hi, seventy-three squared.'" He responded with, "I hate Paul Lynde. He's such a gay bird. Circle gets a square!"

Having watched many episodes of the comedy gameshow *Hollywood Squares* when I lived with my first foster family, the Dersteins, I had to disagree. I loved Paul Lynde. He's one of the best comedians on the show, a real "gut buster," as Mrs. Derstein used to say. But on one occasion, she called him and Jim Nabors very feminine, so possibly Russell was on to something.

"Well, you wanna go, or do you want to stare at fuckin' bark all day?" Russell asked again.

"Let's go," I said with a clap for emphasis.

Halfway down the tree, the calls started. Russell ignored them until we got to the ground, and he shouted back with irate force. *"Coming!"*

Again, his mother shouted, hanging on the last *l* from his name long enough for the neighborhood to take notice. Russell adjusted his heavily faded Darth Vader T-shirt and shouted, "Coming, I said!" and added, "Fuck me, shit," in a forced whisper with his nose scrunched. "Take the bike, and check it out if you want, but call me later about what you find." He karate punched toward the tree with both fists before wiping his mouth and starting home.

It immediately occurred to me I still needed to mow the lawn, and I had lucked out with Russell's mother calling. I glanced at my watch and worried that Pigpie would be ready with some punishment for not having started already.

CHAPTER TWO

Bobos, they make ya feet feel fine. Bobos, they cost a dollar ninety-nine!

2.16-2.6.8.3.95-16.35-145.8.35.4-33.7-8.2.7-26.12.4.33.2.8.16.3.235-33.3.27

Instituted in 1920, Prohibition lasted thirteen years, ten months, nineteen days, seventeen hours, and 32.5 minutes. If you were a law-abiding citizen, that was a long time to wait for a beer. Unfortunately, even with today's freedom to drink alcoholic beverages—and given that tongues replace their 4,600 taste buds every two weeks—most American beer drinkers still aren't sophisticated enough to avoid that Budweiser swill no matter how many chances their buds gave them.

Bud-Wiser. Bull-Shit.

I, Abel Velasco, here on this sunken, cigarette-stinking couch with my inexperienced tongue, am a Pabst Blue Ribbon fan who scoffs at Bud drinkers as those with informed ears should scoff at last year's remake of "Angel of the Morning" by Juice Newton. It is a well-documented fact that Merrilee Rush performed the definitive version in 1968.

In the backyard, Pigpie yelled at what I assumed must be Mister Scratch. "Get out, get out, get out! Sutkin, I know you can hear me!"

By December 1976, about a hundred years after Budweiser was first launched, a little over 411 million barrels had been produced, making it the King of Bilge Beers. I don't know the quantities consumed on the fatal evening of December 14 (I peeped into the knothole too late that night for specifics), but my guess is that Uncle Evert and his friends contributed to Bud's top-selling year by finishing a case. All things even, my uncle guzzled eight before he died in that icy St. Louis gutter, not far from where Saarinen's Arch stands, the city where Bud, and I, were born.

While I found St. Louis unexceptional, Uncle Evert's house worked better than Pigpie's for lodging. My bedroom at his place was top-notch actually. It came equipped with a view of the train tracks and a knothole to the basement. If not for my uncle's heavy imbibing, I'd still be there counting train cars or perhaps eating a warm plate of my uncle's *frijoles negros* with rice and cheese. I suppose if I'm taking peripatetic excursions around the what-if territory, if I still lived there, Mom might be free of her current recuperative quarters in Hoboken to better prepare those beans. Regrettably, none of that is the case. And so, on many occasions, I've cursed that horse piss Bud for delivering me to Hell, or the closest place to Hell on Earth: North Brunswick, New Jersey.

It was turning into a Bud-cursing day already.

My Casio ticked past 4:28:21 p.m. I pressed the side button to get *9-19-82* to show, and again for *SUNDAY*, and again back to 4:28:29 p.m. Maybe I could sneak up to bed, and Pigpie would think I was exhausted from all the lawn mowing. Maybe I could simply fall asleep here on the couch, and she'd leave me alone. Good night, John-Boy, Good night John Boy, Good night John Boy. I'm not tired, though. The seconds continued their tick, tick, ticking. In the 1979 *British Medical Journal*, I'd read that people of Hispanic origin are 20 percent more prone to moles, specifically facial moles, than all other nationalities. I'm not suggesting the gumdrop example on Richard Thomas's aka John-Boy Walton's cheek points to his being Hispanic, and I want it clear that I'm proud of my heritage and its genetic potential, but Pigpie had probably raised that mole count a few percentages all on her own. I'd tallied each of the thirty-one on her peppered visage many times and didn't relish another review.

Clump! Clump! Clump!

The lace on Pigpie's nightgown heaved from overworked lungs as she lumbered forth, swatting away at her corpulent thighs. "How!" *slap* "Many!" *slap* Sunlight retreated from her shoulders and restrained black hair as she entered the TV room, a bulldog-cheeked villain straight out of a bad after-school special.

"How many times do you need to hear I want that lawn kept right?" She tightened her lips and released them with a huff. "So retarded, now lemme see them again." Her tobacco-stained sausage fingers grabbed hold of my calf, as she bent my sneaker to the side and dropped it. "I can't believe it." *slap* "We just replaced your shit shoes. Do you know how much these cost?" *slap*

I kept still, hating her touch and wishing my legs were four feet long instead of my entire body, so the strain of trying to lift them would cause her teeth to crack—even better, wishing I was twenty-one instead of twelve and lived on my own, purchasing my own stupid Bobos.

She grabbed the pillow I'd propped myself up with and tossed it across the room. "Sit up." *slap* "Completely ruined. Why didn't you take them off before you started mowing? This is almost too much. You'll behave." *slap* "You will."

Her slaps and resulting quiver sums had reached twenty-one and fifty-five already today. The potential for her hand to shift from her thigh to my head was rising. She'd only hit me four times since I'd moved in, and I didn't want to increase the average. I had to do something. The number clouds continued their vibrations on my periphery. "Sorry," I said into my armpit. Mister Scratch's barking could have caused her to miss my apology, so I thought of repeating it.

"And you know I don't want him around. That Sutkin thinks just because there's no fence he doesn't have to control that GD mutt." She poked my glasses to accentuate her last sin-avoided *goddamn*.

Pigpie needed a rest after her trip to the porch. She plopped down on the other end of the couch to replenish herself with a noisy swig from her can of Bud and a long, final draw from the cigarette left burning. Marlboro exhaust billowed from her lips and her nostrils flared as she said, "Now, Abel Velaaaasco, get going."

I inchwormed off the couch, grabbed my satchel from the stairs, and darted through the kitchen to the back porch. Pieces of Parkay margarine containers scattered as my sneakers knocked into them. I'd set out some cut-up hot dog I'd saved, but it must not have been enough. Mister Scratch really ripped the container to shreds. Why Pigpie was concerned with what the yard looked like is beyond me since her personal hygiene would suggest she couldn't care less about such matters.

Mister Scratch barked incessantly as I finished cleaning the porch and sat down. Numbers hovered at my eyelids like flies around the collected Parkay pieces. I pulled a journal from my satchel and started transcribing calculations from Pigpie's rant. My head grew dizzy as I wrote. I clapped at Mister Scratch to quell his barking. He stopped for a moment but continued again.

I love animals. I especially love ones of rare distinction like the Goliath frog of Cameroon, which can grow up to thirty-two inches and weigh six pounds, a dynamic amphibian if ever there was one. Dogs, however, unquestionably top my list. I've lived with two dogs separately and briefly, but neither was truly mine. You might guess I'd prefer something a bit more exotic, an *Achatina achatina* (giant African snail) or a *Hippocampus zosterae* (dwarf sea horse), but nothing beats the scents and by-products of dogs.

I clapped my hands again, signaling to Mister Scratch that I'd pet him if he wanted. He sniffed the trash can, picked something up, and bounded happily over.

A spit-coated tennis ball landed between my sneakers. I picked it up and briefly smelled its dog-breath scent as Mister Scratch darted in the assumed direction seconds before the tennis ball left my hand. He zoomed through the mown lines, nails ripping at the ground, purposefully hitting the largest piles and flinging grass blades into the air. Apparently, mown grass made him spaz with delight.

The flitting grass blades incited numbers to buzz about my eyelids again. I used to hear thunder, and it would summon a vision of young calves seeking udders. My mother's voice would bring visions of soft rain in a field or tiny flowers closing for the day. Now, instead of my own View-Master slideshow accompanying dialogue, each word had the effect of summoning numbers. Sentences bring calculations. Every conversation is vivid, filled with computational force.

A minute passed, but the back door didn't open after I thought I'd heard a noise. Sun glimmered off the kitchen windows obscuring the interior. I glanced about for any missed pieces, and finally decided to calm myself by writing out one of my favorite passages.

Unlike simply reviewing an article or book in your mind, writing out another's text can place one in that person's shoes. I'd definitely trade my Bobos for whatever René Descartes wore in the 1600s when he wrote his *Meditations on First Philosophy*. His contribution to mathematics is what truly attracts me, but he falls into Ali Baba–level greatness for philosophical larceny.

I'm positive at this point you're asking, "Oh, really, Abel? Please tell me how you're so sure René pilfered from others in his philosophy." My obvious response, obvious to anyone who knows Jean de Silhon (and Descartes did) would be: "Silhon said, 'It is impossible that a man who has the ability, as many do, to look within himself and make the judgment that he exists, could deceive himself in this judgment and not exist,' which is basically what Descartes said when he wrote, 'I think, therefore I am,' only Silhon said it ten years earlier."

So what do you think? Bullshit master? I think this is indeed the case, but the transgressions are easily overlooked when one focuses on his accomplishments in mathematics.

A clang came from the kitchen behind me. There could be no mistaking it this time. I decided it a good occasion to find that new arcade for fear she'd come up with other punishment.

CHAPTER THREE

Unlikely Friends

3.3400.38.3.33.4-12.13-4.26-33.26.27.38.2.3.61.3.41.10

I retrieved Russell's bike from our secret spot near the blackberry bushes. The bike is silver and has a small transistor radio tied to the back. When I flipped the switch, WJLK 94.3 crackled to life with Paul McCartney singing one of my current favorite songs, "Take it Away." It lacks a little John, George, and Ringo, but it's a great bike-riding song. Static vibrated into the music until the tires hit the smooth surface of East School Street.

I sang along with the song and popped my front tire up to cross over the sidewalk, navigating to the dirt path to kill my shadow in the long beige weeds of Howe's field. It was reborn as I cut across the parking lot of Hanson's factory toward the back of Flynn's Garage at 479 Livingston Ave. Hank Flynn came around the corner when I entered the side lot. He gave a startled small wave and began talking as I approached, but I yelled, "Hold on, hold on!" and rode past.

Livingston Avenue wasn't a hotspot of commerce, but it had a few locations of note. McGinn's shop, across from the garage, was the old train station turned dry-goods store, one of my three favorite stores to purchase trading cards and candy. Inky's and the 7-Eleven were my other two favorites, but the 7-Eleven wasn't on Livingston. Populating the rest of this section of Livingston were Yorston's Savings & Loan and the closed Soap-N-Spin Laundromat across the street.

The hill toward the old Soap-N-Spin became somewhat steep, but Joan Jett urged me on by singing "Crimson and Clover" over and over until I arrived and saw my reflection in the window. I straightened out the hood of my sweat jacket. My hair was blown back, and I tried to pull in my protruding lower lip to fit my *Teen Beat* look. Not bad. A little as if Anson Williams (aka Potsie from *Happy Days*) was Hispanic and about ten years younger.

It was hard to distinguish anything inside because of the reflection, but when I pressed my glasses against the window, the veil lifted, and a row of modern Easter Island monuments greeted me: mysterious and powerful machines that I had no idea about when or how they'd gotten here. Well, maybe some idea. Ms. Pac-Man, the unremarkable and hardly different relative of Pac-Man, was right up front. There also was Tempest, Gorf, and Centipede, and the last, before the dark made it impossible to read, was a game called Journey. I wished it were open now. Looking at a room of unplugged video games was as disappointing as nudes in *National Geographic*.

Russell would certainly be happy to hear about the posted sign: "Join us for our grand opening October 1!" I briefly worried about the effects of his financial status and if he'd ever have the money to join me. Would getting there with him be like our always-talked-about-but-never-done trip to the Pierson mansion? I suppose I could always spot him the quarters.

The railroad signal started chiming just as I turned to ride back down to Flynn's. I'd always considered it lucky if it went off when I was nearby. I turned and rode closer to the tracks as the long, striped arms lowered and the dueling red lights flashed to block traffic. A disappointing nine cars zoomed past. I enjoyed a train at least thirteen cars long or more, but then, I'd be happy if every day could have any kind of spectacular train enhancement. The whistles, the rhythm of the wheels, people and product following regular schedules, and the freedom—yes, the potential for freedom that travel offered—were all so attractive.

I coasted down to the open bay door of Flynn's. Will's head wavered in rhythm to his raised voice as I entered. His back was to me, and his hand with the missing fingers shook above his shoulder as he said, "No way I'm going to be dealt with like some kind of Raggedy Andy."

"If you'd stop sucking down bottles like they were air," Hank retorted.

"Listen, you can't be throwing folks out of places just because they look like they'll fight. I hadn't even started talking to the motherfucker. I hate that racist Speedway, hate it. Don't know why I go back there. I'm decorated, damn it."

"Why don't you go to that place over on . . . hey, hey there, Jukebox," Hank said, noticing me, then patted Will on the arm and shuffled over. "Where've you been hiding? We've got some serious piles needing your expertise." He put his hand out to welcome me as if I'd been away from home for a long time. It'd only been thirteen days since I visited last. "Whoops, that's right, no hand-shaking for Jukebox."

I avoided touching others as often as possible. "Hello today, Hank, and-and-" I started to get stuck in the verbal response. "And hello. Today, you are sixty-nine years and thirty-five days old or twenty-five thousand two hundred and twenty days old, or—"

"Or he's so old he knew Mr. Clean when he had an Afro."

"OK,-OK, and-and I'll accept that, Will, thank you," I responded, a little nervous from the anger I sensed Will still was trying to suppress.

If my skin could be considered an integer of, say, two, a coffee-with-extra-cream brown, Will's would be a Hershey bar eight or nine. At six feet one inch tall, he looked a little like the boxing champ Cassius Clay aka Muhammad Ali, and I often wondered if their resemblance was why he spent so many hours at the gym and in the ring when he wasn't working. The mathematical equation I generated to represent our relationship was a balanced one, so I wasn't that scared of him, although at times he's given me reason to be. On many occasions, he shared his "hellhole 'Nam" experiences, which implied he saw me as a friend, since mostly he didn't want to talk about Vietnam. Two fingers on Will's left hand had been shot off, but he could still do everything with it, even play guitar, though not anywhere near as good as Jimi Hendrix, whom he tried to mimic. When Will played, his eyes opened so wide and looked so bright, you wondered if they glowed in the dark.

"You just missed Mi. She went to get us something to eat. Probably got plenty if you want to join us."

"No, thank you, Will. I will have to . . . eat something my aunt has prepared."

"Oh, hey, listen to this. I got this one just for you. Yo' aunt's *so* fat, she's thirty-six twenty-four thirty-six!" Will laughed, showing me his wrist. "But that's her forearm, neck, and thigh!" He pointed at me with his mouth open and continued laughing.

I stared in horror at the eleven scars on his arm while he laughed. They unnerved me each time I looked at them.

"There's no way you're my son. Anyone related to me would know laughing that hard at your own jokes is in poor taste," Hank said and shook his head.

"Does that mean, uh, inches or, uh, feet?" I asked Will seriously. Both Hank and Will stopped to think about my question and simultaneously burst out laughing.

"There you go, Juke. There you go. Hey, so, you been warned. You know how Mi can be when she wants you to eat. She'll be back anytime now." Will lit a cigarette and took a long drag.

Hank liked to say, "This ole gal has emphysema," when he talked about the garage. I could see what he meant with a quick glance around, everything stained yellow and smeared with oil. I felt tough standing among it all. There's nothing like the great smell of the garage. Cigarettes, oil, and gasoline. Both Hank and Will smoked Pall Malls. I was surprised they hadn't burned the place down with how careless they were leaving lit cigarettes about.

The garage consisted of two bays with one for cars and the other for tools, but the whole place really acted as a big theater. The garage doors were always up when they were open for business, and when Will raised them in the mornings, he liked to say things like, "Let the show begin!" or "Introducing the glorious and world famous, Noooorth Baaah-runswick!" There's a stoplight a block down the street, and the cars and people on the street who'd stop for it were frequently the entertainment or fodder for commentary. Sometimes it seemed a never-ending battle for who could outwit the other, one wisecrack after the next until exhaustion took over or a customer stopped in.

"Come on over here," Hank said, waving me along with him to where they kept the boxes of small parts. "We've got so many piles, it's getting out of hand. When would you like to make a little extra cash if not today?" Hank lifted the cooler open and pulled two bottles of Pabst Blue Ribbon for us from the frosty fog, cracking off the caps with the opener he'd nailed to the counter.

"Thank you," I said, incredibly happy about Hank's lack of compunction over giving me beer. I took a big gulp and squeezed the remaining bitter fluid quickly down my throat. I sized up the bottle, questioning a second swig, but decided I'd been waiting too long for a Pabst Blue Ribbon not to drink it now. The next big gulp forced me to belch.

"Hey, what'd I tell you about that?" Will shouted over.

"Excuse me for the one burp."

"No, not you, Juke, that old fool giving kids beer."

"Didn't hurt you growing up, did it? No wait, scratch that. Here, Jukebox, give me that back," Hank said, jokingly reaching for my bottle.

I raised it toward him, but he waved at me to forget it.

"So dumb he'd take the Pepsi Challenge and choose Jif," Will muttered under his breath.

"I heard that, bonehead," Hank said to Will and looked at me. "So, when you want to come by and give us a hand?"

As great as Pabst Blue Ribbon was, I'd decided all beer tasted like a bathroom attendant's sweat sock. The aftertaste in my mouth stewed, but I took another swig, belched again, and said, "I could come over, uh, after school, 3:40 on Wuh—"

"Did you ask Mom about that, Abel?" My cousin, Shelly, stood in the open bay, giving us all a shock.

I looked to Hank, to Will, and then back to Shelly. "I-I just got here—"

"I know you didn't ask about coming here or about that beer you're burpin' over, and if you don't want me saying anything, you'll come with me—now."

"Hey, it's not nice blackmailing your little brother," Hank said.

"He's not my brother, and who asked you?"

"Wa-hey, listen to little miss thing," Will added.

Shelly put her hands on her hips. "Let's go, or we'll miss the beginning."

I handed Hank the rest of my beer. "Thank you, and I'll see you Wednesday."

"All right, but don't let her get you into trouble now."

"OK,-OK, Hank." I followed Shelly to her orange Chevy Impala parked up the street.

Hank had branded Shelly a troublemaker because earlier that summer when Pigpie sent her looking for me, a box of Chiclets went missing at the station. He said he knew he'd left them on the counter, and when she left, they weren't there anymore. He said any woman that'd steal a man's Chiclets "couldn't be trusted for anything." Hank loved his Chiclets. It was the only brand of gum he'd chew. I liked them, too, but mainly because they were candy-coated rectangles that reminded me of teeth.

I reluctantly slid onto the black-leather front seat of Shelly's car, moving my satchel into my lap and clicking my seatbelt around my waist. The day was starting to feel more complicated than I'd prefer, and my mind raced for an excuse to get back out.

"You should be thanking me. I'm about to do you a big favor. Plus, you shouldn't really be hanging out with those filthy grease monkeys drinking beer. Don't you have any friends your age?" Shelly pushed a cassette tape into the player and turned up the volume.

"I, uh, I forgot about Russell's bike," I said, partly to remind her about Russell being my friend.

Shelly had moved back to North Brunswick with Pigpie a year and a half ago. They'd been living in Washington State in another small town called Kelso, ZIP code 98626. According to Shelly, post-May 18, 1980, there were no tears shed when the police reported her father dead. He wasn't among the fifty-seven official deaths from the eruption of Mount St. Helens, but he was crushed in an ash-related accident on Interstate 5. Apparently, they amassed enough capital from his life insurance to do anything Pigpie wanted, and she decided to traverse the continent to her hometown, back to dreary North Brunswick.

It is Bud and Mount St. Helens I actually blame for my misfortunes.

Shelly taught me a lot about lying. She explained how the stink in her father's car was from "too many cigarettes." Cigarettes smell one way, but when she turned on the air conditioner, this kind of ash scent was like nothing else. Though I must say, it's hard to smell anything over her new air freshener.

With her window down, she ground the gears, shifting into second, and began, "I was just driving around so pissed because they went to see this movie, and Tina tells me she takes the guy, Mike, from the movie, who she says is like one of John Travolta's friends in *Grease*. And Stacy says she always liked surfers and took some guy Spicoli, and they ask who I'd take because I said I'd seen it Friday. They are such high-pitch bitches because I could tell it was all about rubbing in the fact that they'd gone out without me, because they're jealous because I have Tommy." She lovingly touched the cherry air freshener that hung from the mirror.

"I said it wouldn't be right for me to pick someone when I had Tommy, but they said it was just a game and asked if I'd go for Rat or the science-teacher guy. I said no way to Rat and if I had to choose, I'd go for the science teacher, even though he was old. I guessed about him being old because he's a teacher, but they just laughed anyway and said, 'Yeah, right,' and I told them, 'I like what I like,' and they laughed even harder. I told them that Paul Newman's old, and we all said he was hot when we saw *Fort Apache, The Bronx*. I hate them. So, now I have to go see it before we get to school tomorrow, and since Tommy won't, I saw you in there and thought you can go."

Shelly took the road past the Pierson mansion.

"Russell's bike. I have to leave it in our spot."

She screeched to a stop. "Shall I let you out here, or do you want to forget about the bike already? You're going to the movies for free. My God, can't you even thank me?"

I looked at the boarded windows of the mansion and back at Shelly's anger-squinted eyelids. "I always put it ba—"

"Out!"

"I always—" I started again.

"Goddamn it, we're going to be late. It's safe with your greasy friends." She squealed the wheels and sped away from the curb. "Ooh, this is my favorite song. David Lee Roth is so Boss!" She started singing along to Van Halen's *And The Cradle Will Rock...* and banged to the beat in the air. I was now at Shelly's mercy, so I pulled my journal out and wrote down a few conversation calculations from the garage. With the windows down and the warm late-day air, I could almost imagine the school year hadn't yet begun.

Shelly stopped us before we got to the booth. With Pigpie for a mother, Shelly would need many years of private polishing school to make her anything close to cultured. She flipped her long, feathered, brown hair to make it wing and fluff out, pulled her white shirt collar up straight, flipped her hair again so it'd be outside her collar, and breathing out said, "OK, I pretty much know this girl. She said hi to Tina once when I was with her, I'm pretty sure, but don't mention that or anything, because I'm gonna act like I never saw her before unless she says something. She won't ask for my license—they never do for me—but play it cool and don't ask her any of your dumb questions." She smoothed out the fabric on her boobs just before we got to the window.

On the marquee, it read: *An Officer and a Gentleman* rated R, *The Beastmaster* rated PG, and *Fast Times at Ridgemont High* with a lowercase *r* next to it. Shelly looked tough and could usually get what she wanted through intimidation.

Shelly pushed the fee under the glass and said, "Two for *Fast Times*." The girl looked over at me, and before she could say anything, Shelly added, "He only looks young. What person under seventeen can quote Shakespeare?" Shelly looked at me pleadingly. I wasn't sure if her eyes said, "Don't dare say something dumb like you're only twelve" or "Goddamn it, give a quote right now."

The ticket girl looked questioningly at me, and I said, "Act one scene four. *King Lear*. 'Have more than thou showest, Speak less than thou knowest, Lend less than thou owest, Ride more than thou goest, Learn more than thou trowest, Set less than thou throwest, Leave thy drink and thy whore, And keep in-a-door, And thou shalt have more Than two tens to a score.'" Judging by her face, I'd impressed her.

I still felt nervous when Shelly gave our tickets to the old man who ripped them and let us through. The darkness of the crowded theater helped ease my discomfort, and as we found our seats, Shelly harped, "I know she knows me. Bitch didn't even ask how I'd been. God, did you have to say *whore*? You're lucky you're not waiting in the car." She started applying lip gloss as the previews began.

The theater delivered an aroma somewhat like the geriatric section of the hospital I visited Mom at in Missouri: piss, ammonia, and stale popcorn. I didn't have to worry about anyone's head being in my way, so I didn't care about the smell. I'd only ever been to two other movies in a theater. Uncle Ev took me to see *Oh, God!*, and also *Logan's Run*.

Shelly grew incredibly restless after the scene where Mr. Vargas, the science teacher, who had a tiny chance of being a hideous distant cousin to Paul Newman, showed up. After Vargas commented about switching to Sanka, she leaned over and asked me if I wanted to leave. Unless Descartes' remains were in a parade outside, nothing could pry me from my seat when I'd gotten this far through the movie. Shelly twitched, sighed, and cracked her knuckles until the ending credits started. I wanted to applaud and stay to read them all, but Shelly got up. She marched out of the theater with her arms crossed until she snatched her keys from her pocket to open the car door.

The livid steam rising from Shelly's head flowed out the cracked window as we drove. She stayed silent until we arrived home.

"Just let me do the talking," she demanded before we got out.

My watch steadily ticked to 7:04:57 p.m., but I didn't need a watch to know the sunlight had gone. I doubted Shelly mentioned the movie or my going with her. What was I thinking? The thrill I'd felt about seeing an R-rated movie quickly left me when I thought of what I faced. The yellow light emanating from the front porch said, "Caution: Proceed with care," so we snuck in through the back. I left my stained sneakers by the laundry machine. The combined smell of Tide and fried chicken filled my mouth with saliva as we walked into the house. I was starving. Edith Bunker's voice rang out from the TV in the other room.

"Hi, Mom, I'm home. God, your chicken smells great. When's dinner going to be ready?" Shelly said, playing it cool.

"It was ready two hours ago!" Pigpie shouted.

"Oh, really? I thought when I left this morning, you said we'd eat late tonight." Shelly continued her unassuming air with great aplomb.

"Now, why the hairy hell would I say that? You lie as bad as your father did. Have you seen Abel? He knows he's supposed to be in by now. Kid can't even read a watch."

"He's right here with me."

That got her up off the couch and into the kitchen holding her Pringles can. Shelly stood as tall as Pigpie, but Shelly's frame had nothing on Pigpie's girth.

"Where were you?" she asked, hands planted on her hips.

The answer stuck in my throat.

"I took him to the movies. He never gets to go anywhere, and I thought it'd be nice for him."

"The movies, on a Sunday night?" She turned to me. "Irregardless of her being nice, you know damn well you've got school tomorrow."

I nodded as apologetically as I could and squeezed my satchel tightly in response to the torment her superfluous prefix addition to the word *regardless* caused me.

"Shelly, no TV, go to your room, and think about the time I wasted cooking your dinner. Abel, sit down. There, sit at that chair."

I did as told, and she slammed the Pringles next to me.

"But I'm hungry," Shelly whined.

"You're hungry, huh? OK, OK." Pigpie flung open the refrigerator and took out a lump wrapped in tinfoil. She grabbed a paper plate from the pile on the counter, unwrapped the contents of the tinfoil, dropped it on the plate, and shoved it at Shelly. "Take it and move before I move you!"

"But it's just the dirty leftover bones," Shelly griped, holding the plate as far from her as she could.

"Dirty bones!" Pigpie swelled until she burst. "You think if Carl were alive, you'd get away with . . . you want my sweat? That was dinner!" She smashed the plate to the floor. Shelly ran up the stairs.

I pulled my satchel close to my chest. Pigpie walked over toward the counter by the back door and picked up pieces of something. She slammed three sections of the chewed margarine bowl on the table, knocking over the Pringles can. No chips came out of the tall cylinder.

"What did I tell you about cleaning up that backyard? Next time, you'll come get me before you run off." She slapped her thigh. "And I'll inspect and if I find any sign of crap like this . . ." *Slap.* She swept the chewed bowl pieces onto my chest. "That mutt will be dragging itself around by its front legs because the back ones will be broke. And I even told you." *Slap.* "I said Father Mullens was coming, and you embarrass me? I covered for you, and for our not going to church this morning, but don't blame me if they come and take you away."

Laughter came from the TV in the other room. She grabbed the Pringles can and started walking toward the TV.

"I mean, I could tell he thought I wasn't doing right by you when he said you were a sign of God's grace." She halted at the doorway. "Father's trying to make me appreciate you, and I even agreed to his bullcrap. You might know stuff, but it ain't like you have God's phone number, and I am *so* nice to you."

She turned, walked to my chair, and huffed, glaring at me with something else on her mind. "He wanted another freebie, but I talked him into going fifty-fifty. I was going to give you some of whatever we made, but now you'll just do it to pay me back for all I do." She kicked at my chair by her feet. "Do you hear me?"

People on the northern border of Russia and China heard her. She'd never mentioned anything about Father Mullens coming by. It pleased me that I'd missed him, but I needed to prove I'd heard her to calm things down.

"Do you hear me?"

"You said-you said, 'What did I tell you about cleaning up that backyard. Next time you'll come get me before you run off, and and—"

"Oh, it's gonna be cute, huh? You're home after sunset, embarrass me, I cook you dinner, and . . ." She grabbed the used tinfoil from the counter. Her piggish huffing talk came full blast. The moisture in her mouth could fill a small fish tank. "For Christ, you'll learn. You can eat the rest. Chew it." She threw the tinfoil at me.

She'd made me do this once before, causing me to vomit, so this time I balled the tinfoil. I put it toward my lips and showed her that it wouldn't fit in my mouth. She grabbed the ball from me, unraveled it, letting some of the chicken fat drip to the linoleum, ripped off a piece of foil, and shoved it at my mouth.

"Open!" she yelled, and when I did, she shoved it in. "Now chew."

I have five silver amalgam fillings in my mouth— lousy, thin tooth enamel to match my lousy lip genetics. If you've ever rubbed a fork or any metal object against your fillings, you'd have a clue what it felt like to chew on Pigpie's greasy chicken tinfoil. It's a sensory experience akin to maybe licking a battery. Tears started to fill the edges of my eyes, and my gag reflex began.

"Don't start that bullshit. Don't you start." She backed up from me, and the audience laughter on the TV caught her attention. "Get your ass upstairs before I really lose my shit." She put the rest of the foil on the counter and started shaking her Pringles can a little to see what remained. She walked away, and I ran up the stairs, spitting the foil into my hand on the way, chanting *a-hole, a-hole, a-hole* in my head.

CHAPTER FOUR

Liggett Se, Dog Doo, The Infinity Killer

45.6.7.45.40.2.18-11.40.6.7.22.9.40

On May 17 of this past year, just before they told me I could never return to the Paul Robeson Library of Rutgers University, I had in my possession a book called *Monkey on Your Back Math*. Besides obviously being named by some children's book author, the book included descriptions of the most-difficult and unresolved math mysteries on the planet. In no particular order, they are the Riemann hypothesis, Fermat's last theorem, the Birch and Swinnerton-Dyer conjecture, the Hodge conjecture, Yang-Mills theory, and the P versus NP problem. The outdated book included the four-color theorem, which *Scientific American* reported solved in 1976.

This line of pursuit stemmed from my growing belief that without mathematics, progress would halt and society would collapse. Without math, there'd be no TV, no Walkmans, no microwave ovens. The full truth is that without math, we'd have no structure, no beauty. There are sixty seconds in a minute, seven major scale notes, four seasons, ten toes, and twenty-six letters in the English-language alphabet. The potential domino effect of resolving the most-difficult math problems would be akin to becoming president or emperor—not that I was seeking such a position.

On the last day of the school year, with all the excitement the *Monkey on Your Back Math* book generated for me, I mistakenly forgot to check it out. Most likely, as they were known to do, the librarians were snooping on my activities. Instead of kindly reminding me I needed to check the book out, they accused me of stealing. A-holes. I couldn't articulate my explanation when two approached me outside. They gave a short lecture and emphasized their seriousness with added finger wags. In response to their reprimands, I pointed out the commemorative sign dedicating the library to Paul Robeson, which lists his death as *Saturday, January Twenty-third, Nineteen Hundred Seventy-six*. But Robeson, a beloved and respected celebrity, crowned class valedictorian with Phi Beta Kappa distinction, was dishonored because January 23, 1976 fell on a Friday not a Saturday as the plaque states. I told them this mistake disgusted me. With a final act of personal justice, I gave them back their book, dropping it just before they took it from my hand.

OK, actually, I only wished I had the audacity to drop the book through their fingertips, because every day I'd visited the library, the incorrect sign annoyed me. In reality, I said, "Sorry" as I handed back the book, and my skin heated to a deep crimson.

I say crimson but you'd probably say the basic, three-letter word for the color that a tomato or a strawberry is. I have no full explanation for why that three-letter word is so annoying other than certain words torment me more than incorrect dates on a commemorative sign.

The ordeals of language, my private war, are no ordinary irritation. Most people have special words that torment or at least sounds that raise hackles and blood pressure. Mom used to go crazy when someone spoke with extra moisture in his voice or when adults spoke in baby talk. Varieties like the words *colorless* or *nameless* trouble me with their hypocrisy, and I'd love to watch Gauss or Archimedes take on assigning the proper calculations for them. But like the way your brain will quickly silence the occasional ringing created by an inner-ear nerve dying, I've developed similar devices to quell the turmoil these words cause.

The word *infinity* is different. While I can handle for the most part its spoken or written forms, some structures in nature suggest it can cause true havoc to my well-being.

On my trip to the bus stop, to save time, I always take a shortcut across a corner of the Rosens' expansive lawn. Today I'd found a fresh pile to permit me to cross unscathed, but until I learned the trick, crossing Rosens' corner was an almost impossible feat. Shortly after I arrived in North Brunswick, I discovered unbroken stretches of grass fell into the starry sky-and-ocean territory. All three have the potential to make me pass out from their relation to infinity, and without some form of distraction, they're a substantial sedative. It took a few instances of awaking face-down in the grass before I ascertained lawns were a new culprit. Dandelion heads worked to break up the uniformity, but not until I discovered the salvation of dog-shit piles—my favorite dog by-product—did I learn how to navigate suburban yards. The 1981 *Guinness Book of World Records* lists St. Bernards as the heaviest of the domestic breeds. Just imagine what it feels like to step down into the soft magic of one of their king-size curls. The Rosens have a friendly St. Bernard named Biggs, who likes to dump on the back half of the lawn where I cross. Man's best friend.

"Shit, that's like the hundredth one you've stepped in. Don't you ever look where you're going?" Russell said, holding his nostrils closed when I met up with him.

"Hey, you know-you know—" I started.

"Shh, he can probably hear. Keep your voice down," Russell told me as he gestured to the other member of our bus stop's wait list.

"But, I, uh, I went to see—"

"OK, but don't fuckin' raise your voice so much." Russell nodded his head toward him again.

John Berg never said a word to us. He was a smooth biker thug in a thirteen-year-old body, whom we looked upon with fear and jealousy. Russell and I both wished we could stand with him, but instead we talked in hushed voices and tried to see who could kick a stone the closest to the curb across the road without actually hitting it.

"One with real tits, damn. I wish Shelly took me, too."

"Many real ones, but-but no one under seventeen without an adult. The—and the Soap-N-Spin, the sign, the one on the door window said, 'Join us for our grand opening October First,'" I said with a wave of my hand for emphasis.

"That soon? October first is practically already here, fuck," Russell said, shaking his head in disbelief. His pack of Now & Later taffy crinkled in his pocket, and he palmed me one, trying to keep them a secret from John.

"Shelly said forget about the bike already. Your bike's with Hank and Will."

"Where'd you leave it? On the side? I'm not going there to ask for it. If that's the case, you can pick it up, and I'll ride it another day."

"Out front, right side."

"They know it's mine, right?"

"I told them that fact the occasion I first rode it there."

"What? So, they know it's mine?"

I nodded. Russell wasn't allowed to visit the garage with me. His parents thought the Flynns sold drugs. I'd never heard who told them that lie.

Their bus arrived. John's nicotine breath smacked my nose as he stood behind us, waiting for the doors to open. I considered it a much-kinder gesture than his fist, not that he'd ever used his fist on me, but one must prepare with a character like him.

"You want to search for the fort after school?" Russell asked.

"Call me, and, and if it's probable, I'll accept the charges." I put my pointer finger in the air for emphasis.

Russell quickly looked up bemused. "Um, yeah, see ya," and used the metal railing to board. The lady driver gave me a little wave before she folded the doors shut.

Since they won't allow me back at Rutgers—a failed "test of maturity" they called it—I have to attend hateful mind-numbing classes at the public high school again. My bus arrived a few minutes after Russell and John's. The driver reserved the front seat for me. The first two days, I sat with a blond deaf kid who towered about two feet above me and took up most of the legroom. He must've arranged different transportation, because since then I've had the seat to myself.

For the past two weeks, part of my school day consisted of a so-called AP or Advanced Placement mathematics class run by a stodgy Dr. Solomon Limone, 12 Arrowwood Lane. His English accent amused me the first day, but the fun quickly faded. AP math was designed for the "highly motivated" student, and on the class outline, it showed the first half of the year would provide an in-depth study of the concepts and methods of calculus with an emphasis placed on formal proof. Since the second day, I could tell you there are eighty-four ceiling tiles with 443 or 449 holes in each. This averaged out to about 37,464 dots on the ceiling. Last week, I discovered that there are five fewer floor tiles than ceiling tiles. Yes, the class is that exciting.

"Welcome back to our little friend, Abel. How was your weekend, Mr. Velasco?" Dr. Limone greeted me as the class filed in.

I'm his "little" friend, and he's scarcely a few inches taller than I am. I potentially could still grow taller, but he's done. I took my seat without responding.

Phillip Macklehorn, wearing his ironed designer jeans, sat next to me in the front row. Phil, who hates to be called Phil, loved the color brown and wore it daily on his nose. As Dr. Limone began writing some notes on the board, Phil leaned over and whispered, "I think Limone's a little sweet on you. Didn't hear him ask me how my weekend was."

Heat filled my cheeks, and I'd have liked nothing better than necrotizing fasciitis, a rare bacterial infection that can destroy skin and the soft tissues beneath it, to suddenly invade Phil's ChapSticked lips as he smacked them together while the final bell rang.

"Please, pass your homework forward. Once it gets to the front row, pass them inward to Phillip today. Would you collect these and place them on my desk, then, Phillip? Thank you." As the papers were passed, Dr. Limone stood at the front of the class, pulling on his nose and straightening his tie with aristocratic flair. Arrogance stands out like sticky nose-relish on a face, but add a dash of English flamboyance to conceit, and it engenders in me fantasies of physical harm. Plus, Dr. Limone's height gave him the short man's belief that arrogance could make up for stature. The educational world was littered with men like him, but he's my first from the British Isles. Of course, if I don't grow much taller, I'll rescind all that short-man conjecture or make the calculation fit only half of the short-man population.

After his most-gracious placement of the homework pile on Dr. Limone's desk, Phil took his seat. Dr. Limone began, "I'd like to thank you all for providing me with good reason for moderating this class again and for giving me hope for the rest of the school year. With but a few exceptions, all of you got a C on this first of many quizzes."

The class of overachievers collectively groaned.

"It tells me you have room for improvement, and that I will have to work hard to help you along." He placed Phil's on his desk first. It had a circled A- on it.

Even though I was one of the privy few to know the grade Phil received, I'm sure I wasn't the only one in the class who wanted to puke at the sight of Phil's and Dr. Limone's grinning faces. When Dr. Limone placed mine on my desk, he gave a concerned look and waited until I reviewed what he'd commented. Each of my answers was circled with "Where's your work?" written angrily in felt-tip blood. A big zero hovered at the top of the page, with a note in black pen that read, "Please see me after class."

Johann Friedrich Carl Gauss was the first mathematician I thought of when I came to North Brunswick. Like me, he showed signs of genius by the age of three, had an uncle who helped raise him, and never left the town of Brunswick in Germany. I'd shivered at the thought of never leaving North Brunswick. At age seven, Gauss had a teacher named Büttner whose bio read as if his name suited him well. Büttner was infamous for his tortuous educational methods. The story goes that Büttner pushed the class to its limit trying to crack Gauss, and just when they thought Büttner would give them reprieve, he brought forth a problem certain to make the students pull out their hair. But before Büttner finished the last stroke of his chalk, Gauss flung his tablet down and said, "*Liggett Se*," German colloquialism for "There it lies," correctly answering the challenge with ease.

As far as I'm concerned, Gauss sounds like he had a little Phil Macklehorn in him. I mean, half the blame could be pinned on Gauss for challenging Büttner, who then made the rest of the class suffer. Still, I wished I had a tablet to fling so I could write out the proof to what Limone would consider the hardest of the problems on his quiz and shout, "*Liggett Se*" in his face. Or at the very least, I wanted to look him in the eyes and with my best Jeff Spicoli, say, "You dick!" Instead, I nodded at him so he'd know I read the note and spitefully ignored his lecture for the rest of the class.

After the bell, I packed my satchel and put its strap over my shoulder, readying to go, but remained in my seat.

"Ah, Mr. Velasco, I'm so glad you stayed."

I'd learned at most schools since the New City School, if you don't want attention from teachers and classmates, don't get perfect grades. Go for average, champion mediocrity, but I hadn't been in a classroom in a while, and now I'm certain to have to start acting dumb. The number clouds returned to the periphery of my vision.

"You don't like being in my class much, do you?" Dr. Limone said, taking a seat on the corner of his desk.

I stared at my hands, not knowing how to respond.

"You must find it incredibly boring if what I've recently heard is true. I'm not completely convinced, I'm afraid. So let's see." He rose from his desk and took a piece of chalk from the tray at the board. "Someone capable of what you've achieved on my recent quiz should have no issue with this?" He looked at the board for a bit and quickly wrote a problem far beyond what we'd been taught in school, underlining it twice. "You may sit there for as long as it takes for you to figure out what the answer is, and just to be fair, you may jot some notes before adding the answer to the board."

My face felt like it was on fire, and I sat, unmoving and uncertain what to do.

"Hm. OK, well, possibly it was unfair of me, so maybe you'll be able to complete this."

He wrote another less-difficult problem on the board. The force of his tack-tack-tacking with the chalk incited itchy feet. I wanted to leave but remained seated for several minutes before Dr. Limone spoke again.

"This is not looking good for you, Abel. However, this last problem is of the same variety as found on this past quiz. I expect it should be easy for you."

He wrote it out, and after he'd finished again, I continued to stay seated and silent. He stood glaring at me. "It is as I expected. You have duped people in the past, but this is where that comes to an end. You are obviously not equipped to be in my or any advanced class, are you, Mr. Velasco?"

I kept staring at the plastic desktop.

"Abel, this kind of deception is not a—"

I stood up and glanced at him long enough to see his eyebrows raise.

"I have not dismissed you yet."

I went toward the door, the long way around Dr. Limone and his desk, approached the chalk board, and completed all three problems. I drew an arrow down and added a string from some λ-calculus that related to his most difficult problem. I added a calculation for *"Liggett Se"* but reversed it so that there was no possible way for him to recognize my code.

The disdain and challenging look on Dr. Limone's face barely melted.

"What is that last bit there?" he said in a slightly gruff manner.

I decided to respond to the computer code and not my personal retort. "Lambda calculus is a formal system for function recursion and relates to some computer languages, particularly LISP."

He looked around the room and started acting a bit frantic, seeking something. He went to his desk and opened a book that had *Topology* written on the cover and flipped to the back of the book where a marker had been placed before laying the book in front of me. "Can you tell me what each of these four diagrams is an example of?"

I'm not sure at what point a person would be taught about topology, but I knew it wasn't in high school. I noticed there were the four branches of topology, so I said, "Um, that is algebraic, that is differential, that is low-dimensional, and that, um, is, um, point-set topology."

He gently took the book from in front of me and closed it. "Why in God's name are you in a class like mine? I was dumbfounded by your answers to my quiz. I thought no one could be so stupid as to cheat and not at least try to make it look like they'd factored it on their own. I was sincerely upset with you—"

"I didn't cheat," I managed to say as I fought to will the discomfiture from my face.

"Oh, my dear boy, of course you didn't. They really should offer more information on special students like you. But the inept ones in administration . . . two weeks putting up with my blather, I'm terribly sorry. They only said you'd skipped some grades and were good with math. There is no record of what you were studying at Rutgers, but there is documentation of some theft? Stealing isn't a milestone one likes on one's record, unless you're Robin Hood, I'd say."

"I-I didn't—"

"Well, they think you did, but you have no other black marks on the few records we have for you, so I'll choose to believe you and not them. You haven't made it easy on me to discern your intellect, you know. You could have participated in class more to give me a heads-up, but I suppose it's not easy acclimating to such situations." He looked at the blackboard and back at me. "I know as an adult and as a teacher, no less, I'm thought of as the enemy, but I'd be most pleased if I could help you out. Would you give me a few days to queue things up? I'd like to make some calls, and if the responses are what I'd like, we'll see about making life a little more exciting for you."

His being kind to me, without obvious arrogance, became an obstacle to the faith I had in his character.

"You're really not a talkative fellow, are you? No bother. So, instead of your regular classes, I believe your time would be better spent in the library. Until I've gotten my replies, that is. Would that suit you very much?"

His grin allowed me to look at the heavy yellow buildup on his teeth. I nodded.

"Fine, fine, then. Check in with me each morning, and I'll speak with your other teachers. Oh, and I'll make certain administration understands the situation also. 'bout time they were up to speed on you."

I got up and started walking out the door when he shouted after me, "I should have something for you by the end of the week. I hope the library will suffice."

I simply waved. Repeating it, he probably wanted more gratitude, but I wasn't sure he deserved it yet. I dropped my sweatshirt at my locker since they set the heat in the building too high. My armpits were excessively moist. On my way to the library, someone walked behind me.

"Hey, retard, your fag tag's showing."

I didn't turn around, but since I was the only one in the hallway, I knew he meant me.

"Hey, retard, are you deaf, too?"

His distinctive, odd, nasal voice revealed its owners identity: Kevin Schmill, the tallest and the oldest of the Kevins. Russell and I had seen him around town with his other friends, Kevin Hudrick and Kevin Groter. Schmill was the dumbest of the three, not that it was much of a competition.

"I said, your fag tag's showing, fag." Schmill pulled hard on the tag on the back of my collar, ripping it out and knocking my satchel from my shoulder. I almost lost my balance but hooked the satchel on my elbow and managed to stay standing. He laughed and walked past, tossing my tag to the ground. The sound of the library door closing behind me offered minor relief, knowing he wouldn't follow. Yet another example of how libraries are security against ignorance.

CHAPTER FIVE

L'Ecole des Filles and the Allure of Abandoned Dwellings

48.6.35.48.75.48.35.26.9.30.27-9.6.35-9.1.38.48.11.26.5.26.27-4.5.30.2

My phone rang at 3:49:39 p.m. Russell, no doubt, called within thirty seconds after arriving home from school.

"I got a tip on the fort, but meet me at the tree, OK?"

Pigpie yelled something at me while the door was closing, but I pretended not to hear and kept walking. Mister Scratch ran along, and as I swung from the limb onto the tracks, I was surprised to find him still by my legs. I thought he stopped following, but a few yards past the blackberry vines, I heard the whining begin. Mister Scratch may have some German shepherd in him but not enough for membership in the "smart dog" club. He'd gotten caught up in the vines. A step to the side and the thorns would have been avoided, but Mister Scratch couldn't see that. I used my jacket, tucking it around his body to help, and received contented leg and crotch sniffs with matching tail wags in return for his freedom. After a little ear scratching, he trotted back home without me. Not surprisingly, my jacket smelled of dirty dog when I put it back on. Nice.

"Hey!" Russell shouted down to me from the top of the tree.

Russell was busy focusing his binoculars when I reached him.

"Jerry Hampton told Bill Necks's brother, Mike, who told me that it's covered with pine branches, so no wonder we couldn't find it because it's fuckin' invisible in the summer, but now that the leaves are almost gone, it sticks out like crazy. He said it's near the tower near his house, which is near Mank's." He looked down at me. "Shit, you're a slow climber."

Jerry Hampton, 223 Bains Street, bought and resold gum at school. He was well-known but mainly hung out with other troubled kids. Jerry lived in a house past the lake, so he might actually know something about the fort, but even at our elevated height, I had my doubts Russell would spot it. As Russell scouted the area for the fort, I slowly peeled a big piece of bark off the trunk, trying to get it as big as I could like sunburned leg skin in the summer.

Three palm-size pieces of bark later, Russell proclaimed, "There! I see it there. Here, take a look."

I glanced in the direction Russell pointed and saw some pine trees.

"See that space by the water tower? Just over to the right of it."

I put the binoculars to my eyes, and at first, I had trouble seeing anything but two dots of white light at the center of each lens. I finally focused and noted that plenty of pine branches grew but nothing I could identify as a fort, or anything other than treetops, really. I shook my head.

"Over to the right of the tower, it looks like a shield of pine trees."

I found the water tower and kept looking for another minute, but Russell started climbing down.

"Come on, I fuckin' bet I can find it over there."

The ride there would be long, and I doubted we'd find anything, but I knew the two library books I'd checked out wouldn't last all night.

I mostly hated sharing a bike ride with Russell, but he took great offense the time I tried to say I didn't want to. Russell pedaled as I rode because he said he knew the area better than I did, but I knew the full reason was because we'd be going downhill, and he wanted me to have to pedal back. Luckily, that meant he didn't have his arms wrapped around my waist, and I could hold onto the seat for balance. The batteries in our radio were dying, and between the static we caught snatches of what I thought was The Archies, but revealed itself to be the "Stars on 45 Medley" before the radio went silent. I didn't much like the song, so I didn't care. We cycled along Georges Road across the highway circle and past the old National Musical String Company buildings. The slope of Farrington Avenue angled toward the lake, and we coasted down it until the bend.

After about twenty minutes, we could see the water tower clearly. "I think this path leads to the dam," Russell shouted back through the breeze. Normally, we walked, so this was our first ride to the dam.

Even though he gave a heads-up, it still surprised me when the bike quickly turned off the street and down a dirt trail. We bumped along it through some trees and the lake came into view.

"Geesh, we must need rain. Look how low the watermark is," Russell repeated what we'd heard a couple of anglers say last time we visited the dam.

Russell's one hand on the handlebars wasn't enough to sustain our balance, and the bike started wobbling. We quickly came to a graceless halt unhurt—me falling off into the field, him with his leg through the frame. I got up from the ground as Russell laughed, unconcerned over whether I'd been hurt, and began pushing the bike farther into the tall grass.

After a few paces, Russell said, "Let's just leave it here," dumping the bike in the weeds.

"You can see the other end of the lake is where the tower is, so over there near Mank's Creek, probably." Russell slapped his neck when something bit him.

"Wouldn't that, uh, wouldn't that mean June ninth?"

"What's June ninth?"

"Three glass Coke bottles, next to the burned trash, remember? June ninth. It is a fact. I got one. You got two." The folks who owned the house where we found the bottles saved money by burning refuse instead of paying to have it hauled away.

"What'd you expect? I found 'em. You're fuckin' lucky I gave you any, right?"

"No, uh, no, I mean, that was when we walked Mank's Creek."

"Oh, right, but that was summer. We could've missed it."

The air by the lake edge was cooler, and the scent of the algae mingled with the strong scent of pine, creating a pleasant effect. I wished it wasn't only good-smelling but also an insect repellant because the no-see-ums and gnats were swarming. One flew up my nose, causing me to cough when it hit the back of my throat.

"Let's go check it out, anyway. We could find some more bottles maybe." Russell walked ahead. A frog jumped into the water from the bank, which made us pause to see if we'd view him surface. No luck. We'd spent hours trying to catch frogs or crayfish or minnows, only to let them go. Unless Russell killed them, that is. He did that sometimes for no reason.

Mank's easily ranked as one of the best creeks to explore due to the plentitude of animal hiding spots. An amazing fact, since I mainly considered the water to be poisonous, but we'd seen frogs, minnows, carp, sunfish, a raccoon, muskrats, snapping turtles, painted turtles, box turtles, tadpoles, crayfish, too many types of insects to list, too many types of birds to list (except for maybe the herons, which were my favorite), mice, regular rats, cats, chipmunks, possum, and plenty of snakes. The abundance of great, flat stepping-stones made it even better to travel along, but you needed good balance at many spots. At a few locations, you had to get back on land, but mostly, you could stay right with the water without getting wet (unless you fell in) until you reached the sewer plant, always the final destination. The first time I saw the "stew-of-poo," as Russell called the large processing vats, I wondered about the quality of the water that poured into the creek. I never drank from Mank's, no matter where or how fast the water rushed by. Russell said it was OK to drink if the water was rushing.

    We arrived at the mouth of the creek and started following it toward the processing plant. I thought about the location of the creek and how Jerry's house wasn't that far. There were two other houses along it, and I bet if the fort existed anywhere, it'd be near the one that didn't have the barrel, because there weren't that many trees on the barrel property.

    We'd just passed the barrel when Russell's body stiffened and his vocal cords went tight. "There." I should never doubt his bloodhound nature. He pointed and started quickly toward it. It was only a corner of wood, but obviously, its sawed edge wasn't part of a tree. He kept murmuring, "Jackpot, jackpot, jackpot . . ." as we hiked through a grove of smaller pines. I found myself echoing his chant, "Jackpot, jackpot, jackpot."

    "Shh, see if you can hear anybody up there." His mouth-corner spittle made the *shh* a sloppy spray.

    We listened quietly. The fort nested between a *v* of a sizable oak, camouflaged with pine branches on all sides, sort of like a giant Russian winter Ushanka hat. A rope hung down from the door at the bottom of the fort. The rope didn't come all the way to the ground, though, only to about halfway to where they'd nailed a slat ladder like on the sycamore.

    "Do you hear anything?"

I shook my head.

"I think it's empty, and if anyone's inside, we'll just say we thought it was abandoned. All right?"

Russell wiped his mouth on his sleeve as I nodded.

From beneath the fort, the height of the tree appeared daunting, but Russell went ahead, making the climb seem much easier. At the first good foothold, I read the door in the tree-fort floor. *Stay out or U R DEAD meat* was written in white paint. I alternated between looking at Russell's sneakers and the tree trunk as I climbed. The tricky part came at the top slat, and even Russell hesitated when he realized what we had to do. The trunk divided into two at this junction, and while our part of the trunk had the climbing slats, the dead-meat door entrance was above us on the other side. Our trunk had a little platform where you had to stand, lean out, and grab the rope so you could climb up to the entrance. It was fairly ingenious, really.

Russell stood on the platform, looking down at me. The rope was too far, so he leaped to it at the last second and swung, laughing with relief. The fort moved a little as he dangled. He waved over at me once he was secure. "Schmeasy," he said and climbed from knot to knot until he could push the door open and stick his head through.

"Shit, you're not even gonna fuckin' believe it!" he cried as he pulled himself in.

I waited nervously on the platform for the rope to stop swinging. I could feel my heart in my throat and considered climbing back down, but Russell oohed and wowed over whatever he'd found inside, so I had to jump and soon.

"I might be too short," I said to the rope, turning around to see if I might climb the trunk into one of the windows instead. Russell's head popped out the doorway.

"Come on, Apple, don't be a pussy. It's paradise, better than buried treasure."

Russell's description was correct, and from my evaluation, it must've taken quite a long time to make. The fort could clearly hold six people and was nineteen feet off the ground.

I estimated the rope hung fifty inches from me. The probability of my missing it resolved at next to nothing, but the chance that I'd slip or not grip it correctly was significant, as was the drop if I did.

Russell stuck his head out of the door. "What are you fuckin' waiting for?"

I looked at him, wished I had Steve Austin's bionic legs, and looked at the rope again. There was nothing left to do, so I counted to seven and leaped. To my surprise, I caught it easily and held on until I secured a knot under my sneakers and my ass. Schmeasy, indeed. I finally arrived at the door, and Russell helped pull me inside.

"Shit, finally. Wait'll you see," Russell said. I moved in, and he raised the rope up and dropped the hatch shut.

Shadows huddled at every nook, but the three small windows allowed enough light to see most everything. It felt like some ancient tomb. The trunk ran up one side and had more slats nailed to it for climbing to the roof. The builders added shelving on each wall. Old magazines, a can with dried white paint dripping, a piece of broken mirror, a mud-encrusted bucket, and a somewhat-out-of-place set of bound copies of *Reader's Digest* were stored on the shelf closest to me.

"Lookit this stuff." Russell propped his foot on a bench with a blanket draped over it and swelled with pride, as if he owned the place already. It suited him somehow. Pine needles mashed into dried mud coated the walls—a hairy square cave, an abandoned bird's nest.

"Mike said they built this from stuff they stole from the mansion. Feels like it, doesn't it? I bet they covered the walls with this crap to cover over the blood." He looked at me with wide eyes, scaring himself.

The Pierson mansion, as town legend would have it, was where a father killed himself and his family. Apparently, the house has never been inhabited since. Russell told me this as we viewed the mansion's strange roof in the distance on one of our creek walks, and I can't say I believed it, but from a distance the mansion certainly had a classic, haunted quality.

Russell pulled a rope strung around a pulley. Suddenly, the pine limbs that covered a large window lifted away, brightening everything. With the added light, I surveyed the interior and noticed words written on a hatch in the ceiling: *Dead Man's Drop.*

"Cool!" Russell exclaimed, excited by the rope trick, and we looked at each other, moving closer to the window to peer out over the lake. We felt a kind of majesty, something delivered by being inside and high above, but it was short-lived. He let go of the rope, and the window slammed shut with a little gust of wind, making us both jump back. Russell nervously laughed.

"Oops. Sorry!" He moved over to one of the full shelves. "Look here, it's like someone was fuckin' readin' my mind for what I'd always wanted." He opened an old cigar box to show me a pack of Marlboro cigarettes, several packs of matches, a folding knife, and a container of Love's Baby Soft body lotion. He put the box down, leaving the lid open, and showed me a small pile of magazines.

"And look, can you believe it?"

One *Hustler*, two *Playboy*s, one titled *Oui* and one titled *Scandinavian Sweethearts*. I felt more nervous joy than fear and couldn't believe our luck. I decided no matter what happened now, it was worth it. Russell handed me the *Oui* and one of the *Playboy*s and kept the rest for himself.

"I was saving this for the weekend, but I feel like it's a better time now." He pulled a pack of grape Hubba

Bubba from his pocket and handed me a piece. My reflection grinned at me from the broken mirror as I unwrapped the gum. Dark streaks of dirt slashed my neck, and I continued to watch as I lit the cigarette Russell handed me. Shadows warped the angles of my face, and when the match light faded, I looked like an undertaker or a killer from a late-night TV movie as the smoke seeped from my mouth. I stuck my tongue through the gum and blew a small bubble. Hard to believe how great they tasted together. Grape Hubba Bubba and cigarettes.

We stood at separate windows for decent light, flipping through the magazines. I'd doubted Russell understood that *Oui* meant *Yes* in French, but disappointingly, the magazine was written in English. It'd have been good fun to translate for him. I fanned the pages to get a feel for its contents. Unbelievable.

"Holy shit, holy shit, look at that." Russell brought his hand with the lit cigarette to his mouth to cover his triumphant grin as he tilted the magazine for me to see and revealed a close-up of a woman's vagina.

Russell had practiced fancy ways of inhaling, letting the smoke leak out some and quickly sucking it back in his mouth or up his nose. Every time he pointed something out to me, he inhaled like that and ashed his cigarette out the window. I couldn't help but notice Russell's inflated pants. He moved closer to me on the bench, and I tried not to think about him having a boner. It was monumentally difficult.

Playboy turned out to be a disappointment because the majority of the magazine was stuffed with articles, ads, and cartoons. So I picked up *Oui*, which had spectacular visions on almost every page. One photograph included a beautiful, glistening black woman about to lick the long, hairy shaft of a tubby white guy with only dark sunglasses on and his pants around his ankles. In the next panel, she had it between her amazing bulbous lips. His boner looked about three times the length of what nature provided me with. I needed to shift mine because it'd become lodged awkwardly against my thigh. When I looked over at Russell to see if he saw me do it, I found him squeezing his. He must've sensed my gaze because he lowered the magazine, covering it, sheepishly took a drag of his cigarette, and blew the smoke toward the window as if to say, "I've got all the time in the world."

"In 1650, modern pornography had its beginning," I recited from the 1965 *Encyclopaedia Britannica*.

"What's that?" he asked with annoyance.

"'*La Puttana Errante*, translated from the French meaning 'The Wayward Prostitute,' and *L'Ecole des Filles*, meaning 'Girls School,' were translated into seven major languages. These novels became models for all later pornographic books and movies.'"

"What are you talking about?"

I held up my magazine showing him the cover. "*Oui* is French."

Russell scrutinized it half interested, rolled his eyes a little, but kept looking my way in a partial daze. "Just leave me alone for a while, will ya?" He suddenly ducked to the side of the window, listening intently. It was with such intense drama, I thought something possibly flew in the window and hit him until I noticed he wasn't clutching himself in pain or swatting anything.

I started to shift away from my window, and he shushed me with a pointing downward motion as if to say someone was there. We waited about ten seconds, not moving, and as I started to crouch, he began laughing. "Ha, you were about to shit your pants. Don't try to deny it, ya dweeb. I got you good."

I didn't react except to move back into the position I previously held. He put his hand in his pocket with a big satisfied grin and went back to the magazine. I returned to *Oui* immediately, forgetting about his trick when I turned to page twenty-three, where it showed a man having sex with a woman. I turned my back to Russell when I found it, fearing he'd see and take the magazine for himself. The picture showed it half inside her. I flipped ahead to see if there was anything better but returned to twenty-three several times. I looked over again to discern whether Russell could view my erection, and this time I found him looking at my crotch. He must've known I had one.

"Hey, you know. You know, I have to be in before the sun sets." From the height of the sun, I could tell I still had about an hour.

"You have short poles on top of your bedposts?"

I faced him again but looked out the window and figured it might not be a bad idea to start home now, as I had no idea the time it might take to climb down.

"I have to be in before the sun sets," I repeated.

He continued to ignore me and with an odd excited voice said, "Don't fuckin' say anything, but I know you would do it, too, and think it feels so great, because it does. But when I get out of the bath, I sometimes sit on those short poles on the top of the bedpost. It's hard to balance, but if I pull my desk table over, it's not a problem. It feels really good, so don't fuckin' say anything."

I wasn't sure how to respond. The calculation for Russell's private activity stuttered a bit in my head before I finished working it out. I blinked a few times and looked at the Love's Baby Soft bottle in the open cigar box. I knew what being gay meant, men who liked to put their dicks in each other's rectums, and it sounded a lot like Russell would want to do that. But I decided that x in this equation wasn't equal to Russell liking dicks but simply the fact Russell wasn't that intelligent.

I don't think he read my mind, but he defended his action. "I'm not a gay bird. I don't want a wang. The pole just feels good. I still like porking women, you know."

"OK, but, I think the, the sun will set soon." I moved the magazine over my crotch.

"Jeez, it's just bed poles. I don't want your wang."

I pulled the door up, and a rush of air came in. So did the sight of the ground far below. I stepped back.

"Hey, watch out!" He grabbed a group of the thin volumes of bound *Reader's Digest*.

For a moment, I thought he meant to hit me with them, but he shoved two through one of the windows and stuck his head out to watch them fall.

"Come on, we don't want these." He shoved a few forcefully at me, so I threw them one by one out the window as he watched. Then he did the same, and I watched as the pages fluttered each volume to the ground.

He threw the paint can down through the door. It clattered on the ground below and the lid popped off, splattering a small amount of paint.

"Great, fine. Now let's go. We can come back this weekend, right?" he said, acting somewhat upset still.

Russell dropped the rope through the opening and held the sides of the doorway while he lowered himself onto the first knot. I stared at the three volumes left askew on the shelf before I worked up the nerve to follow. My erection quickly subsided when I saw the distance I had to climb. I figured it'd be easier than climbing up, so I kept my eyes on the rope and proceeded down.

Russell's continued anger was made apparent by his silence on the ride back. I wished we had extra batteries because I knew if the radio worked, he'd be commenting or singing. The sun hung low in the sky and put a bright-orange outline around Russell's shadowed face when I got off the bike at our hiding spot.

"You won't say anything about what I told you, right, because that was pretty much a secret. I only ever think about women." His shoulders were tensed up near his ears with his elbows raised, and his hands wrapped around the back of his neck like he'd beat me with his elbow wings.

"Russell's no gay bird. Likes, he likes porking women."

"That some kind of joke?" He dropped his arms and moved toward me, getting angry.

"No, no." The calculations were blocking me.

"So you'll keep my secret, and that's it."

I stepped back as he moved closer and finally the symbols settled into place. "Like Bruce Wayne's Alfred," I said, trying to get on his good side.

"Just keep it a secret, OK? See you tomorrow." He ran off toward his house, and I took the darkening train path back home.

CHAPTER SIX

The Dreams of St. Martin and Descartes

7.2.1374.7.46-16.8.46.7.2.17.41-26.45-41.2.7.17.16.22.2.41

For most of the morning, I'd watched the tape and staplers fly. The three vested-with-slacks lady librarians filled with delighted cackles and hushing fun were decorating for Halloween. Handcrafted cardboard monsters and bats hung from every wall and desk of the library. Mom loved this time of year. She'd have been cackling along with them. I'm certain the Halloween holiday directed my eye toward *The Illuminated Text of St. Albans Psalter* in the card catalog. I hadn't viewed the grand illustrations since just after Halloween on November 2, 1980, when I lived with the Chungs. I'd completely forgotten to follow up on the questions I had back then after finding the St. Martin quire mark. I pushed the card drawer back and let the Dewey decimal system usher me to the art section, where the big books lived tortured lives on cramped shelves. I took 753.1 *The St. Albans Psalter* to an empty table decorated with an expandable pumpkin made of tissue paper, and started flipping to locate the quire mark again.

The St. Albans Psalter is made up of five distinct sections that contain (among other items): a liturgical calendar, forty full-page miniatures showing the Life of Christ, the psalms and prayers, a diptych showing the martyrdom of St. Alban, and not least, the illustration of St. Martin.

St. Martin himself only tangentially interests me because of the religious transformation in his story and its relation to Descartes. St. Martin's story in brief goes like this: Martinus, a Roman soldier, lived from 317 AD to November 11, 397 AD. The Roman armies were conquering everybody, and Martinus's unit marched to Amiens in Gaul during winter. A shivering, half-naked beggar approached Martinus at a gate. Martinus jumped down from his horse, cut off half his green cloak, and gave it to the beggar. That night Martinus had a dream where Jesus, glowing with one of those aureoles about his head, was wearing the half cloak Martinus had given the beggar, according to the illustration in *The St. Albans Psalter*. In the dream, Jesus told some angels about the greatness of Martinus but mentioned that Martinus wasn't baptized. Despite that obvious guilt trip, Jesus thanked Martinus for his generosity and gave him back the cloak. When Martinus woke in the morning, his cloak had been fused together again with supernatural magic. The dream made such an impact on Martinus, he got baptized, left the army, and became a monk. He was later renamed St. Martin.

The exceedingly interesting aspect is that in *The St. Albans Psalter* where the illustration of St. Martin is, there's a small curved *i* drawn at the top of the page—above the left angel in the margin on page fifty-three. It could be a quire mark. A quire mark is used in manuscript bindings, but there are no other quire marks in the remainder of the book. Why only one quire mark when there should be more? I think of it as a declaration of being, like saying by adding this modest little *i*, you and all others that look upon this book will know that *i* am, that *i* existed. Some quire marks are signatures, but this one isn't at the end as ones used as signatures often are. One must wonder if Descartes ever knew of St. Martin's story or had seen this text before his own similar dream.

In parts of Germany and the Netherlands, they celebrate St. Martin's eve November 10 in a similar fashion to the way we celebrate All Saints Day Eve aka Halloween on October 31. Kids get dressed up and go begging door to door. Interestingly, All Saints Day is November 1 and St. Martin's Day is November 11, but that's not an item I have questions about, merely a noteworthy calendrical fact.

My hero Descartes, the great scientist, mathematician, philosopher and head of the pack for creating declarations of being like that little *i*, traveled in Europe from 1618 to 1628 to study, as he said, the book of the world. While traveling in Germany on November 10, 1619, the eve of St. Martin's, Descartes had three connected dreams that, like St. Martin, changed his life.

In the first dream, Descartes is blown by evil winds from the safety of a church toward a third party, whom the wind cannot budge. In the second, he watches a frightful storm through scientific eyes and realizes that once the storm is seen for what it truly is, it can do him no harm. In the third dream, Descartes is reciting a poem of Ausonius, which begins with the line "What way of life shall I follow?" In the first two dreams, godlike forces seem to point to the answer of the question that the line of poetry in the third asks. In the first dream, Descartes sees that the church doesn't have all the answers; in the second, he uses science to understand something mysterious in nature, killing the fear of it in the process; and in the third, he looks to the arts for wisdom. Descartes woke feeling the solution to the foundation of all the sciences had been shown. After reviewing the dream, he exclaimed he'd devote himself to the pursuit of knowledge for the benefit of humanity.

So again, René's dream, where his life is transformed and focused in the way Martinus's was, happened on November 10, St. Martin's Eve. If nothing else, it's an interesting history-book coincidence.

I don't necessarily believe that either of them had these miraculous dreams. Of course, everyone dreams and both of them probably had some strange ones in their time, but God or Jesus appearing and directing you in your dreams seems like a lot of bullshit to me. Mostly it's the date of René's dream, the *i* mystery from the St. Albans text, and how it makes me think of Descartes's "I am" business that captures my attention.

Also somewhat attractive is the fact that Geoffrey de Gorham, the abbot of St. Albans, had the book made for his secret lover, Christina of Markyate, a woman who left her husband on their wedding night, hid out with monks, and eventually became a nun at St. Albans. An unconsummated love affair united the abbot and the nun and produced this wondrous text. I suppose that only interests me because Christina is also the name of the queen from Sweden who also never married but basically hired and killed Descartes—well, Queen Christina forced him to rise very early during freezing mornings to tutor her and hastened his death by pneumonia.

After I'd returned the book, I looked to see if by some odd chance the library had more on illuminated manuscripts, but high-school libraries often aren't extensive enough to stock such worthy texts. As I thought, no luck, so instead I picked up two phone books from the community section. While there, I heard someone on the other side of a shelf say, "*Come mierda,*" which translated from the Spanish means "Eat excrement" but was also slang for *idiot* or *annoying*.

As I peeked through an open space, I was shocked to learn it was one of the five students seated around a table. The teacher directing them barely seemed troubled. In fact, the only signs of frustration could be detected in her mildly raised voice and the continual tapping on her book with pencil.

"Franco, see, see, like Jose and Julian, please turn to page seven. Page *siete, siete por favor.*"

Franco was fanning the pages at himself, looking at her in a challenging way and talking to the other two students about their cow-faced teacher who doesn't even speak Spanish. Jose tells him to please just do as she says because maybe she's just playing dumb to see what they'll say, and Franco says she barely knows numbers and that he could tell her to clean his backside and she wouldn't get it.

Two girls conversed in Hindi as the teacher tried to turn Franco's page for him. Girly and fragile next to the three coarse boys, the girls appeared to be about a year apart in age. They had a lovely birdlike twitter, discussing with hushed voices about whether their father got indigestion from their mother's or their aunt's special vindaloo.

The teacher tapped at her notepad harder and harder because she couldn't gain control of the students. I looked about to see if a librarian would help when I noticed Dr. Limone waving from the other side of the library. The blush hit my ears before he got to me, and I hoped it might fade as fast as it appeared.

"Who're you trying to call?" he asked, pointing to the books.

"Uh, no one." Maybe I could pass the crimson in my face as a mild form of rosacea or acne. I had gotten my first real pimple forty-two days earlier, so it wouldn't have been implausible.

"Why the phone books, then?"

"Uh, Dr. Solomon Limone, twelve Arrowwood Lane, seven three two seven three eight zero three seven three."

"That would be me. No need for phone books; you could've simply asked. I'd have shared that with you." He questioningly cocked his head sideways to read their spines. "Those aren't for New Brunswick."

"No, Secaucus and Hoboken."

"Mm." He seemed to be mulling that idea over. "My address and number wouldn't be in those."

I thought it odd he'd say that when we both knew where he lived.

He continued, "I'm surprised we have copies of those. Well, you won't have to worry about finding the resources you want from here on out." He directed me over to a table next to where Franco was still defying the teacher. "Let's take a seat."

I slid the phone books to the side of the table, sat down, and set my satchel on the floor. Franco passed us and walked to the periodicals while the teacher continued with the remaining students.

"First, a bit of advice: Always hold on to old friends, my boy. One never knows when you'll need them. I contacted a brilliant fellow by the name of Conway whom I've known since my formative years at Cambridge." He gazed off for a second, posing with a those-were-the-days look. "An amazing individual. Why, just this year he's been elected a fellow to the Royal Society of London. Can't imagine that means much to you, sorry. I explained a little of your situation, and after the usual ribbing he gives about my career path, he agreed that this was a case where I could really make a difference."

He reached forward and momentarily grabbed the back of my hand with excitement, startling me. I quickly pulled mine away.

"He's made a few calls, and to make a long story short, we've arranged for an interview for you to see if instead of having to continue attending here, they'll let you use the library at Princeton University. Yes, the home of the likes of Einstein and Gödel. I said you'd been used to self-directed study and would that be OK until I'm able to drum up a grant or scholarship for a decent private school." He spread his arms wide with great pride. "So, what do you think?"

"When were your born?" I asked.

"Sorry?" His eyebrow arched again, and he smoothed out his tie.

"What, um, what is the date of your birth?"

"That would be January fourth, 1937, but—"

"It is a fact: You were born on a Monday and are forty-four years old. You are lucky because on January 4, 2002, you will be sixty-five and eligible for full retirement benefits. You are also lucky because that will be a Friday, a good day for a party. You are also a Capricorn, sign of the goat, or on the Chinese calendar, you are an ox. Oxen are quite dependable and possess an innate ability to achieve great things."

"Indeed, by sixty-five, I will be an old goat and hopefully will have achieved great things or, if not myself, have helped others to." He winked at me. "Thank you for all that." He thought it over for a second. "I'm afraid that doesn't answer my question. Do you think you might like to direct a bit of your life's path along the aisles of the Princeton University library, then?"

I tilted my head up and down like a Ken doll to his bride, Barbie. I imagined that a big-time university like Princeton would have a library where dreams are made. No more dealing with high-school students.

"What I'd like to do before I take you for the interview—which I've set for next week, by the way—is, well, preinterview you. Your records are very incomplete I'm afraid."

The number clouds rolled into the periphery as my heartbeat quickened. In the past, *interview* has been a code word for inspection or examination. I stared at the desk, trying to think of how to get out of his interview and still get to Princeton. These always started with an interview and led to a multitude of other tests.

"Would that be OK? I have time now if you do." He opened up a folder and pulled out a tablet.

"There, uh, there should be files on me already, OK."

He gave me a shifty look as if on the verge of irritation.

"Oh, yes, I've read those. Let's see, I'll just start at the top. Family records, all right? Your father, um, it mentioned his whereabouts are unknown but doesn't mention any history whatsoever. Have you ever known him?"

I looked at the desktop, hoping that would convey my discomfort over any discussion about my nonexistent father. I knew almost nothing besides his making my mother pregnant, going missing before I was born, having one obese sister who never speaks of him and one niece who knows as much about him as I do. Dr. Limone's stare required an answer that I didn't want to give.

"Descartes's housekeeper gave birth to his daughter, Francine. Francine died of scarlet fever when she was five in 1640," I finally managed.

Dr. Limone hesitated a few seconds, looking as if he may have been considering what I said, but if he was, he didn't address it. "Um, OK. Very good, thank you. And your mother was placed in care when you were six, currently at St. Mary's in Hoboken. Do you visit often now that you've moved closer?"

"No." I considered adding that Pigpie has never consented to my request to do so but did not.

He waited for a longer response and gently added, "Possibly you aren't old enough yet. So, you were placed in the custody of your uncle when your mother obtained help, but your uncle passed away when you were seven. Since then, you've been to three different schools, one for each of the three foster families you've lived with. Mediocre grades at each school, and a record of steady truancy."

Part of me thought of telling him the truth, but I held back. Of course, my grades were mediocre—it wasn't like I attended the Royal College La Flèche or something. Who'd care what those mental invalids thought or taught you?

"Only the last school recognized your math skills but didn't have the capacity to address them. Then your aunt was found. You were relocated here last January, which again, placed you in the hands of those that did not have the means, and since your aunt pushed the issue, they sent you to Rutgers to explore the library. Not too shabby. Your progress was monitored at Rutgers. They reported you did well on your own until the theft incident, which I know you have stated is false. Your aunt didn't make it easy for us to get you back to Rutgers. Even if one has connections, one can't go around calling others names in the way that she did and expect them to want to continue to offer special services."

Pigpie mainly insulted them because, as she said, "Now you'll be crappin' around the house all summer instead of going to that school, GD it!" not because she'd ever defend me.

He flipped the page of writing over to check the second page. "Our administration thought they'd try you in advanced-placement courses this year. Besides the calculus that you are obviously far beyond, it's too early to say how you'd fair in the other classes, but I'd imagine similarly. Although, it, um, seems you've had some trouble with Coach Banks." He leaned toward me. "I never liked gym class, either."

I only half paid attention to Dr. Limone but began to refocus on what was said as his face inclined toward me. Dr. Limone reminded me of Father Mullens when Father Mullens gave an equally excited description about the potential of gaining access to the Rutgers library. I made the mistake of commenting to the Father about how Pigpie had said Rutgers would be a gold mine. Father Mullens still agreed to help get me in, so I don't know why I was in trouble when he left. One could only hope Pigpie would be equally excited about Princeton.

"You're currently staying with Cecelia Stacks, your aunt, now widowed from Carl Stacks. Your cousin, Michelle Stacks, who goes by Shelly, whom you also live with, is in the senior class here, and that's it. Besides specifics of the dates and your grades, that's almost your entire recorded information, and to me, that isn't very much. So, do you mind some questions, or would you prefer to continue reading phone books at our lovely library facilities here?"

I took that as if I didn't answer his questions, I wasn't going to Princeton.

"Uh, you, uh, go ahead." I continued studying the grain of the table.

"Oh, good. Have you ever had your IQ tested?"

With that question asked, my system went off-kilter. It's the second sign of trouble. First, they say it's just a little interview, then they ask you to take IQ tests, then all the other inspections.

"Yes," I replied and banged my fist on the tabletop. Dr. Limone looked at me curiously but continued.

"OK, anything you want to share about it?"

I shook my head.

"OK, when was the last time you were tested?"

"When I, uh, was six."

"Who did the testing? What was your score?"

"New City, Ms. Crups with tan shoes and Mr. Patterson, always a blue tie. Ms. Crups said 'You did extremely well, my dear.'"

The black ink rolled out. Dr. Limone's thin, precise lettering quickly looped *Crups* and *Patterson* onto the page. I hated it whenever Mom took me for testing. All those doctors coming at me with wires, the pages and pages of questions and a promise of seeing Mom again soon if I'd focus on what they asked. Days spent away from her, no bike rides, no sing-alongs with my uncle. Trapped in the light-blue rooms where they'd do ridiculous things like tuck teddy bears into bed with me as if I cared about a stuffed toy.

"How long were you at New City School?"

The number clouds forced their way in front of my vision. "Dr. Schlety held a banana up to his ear and said, 'Ring, ring. Hello, hello. Abel, are you there? How are you?' He's too close to my face with his stupid banana. Dr. Schlety asked what he was doing. I said-I said, 'You're putting a banana in your ear.' 'Why would I do this?' Dr. Schlety asked. He kept putting the banana near his ear and taking it away. I said, 'Because you-because you don't know you eat a banana, not stick it up your ear?'" Dr. Schlety was a real a-hole who always treated me like a toddler.

Dr. Limone repressed a smile and looked at me curiously. He repeated his question. "How long were you at New City School?" The serious look on his face didn't ease my anxiety.

"For a semester, one hundred and eighty two days, then Mom . . . Uncle Ev didn't want me away from him."

Dr. Limone studied my face a little and reviewed his questions again. "What kind of things did they teach you at the school?"

"In the 1973 *Encyclopaedia Britannica*, it's reported that the world total of languages and dialects still spoken is 4,974. Chrichton, who lived from 1500 to 1585, had learned ten before the age of fifteen. Cardinal Giuseppe Mezzofani, 1774 to 1849, was able to speak fifty and translate from one hundred and fourteen. Sir John Brown, British diplomat, spoke one hundred and read in two hundred. I was seven and spoke one for each year old I was: English, Spanish, Russian, Italian, French, Korean, and German."

He gave me another look of disbelief and jotted a few notes.

"So, they taught you languages. Are you telling me you speak seven languages?" he said in French.

"No, eleven, or sixteen with the computer programming languages: Smalltalk-eighty, ANSI standard, AWK, Franz LISP, and Modula-two." I responded in French as well.

Dr. Limone's nose waved back and forth at me as he shook his head and continued writing. "My goodness, computers. So, what kinds of things were you interested in back then?" he continued in French.

I shrugged.

"Name two for me, if you would."

"Uh, calendars, and, uh, trains."

I waited for him to finish writing and considered the multitude of other things I might have said.

"Did they start you with your math education then?"

"No, at the Chungs."

He flipped to look at my documents. "This was when you were living in Wildwood, or was that Kirkwood?"

"Yes, Wildwood, Missouri, not New Jersey. Kirkwood was the Melvilles."

"I see that here. Yes, you lived with the Melvilles in Kirkwood. The Chungs in Wildwood, Missouri. Was it the Chungs that taught you math, then?"

"Im Chung, their oldest son, liked geometry a lot. I asked Im if I could borrow his book."

"So, you've learned none of your math in school? I see you had some classes. What did they teach you in the last formal math class you took?"

"To my left, every day, Brendan Wickerscham drew cartoon pictures of turtles on his yellow tablet. One turtle had a bigger head than the other turtle did. Turtles having sex or turtles on walks that ended with being flung from rubber flowers and then, turtle sex again. He shared them with Melanie Fox sitting next to me on my right. I was their courier. I stopped going to class."

More writing on his pad. "Impressive. Abel, Please don't take offense, but I'm hoping very much that what you're telling me is true. A natural talent. Would all of your math knowledge be self-taught, or did you have a tutor of some kind?"

Jubilant might be the word I'd use to describe Dr. Limone at this moment. It's a sunshiny, a sunshiny day. It's a sunshiny day.

Franco ran by again and started tugging at Julian's sleeve. The teacher finally snapped. She took Franco by the arm out of the library. Everyone stopped what they were doing and watched.

"Can I have only two more?" I said, refocusing on Dr. Limone and using English again.

"Two?" He looked at his notes. "I wouldn't say that-"

"I have two more answers left."

"I see." He put his tablet down. "Very well. I'll try and make them easy." He looked up for a moment. "Could you name any teachers that may have significantly helped you since your brief stay with the New City School?"

"No."

"No?"

"No."

"Is that no, you won't answer, or no, there haven't been any teachers?"

"No teachers."

"Mm. OK. What will you be doing for the rest of the afternoon, then?"

I pulled the phone books toward me, not really answering because that officially totaled three questions.

"Right, OK, then. Well, I suppose I know where to find you when I have more information. I'll leave you to it." He patted the phone books and left with a wide grin on his face.

I worried for a few minutes if I should've answered more questions and whether that would affect my acceptance to the Princeton library. Those thoughts faded by the time I got to Applethwaight, 9 Center Ave.

CHAPTER SEVEN

Records Spun and Broken

16.2.6.5.8.4-8.18.1.1.19.20.2.8.10.4.2.18.20

Mister Scratch had found some paper plates in the trash to rip up, and they'd migrated to the side of our yard. Pigpie might consider them as still being in Mr. Sutkin's yard, but I couldn't chance it, so I cleaned the shredded bits before I left. I pulverized an aluminum can, many dried leaves, and a Baby Ruth wrapper into the sidewalk as the liquid crystal seconds of my watch demanded more speed. They spat 3:52:07 p.m. at me when I passed under the Flynn's Garage sign. Twelve minutes seventeen seconds late. I tapped crossly at the face of my watch.

Hank was polishing a shiny new vending machine in the front office. The gold knobs and silver trim gleamed.

"Juke, just in time, just in time. Come 'ere. Won't take you but a second, not even, but count 'em. Four kinds." He tapped on each area of the glass in front of the peppermint, spearmint, cinnamon, and fruit-flavored Chiclets. After popping some change in the slot, he pulled the plastic knob, which sent a box of the peppermint shooting down to the dark retrieval area.

"Easy as that." Hank shook the box at me with a grin, ready to chew. He took a couple for himself, then handed me the box. "That's a gift and don't worry: It's not coming out of your pay." I preferred fruit-flavored but didn't mention it.

He polished the knob he'd just pulled.

"Won't have to go back to that racist Horace Inky Davis's anymore now, will I? You couldn't pay me to step in there, and I don't even like pool," Hank announced to the machine, giving the window a little extra polish before he tucked away his rag.

I remember on my second day in town, Pigpie showed me places she hadn't been since she'd left for Washington. Inky's, she explained, would be a treat. As we climbed the steps into the old brick building, she told me how Inky's had been around forever and that she spent many hours there when she was Shelly's age. The place had a grand glass display case in front, loaded much like the candy store in *Willy Wonka & the Chocolate Factory* shown on TV around Easter.

I stood at the section of the glass where packs of trading cards were stacked in boxes and listened to the other kids ordering penny candy while Pigpie talked with some of the men playing pool. Before we left, she came over and said hello to yellowing-teeth, yellowing-undershirt, yellowing-from-nicotine-fingertips Inky. Probably more for Inky than for me, she offered to buy me something. As they smoked and chatted while I made my decision, I overheard Inky ask Pigpie if she could still "whoop like Betty Boop." I looked up just in time to see Pigpie blush and comment on how those days were ancient history, then shake her head and gesture in my direction. Inky continued anyway about some guy named Bill who used to really make her whoop, how sad it was he gave Pigpie the heave-ho, and about how no one would touch her after that. Pigpie changed the topic by reminiscing how Inky served her candy when she was my age and nudged me to hurry up. Inky chuckled and lecherously said he still could.

His character rather sickened me, but Inky's candy selection was beyond reproach. BB Bats, Saf-T-Pops, root-beer barrels, licorice pipes, caramel creams, Big League

Chew, Abba-Zaba bars, Bubble Tape, Jelly Bellies, Starburst, Whistle Pops, Ring Pops, Spree rolls, licorice laces, Swedish fish, Tangy Taffy, Cherryheads, Lemonheads, Dots, Blow Pops, Mamba bars, Razzles, Black Taffy, Hubba Bubba, Bubblicious, Bubble Yum, Freshen-up spearmint gum, Hot Dog! gum, Beemans Gum, Mary Janes, Lifesavers, Nerds, candy lipstick, Bazooka gum, Atomic Fireballs, Sugar Daddies, Charleston Chews, Boston baked beans, Sugar Babies, Bottle Caps, candy cigarettes, candy necklaces, Chick-O-Sticks, wax lips, Fun Dip, Gobstoppers, Now & Laters, Pixy Stix, Smarties, Zero bars, Bit-O-Honey, Dubble Bubble, Tootsie Rolls, spearmint leaves, and gumdrops. I'm sure he added options I never saw.

The choice was torturous. Although I really wanted a pack of *Star Wars* cards, I decided not to be too greedy and instead chose what some of the others had. I politely requested ten of the one-cent "nigger babies," which were little sugar-coated, black-licorice men with top hats. Inky chuckled at me and started to bag them, but Pigpie slapped me hard on the ear and dragged me out of the place while the men by the pool table laughed. I barely knew her at that point but learned most of what I needed to know by the end of that day. On the street, she yelled about my embarrassing choice of words. Something did feel wrong when I said it. I knew that one shouldn't use *nigger* regularly, but I assumed that when used in reference to candy, it meant something else and was not derogatory. I'd heard people call other people *motherfuckers*, but I'd also heard people say, "That's fucking great" and they meant it as "That's really good." Plus, yellow Inky, who was a white man, didn't chuckle or seem shocked when the other boys ordered them using the term. I wondered now if Inky had a special name for Chiclets, too.

As Hank turned to me, I became filled with the desire for him to be my real father. If my real father could be anything like Hank, and he found me one day and bought me a box of Chiclets, well, that'd be something nice.

Mom and Uncle Evert never talked about my biological father or any of his relatives. It was an off-limits topic, and I gave up asking by the time I was six. When the foster system located information on my dad's sister, Pigpie, I immediately doubted its veracity. Hank was probably better than my real father, anyway.

As a smart marketing ploy, Hank made a sign that read: "Have a treat while you wait," with an arrow pointing to the machine, and placed it on the counter where people paid for services. Yelling came from the apartment upstairs, but I tried to ignore it. Hank led me to the plethora of boxed nuts and bolts. He said he sold some, but I had a hard time believing the market was that hot for the excessive stock stored along the far wall. At least nine new boxes rested among the multitude of rows since the last time I counted.

Will's record player sat on the workbench, down from their apartment, along with a couple of crates of albums. The eighth track of Stevie Wonder's *Music of My Mind* repeatedly asked why I keep on running from his love.

"This album is great from rim to hole, right?" The song was one of Will's favorites—a member of the large group he used to avoid working. Hank liked it a great deal as well.

"Oh, hey, that's right. What year was this put out again?" he asked, feigning ignorance and lit a Pall Mall.

"1972, and-and seven months later the same year he put out *Talking Book*, which is known by you but not by Will to be a far superior album. 'Superstition' went to number one on the charts."

"Damn straight, it's superior. 'Superstition,' 'Blame It On The Sun.' Can't beat 'em," Hank stopped to listen and took a long drag off his cigarette. "I'll get you a soda, but you can go ahead." He waved at the boxes. "Will should be right back if Mi hasn't killed him."

Hank seemed excited to have me around. As soon as he disappeared, Will's large boots thudded down the stairs from the apartment. I pulled down one of the full, unmarked boxes and grabbed an empty from the floor.

"No, I didn't!" Will yelled from the stairway. He reached the bottom and looked over at me, Mi yelled something else at him, and he yelled back, "Everything dies."

Whenever I saw them they were either arguing or busy making up. I preferred the making-up visits.

"Whattaya say, Jukebox? When'd you get here?"

"*Keep On Running* from *Music of My Mind*. It's your favorite."

"That's right, Juke. You know he played all the instruments on this one, right? Listen to that." Will immediately calmed down and bobbed his head to the rhythm. "I've missed most of—"

"This stink bad. It no stay. You wrong." Mi wandered down the steps, pouting angrily as she held a fishbowl half-full of water with a goldfish floating dead on the surface. As she walked to Will with defiant purpose, the water sloshed onto the floor, but the fish stayed inside.

Will looked at Mi holding up the bowl and said, "Smells like your cookin'. Get that out of my face, and throw 'im out already." He turns to me. "So stupid, she'd sell her car for gas money." Then he smiled and put his hand out for me to slap him five, which I'd learned would anger him if you didn't. I pretended to smack his palm and managed not to touch it, but I had to turn mine over. He slapped mine as Mi mumbled something in Vietnamese and angrily stomped away.

"You ready to get back to work yet, Will?" Hank asked, returning with a Dr Pepper.

"Quit rushin' me, old man."

I grabbed a handful of the bolts and dropped them in one of the white trays, making a lot of noise when I did it. Hank and Will don't exhibit the same interest in my counting the bolts as they once did. It took a few recounts for them to believe my accuracy at first, but that ended long ago. They loved the thought that I'm able to count the bolts in a glance, but without the noise, it doesn't seem to impress.

Hank left the Dr Pepper on the counter near me and pulled the dolly toward a green Mustang. It appeared effortless when he dropped to his back and rolled under the car. "Damn it. Can you get me that three-quarter, Will? I grabbed the bad one."

Will slid a socket wrench beside Hank and dug around in his pocket as he walked over to me.

"Now let's see. So many good ones." He fanned himself with the dollar he found.

I let a big handful of bolts clink into the tray. Will crab-clawed my shirt by the pocket, stuffed the dollar in, and patted it to my chest.

"Let's go with Richard Pryor. How 'bout . . . *Is It Something I Said?* Track, oh, say, whatever, track three."

"Track three of the 1975 album . . . *Is It Something I Said?* would be titled 'New Niggers.'" I said the word a little cautiously.

"That's right, that's the one. Good. Go ahead." Will leaned against the counter, waiting for me.

I made a little *swish-crackle* (pause) *crackle* (pause) *crackle* as the album did between tracks two and three, and in my best impression of Richard Pryor, I began. "White people don't care for us anymore. Been findin' new niggas. The Viet-dirty-knees." If the audience clapped, I clapped; if the audience laughed, I paused but didn't try to imitate their laughing because usually Will and Hank would be. I clapped briefly. With a white man's accent, which I did by trying to sound like a robot, I said, "Brought them here.

Brought tons of them here. " I deepened my voice for Pryor's accent: "Nobody asked me nuthin' . . ."

"That's right, that's right, Rich," Will said.

I continued. "Us the folks gotta give up paid work for 'em . . ." More brief clapping.

Hank waved a wrench at me. "Nah, he needs to lighten up like he does on some other tracks. Move on to that Mudbone story. The one with the witch, and hey, you, you been eating magnets again, or is there some other reason your ass is stuck to the counter and not over here workin'?"

"Just 'cause he mentions Vietnam, what you got against us 'Nam vets, anyway? It's every damn time with you. I can't get a word out about it, but bring up Korea, and we can talk all day, right?"

"You must be some serious kind of chowderhead." Hank rolled out from under the car and sat up. "Did you hear the same thing I just did? You've heard it before, right? Knew I should've sent you back to kindergarten when you needed a tutor to learn how to scribble."

"Man, that's so stale. I have some clippers for that ear hair. Maybe we should put on the real thing so you can hear the audience getting it."

"Just keep kickin' mud, why don't you. He was talkin' about your wife, you know. You should be insulted, but you clappin' and laughin' along like a seagull chokin' on Alka-Seltzer."

Will shook his head in disgust. "Oh, oh, you off today. Besides, you see her pulling in any green? 'Cause I don't. Only job she's good for is dumpin' dead fish, and nobody's competing with her for that."

"Respect, boy. Find it. And you're not gettin' paid to stand around. Move."

Mi walked in carrying the empty fishbowl on her hip and walked up to me. "Oh, good, good, Ah-bel. You stay for food, OK? So good you look. Han-some." When she stood next to me, we were shoulder to shoulder. She looked at Will. "You should take a look at Ah-bel. This a real man. Know how to treat a woman good. No listen to him, Ah-bel. I get you food, OK."

"We just ate lunch like an hour ago. Juke's not hungry. Get him some pie or something."

"Pie for dessert. No, this time, this time good food, healthy."

"You heard me."

Mi walked up near him defiantly, huffed, and left.

Will took a long drink from his soda.

"Go ahead then, Juke. Give me that Mudbone, would you? Will, put another quarter in his pocket already."

"He's good from the last; he didn't even finish." Will went into his pocket again and dropped a coin in my pocket. "Go on, Juke. Old man likes old man Mudbone. Can't help it."

Hank loved listening to Richard Pryor do his Mudbone, which was a heavily accented character that I had a hard time imitating. I delivered it word for word with the same pacing and pausing, same act but no accent.

The story was about a voodoo woman who Mudbone took his friend to for help with his hexed swollen feet. Toward the end, she shrinks them much smaller than he wanted with her own pee. This had Will and Hank laughing so hard, they could barely breathe. I didn't fully understand why they found it so funny, since they'd heard it many times. The punch lines really only made me smile some. Mi walked in the room holding a tray with a brown bowl and listened to me finish.

"Nigga grabbed the ape toe off her necklace, ate that. Bad idea. They took his toe-eating ass to a cage. You can visit him if you want. He's the stork with little tiny toes," I finished.

"Now, see, that was pretty good until the end. Even when Rich tells it, I never got the stork part of it. A monkey or a gorilla, he coulda turned into those, but a stork? A stork makes no sense," Will said.

"Next time you get off stage with your stand-up act, you can ask Rich what he was doin', all right? Until then, maybe you think he was sayin' that turnin' into a whitey animal with tiny feet in a cage wouldn't be ideal. Them's great guns you got for killin' jokes." Hank shook his head and ducked back under the car again.

"This a snack for Ah-bel. Quick here. Healthy for you." Mi held the bowl in the air, waving me closer.

"Where's that pie?" Will asked.

"We no have pie, only salted snack." She put the tray down on the table and smiled at me.

"Beans? Man, no one eats this shit. I've had it with you today," Will complained, walking over and trying to grab the bowl.

Mi moved the tray away before he could. "Ah-bel eats it. He likes everything, not like you. So picky, picky, picky."

Will gave her a sharp smack on her face and looked directly over at me, as if he faulted me for watching. It was an anomaly in our normal formula for arguments. Usually, in argument, all were given free reign to say what they liked with only a verbal retort as part of the likely product. They played what they called "the dozens," which I thought highly inaccurate because they rarely went past three or four of the individual "snaps," but I read that term came from the sale of slaves that had been beaten until they could only sell them cheaply, by the dozen.

Will looked down at the beans, and I thought for sure he'd throw them or pound them with his fist, but he picked up a little with his fingers and ate it. He made a big show of smacking the food against the roof of his mouth.

"Mmm, these are pretty good. Give 'em a try, Juke, if you're hungry." There was an odd tone in his voice and also in the pacing in his walk back to the engine, casual but not his normal stride.

The dish contained heavily salted lima beans. I've always hated lima beans. Their size and shape makes me think of testicles, and once you start thinking like that, you can't turn back. I scooped up a few like Will did and quickly swallowed them down and smiled at Mi. Mi wasn't looking at me because her head hung toward the garage floor.

"It is a fact. In 1979, Norma McCoy of Hubert, North Carolina, grew a lima-bean pod that was fourteen inches in length," I said after I took a huge swig of Dr Pepper.

Mi slowly rubbed at her cheek and stayed composed.

I belched. "Same year, Martin Moore in Brighton, England, ate 2,380 cold beans one by one with a cocktail stick in a half hour."

"Is that so, Juke? Some folks'll do anything to keep their cars on the road, I guess."

Hank's joke at another time might have had us all laughing, but Mi continued to rub her cheek. She didn't lift her gaze from the floor while moving the bowl closer to me. When it rested at my counter, the curve of her smile grew warm, but its meek slope did not compare to what it normally averaged. Mi walked casually to the steps, but once near, she dashed up them. I thought I could hear crying above the click of her little heels.

Everyone returned to work for a while, even Will, until Hank interrupted the tools' clatter by starting an Art Blakey album. We listened to the drumming without comment for the next half hour when Hank asked me to tell them something about the music. I didn't know much about Art Blakey besides him being a jazz drummer and the title of the album was *Moanin'*. It'd been stored in the album cover for Miles Davis's *Miles Smiles*, so I never got the chance to read the *Moanin'* cover for any information it might have.

"The slaves who were originally brought to the United States from West Africa were the creators of jazz. During their breaks from working, they would make music. It was a reminder of their home; full of syncopation and special rhythmic complexity." I'd read this in a *Time* magazine article on Miles Davis.

"Hear that, Junior? Listen up, you'll learn something about where our jazz music comes from."

"I don't need to be schooled today now, do I? Who's the musician here? Listen, you won't have to worry about any lessons when I move west."

"So, there'll be more room in the apartment, but hey, where you going now?" Hank said as Will wiped his hands on a rag. "Won't be affording that move by not working."

"I'll be making my money at the match Friday night." He stomped away, and a minute later we heard his car speed out of the lot.

"Well, Juke, it's me and you again. Put on what you like over there."

As the record spun to the end, I lifted the needle and started it over. We didn't say much for a while as I wrote the counts on the last of the four boxes I finished.

Hank started cleaning the tool he worked with. "Did Will ever tell you how he and Mi met?"

"They met during the Vietnam War."

"Yeah, yeah, that's the bones of it, but . . ." Hank tilted his head, thinking. "There's lots more nerve and meat to that story." He wiped his hands on his coveralls and retrieved two bottles of Pabst before taking a seat. He liked to sit in one of the chairs looking out onto the street. He waved me over. I could smell a little BO coming from him when I sat down. He handed me a bottle.

"Not my place maybe, but I'd rather you didn't think badly of Will. It's been tough on him moving back here with me. He's still trying to find his bearings, and that anger, don't let it fool you. He's a boy with a big heart." Hank put the wrench on the ground next to us as a car pulled to a stop at the stoplight. "Vietnam, mm-hmm, Vietnam had lots of young men living inside themselves, you know, living every day with the fear of death. Will was no different, not one bit. He sought out women to keep sane like so many of them boys." Hank lifted his bottle and drank. "As I heard it, there were lots of women like Mi, trying to find a way to survive by taking care of soldiers. Same women I found in Korea. But Will didn't do like the others, you gotta believe me. His mother and I brought him up to respect women. There were plenty of soldiers there that'd tell a woman who was just tryin' to survive that, sure, they'd come back for her, and take care of her, if she'd only give him some lovin' that night, but they never did."

The slight yellow tint of his eyes emanated warmth, sending it out along the long, fluttering lashes. He swallowed a third of his bottle and released a slow, muffled burp. "If April only lived until he got home, but-but see, no, sir, Will Flynn wasn't that kind of man. When he told Mi he'd be back for her, he meant it. When he finished his tours, he had her come back to the States with him. I never raised a hand to April, never once. Will saw plenty of our fights. I've learned, see. You gotta look the other way if he gets that way with her, because I wasn't in Vietnam, and you can't understand a man's actions that's been through what went on over there. The man gave his hand. I guess he should be able to use it for what he wants now."

We sat and listened to traffic pass and belched while drinking our beer. I thought about how they'd treated me since my first visit. On top of what they paid me for the counting, every time I'd come, Hank or Will would put extra in my pocket for any little thing I did. They always laughed and laughed and sometimes they'd stick other things in my pocket besides money, like used tissues and bottle caps, but I'd keep reciting stand-up even if that's all they ever stuck in there. These were the types of guys you care for as if they're your relatives because they're better than the ones you see on TV, and at least as good as my uncle. As long as Will wasn't slapping me and as long as Mi still showed how much she loved Will the next day, then I figured it's OK to go on loving them, too.

"Will's moving. So that means, it means you are moving, too."

"I been here thirty-seven years. I'll probably be here when you move away and probably until the big guy comes and takes me away, but I'll be living over there in Tri-Pyramids home at that point. Nice little slice of Heaven from what I can see."

We looked over and saw a group of elderly people moving slowly on the grounds. The lawn and shrubs were well manicured, but other than that, it didn't look all that special to me.

"It is a fact. The Seven Wonders of the Ancient World were the Great Pyramid of Cheops, the Hanging Gardens of Babylon, the Statue of Zeus at Olympia, the Temple of Diana at Ephesus, the Tomb of King Mausolus at Halicarnassus, The Colossus of Rhodes on the Isle of Rhodes, and the Lighthouse on the Isle of Pharos. The Great Pyramid of Cheops located on the Giza plateau is the only one still in existence. It was built in less than thirty years. Memphis, Tennessee, is named after Memphis, the necropolis, or burial city where Giza lives. There has been speculation that the Pyramid was built by aliens or perhaps Atlantians. Many people don't think of Egypt as being part of Africa, but the pyramids were built by a proud group of intensely hardworking Africans. You know-you know I'm of African descent, too, Hank."

Hank had been looking at me with wonder, then smiled wide, exposing his dark gums. "Is that right? Well, you got color. I'll give you that."

"We all are. Because of the fact that the earliest woman, Lucy, she was from Africa. We all must have some of her blood in us."

"I imagine you're right, that is, unless we came from aliens," he continued with his wide grin.

"Or the Atlantians, but I should be going home now."

"Already? Well, come by again when you can. Don't want me counting them bolts. I'd be all week at it." Hank pulled a small roll of bills from his pocket and tucked a five in with the Chiclets.

"OK bye," I said and tried handing him the Chiclets.

He took my quarter-drunk bottle instead. "See you later, Juke."

The automobile Hank most resembles is a Volkswagen Beetle. I say this not because he's a fat, squat man with bug eyes, although he sort of is. I say it because blue whales have hearts the same size as Volkswagen Beetles. Maybe it'd be better to say that Hank has the heart of a blue whale, but that'd be a frightening physical impossibility.

CHAPTER EIGHT

Douche Bag vs Scumbag

12.13.19.38.14-10.5-26-29.13.14-13.50-5.185.3.19.1

Occasionally, I'd sneak behind the chair out of Pigpie's view and watch the good TV, but only on rare nights would I risk it. Who can enjoy a sitcom when you can't laugh or make a noise during the show? *The Dukes of Hazzard* was on last night, but Pigpie preferred *Benson*, so I spent my time in my room with Williamson's book *An Elementary Treatise on the Integral Calculus.*

The old console TV in the basement was a safe alternative on weekend mornings because of Pigpie's difficulties navigating the stairs, but it took ten minutes to warm up and only got two UHF channels. On those mornings, I watched it in the dark with the volume turned down while sitting on the fungus floor. A dank, smelly basement was the price of quality entertainment in our house. The post-chore debate I'd been having with myself this morning forced me to choose between continuing with Williamson's book or watching that crappy TV. It ended when I recalled *Emu's World*. One of the UHF channels broadcasted this British TV hour on Saturday mornings where I could often watch a children's show called *Emu's World.*

Emu was a big, grotesque puppet who I thought of as an evil *Sesame Street* character. Emu looked even less real than the man in the Big Bird suit, yet he acted like some of those carrion-loving birds in PBS documentaries, so I thought of Emu as being more plausible. The frizzy blond-haired Rod, Emu's keeper, cultivated a hapless, British-gent quality, but lurking beneath it, I detected a certain cruelty. Rod had Emu stuck perpetually under his right arm. Most anyone upon close inspection could figure out that what you thought was Rod's right arm holding Emu was a con. He fooled you with a false limb to distract from the real one inside Emu moving the neck, head, and beak.

Emu's World wasn't scary as much as sickeningly cute. I took great pleasure in some of the unusual actions, like when Rod's nemesis Grotbags would cough on children, but I suppose I mostly enjoyed the show because of the odd fear Rod and Emu brought out in me. I'd seen Rod and Emu appear as special guests on several comedy shows, which instilled in me the initial dread and fascination. In his comedy appearances, Emu was a mean a-hole. He did not talk or do tricks but specialized in attacking people. The bird was a horribly vicious creature, rabidly taking offense at anyone who spoke ill of anything to do with the world of feathered vertebrates or him personally. If you were in his presence and whispered about going to Kentucky Fried Chicken, Emu would go for your crotch or throat. Emu has attacked a multitude of celebrities, even the Queen of England once. The Queen apparently loved it.

The crowd of kids on *Emu's World* started to chant, "There's somebody behind the door! There's somebody behind the door!" when the phone rang upstairs. Shelly yelled my name. It always felt like a present when the phone rang for me.

Russell and I had barely talked since the blessed tree-fort discovery. In fact, our bus-stop mornings consisted almost entirely of the "who can kick the rock closest to the curb" game and TV trading-card swapping. Potentially, John Berg could hear, even through his headphones, so the fort was never mentioned. Part of me was surprised when the first thing Russell inquired after I said hello into the receiver was, "Hey, Apple, you ready to go?"

I knew exactly what he meant, but I asked for clarity, anyway.

"Back to you know where. I'll bring the rest of the Hubba Bubba. I saved it. Meet you at the bike in twenty, OK?" He hung up, and I ran upstairs. Shelly dumped laundry in a pile by my closet, and I rooted through it to get my dungarees. I zipped them on quickly and grabbed my satchel.

"Where're you running off to?" Shelly asked as I passed. She was flipping and combing her hair in the hallway mirror.

"Russell's."

"Did you finish your chores? You better if you didn't."

"I did," I answered as I ran down the stairs and out the door.

Mister Scratch furiously barked at some younger kids riding their bikes up the train tracks when I got to him. He couldn't chase after them because he'd tangled himself in the clotheslines that must've been hanging on the ground. It took me a minute to set him free and wrap the lines back up.

The stink of Mister Scratch on my hands could just be smelled over the scent of burning leaves that filled the air when I reached Russell. Russell busied himself cross-eyed, staring at a gum bubble.

"'Ook at 'iss. 'Ook at it." He pointed at the bubble he'd blown to almost the same size as his head. He pushed it to the popping point and slurped it back in. "Damn. What took you so long?"

I looked at my watch, knowing I'd made it within the twenty-minute time frame and also knowing this was more of a taunt than a question. To him, it'd been an unstated race. I played it dumb.

"Mister Scratch was tangled, and Shelly—"

He interrupted me with the pack of cigarettes in one hand and wiggling matches from his other. "We're set. Time's a wastin'. Let's ride."

I drove while he was the passenger this time. We stashed the bike near the creek at the drainage pipe where we often saw muskrats and ran to a decent hiding spot near the fort, watching for any other occupants.

"Shit. Fuck. Someone else knows about this place. You fuckin' blabbed, didn't you?" Russell said with his sour-gum breath right in my face.

"Nope."

"Well, the shit we dumped is over there stacked up, and we didn't fucking leave it like that."

"Nope."

I rarely used common expletives, but there was a day this past summer Russell realized he could curse when his parents weren't around. Since then, he tries to use them as often as possible. I honestly don't understand most adults' fear or annoyance over their use. It sounds idiotic the way Russell uses them, but if someone is stressed and says *shit* or *cocksucker* or *asswipe*, aren't they all just words? There are many to choose from if one wants personal satisfaction. I prefer words like *curpin* because it makes me think of belching and means the ass of a chicken. Better still, *aerocolpos*, which when said with an emphasis on the *colpos* part, has a harsh force. Aerocolpos suggests Greek mystery and is a much better verbal alternative to emasculating men than the word *fag* because *aerocolpos* means vaginal flatulence. Still, a good old-fashioned *bullshit* shouted at an opportune moment is hard to beat. While the world doesn't fall to pieces when a cuss word is muttered aloud, I've noticed I feel better knowing that saying those words is one of the small freedoms I'll always possess.

"Come on, there's nobody up there now." Russell slunk to the tree with his arms out and his body bent forward.

He quickly scrambled up to the platform. I wasn't so sure about the coast being clear, so I crept over, continuing to listen intently. Unless they were sitting perfectly still in the fort, waiting to ambush us, it was OK. I lingered until Russell climbed inside to be sure. No screams of pain, so I started my ascent. The counting to seven helped me jump again. Russell had already said, "Hurry the fuck up" three times when I pulled myself into the fort.

A lit match burned between his bony fingers. "You missed it—there was an owl sitting in the window before you came." He lied terribly.

"I missed it."

"You sure did. Ugh, when did you step in that one? Yeech, it's too fresh." He snickered a little and lit another match.

I hadn't stepped in one since I left the yard. You would have thought he'd have smelled it sooner than just now. Its mild scent blended curiously with the pine-mud walls, though, a special hint of aged meat and deviled egg.

The place looked different. The blanket that covered the bench was now bunched up next to it, and scattered around the fort were eleven candles. I checked out the bottom of my shoe when Russell started to light the ones on the shelf behind me.

"Oh, Jesus Cah-rist, we're in deep shit."

The candle illuminated a board leaning against the hairy wall: *We know who u r and u r DEAD.*

Russell quickly closed the hatch in the floor.

"There's no way they know who we are unless you said something because I didn't say anything for sure. Did you?" His brows deeply furrowed, almost leaning on me.

"No," I said, feeling guilty for no reason, and put my satchel on the bench.

"Well, I didn't say anything, so there's no way they know, so let's just enjoy it and then leave everything like we found it, all right?"

I nodded but really didn't feel like staying. Sitting dorks with no escape. It was Saturday; all the probability calculations marked us at a high percentage that we would be DEAD soon.

"I'm not afraid of them, anyway, unless they're sixteen or something." Russell karate punched toward the candle flame in front of him. "I should've brought my nunchakus." Russell's nunchakus mainly struck Russell plus the occasional tree trunk or bush, but he often bragged of how he'd use them against anyone that might give him trouble.

He casually passed me a cigarette and lit it, but the smoke entering my ill-prepared lungs caused several minutes of stifled coughing. Russell ignored me and smoked while seated at the window, monitoring the creek for any danger. Plume after plume wafted out and, by the time we'd crushed them into the tray, like stunted Marlboro men, our fear subsided.

"Did you notice?" Russell unexpectedly jutted his mouth toward me, moving his head into the light from the window.

I looked closely at his mouth, thinking it a gum-stained lips exhibition, but didn't see anything unusual. So I just kept staring until he said, "My mustache is starting to come in."

I continued looking and nodded in acknowledgement but noticed nothing except maybe the same kind of peach fuzz that grew on his cheek.

"Oh, hey, I almost forgot." He ripped the rest of his Hubba Bubba open and handed me a piece. "Guess we'll have to have another." He gave me another cigarette from the almost-empty pack. It felt like we were gorging ourselves. Normally, if we got our hands on cigarettes, they were half-smoked and scavenged from the sand bucket outside the 7-Eleven. We chewed the gum with great vigor and carefully dropped our ashes in the tray, making a big show of it this time. I couldn't find the box with the Love's Baby Soft, but they'd left the stack of magazines and some new additions: a plastic bottle of Jergens hand lotion and a small nondescript box. Russell grabbed both. The bottle made a farting noise when he squirted a little on his hand, which made him look at me to see if I'd laugh. When he saw my blank expression, he laughed through his nose.

"Disgusting," he said, still grinning, and turned his attention to the small cardboard box. "Holy shit, check it out." He pulled out three small square packages, but I still couldn't see them clearly. He started ripping open one, and I wondered what kind of candy he'd found.

"These are unused scumbags," he said.

I finally saw what he had.

"I thought, I thought they're condoms."

"Yeah, they're called that if you don't know stuff, but women have stuff that cleans out their pussies, and when they're done with them, they're called douche bags and when guys are done with these, they're called scumbags." He unrolled it, letting it hang limply from his fingertips like a piece of diseased flesh. "You want it?"

I shook my head.

He drew it toward his nose and sniffed. "Ugh, it smells like a bike tire."

I thought bike-tire rubber smelled pretty good, but I acted like it stank after I'd sniffed.

"Here, you can have one, and I can have one."

I accepted the small package, examining it briefly before tucking it away in my satchel.

After such a find, it was inevitable that our attention would turn to the stack of magazines.

Russell moved to stand in front of them and checked to see if I was looking. Instead of handing some to me, he started turning pages of one of the remaining bound *Reader's Digest*s.

"My mom reads these sometimes," he said with fake excitement. While he was busy thumbing through the pages, I decided to see what was the farthest landmark I could recognize from the windows. But all I saw were limbs and leaves. As Russell kept up his fake reading, I figured the magazines were as much mine as they were his, and so I finally reached for the top one as easygoing as I could.

"Hey"—he put his arm out to block me—"we should save those for last, shouldn't we?"

I knew it's what we were most excited about, but I returned it and picked up a boring *Reader's Digest*. I knew he could sense my displeasure.

"I mean, we could even try to take one home, don'cha think?"

I examined the rope used to open the secret window.

"Don't you? Come on, don't be a pussy. I can't take one unless you do."

I started to tell him that'd be fine when we both heard it, something similar to voices. Russell chucked his cigarette out the window on the opposite side of where the sound came from and got down on the floor. I stood still, listening. Russell found a slot to look through, and I crouched down beside him.

CHAPTER NINE

Rod Hull's Legacy

65.9.8.8.4.18.9.8.31-15.2.30.30.9.5-27.26-27.7.15.9.26.35.2.8.9.31

"I can't see anything but the ground," he whispered.

I stared at a board below me as if I might suddenly gain x-ray vision. My shadow's outline from the candlelight quivered from Russell steadily kicking the floor in fear. The voices grew in clarity and volume. Russell jumped up suddenly and started blowing out candles. I grabbed one of the bigger ones and blew it out, but the hot wax splashed all over my hand. I held onto it, anyway, and grabbed another, trying not to let the wax spill, figuring I could dump it down on them if I had to. I scanned for something else but quickly forgot about it when I noticed the steps to the top of the fort. Abandoning the candles on the shelf, I grabbed my satchel and started climbing. Russell followed, and we were surprisingly quiet getting up there. They couldn't have heard.

Russell pushed me back when I went to look. He stared at me with as much earnestness as he could muster. He put his fingers to his temples, notifying me he wanted to convey something telepathically. It took all my reserve not to roll my eyes at him. Instead, I nodded my head to say, "I got it," and speedily ducked low to the roof, waited for him, and crept to the edge.

"Holy shit, you did it." He grinned so hard, he probably forgot our trouble. My action completely lacked superhuman merit.

From a distance, their long hair might have deceived some into thinking they were boys and girls, but we knew differently. Approaching the clearing were the Kevins and Jerry, the gum salesman, carrying a big radio.

"They fuckin' better not be, because I'll have a shit fit," Schmill, the Kevin who'd ripped the tag from my shirt the week before, exclaimed in his odd nasal voice.

"Ah, if they're smart, they're not, right, Rick?" Jerry used a mock Bugs Bunny–like accent. I imagined Jerry only got away with it because he was the same size as Schmill.

Kevin Hudrick, aka Rick, replied with the same Bugs Bunny accent. "Ah, who'd return to the scene of a crime, doc? Especially if it'd cause Schmill to, a, have ah shit fit."

"I said cut that shit out already." Schmill punched Rick on the arm, which Rick ignored.

Kevin Groter inspected the piled paint can and *Digest*s.

"I wore my ass-kickin' shoes if they returned," Schmill said as he lifted his foot, clumsily hopped twice, and placed his sneaker on the first step of the trunk.

That was our sign to retreat from the edge. We lay on our stomachs and listened to orders from Schmill to hurry up, which must've gotten them moving, because their shoes clomped the wood planks beneath us in no time.

They recognized our recent occupation immediately, and I figured we had seconds before they'd be up and throwing us off the roof.

A nasty mélange of scents wafted off Russell that I'd never smelt before resembling a ham hoagie gone bad mixed with fresh nicotine and bile grape. He panted in fear next to me. His hot breath felt like it left a film on my ear when he whispered, "I'll fight two; you fight two. I got Jerry and Schmill." I knew he offered because he figured

Jerry wouldn't fight him due to the potential loss of future sales. Everyone knew Jerry cared about one thing above all else. But Russell was as afraid as I was and dumb about taking Schmill, who'd be the most difficult to beat, not that I had a chance with any of them.

Russell put his fingers to his temples again, trying to tell me something. I wanted to smack his stupid fingers away. I'd never play that idiotic game again. We both were on top of the door, so I figured they might not be able to push it open. Only one at a time could climb the steps to get here. Minutes felt like an eternity as they were busy talking about kicking ass and what they'd do once they found us, who did we think we were, and how we must be so dumb, we can't even read. Their chatter got them even more worked up, and the fort started tilting back and forth.

Schmill squealed, "Those fags are fucking dead." And we heard something crash against a wall. "I can't take it, let's go."

"We just got here. Forget about those fags," Jerry said.

"We stay here, we're the fags. You gonna let them call us fags? Stay if you want," Schmill roared.

The fort jerked, as they must've started climbing down the rope ladder. I felt spellbound by the remnants of the spilled wax clinging to my hand like old scabs. Numbers and symbols flew. My focus shifted to Descartes's *Second Meditation*. In it, he considers a piece of wax. He tells how the senses are the tool used to discover its various properties:

> "Let us take, for instance, this piece of wax. It has been taken quite recently from the honeycomb; it has not yet lost all the honey flavor. It retains some of the scent of the flowers from which it was collected. Its color, shape, and size are manifest. It is hard and cold; it is easy to touch. If you rap on it

with your knuckle it will emit a sound ... bringing it close to the fire. The remaining traces of the honey flavor are disappearing; the scent is vanishing; the color is changing; the original shape is disappearing. Its size is increasing; it is becoming liquid and hot; you can hardly touch it. And now, when you rap on it, it no longer emits any sound."

Basically, Descartes asked how the hell anybody still calls it wax when your senses tell you it's so exceptionally different.

I wished I could pour out my mind. If only the sun would turn me liquid, ease me to the weeds, to the creek, and let me flow away. I wished more that the Kevins were simply an inspection on the part of my mind, that they were mental creations and had no physical extensions like the potential Descartes described with the wax. If that were true, neither my body nor my mind was buying it.

A shadow drifted over my fingertips, and the trembling in my body made the shadow seem three-dimensional. At first, I thought the shadow was my own, but then I noticed it on top of me, not below, and the idiot, the incredible idiot Russell, stood with his arms in the air. Who could fathom why he'd stood or where he found the nerve.

"It's ours, and just 'cause you found it after we did doesn't mean you own it!" His bony frame shook as he shouted down to them, the spittle forming in great, bubbly, nervous clumps.

It was all over now.

He said *ours*, and since I'd been exposed, I stood and backed away from the edge. My legs didn't want to hold me, and I doubted they'd have the strength to climb down. My real shadow laughed up at me, stumpy and dwarflike.

"It's that alien kid and that kid that used to be in our grade," Groter shouted.

"Get your asses out of our tree!" Schmill screamed like a weird woman, his shoulder-length hair enhancing the auditory allusion.

"Get your fuckin' asses down here right now!" Rick yelled, struggling to seem in charge.

"We don't have to leave our fort. We found it first!" Russell shouted with an odd, high pitch himself and sat down on the edge of the roof, goading them.

"You stupid dick bag, you ah!" Schmill yelled with his mouth open as wide as it might go. "We made that fort." Barely keeping his skin on, he punched his fist into his hand.

"I made the fort, but it's ours. Now get out," Rick demanded.

"Fuck them! You stay right there, right fuckin' there." Schmill moved under the fort, out of sight.

"Fine, fine, we'll come down." Russell's fear must've helped him realize a lower elevation might work to our advantage.

We descended as far as the hatch, but Schmill had already climbed halfway up the rope.

Russell whispered to me, "Don't worry, I've got an idea, but forget about taking two." I wanted to grow wings, but our only option was to face the ineluctable pain.

"Look the fuck out, I'm coming up."

"We're coming down. This isn't fair," Russell whined.

"That's right shit dick, it's not fair." Schmill backed down the rope a little out of breath.

Russell desperately held back tears. "Some of you guys are two grades ahead of us." If this was Russell's plan, we weren't escaping without losing blood.

"You flunked, anyway, so you're as old as some of us," Rick said.

I could tell Schmill wanted to fight. Schmill jumped to the ground and stood to the side, arms crossed with temporary self-control, lips pursed like an asshole. His sharp-angled face with orange hair withering in tangles to his shoulders reminded me of Rod's Emu in human form, waiting to peck Russell to death.

"So did he." Russell pointed at Schmill. "So it's still not fair." He dangled at the bottom of the rope, afraid to drop.

"You dickle fag," Schmill said as he grabbed Russell's leg, pulling him to the ground with a heavy, hollow thud.

There were a few motionless seconds where we waited to see what would happen, but Russell appeared OK, just afraid to stand up. He dusted the dirt from his pants leg, and tears moistened his cheeks. He moved out of the way, and I landed beside him.

"I didn't know you flunked," Jerry said.

"Did you really flunk, Schmill?" Rick asked.

"You believe this fag? He's a lying shit, and don't think you're not dead, too, you . . . alien ass." Schmill's brain worked overtime.

"Heh-heh, that's even better than dickle fag. What's an alien ass, someone with three assholes?" Rick said.

"Yeah, a spaceman Play-Doh factory," Groter added.

Schmill punched Rick on the arm, and Rick punched him back, but they weren't after each other. They stood in a line in front of us: Advertisements for AC/DC, Black Sabbath, and Led Zeppelin were ironed or silk-screened on their shirts. Jerry's didn't have a logo, and Rick was the only one who didn't cut his three-quarter length shirtsleeves to a fifth.

Russell turned to Groter and Jerry, feeling safe talking to them. "What, do you want to not beat us up?"

A WHOLE LOT

I thought his tears would get them to forget about violence, but you could see Schmill only needed one of the others to ask him something more about flunking.

"Nothin', you can't give us nothin', you already screwed with our fort," Rick said, tucking his long hair back behind his ears.

"You ripped us off, too." Schmill pounded his fist in his hand.

"Hold on, guys, this could be profitable," Jerry offered.

"What're they gonna give us?" Rick poked at me. "It'd take five..." He poked me again. "No, ten bags of weed for me to forget about it, and there's no way you could get it for me, you little spic."

The calculations flooded my eyes, obscuring the features of Rick's face.

Rick poked me one last time painfully on the same spot. "Do you even know what weed is, E.T.?"

"What's with his eyes?" Groter asked.

Did I know? By the age of four, I knew. I took a long look into the back of my eyelids, where the number clouds roiled like smoke trapped on a ceiling before I exploded like a 45 record at 33 rpm.

"It is a fact: Cannabis is short for *Cannabis sativa*. Tetrahydrocannabinol, or THC, is the psychoactive chemical in cannabis that produces the high. It is a fact: Cannabis was sung about in the Indian Vedas as one of the divine nectars. The song is about how cannabis supplies man with good health, long life, and revelations of the gods. Other uses are food, cleaning materials, textiles, shoe polish, plastics, and medicine. It is a fact: George Washington and Thomas Jefferson farmed it. It is a fact: Jesus was initiated with cannabis holy oil. Its recipe, if properly translated, is in Exodus thirty, twenty-two twenty-three." I took a quick breath. "Even Descartes must have smoked it. Everyone smoked cannabis when he was a soldier in the United Provinces. Pot, grass, weed, wacky weed, wacky tobacky, Mary Jane, dope, reefer, hash, bud, doobie, tea, herb, super skunk, sensi, ganja. And-and-and it is a fact: If you are a master smoker in Greece, you call yourself an aerocolpos, which is-is a god of smoke."

This unexpected, voluble action had everyone, including Russell, in suspended animation, gaping incredulously.

"You *are* an alien." Russell commented, appearing to have joined their side.

"Holy shit, I think he said Jesus smoked pot." Groter lowered his hand to his hip to cross himself.

"I don't care what that freak said. They're still gonna get it." Schmill grabbed Russell by the shirt and punched him hard in the stomach. His coughing and wheezing had me frightened that he'd never stand up straight again.

Schmill was just waiting for Russell to compose himself so he could unleash his anger again, but Russell looked up and pleaded, "Wait, wait, we can't get you weed, but we could get you money for it."

"How much?" Schmill grabbed hold of Russell's hair.

"It's in the haunted house. Everyone knows there's a ton of money in there." Russell wiped his eyes.

"Bullshit, you wouldn't even go in there," Jerry insisted.

"You couldn't make it past the albino village," Rick added.

Schmill let him go, and Russell backed away and smoothed out his hair.

"My father told me there's not even any such thing as an albino. Someone just hung those signs to scare you away from the house. We've never seen any albinos, right, Apple?"

I didn't move as I knew nothing about an albino village. Russell's lie could only prolong and increase the pain.

Rick grabbed a stick from the ground and poked us with it. "All right, we'll give you and E.T. here a chance to pay us off."

"We will not," Schmill said.

Rick turned to Schmill, "Do you have any extra cash for weed? 'Cause I don't, and if they don't get it for us, we can still kick their asses. So, what do we have to lose?"

"I'm getting paybacks at least somehow." Schmill pushed Russell.

Jerry led us along trails around the lake. We had to cross a creek and climb its banks using the roots of a tree, then climb to the top of an old concrete bridge the train once used. Ahead, amid the tall grass that obscured the tracks, the first warning sign became visible. It read, *Privat Propurde*. People with that level of spelling usually make up for their deprivation with firearm expertise, or at least that's how they're portrayed on TV.

We kept along the tracks. At the entrance to a tunnel, there were more wooden placards, painted in maroon, white, and blue. The topmost one in white on blue read:

Tomb of Alexander Bino.
Vote for J, He's for you!
John (Albino) and King for Mayor

In maroon on white, a small sign at the bottom read:

Founded Thursday 18th, 1804
Original village founded by Alexander Bino (Al Bino)
For the purpose of creating a master race

These couldn't have been original signs made on a Thursday the eighteenth in 1804 because that would make it October, which was the only month in 1804 where the eighteenth fell on a Thursday, and which also means they'd have gone through 177 winters. That's an exorbitant amount of outdoor wear and tear on this paint for it to continue to be legible.

The third sign in blue with some letters having white painted over the blue said:

Characteristics:
Short stature
Pink eyes, translucent skin, white hair—fierce nature!

And in big letters on the side of the sign:

Beware of Albino Greyhound!

"Have any of you guys ever gone through? My brother Jim said they've got traps set up at the other side of the tunnel," Jerry asked.

"Flunky here said he'd been through millions of times." Rick turned to Russell. "So, there mustn't be any traps, right?"

Russell stayed quiet, and I could tell by the look on his face he'd probably never even gotten close enough to read the sign.

"Right, flunky?" Rick repeated. "Well, you can keep your mouth shut all you want, but you and E.T. are going through first."

Rick's stick directed us and poked at the small of my back while we started in. As shadows enveloped me, their low, triumphant howls worked on my spine at the same spot as Rick's stick. I stalled until my eyes adjusted. Possibly fifty yards lay between the end of the tunnel and us but hard to properly estimate with the junk strewn about the tunnel. We breathed in toxic fumes from old solvents and poisonous fungi spore, no doubt. My focus kept jumping. The various formulae I tried using to process-volume estimates didn't work with the intrusion of all the sensual data. Marooned necks of broken bottles threatened my ankles. Broad areas of deep shadow stirred. To the right and center of the tunnel, it became necessary to climb up a heap of bloated plastic bags. Russell and I waited for the rest to navigate, and our gazes questioned if escape was possible.

Russell's thoughts wrestled on his eyebrows. Should we run? Could we make it? No way to know, so we continued on. Past the rusted bedsprings and the legless chair, over the smaller piles of unrecognizable misshapen objects, through the water sludge area and finally out the other side as quickly as we could. Minor relief hit when we reached the light, but shadows still clung with thick dread. We waited by concrete steps, and I searched for other trouble.

The tracks continued, veering off to the left, and shacks lined a dirt road to the right. I'd never seen anything like the shacks. A poor man's art gallery. Painted tires and concrete birdbaths were planted in the ground along what might be called a fence. Scary faces painted on plastic milk cartons with pens and pencils embedded for hair sat on top of poles tied together with wire. More painted signs that were too far away to read hung from the wiring.

"The albinos must live in those," Jerry commented as he joined us.

"They don't look like anyone could live in them," Groter said.

"Just stay away from that side of the tracks. They've set up real voodoo and mojo," Jerry said.

The stillness of the shacks seemed unnatural. No albino greyhound barking, no noticeable animals of any kind, not even a breeze to ruffle the tall weeds or kick up some fallen leaves. Our running created the only motion. The Kevins and Jerry ran in fear ahead of us. Russell leaned over as he jogged beside me and said, "When we get into the house, just run right through to the back door. We'll find our way home somehow."

This was his best plan, and while I knew his prudence to be less than trustworthy, I couldn't construct a better one. If his plan consisted of more, Russell didn't get a chance to convey it before the others slowed at the sight looming ahead. I wasn't sure if the estate included the surrounding forest, but the dark trees certainly added a menacing frame. Waves of dense crabgrass and thistle spread out before us, slowly cresting toward the center, where the remnants of a grand mansion lay. It gave the impression of floating above the rest of the county, although the hill it crowned rolled out gradually. Carved into the cement at the midpoint of the walkway to the house was *269 Seawell*. I searched my memory for listings to that address in North Brunswick but couldn't locate any 269 Seawell. Four pillars with empty planters at the tops surrounded us, and at least sixty yards separated the spot from the front door.

"We're stopping here," Rick said. "E.T., you're going in. You're the smart one, so you'll know where to look. Flunky, you're waiting with us."

"I should go with him. I mean, we were both in the fort, and what if he finds giant bags of money? You'll need more than him to carry it out."

"No. If E.T. don't return with some cash in, say, a half hour . . ." Rick checked his watch.

"A half hour's too long. Give him twenty minutes," Groter said.

"A half hour's plenty. It's a big house. Hell, we got all day, and E.T. won't wanna come back and find his best buddy here beat to shit, 'cause he'll know he's next."

"Fuckin'-A right, he's next," Schmill said.

"I got one seventeen. Lemme see yours." Jerry took my wrist. "By one fifty-seven, you better be back here with the cash."

I nodded, deciding against correcting him about his mistake with the time and met Russell's eyes. We locked for a moment, no apology shared, only fear and pleading. Russell couldn't be blamed for his weakness under pressure or for both of us entering the fort, but we wouldn't be in this mess if only he had stayed hidden.

"Hurry up, E.T., ah, Apple," he added with great dread.

CHAPTER TEN

Crimson Gold

43.4.12.18.60.4.43-14.12.13.11-9-41.13.43.217-9.12.4-47.13.2-14.13.28.9.43

I could be called brave at this point, although I'd need an epic poem or at least a cheerleading squad to convince me of it. I felt more like a poorly calculated quotient, or some early American explorer like Francisco Vázquez de Coronado made to work for the high council of Spain, cut off and onstage as I walked quickly along the path toward the door. All the front exterior windows were boarded, but a few toward the third floor were cockeyed because they'd lost some of their bindings. A bioluminescent light flashed through one of the cockeyed ones. What kind of lightbulb produces that? I squeezed through some overgrown evergreen shrubs that stood sentry and was informed of the house's owner. The name engraved on the large brass plate above the bell said *PIERSON*. So, that part of the story I now knew to be true.

  A daddy longlegs crawled along a piece of decaying yellow police tape that draped from the nameplate to the ground. Another piece dangled from the simple latch I lifted to open the door. Several feet ahead, a second door slightly ajar led into a place darker still. This wasn't a foyer or breezeway. Between the first and second door was a murky void about five feet wide. The void spread left and right, with no roof nor constructed floor. It felt more like an area for insulation or something I couldn't imagine. Even if it were for insulation, it'd take a hell of a lot of insulation to fill it. My skin pimpled from a chill in the air. Not wanting to move all the way into the house, I stepped down into dry grass. This zone was still safe, like a purgatory without the need to resolve sin, allowing me to live with some light awhile longer. I looked up along the wall past some of the silhouettes of bracing and was fairly certain I could see the sky. There may have been shiny metal strips at the top, reflecting light that dappled parts of the walls, but I couldn't figure it out. It reminded me of the way light bounces off swimming pools. The mysterious light through the windows out front obviously emanated from something. Maybe mirrors?

One step forward in the dried grass, then up again to enter the house. I left both doors open for sunlight. Surprisingly, when I flipped a switch, I found the bulb actually stirred to life. Even with the lamp, the foyer I stood in wasn't very bright, and the doorway continued to be my main source of light.

The foyer offered three options, each ominous in its own way. First, an open stairwell to my left, which led up and curved over a corridor straight ahead—my second option. Third, I could go for the archway to my right.

"Hello?" I tried, knowing no one would answer but feeling it the appropriate thing to do. The fear of not finding money wasn't my immediate concern. It's the natural syllogism. Spirits of the dead haunt all old, dilapidated mansions. Jealous and hungry spirits want the living to suffer as they do. Therefore, I would have to suffer—and probably very soon.

Perhaps ghosts of murdered children would not haunt other children, but I didn't want to chance it. So to dispel the ghosts, I spoke in a mocking voice, "Angel bright, life in death, get off the road. Don't suck my breath," and swung my satchel to cover my stomach. I tried fortifying myself with Descartes's thoughts when he ditched all previously created philosophical notions about the nature of reality. It seemed fitting. He'd considered everything that was merely probable to be well-nigh false. Therefore, I, too, would declare all my concerns over ghosts and matters of horror to be well-nigh false.

    I had to locate some item that looked expensive, something portable I could use to convince them it'd bring a great pawnshop price. A box filled with jewelry, even fake, would be spectacular. Jewelry was often found in bedrooms, and bedrooms, of course, were almost always the scenes of bloody massacres. I took a deep breath. Master bedrooms would be upstairs, so I went in that direction.

    Unfortunately, the hallway switch at the top wouldn't work. I held the air tightly in my lungs as I inched forward along the wall. The darkness enveloped me, slipping coldly beneath my clothes and raising more bumps on my skin. One expects darkness at night, but something makes it more insidious when you know it is the middle of the afternoon outside. The idea of yelling something out about not being afraid came to mind, but I couldn't do so convincingly. I should've saved a candle from the fort. Walking without the support of touching anything made me fear I would accidentally touch an item I did not want to, and sliding my hand along the wall was only slightly better than having it land on something hairy or slimy. None of the doorknobs I encountered helped me find a watt of light. I tried imagining what could possibly make this creepier and felt happy there wasn't any howling or screeching.

    The hallway jogged to the right and then left again. Light far down at the very end greeted me as I turned. The floor began to slope slightly toward the ground and had stiff sponginess to it with each step, like when you get off an elevator. I wished I could feel hope or ease my tension with the sight of the light. As I approached, the rectangle of light became clearer. Instead of finding a door open to a room with a thousand-watt bulb, I discovered a wide space with light from the cloud-streaked sky. It was as if Moby Dick had crashed through the roof and crushed everything in its path. I peered down to a room of the house where large slabs of flat, white rock, possibly marble, were broken and scattered like a puzzle among cracked bones of joist and beam.

A little vertigo wobbled my knees, so I turned back down the hall, moving faster this time, knowing no chairs or objects barred my way.

The passage beneath the stairs seemed the best choice to gain a better view of the fallen slabs, so that's where I went. Another switch at the end of the passage revealed a grand high ceiling. Tiny ensconced light fixtures came on around the room's perimeter, exposing what might have been a dining room at one time. A long table sat at the center of the room without any surrounding chairs. The chandelier hung above the table and needed only some water currents to emphasize its seaweed-creature appearance. An ocean floor of dust-and-cobweb-connected plastic coverings started the snaps from the *Addams Family* theme song in my head. If Thing had run on all four fingers across the floor and beaconed me toward the room with the marble slabs, it wouldn't have shocked me.

I swatted through the webs to a short hallway where a small amount of light bled through cracks from the area of the cave-in. A section of one of the slabs blocked the way. I gave it a quick wipe but found only a smooth marble surface. The angle and debris made it impossible for me to climb beneath, and it'd clearly be too heavy for me to move aside. If only I had a lightbulb and could pull an Uncle Fester, I'd be able to search for another way in, but as it was, I returned to the dining room.

All of the rooms were glazed softly with plastic drapery except for one. I swiped my way through and reached an impromptu bedroom next to a fireplace. A cot with a rumpled blanket and pillow, which still had a head indentation in it, lay alongside a colossal desk with mounds of books and bundles of newspapers and magazines.

The dust masked every item on the large desk. Most dust in any room you encounter is composed of shed human skin cells. The human body is composed of about sixty trillion cells, and as we move, we continually shower them on everything around us. I wondered if ghosts lived on using our dead skin as a conduit. Our life energy surging through layers of discarded old cells... although how many people would have had to live here to create such a layer? Probably also generated from the cave-in.

I pulled the metal cord of the desk lamp and lit up a clouded, empty drinking glass and a framed picture. Both were plain and of little worth. I wiped off the picture to see it, anyway—a black-and-white image of a happy, dark-haired woman holding a girl on her knee. Without the dust, the picture looked fresh and new.

What appeared to be months, maybe years' worth of aluminum TV-dinner trays were piled in an archway to a pantry. This gave the impression of a vagrant who had set up home for a while, but what vagrant kept pictures like this? Or used all these books for whatever studies took place here?

I picked up a folder from one of the stacks and opened it. Dust flew up into the air, choking me, and I had to move out of the area until it settled and cleared from my lungs. Inside the folder were delicately painted pictures of flowers. The first, titled *Chippewa Star* had three lilies; the second, five buttercups. Each image a different flower and number in the bouquet: eight delphiniums, thirteen marigolds, twenty-one asters. I tried the folder underneath it and found images of the Parthenon from Greece, again painted in meticulous watercolor. I doubted the Kevins could be calmed by paintings or that I'd be able to convince them a book was of great value.

A WHOLE LOT

A single large volume rested prominently at the front of the desk. Clouds of dust lowered onto my Bobos and the floor; I shook it off. While waiting for the dust to clear, I guessed it'd be an Agatha Christie novel. If so it'd fit well with the setting, and as she's the top-selling crime novelist, the percentages were high one of her books would show up. I should have gone with the top-selling book of all time, the Bible. This one was written in the Bible's original language, Hebrew, and as I turned the pages, I found handwritten numbers between each printed line reminding me of that single quire i in the St. Albans manuscript, demanding recognition of the writer's existence. I flipped to the beginning and below the printed words *Textus Receptus,* I found a name scrawled in ink: *Richard Pierson, December 1966.*

A quote written below that read: *"Trials are medicines which our gracious and wise physician prescribes because we need them; and he proportions the frequency and weight of them to what the case requires. Let us trust his skill and thank him for his prescription. —IN"*

Someone, probably Richard Pierson, crammed whole numbers but no formulae into every section of the following page. Lists and lists of numbers on each available blank space, then the next line and the next until the page darkened from their density. They reminded me of a kid named Christopher Pollen from New City who spent most of his free time writing as small and compact as he could. When Christopher finally allowed me to read his writing, I found he'd only rewritten notes from class. He attributed all his educational successes to this activity. It was nothing nearly as exciting as what the discoverers who used magnifying glasses to look at Jan Van Eyck's paintings for the first time had found. No tiny people or poetry.

I scanned the number list in the title pages of the book. I hoped to find some addition, multiplication, or any special symbol that might reveal Pierson was working on a calculation of an immense number, but I couldn't find one. The exceedingly curious aspect of the uninterrupted dense numbering was that a list of numbers could arouse such interest in me. They appeared to be mere idiocy, but I wanted to keep reading.

This version of Genesis had one Hebrew letter printed after the next without spaces between the words except for above and below the sentences, where plenty of unprinted space existed. Handwritten numbers filled those areas, too. I flipped through every page to find numbers coating the entire text.

The more I flipped, the more manic the numbers became. I read the numbers and the text itself for a few minutes until I came across a line about *paying the price of our sin* and I recalled the need to find cash. My watch ticked to 1:41:07 p.m. I glanced around the room but gray webs and dust gave little promise. Normal desk supplies filled the top drawer, but in the bottom, two objects were wrapped in yellowed paper. They turned out to be bookends shaped like sunflower heads and were vibrantly shiny—dazzlingly shiny, in fact, and probably made of brass. To an undiscerning eye, they might just pass for gold.

Outside the house, I found Russell begging.

"Come on, seriously, I gotta go. Let me go up there behind the shrub near the front door. You could easily see me."

"Just sit on it and quit asking," Rick said and kicked the pillar next to Russell's body.

I watched as Russell shifted his weight from his right foot to his left. He did this for another minute, then chanced asking again.

"I swear, guys, I'm gonna pee my pants. This isn't funny."

Kevin Groter started looking closely at Kevin Schmill. He stood up. "That's it! You were the kid in the fourth grade that wet his pants during the Halloween assembly."

"No, I wasn't."

"You were the Dracula that wet his pants?" Rick said, looking closely at Schmill.

"Shut up! No, I wasn't."

"You were. You were that kid who pissed himself onstage during the costume parade," Rick said, moving up to show he wasn't afraid of Schmill.

"Man, all the third graders laughed for days about that. Remember how we pretended to fall and drink our own blood?" Groter said to Rick.

"It wasn't funny. How 'bout I knock you down some stairs, and you can sit at a doctor's with wet pants while they fix your teeth." Schmill shoved Groter.

"There were only two Kevins in the third grade, me and Groter, and in the fourth everyone talked about how there were three. Three in the fourth, remember?" Rick said.

"Shut the fuck up with this." Schmill went over to Russell. "See the shit you've started? See this shit?" The dirt from his hands left prints on Russell's shirt as he shoved him to the stone pillar, knocking his head against the empty concrete planter at the top.

They were so busy with their arguing that my return remained unnoticed until Russell's head hit, and I spoke up.

"Hey," I muttered.

"No, uh-uh, no stopping now. This kid's gonna piss himself, and we're all gonna laugh in his stupid fuckin' face." Schmill poked Russell.

Russell cried pathetically into his wrist.

"Hold it, Schmill." Jerry turned to me. "Where's the money?"

"Did you see any dead bodies?" Groter asked.

I nodded.

"Yeah, right. How many?" Schmill asked.

"Two adults, two children, parts of their bodies from under—"

"Bullshit. Now where's our dough?" Schmill persisted.

I waited until I was sure he wasn't going to continue beating up Russell.

Rick hawked and spat on my Bobos. "Where's the—"

"It is a fact: The greatest distance achieved at the annual tobacco-spitting classic in Mississippi is thirty-one feet and one inch by Don Snyder on July twenty-sixth in 1973," I said.

Rick shook his head with annoyed disbelief. "That supposed to be some kinda joke? Because I don't see any cash, and Schmill here is—"

I pulled the bookends from my satchel. Everyone stopped and stared as I held them up.

"Crimson gold," I spoke softly, trying to make the brass sound glamorous.

Russell looked up after wiping his eyes. Rick took the first from me and started examining it.

"The pawnshop by Bradlees near Stop & Shop. It says top dollar on the window," I explained, afraid to move.

"Lemme get a look at that." Jerry grabbed the other. He turned it over and looked closely at the name engraved on the back. "I think he's right, Rick. I mean if there's one thing alien kids like him probably know it's crap like this." He held up the bookend for Schmill to look at.

Schmill pushed the bookend away. "That's... my nana has bullshit flower crap like that, and it ain't worth shit."

I didn't want to show what else I had because I wanted it for myself, but I hoped it might have a calming effect on them, so I pulled the Bible from my satchel. I tried displaying it with as much honor as I could convey. "This, too."

Schmill grabbed it from me. "A fuckin' book, you dumbass spic." He started ripping pages from the back and throwing them to the ground. He got about three handfuls, ripped the cover off it, and chucked the book as hard as he could into the field. The eagle spiraled on one wing and flapped to gain balance, but its flight was brief and death swift. A whimpering soul tried to escape to the heavens on the two pages that fluttered away before the final grounding.

"It was a Bible," I explained as tiny rows of numbers called from the paper carnage around me.

"Holy shit, Schmill! You stupid . . . you killed a Bible. That's a mortal sin," Groter said.

"I didn't even know it was a Bible."

"That doesn't matter. You're going to Hell."

"Shut up."

"You can go to purgatory just for closing a Bible too hard. You're gonna burn." Groter started backing away from him.

Either Russell's bladder was about to rupture, or he was at his wits end. Regardless, Russell didn't try to signal me before he bolted toward the albino village.

"You shit, you can't run. I know where—" Schmill grabbed the bookend from Jerry and started running after Russell.

"That's for splitting between all of us!" Rick shouted and started chasing him. "It's not yours. Hold up!"

Groter and Jerry ran to catch up.

I searched for where Schmill threw the Bible, but I could see nothing except tall weeds, so I held my satchel close to my side and started running after them, too. Russell may not deserve my help, but he deserved to get beat up alone even less. A dog started barking in the distance.

When I caught up to them at an embankment, Schmill scurried along the edge, trying to figure out a way down to where Russell had obviously slid. A shaggy black-and-white dog jumped against the fence in the yard of one of the shacks.

"Get up here, you retard!" Schmill shrieked, holding onto a small tree trunk.

Russell froze in a physical stutter, trapped between the choice of the dog and shacks or climbing back up. Schmill crept to where I thought he'd start down. His small brain must have figured he'd never be able to manage it with the bookend and instead decided to stay put as Russell made the poor choice of climbing up. The pain and fear in Russell's eyes suggested he might not be able to climb all the way.

"I'm comin', but you better get the hell away from me," Russell insisted frantically.

"I better what? I better nothing, you shit. You fuckin' ass."

Schmill's arm wound back like a pitcher, and he threw the bookend with all he had. At first, I couldn't tell if it would hit Russell. Before I could calculate anything, it caught him on the shoulder, and he dropped. He hit the side of the embankment, then rolled headfirst through weeds and blackberry vines to the bottom.

"Holy shit! You killed him." Rick went over to where Schmill was standing.

Schmill looked surprised and hung onto the tree trunk, looking down, then realized we were all watching him. He glanced over at us. "It's your fault. I never wanted to go to that house. It's your fault." Schmill looked as if he might cry. He snuffed loudly and started running toward the tunnel, where he vanished into its interior.

"Hey, none of that is my fault, either, guys. Don't say anything to my brother, all right?" Jerry looked frightened. Groter hadn't flinched since Russell was hit. He kept watching to see if Russell would move.

"OK Rick?" Jerry asked again.

"Nobody cares about your dumbass brother, Jerry." Rick dropped the other bookend and ran off into the darkness, too.

"Come on, Kev, there's nothing we can do." Jerry nudged Groter, who snapped out of it. They left me to figure out what to do on my own.

Taking into consideration the force that Schmill could possibly generate, the addition of gravity, plus the many sharp petals that outlined the flower, and the way he landed, my stomach felt queasy. I couldn't manage much alone, but I thought of Hank and Will. Will's got a fast car. He could drive it very fast to the hospital.

"Hey, hey . . . it's me, Apple!" I felt ridiculous hanging maybe a fifth of the way down the slope with my satchel hooked to a rock. I'd have to hike over to where the steps were to get down to Russell, but I could see his wound from here, a frightening, bright crimson blotch on his shoulder. I looked over at the closest shack and thought I saw a curtain move but couldn't be sure. My heart said go check for a pulse. My head said go get Will. The curtain moved. I was sure of it this time.

Spit and shit and cobwebs, it didn't matter, my Bobos flew into action. I ran past the steps into the darkness. The glass and rusting entities bounced from my feet as I scrambled through the tunnel without care. I scraped the shadow off me and pushed on, finally arriving at the lake. I slipped quickly along the path at the water's edge as my lungs constricted, and I choked on the phlegm in my throat, but the static image of Russell's damaged body compelled me onward. I wheeled the bike onto the path. My satchel hung across my neck, choking me and banging into my back as I pedaled, but I didn't care. I picked up speed on the flat part of the path and flew up over a hill, thinking the road would be there. Instead I shot between some shrubs into a freshly mown backyard. I tried to look for some object, some dogpile to break up the uniformity. I needed to break the grass into sections. The sidewalk seemed like a million miles. Infinity took my shoulders and slowed my pace. I could, I . . .

A graying beard replaced the tessellated patterns beneath my eyelids as I came to.

"Grace! His eyes are opening. Son, son . . . hey there, you OK? Sure you are."

His arms wrapped around my back on the concrete slab next to a house. My hip ached, but nothing was broken.

Grace towered above us. Her marshmallow face peered down as she took me from the man, and he took her place above. She draped a cold cloth on my head and took another from her shoulder to wipe my arms.

"You'll be fine. You had a little accident." She smiled politely. Her white skin tempered with powder sifted down onto my face. "Now, what's your name?" She had a tough German quality about her.

"Abel."

"OK, Abel. Well, you fell off your bike, and we need to know who we should call to come get you," she continued firmly, wiping the mud from my arms.

"Three-four-eight, six-three–three-three," I said.

"Hold it a minute." The man pulled a pen from his pocket. "What's that again now?"

I told him again and added Will Flynn's name after I finished.

He wrote the number on his own arm and ran to the house. Grace continued wiping me. I felt like a toddler as she kept my hand in hers until the man returned with a glass of pink lemonade. He explained that Will was on his way. The garage wasn't far, and I finished only about a quarter of the glass before I heard his engine out front. My blood pulsed through my body in a wave from the skin of my scalp to the veins of my stomach. I allowed Grace to help me walk to the car. I stared at the liver spots on her hands to avoid the lawn.

Will opened the passenger door from inside. When I leaned in, his beat-up carbuncled face ballooned out like clumps of darkened fungus. He'd obviously been in the ring recently. The man, who now stood beside me, quickly moved next to his wife when he saw Will.

"Hi, Will. Will, it's four fifty-seven."

"Almost dinnertime, Juke. You OK?"

"He'll be fine. He must've taken quite a spill. Name's Roland Bean." He wheeled the bike over and immediately stopped when Will got out. Mr. Bean's eyes kept darting toward Will's battered face as he put the kickstand down and backed away from the bike.

Will walked over. "Will Flynn. Thanks, I got him now." Will's eyes did a similar thing as Mr. Bean's. His eyes kept glancing at Mr. Bean's face and back to the bike until Will finally picked up the bike and loaded it into the trunk. Will wasn't much for small talk with white people, even when he sold service to them at the garage. Anyone could see the Beans were afraid.

"Don't know why he rode his bike into our backyard, but that's where we found him," Mr. Bean added.

"Take care now, and I'd practice riding in your driveway before visiting those paths along the lake again," Mrs. Bean said and waved good-bye.

As soon as Will backed out of their driveway, I started in like we were in a cop movie. "The albino village, step on it."

"Say what? Who's been choking you?" Will took me by the chin and examined my neck.

"It's a-a brush burn," I explained, understanding the aching sensation at my Adam's apple better now. "Russell's hurt at the albino village."

"That kid with the eyebrows?"

"He-he could be dead." I pressed my palms into the dashboard to try to get him to go faster.

"OK, OK, calm down." Will stepped on the accelerator. "Brush burn . . . how the hell you make a brush burn like that on your neck?"

I showed him with my satchel around my wrist and made it run along.

Will knew the back roads, and when we hit a dirt turnoff, I could see part of one of the shacks. We came around to the painted-head fence. Russell no longer lay at the bottom of the hill. There was no dog barking, either. I glanced along the blue-and-orange paint of the fence, worried I'd see some other color dripping from a freshly decapitated head. I knew it was a stupid thought, but it came to me that maybe they'd replaced one of the painted jugs with Russell's.

"Here," I said. Will applied the brakes, and the car briefly slid on the gravel. Dust hovered in the air as we looked around.

"You want me to go knock on these shacks?"

"He was there." I pointed at the bottom of the embankment.

"Well, he's not now. Hang on." Will left the car running, got out, and wandered around. He went over and kicked some of the tall weeds aside, then marched over to the second shack and banged on the door. I waited with "Beetles in the Bog" by the group War playing on the eight-track. In the background of the singing and the music, a "hey" shouted at irregular intervals, which made me think someone outside the car said it. Each time I jumped a little, frightened that Al Bino, the Mayor King, or the dog would leap out, but nobody came to answer Will's pounding.

Will went to the first shack and banged. Again, nobody answered. Maybe they saw his muscular body and swollen face. He gave me a shrug as he waited, then finally came back to the car.

"Hey, it's OK. Juke, we all grew up scared the Albinos were gonna get us. You'd think they were long gone, but look at this place. You sure you didn't dream Russell died when you fell off your bike or something?"

I shook my head. It was all too much for me to explain.

"Did you win?" I asked, staring at the plums expanded from his eyebrow and cheek.

"You wouldn't know it looking at my face. Yeah, man, I won. 'Nother couple of months winning like this, and I'll have enough for the move."

I scanned the area where Russell had been.

"You gonna come watch me when I fight in LA? Some say I'm too small for a heavyweight, but they'll see. I'm almost there now."

"Robert James Fitzsimmons from England," I said as I rolled down my window to get a better look at the bottom of the hill.

"OK, I'll bite. Who's that?"

I could see the path where he'd slid. Some of the rocks were out of their moorings, fresh dirt was exposed, and plants were bent downhill.

"The lightest heavyweight champion who won the title by knocking out James J. Corbett in fourteen rounds at Carson City, Nevada, on the seventeenth day of March in 1897. He weighed 167 pounds." I scanned for the bookend that would be shiny and easy to spot but couldn't locate it, either.

"See that, right there. That's what I'm sayin'. I can't lose now, can I? And worst case, I could become a movie star instead, right?"

We drove past Russell's house, which remained dark without a car in the drive.

Will pulled up to the curb. "Don't know what to tell you."

"Mm, yeah, mm, no one's home. Pop the trunk, OK?"

I placed the bike on the side of the driveway for Russell. He'd surely worry about it when he came home.

"Maybe you could call him later tonight," Will said three stop signs later. I nodded, and we continued to drive without much conversation. We pulled to the stop sign near the top of my street.

"Please, I will get out right here."

"What? Not to your house?"

"No, thanks." I waved good-bye after I closed the heavy door.

He didn't pull away and called out of his window. "How 'bout you? You sure you're all right? Them white folks looked pretty shook."

"I'm A-OK," I said, making the OK sign and starting to walk away.

"Hey, you want to come back to the garage? I'm forgetting it's Saturday. We could get a couple of pizzas with Dad and Mi."

"I've got church tomorrow. Good-bye again." I turned one last time.

He revved his engine and did a great little squeal of his tires for me as he left.

CHAPTER ELEVEN

A Strabismus Tiger Clears Up The Miracle Boy Blues

39.6-14.3.21.39.88.39.13.5.4-10.13.13.114.4.101

The Sunday before school started, we went to Wildwood, New Jersey, which was one of the best locations Pigpie had me work. Wildwood is like taking twenty local carnivals and lining them up along a wooden walkway on the ocean. Pigpie's notion to start marketing my abilities all over New Jersey happened one day after church services. I practiced some fellowship by finishing the full quote to a verse this kindly old man had begun, and before I knew it, people had lined up around the block to have me recite a chapter and verse number. I don't think all of them even went to St. Christopher's.

In between the shows at Wildwood, I at least had time to construct algorithms for extracting cube roots or watch the monkeys' dancing feet through the crack in the tent. However, I went more than two hours without a break that first day at the church, except for the brief respite before Father Mullens collected their "donations."

"What're you wearing? Get upstairs and put on that shirt and tie I bought for you, and do you have to carry that dumb bag with you everywhere?" Pigpie unrolled her curlers and dropped the little pink cylinders in the sink.

Pigpie bought me a special church outfit when she acquired my new school clothes, but the church shirt was too small and the clip-on tie that accompanied it didn't stay clipped. I hoped to fool her by wearing my usual T-shirt-and-bowtie combo. Although the T-shirt didn't go with a bowtie, the bowtie actually looked smart and felt far more comfortable than the new church combo. I went back up to change again, and as a result, there wasn't time to toast some bread. I ended up having a slice of plain Stroehmann's white for breakfast. Waiting for lunch would feel like an eternity.

Father Mullens, with his pristine shoes and gold rings, looked like he'd been shipped straight from some affluent part of Ireland to convert us wayward Americans. I overheard a member of the congregation, Tim Brown, telling Pigpie that Father Mullens was actually from Boston and worked the Irish brogue to impress his flock. I can't comment on his preaching skills, as I always fill my ears with moistened cotton-ball plugs when we've gone to church. This tactic allows me to still mostly understand what Pigpie says, and it makes Father Mullens's voice a soothing underwater symphony.

"Ah, I'm so happy you could make it today." He pronounced *today* so that it almost sounded like *teddy*. His accent was charming, but I had serious trouble listening to him, as the numbers made ugly patterns because of his whistling *s*.

"Abel Velasco," I said to be certain he introduced me correctly and not as Abel Stacks.

"Oh, dear child, I know your name, and while you don't come as faithfully as you should, you come enough that your name is well known. And my goodness, how could I forget it after our special day together." He turned to Pigpie. "Cece, that's a singular coif you've got there. I'm sorry you didn't show it off at services earlier."

Lucifer sent the last sentence to torment me. When he whistled the word *services*, I could practically feel one of the tiny bones of my inner ear fracture.

"I thought sharing the miracle"—she placed her arm around me—"would pay off my time to God."

"Yes, but I wrote some kind words in today's sermon just for you. Maybe you'll join us next Sunday?" He looked down at his Spic 'n' Span shoes and bent to wipe some unnoticeable thing from the left one.

She apologized, and they went on with massive piles of blather about how God smiled on me and weren't we all blessed I came to them. They set up a sign on the road that read: *Come talk with the Miracle Boy! Sun., Sept. 26, 11 a.m. to 4 p.m.* on one side and *Ask God a question, he'll share a miracle! Sun., Sept. 26, 11 a.m. to 4 p.m.* on the other. I hoped possibly Russell or his parents would see it and know to stop here to let me know how he was.

Pigpie and Father Mullens walked me out to the parking lot at the back of the church so the long line of people could get a good look at me. I became a human sound dampener. The decibels of the chatter increased as I passed and lessened as I approached. The heat in my face grew almost unbearable and made me wonder why anyone would want to become famous.

At the tent door, Father Mullens gave a short speech in which he never said my real name, only calling me "the miracle of St. Christopher's" and pointed out the donation box at the entrance. He directed me inside to my sad stage. The tent's interior design consisted of a folding table with a Bible resting on top, two metal chairs, and a latch-hook rug of Jesus with a bleeding heart. Who wouldn't feel God's grace in here? Pigpie and Father Mullens left me alone and stood outside by the cash box, inveigling donations.

They let each visitor in one at a time unless a mother brought her children. Most people weren't prepared with a question. They entered, sat down, or stood next to the extra chair, waiting for me to say something. I finally figured out how to speed it along by asking them what I most wanted to know if they didn't have something prepared.

The exchange inevitably went like number thirty-one:

Man with four missing lower teeth, in jeans enters leaving wet streak—probably sweat—on the canvas flap. He doesn't move very far into the tent, faces me without speaking.

"When did the misfortune of birth overtake you?" I asked.

"What?" he replied.

"When were you born?" I repeated.

"December second 1941. Why?"

"It is a fact. You are forty years old. You will be forty-one on a Thursday this year. You will be eligible for full retirement benefits on June second 2007, which is a Saturday. The day you were born, the *SS Brynmill* cargo ship on route from Blyth to London was sunk by a German aircraft off East Dudgeon Buoy."

"What're you, a robot? 'Cause you sound like a robot. I heard about you, and I told the guys you're probably just a robot." He scratched his chin.

"It is a fact: On December second 1941, the largest roller-skating rink outside of New York City opened in Peekskill, New York."

"Yeah, so?"

"Thank you," I said, dismissing him.

"What a rip-off. I told the guys you'd be a rip-off fake."

Sometimes people would come in looking for a repeat performance from my first show and give me a verse and chapter, or ask me if they could speak to one of their dead relatives like the one aggrieved woman with her grandson.

No hellos and only one introduction.

"This is George, my grandson. Let me speak to my husband."

We stared blankly at one another. I didn't say a word.

"Fine. OK. Listen, Bill, I can't find where you left the key to the shed, and I know that's where you hid the white leash with the flowers on it for my little Mooshie. Now tell me where it is."

She leaned forward, and I could see the cracks where she'd applied her makeup too thick. She seemed to be looking through me. George looked around impatiently. She sat back and began to cry. When she composed herself, I asked for her birth date and she gave it. I told her it'd fall on a Friday this year, a perfect day for a party. She didn't know what to say, crossed herself, and left.

This went on for 167 minutes until Father Mullens stuck his head in and said I'd be getting a five-minute break.

My butt needed some relief from the metal chair, so I stood. I reached up to stretch my arms and touch the tent roof when a new woman walked in. She confidently tucked the entrance flap in place and winked at me as if to say, "Now we're alone." I don't know why I left my arms in the air, but when she winked, they dropped as if she'd shot me.

Her beautiful, asymmetrical eyes froze me in place like Medusa's would. I wanted to share information about Descartes's predilection for women with strabismus. I wanted to share how before I even knew of his tastes, my first crush happened over Stacy Pahrel, who could play piano as well as Mozart and could be deemed one of the greatest strabismus beauties ever. In fact, since Stacy, I've been attracted to other girls, and aroused by a few ladies in magazines and movies but none who truly plucked my heartstrings until just this moment. All I could do was stare.

Strabismus is a term for an eye condition alternately called cross-eyed, wall-eyed, wandering eyes. While movies and TV always portray those blessed with this condition as gooney or crazy, I knew better than to believe this stereotyping. I'd once heard you were supposed to look them in the eye that looks directly at you, but I preferred the wandering eye—I accept the parts others choose to avoid. I couldn't actually look at either of her eyes, so I looked at everything else. She had long brown hair, skinny long legs with no hips, and was wearing a fuzzy blue-green-and-white striped sweater over a short white skirt. She might have been the most beautiful woman I'd ever seen.

"Hello," she said with a Marilyn Monroe voice as she sat down next to me. Her breath smelled of onions. I was in love.

I wanted to impress her by saying I'd just gotten back from the Bahamas or some other exotic island resort. I knew she knew I was blushing, and I loved her even more for not mentioning it.

"Honey, I'm not even sure why I'm here, but God knows I could use a miracle." She grabbed her shirt by the shoulder and adjusted her bra strap.

I looked at her chin to avoid appearing lecherous.

"So, how does this miracle stuff work?"

I wanted to start rattling off the factors of pi as far as I could go, but instead I managed, "Uh, well, uh, what's your—what's your birthdate?"

She put her hand on my forearm and left it there. My body tingled, unlike most times when others touch me, and all the numbers calculated into crystal formulae, creating an effect that was almost as beautiful as she was.

"Is that, like, what's my sign? It's November seventeenth, 1962. I'm a Scorpio, darling, watch out."

She seemed much older, but she was old enough to be drafted and almost legal to buy beer.

"It is a fact: You are nineteen years old. This year you will be twenty on a Monday. You are a tiger in the Chinese zodiac. Tigers have a fighting spirit. Tigers are aggressive and courageous. Tigers are sensitive deep thinkers who are true-blue friends. Tigers should marry a horse or a dog, but beware of the monkey. I'm a dog." I immediately wanted to detract the last phrase.

"Wow, you know, my father said I'd marry a dog. Now, I hope he's right." She rubbed my arm a little.

"Uh, it is a fact: Georgia O'Keefe was born the same day as you."

"Who's she, honey?"

"Beverly D'Angelo, who was in such movies as *Annie Hall*, *Every Which Way But Loose,* and *Coal Miner's Daughter,* was also born the same day as you, only she was born in 1954, so she's a horse."

"Well, I guess I should marry her then, too. Then I could ride her the hell out of this town." She looked at the side of the tent with frustration but composed herself and rubbed my arm again, forcing a smile. I wondered if she could see my lap from where she sat. I didn't know what else to say.

She looked directly into my eyes with her one eye.

"You're not just a miracle; you're a handsome miracle, aren't you?"

I shrugged again, and a wonderful formula came to me.

"You there? Where'd you go, handsome?" She snapped her fingers in front of my eyes.

"You'll be part of my future," I said.

She stood up and came around the table. "Oh, honey, you're giving me goose pimples." She hugged my face to her chest, and I wanted to say, "Lady, you should call those two North African ostrich pimples."

"Of course, I'll be part of your future. We'll be getting married, right, sweetie?" She kissed my forehead. "This was so much fun. I'll have to look for the sign so I can come to your next show. Thanks for the good time."

She waved a cute little good-bye as she pushed through the tent flap. She didn't even tell me her name.

After she left, the day seemed to slug past. By four, my stomach compressed with hunger as if I'd descended a thousand feet in the ocean. If they didn't bring food soon, I'd surely get the bends. I couldn't move the people out quick enough.

After the last person came through, Pigpie and Father Mullens brought the box into the tent and split the money. I felt like I took part in some crime as they tucked their wads of cash away.

"Let's go shopping, and we'll buy you whatever you want for dinner first," she offered, wrapping her flabby arm around me for the second time in one day. I bit the side of my cheek hard. Luckily, I had the memory of Marilyn to comfort me. I decided to call her Marilyn because of her voice, even though Marilyn Monroe had eyes that looked in the same direction and wasn't half as pretty as my Marilyn.

"That sounds like a grand idea. Our boy here has done quite a service for the church today. God is smiling on him for certain." He appeared sincere, but I sincerely wanted his tongue to melt out of his head. I bit the side of my cheek again, this time to numb the pain of hearing the "smiling-certain" combo from Father Mullens and felt so hungry I could've eaten the part of my cheek that I bit.

I rested my head on the window as we drove the back roads through housing developments. I couldn't shuck the grin from my face no matter how many unpleasant pops and gurgles my stomach produced. Damn. I should've asked her what troubled her. I should've found out where she lived. I'm so stupid. There are a hundred questions I could've asked, and she would've answered. While the "what ifs" swirled around me, I took refuge that I'd eventually see her again, and this realization filled me with joy. Listening to Pigpie sing along to Anne Murray's "Danny's Song" on AM Gold was even pleasant now, if not bizarre.

At one part, she actually touched my leg as if I were the guy she was going to take home. It gave me the shivers. Then she sang along to the part about having no money and patted her purse. It made no sense.

As we passed a couple that came to see me, Pigpie waved as if they were old friends. I don't think she actually knew them or that the couple noticed, anyway, because they were in conversation. They caught up to us as Pigpie backed the yellow Buick into the parking space at Doyle's, but she didn't acknowledge them a second time, nor they her. The woman born on July 11, 1947, who'd also hugged me when I gave her retirement date, cracked a recognition smile at me when our eyes met. But I barely had time to smile back since the smell of deep-fried food filled me with delight as soon as my foot hit the pavement.

Pigpie and I stood for a minute until the hostess arrived. She guided us to a booth near the front windows. I couldn't get the menu open quick enough.

"Oh, look, Abel, they have grape placemats now. Isn't grape your favorite color?"

Who was this woman? She had no idea about my favorite color. Grape? Another of my word tormentors. How is one to factor the word *grape* used as a color? Grape is not a color. It is a noun whose definition is: a smooth-skinned, juicy, greenish-white-to-deep-purple berry eaten dried or fresh as a fruit or fermented to produce wine. Green or purple. The placemat was blue with maybe a minute amount of purple to it. Maybe she's color-blind. I pounded the top of the table from behind the menu to release some of the strain I felt.

"Hey, cut that out. She's coming now, and I'll take you right out of here if you try that again."

The waitress arrived and must've thought chewing gum with her mouth open would be acceptable. It wasn't, and I pounded the table again.

"What the hell is with you? Do you want to leave now?" Pigpie turned to the waitress. "I'm sorry, miss. He's got some disabilities." She whispered *disabilities* as if I wouldn't hear it.

The waitress nodded with understanding and started rattling off the dinner specials. Pigpie asked about the chef's best dish and laughed at what the waitress suggested. I failed to see the humor. There's nothing funny about meatloaf. I might laugh if she said, "lopadotemachoselachogaleokranioleipsanodrimhypotrimmatosilphioparaomelitokatakechymenokichlepikossyphophattoperisteralektryonoptekephalliokigklopeleiolagoiosiraiobaphetraganopterygon," which is the 182-letter transliteration of a 171-lettered Greek word for a fricassee of seventeen sweet and sour ingredients including mullet, brains, honey, vinegar, pickles, marrow (the vegetable), and ouzo—a Greek drink laced with anisette. It's from *The Ecclesiazusae,* a comedy I read by Aristophanes. If she tried pronouncing that word, it would be hysterical but laughing at meatloaf only made me want to pound the table again.

"*Khazzer,*" I mumbled, looking at Pigpie's placemat. It means pig, foul, or gluttonous in Yiddish.

"What do you want me to say? Bless you? Maybe if you deserved it. Now, what do you want?" Pigpie asked and started rooting through her purse until she found a tissue that she forced me to take.

I looked down the numbers of the menu. Menus without numbers made it difficult to order, and in the past I had to go with whatever the person on my left ordered if there weren't any. Number nine on the menu was the meatloaf, which made it easy.

"Number nine."

"So, ya want the special, then?" The waitress said with her gum still visible.

"The number nine."

"Honey, the special and number nine are both meatloaf."

"I'll have number nine," I repeated.

Pigpie cleared her throat and made an odd face toward me for the waitress's benefit. "Make that two of the specials."

We gave over the menus, and I started wiping my hands with the tissue.

"What is with your..." Pigpie began to say but then got distracted by her purse. She pulled the wad of money out, separated it by denomination, and counted it again: $314. She didn't get up to wash the money filth from her hands when our dinner salads arrived. *Khazzer*. Maybe I should thank her, though, because it gave me a great excuse to avoid her slopping the lettuce into her mouth. My stomach rolled with hunger, but I showed her my hands and got out of my seat.

"Where are you going?"

I showed my hands to her again and pretended to wash them. She looked disgusted and starting aggressively spearing her salad.

I weaved through a few tables and turned the corner, following the pointing hand labeled with restrooms and heard a woman say, "And you'll see my name, Kate Crawford, up in lights." Her companions laughed at this. "Hey, can you believe it? Did I tell you he was a miracle boy?"

The two other women at her table turned to look at me.

"Believe it or not, this is my future husband I was just telling you about. What ya say, loverboy? Aren't I going to Hollywood?"

I'd already located page fifty-two of the telephone directory for Milltown, New Jersey. There wasn't a listing for a Kate Crawford in North Brunswick and only one number listed for a Kathryn Crawford in Milltown with 391 Broad St., Apt. 2B, as the address.

"Look at those red cheeks," the woman sitting across from Kate said.

"Oh, leave him alone, would ya, Sylvia?" Kate looked to me again. "You having dinner here, too?"

I nodded, noticing Sylvia's hair was the same color and length but with more curl than Kate's.

"Hey, show them what you can do, would ya? Syl, tell him your birthdate."

"March fourth."

"You have to tell him what year, too," Kate said.

"Hey, do me," the woman next to Sylvia said.

"Wait your turn, Meg. It's 1961."

I looked at their placemats.

"March fourth, 1961, was a Saturday. Today, you are seven thousand eight hundred and seventy-six days old. You are an ox. An ox is a symbol of powerful individuals with unyielding and stubborn personalities. They are leaders who typically succeed when given the chance and will make outstanding parents. They are upright, inspiring, easygoing, and conservative. The ox would be successful as a skilled surgeon, teacher, or hairdresser. Ox gets along with Snakes and Roosters, but not Sheep."

"Didja hear that? I'm upright and gonna have kids. He doesn't have a clue." She turned to me. "I can't have children. Thanks."

"Quiet, Syl. Where's your manners? It's a freebie. Besides, he never said you'd have kids. He said you'd be a good mom." Kate put her hand on my shoulder, and I backed up so she couldn't keep it there. "That was great. Don't listen to Syl. She doesn't believe anything. You're absolutely right. She's as stubborn as they come."

"Hey, fine! Thanks, kid. I guess he did say I get along with snakes." They all laughed.

A waitress showed up with a full tray and placed a soft drink in front of Kate.

"Come on, don't make me look like a hog. Order something else, Kate," Meg said.

"I told you, I had a hoagie like an hour ago." She thanked the waitress and took a sip.

I felt out of place and left as the waitress handed out the rest of their order. I passed them again on my way back. Kate talked with a mouth full of food as I passed. She didn't seem to notice me, so I avoided interrupting her.

"Hey, you leaving without saying good-bye? See, girls, he's already acting like we're married," Kate said, putting Sylvia's cheeseburger back on her plate.

"Bye," I said.

"Bye-bye, sweetie. Call me soon." Kate and the others giggled.

Pigpie had already emptied her plate when I got back to the table.

"You don't think I was going to wait, did you?"

I shoveled the lettuce and cucumber slices into my mouth, swallowing without stopping to taste it all. Pigpie didn't say anything when I used my finger to get the last of the ranch dressing from the plate. We inhaled our meatloaf without talking, not that we ever talked during dinnertime much. I should've tried it when she sang along with Anne Murray, and I just realized I could've asked her for a visit to St. Mary's to see Mom on a day like today. Idiot. I bet the hour drive would've been no big deal. I tried not to think about the missed opportunity and instead wrote out conversation calculations in my journal while we waited for our check. The swish of recounting the bills apparently held Pigpie's focus from the usual harassment about my scribbling.

I grew a nervous tickle in my stomach on our way out. Kate and her friends finished paying just as we arrived at the register. She didn't say anything to me but looked

Pigpie up and down and smiled with a little wave to me as she left. I watched her and the others get into a poorly repainted green Pinto while Pigpie handed over some of my earnings from the day to the cashier. The ride wasn't that far to Milltown if I could get the bike. I needed to call Russell's house. Sunday nights the Ghetys were always home for their ham-and-mac dinner.

It was no surprise Pigpie went straight home, skipping the shopping she said we'd do. Not that I expected any less. It allowed me to try calling Russell earlier, anyway.

"Hello?" Mrs. Ghety answered. I hated it when his parents answered before he did.

"Hello, is Russell there?"

"Who's this?"

"Abel."

"Oh." Mrs. Ghety's voice changed from a semi-friendly phone tone to annoyed once she knew who it was. "He's in the hospital, Abel, and won't be able to-t-t . . ." Mrs. Ghety's voice cracked as she started weeping. I heard a clank as if the phone had been dropped.

"Who did you say it was, Betts?" Mr. Ghety asked in the distance and at the receiver then said, "Hello? Who is this?"

"Abel," I replied.

"It's Russell's friend, Apple," Mrs. Ghety told Mr. Ghety.

"Listen, Apple, Betsy, Mrs. Ghety shouldn't be upset anymore this weekend. Russell might be in the hospital for a while. He'll call you when he gets out." Click.

CHAPTER TWELVE

Barking About the Firestone Library

12.21.12.109-12.3.21-2.66.2-3.12.109.2.21-5.13.2.9.8

Cows are some of the greatest belchers on the planet. They have no upper teeth, a four-segmented stomach, and add nearly as much hydrocarbon into the atmosphere as cars—some hundred million tons annually—and this is accomplished mostly by belching. Since I found this out, I can't pass a herd without thinking of them gumming cud and burping. It makes me grin every time. As Professor Limone drove, we passed a herd, and I almost told him about their belching, but I doubted someone like him would see the humor. He seemed the type who if he ever dared to burp would do so in private and immediately excuse himself.

"It is a fact: Twelve cows together are called a flink." I explained about the twelve in the field.

"Um, you don't say?"

Those were the first three and one partial words he'd used since he told me to put on my seatbelt when we left school for Princeton. He looked nervous.

"There are five main breeds of dairy cattle in the US. Those are Holstein; you can tell by the black-and-white blotches. The others are Ayrshire, Brown Swiss, Guernsey, and Jersey."

"One might guess they were Jersey cows in this state."

He smiled wide with high eyebrow arches after saying this, but his overenthusiastic eyebrow use prevented me from smiling back, so instead I turned and took in a deep breath. We drove in silence for another five minutes. I tried to practice my usual conversation permutations, but having no idea who might interview me made the preparation far more difficult than usual. Normally, I'd know whom I would be speaking to and could prepare by whatever I'd cataloged their interests to be and what the meeting circumstances were.

Dr. Limone turned up the news. The commentator explained about a recent child abduction, and in the background, I could hear a grieving mother.

"Did your mother teach you all that about cows?" Dr. Limone asked. He changed the channel to WJLK 94.3 but turned down the radio as the DJ introduced Laura Branigan singing "Gloria."

"A cow must give birth before she can give milk, and then she must have a calf each year in order to continue producing milk," I offered. I figured he was fishing for information about my mother.

"Yes, think of the exponential growth of the cattle industry. Er, well, I suppose they must have to kill off so many in order to stem the milk-tide, so to speak. Mm, cheeseburgers. I love cheeseburgers."

Luckily, the cows were out of sight now, and I could focus elsewhere. I rolled down the window and let the cool air flow over my glasses. The only thing better than having wind deflected from one's glasses was standing beneath an umbrella in a downpour.

"Er, uh, now, I'm certain you recall they'll be interviewing you today."

I touched my bowtie in response, but I don't think he understood.

"You might not have an option to refuse to answer the large number of questions they ask. Also, they'll expect thorough answers and complete honesty. We must be very careful to give them the proper answers. I'm sure you'll do great. You brought the form I gave you for your aunt to sign?"

"Yes." I felt like explaining that I'd forged her name and hadn't mentioned Princeton to her, since I knew it'd be out of the question after what happened at Rutgers.

"Good, good. Well, thar she blows," he announced using one of Russell's expressions. I missed our morning bus-stop socializing more than one would guess.

We drove into town on Nassau Avenue, and he pointed out a few of the sights.

"Old Al Einstein lived, worked, and died here, you know." He explained this with great excitement as if it wasn't common knowledge. He pointed out where the buses stop on the corner of Washington and Nassau and with a slight trembling pleasure, the Firestone Library. I felt the same thrill Dr. Limone exhibited. The campus buzzed, lively with sports coats, sweatpants and plenty of bowties. This was my kind of town.

We parked the car and entered Firestone. A guard directed us to a side room where a woman with large gums and tight, curly brown hair greeted us.

"Happy to see you today, and what's your name?"

"Abel."

"Welcome to the Firestone Library, Abel. Is this your first time here?"

"It is his first time and mine as well, thank you. Would you mind telling me how I'd get to Dr. Langdeer's office? We have an appointment with him at eleven fifteen."

She checked an appointment book and handed us guest passes.

"Welcome to you both then." She leaned over and looked at the badge Dr. Limone filled out and pinned to himself. "Dr. Limone, Dr. Langdeer's office is on the other side of the building. Go right when you leave our office and straight down the corridor. You can't miss it. I'll inform him you're on your way."

We went back out into the lobby and turned down the corridor. I could tell from the outside that the library would be enormous, and walking inside only made me even more impatient to get these interviews over with. Dr. Langdeer greeted us at his door, which had *Senior Librarian* stenciled on the frosted glass.

"Hello, gentlemen, glad to see you. Dr. Limone, is it?" he said, extending his hand. "And this must be Abel. We're all very hopeful you'll be joining us. Let's get started right away then, shall we?"

Dr. Langdeer was a short bald man with a white mustache and a necktie resting on his potbelly. He led us to a room with a long table and spilled a little of the coffee from his mug as we all took our chairs. Dr. Limone immediately helped clean up the spill and, with a special panache, lessened the awkwardness by pouring each of us a glass of water from a pitcher obviously supplied for us.

"Since Dr. Limone has given you such a shining introduction and Dr. Limone's friends at Fine Hall vouch for his character, there is little I will actually need from you, Abel."

I felt both relief and disbelief at his comment as I'd been prepared for a protracted torture session.

"There is one problem, though. Dr. Limone explained to me about the difficulty with the administrative staff at the New City School. They've yet to deliver your records. The school's reputation is established, and they should have all we need to know about your capabilities. I'm disappointed they haven't sent them but more disappointed with our public-school system, to have done such a shoddy job with discovering your abilities. Three schools and all so ignorant."

A large painting hung on the wall depicting a hunting scene with eleven Springer spaniels.

"I'm hoping to rectify that," Dr. Limone added.

"Yes, of course, and concern such as yours is what has made our public schools great in the past. I will be looking forward to whatever you hear from New City. Until then, I'll accept the folder of his progress under your tutelage that we received. I'm certain Abel is very appreciative of your efforts and also for taking the day off work to join him here."

They both looked at me waiting for a response, but I held back my smile, concerned more with the fourth dog from the right's attitude toward the fifth. She thought his ear a good place for her nose, and I imagined it made it hard for the fifth to hear the orders to hunt the rabbit from the men on the horses.

"Abel, I have a question for you. This is serious, and as Mrs. Reagan, the first lady of our country, is so wisely bringing to the forefront of our consciousness, are you saying no to drugs? It has been explained to me that you have the potential for a genetic disposition toward them."

This was a poor place to start if he wanted real information from me. Others more adept were wise enough to talk for some time on topics that might interest me before they started prying. Bad-mouthing my mother was not a shortcut to my good side.

"I don't know who else you may have spoken with at the high school, but while Abel's cousin, Michelle, may have a few black marks on her record, I can assure you Abel is not that kind of boy. You say no to drugs, don't you?"

I shook my head.

Dr. Limone looked worriedly at me, then at Dr. Langdeer.

"Maybe we aren't being clear, Abel. Do you or are you using any drugs?"

"Yes," I said and pounded on my leg instead of the table.

Dr. Langdeer sat back and smoothed his tie over his belly. He picked up his coffee. "Well, at least he's an honest boy. Maybe he needs a different kind of program—"

"Hold on a second. Abel, could you tell me what drugs you've used or are using, please."

"Everything we eat is composed of compounds, or drugs, substances that chemically alter our bodies," I quoted from *Living Nutrition*, an incredibly bland book I'd read last year.

"That's not the kind of drugs we're referring to," Dr. Langdeer added.

They exchanged understanding looks, and Dr. Langdeer asked, "You've never experimented with any of the illegal narcotics such as cocaine, marijuana, or methamphetamine, have you?"

I shook my head, lying and thinking about the nicotine in cigarettes.

"Good, that's what I thought you meant." He inhaled a heavy breath through his nostrils and released it. "I thought you'd be smart enough not to, but one never knows with the youth of today. I've had little contact at your school except with you, Dr. Limone. So let's see." Dr. Langdeer sat back down and tapped on the table. "Do you know much about the Dewey decimal system, Abel?" He stroked the hairs of his mustache as if he were petting a cat.

Talk about unprepared. If the scope of his questioning included only these, it was pathetic.

I nodded.

"Good. So tell me then, um, what would you find in, say, the two hundreds?"

"Richard Pierson would be a good subject," I said, hoping to learn something about the owner of the house.

"Richard Pierson. The name sounds familiar, hold on. Pierson, right? Oh, I've got it. No, you wouldn't find him in the two hundreds because that's the section in which religious topics are found. His books would be in the five hundreds under natural sciences. Well, that's not a problem. Nothing a little introductory library science won't fix. Anything else?"

I'd already read Euclid's *Elements* when I was ten, a year before Bertrand Russell had, and knew it would impress him so I said, "*Elements*."

"Elements? I recall a delightful chemistry set I was given for Christmas at your age, too. You'll be careful not to blow up any books you borrow. Damaged books would incur a harsh penalty, if not expulsion for you."

"Euclid's *Elements*," I clarified.

"Euclid's *Elements*? That's a horse of a different color entirely. Hm, gosh, you do know there are many volumes to it. That's a Herculean task for someone your age. I think you'd do better to start with something by, say, um, yes, well, I know a few of the famous ones we house here at Firestone, and those are probably too advanced for you, too. Honestly, the Romanticists are more my forte. I had the worst time with fractions if I recall my prep-school days properly. Maybe Dr. Limone could direct you better, but that sounds fine, fine. Or, oh, well, yes, if you mean, you are right. *Elements* would be found in the five hundreds, too. Natural sciences and mathematics would be in the five hundreds. Maybe eventually we'll take a trip down to Fine Hall. You'll locate most of the math books in the library there. I'll tell you, Dr. Limone, I can see no reason why Abel couldn't join us. Let's just say so here and now."

I thought I'd jump out of my pants. That was it?

"That's a good question. What would be the limitations of his library interaction? Numbers of book taken out at a time? Books he'd be restricted from, et cetera? Where he should stay seated, if you had any particular spot in mind," Dr. Limone questioned.

"Let's start him off in the main library. Three books out at a time should suffice. No access to the rare-books collections or microfiche section yet."

He obviously made this up as he went along. I was disappointed about no microfiche, but beggars can't be choosers. I probably wouldn't have time to go through half of what I wanted to read with the books alone.

"What do you say to that?" Dr. Limone asked with a little pride.

I didn't say anything but smiled a little and thought about how I'd enjoy barking excitedly with some of the dogs in the painting.

"I'll set up some appointments with you to check on your progress. You'll need to submit regular lists of books you've taken out so I can talk to you about any I might know something about. Please come to me with any questions the desk librarians can't answer for you." He nodded at me and stood up. "I guess that will do it then. Thank you, gentlemen. The secretary that gave you the guest pass will also provide Abel with his library card and a bit of paperwork."

He walked us to the door, and Dr. Limone thanked him and shook his hand again while I started down the hallway to get my card.

On the way home we didn't take the same roads and I decided that maybe Dr. Limone would drop me by my house instead of back at the school. I didn't recognize any of the streets, but when I saw the sign for Arrowwood Lane, I looked over at Dr. Limone and he looked back enthusiastically at me.

"I thought you wouldn't mind a little surprise to end this special day."

I'd never been to a teacher's house before and wondered what Dr. Limone considered a little surprise. His house was much smaller than I imagined, with almost no landscaping and a tiny front yard with one of those shiny, metallic, blue gazing balls on a pedestal. I thought the British specialized in landscaping, but maybe he'd lost that sensibility while living in America. He shouted a long hello when we came through the garage into the kitchen door. His house had the smell of last night's roast. Part of the reason I hate visiting other peoples' houses is this kind of smell. All those minute particles joining with your body. I loathed the thought of eating his leftovers. He had a sink full of dishes and a pile of mail on the counter.

"Mrs. Limone should be around here somewhere, hang on." He went out the back door and shouted as I peeked at the backyard through the kitchen window. A black woman came from behind a shed with her arms full of dried and twisted plants. He returned and switched a burner on.

"Busy tidying up our garden, I'm afraid. No bother. We'll put a kettle on for tea ourselves, shall we?"

I don't know why it surprised me, but I'd never imagined uptight and white Dr. Limone to marry a black woman. Actually, I couldn't imagine him married at all. If anything, I saw him living with his mother, or sister, or even his aunt. I stood with my hand inside my satchel, flipping over my new library card, and waited for him to finish filling a teapot.

"While that's working itself out, why don't I give you a show?" He smiled and took me to a door with stairs leading down. It became pitch dark after only a few steps.

"Sorry 'bout this. The switch is at the bottom. Just a second."

I bumped into his legs and fell back on the step. I sat there for a minute, and the light came on.

"Sorry, oh, sorry. I should've set things up before I had you follow. My mistake. You'll be all right, won't you?" He called and walked back around the corner to see where I was.

I stood up and wasn't sure I wanted to follow him. His basement acquired a similar mildew scent to the basement at Pigpie's, and I could've used another lamp or two. As I turned the corner, he was shoving boxes against a wall. He went over to a desk, where he turned on another light and set up a second folding chair. His basement was a grubby little space, but it had a large shelf of books and a big old-fashioned radio with vacuum tubes.

"When I was your age, several boys and I had a teacher who started a chess club with us. I thought about it, about gathering a few fellows to start one. You'll let me know if that interests you, won't you? I didn't want to force a game of chess on you today, but I wondered if you wouldn't very much like to give this a try."

I expected a CB radio—with Dr. Limone, I wouldn't have been surprised—but he pulled the tarp away to reveal a computer.

"It's an Apple two plus," he gushed. "I splurged and went for the full forty-eight kilobytes RAM. It's almost twice the price, but the other model had only four. This one's much faster. Mrs. Limone wasn't very pleased when I came home with this filly, but sometimes you have to address the future. I'd put it off until they'd been developed a little more." He removed the cover. "Now, come over here and prepare to be dazzled."

I walked closer, and he moved out of the way so I could peer inside. He stood behind me and started pointing out parts of the system.

"There's the expansion slots. That's the motherboard, and the keyboard is built right in. And if you think this is impressive, well, hold on tight." He replaced the cover and turned it on. The monitor came to life, and the Apple II logo blinked on in color instead of the monochromatic green or amber I was used to. I'd seen the advertisements for these, so it wasn't a huge shock.

"Like when movies went from silent to talkies, if you ask me. Not that I'm that old but, well, it's got a six-color display."

He pecked slowly away at the keyboard to show me what he knew of DOS. I knew he knew about my computer-language knowledge and I wanted a turn, but with the close quarters of the dingy basement, the scene felt a little creepy.

As he pressed the Enter button, the screen cleared and a question scrolled across the top. "What is your name?"

"Go ahead. Type your name in." He stood up to retrieve the kettle that started whistling upstairs. "Better get that. You can stay here if you want."

I typed my name in, already knowing what would happen as I pressed Enter. Abel started filling the screen. Unimpressed, I left it scrolling and followed him up the stairs to find Mrs. Limone in the kitchen, spooning brown tea leaves into a teapot.

"Maddy, this is Abel. Abel, this is Mrs. Limone, my wife."

"Oh, geez, he is sharp looking, isn't he? Nice to meet you, Abel." She extended her plump hand but dropped it when I didn't raise mine. "Solly's been raving about you for weeks now. I've just started some Irish Breakfast, ready in a wink." She put some cookies on a plate and had that waiting-for-me-to-respond look people get in their eyes. "So, has Solly been sharing his latest bankrupter with you? He'll be buying flights to Mars next." Mrs. Limone handed the plate over to Dr. Limone with a comical look on her face.

"Your aunt won't mind you having a few biscuits before dinner, will she?" Dr. Limone asked, holding the plate of cat-and-mouse-shaped cookies in front of me.

"No," I said and took one from the plate. My watch

only read 3:40 p.m. Maybe they ate dinner earlier than we did.

Mrs. Limone's girth matched nearly the size of Pigpie but not as dumpy or dirty.

"How did the visit to the university go, then?" She strained some tea into a teacup and set it in front of me. "Milk and sugar, sweetheart?"

"Best take her up on that offer, Abel. She makes it strong enough for mice to trod on."

"Yes," I answered, not really knowing how tea tastes best. I'd never had anything but iced tea. The Chungs drank tea with every meal but never offered hot tea to children.

"They let us off easy, and Abel impressed them just enough." He smiled at me. "They gave a great tour of the library before we left, too. You should see it, Maddy. I'm jealous of what Abel has in store starting tomorrow."

Two friendly beagles came bounding into the room.

"Now, where have you two been? Better not find that bathroom rug mussed." Dr. Limone patted them, and they sat at his feet. "This is Fergus, the master bone burier, and this with the lovely pink collar is Godiva. I hope you're not bothered. She's not much for clothes I'm afraid," he joked, trying to utilize the historic Lady Godiva's fame for humor.

"Oh, Solly, not with our tea. Do you like dogs, Abel?"

I squatted down, which must have been the signal for them to run over and start licking my face.

"Looks like they approve. Here now, you two leave him alone." She picked up her teacup. "Shall we move into the parlor?"

The dogs trotted after me into the living room and sat by my legs. An air of simplicity adorned the small and sparse room with its single lamp and freshly cut flowers in vases. On the fireplace mantel rested several pictures of the

Limones, including a girl. In one of the pictures, the girl as a young child rested in Mrs. Limone's arms.

"I see you've noticed our Brenda," Mrs. Limone said to me and got up to dust off the pictures. "These are old now. Oh, my, look at my hair here. Quite poofy, isn't it?" She handed the picture to me of her with the young child. "Sweet girl. Brenda's living in London now, finishing up her freshman year."

"She's another smart one with numbers." Dr. Limone smiled at Mrs. Limone and turned to me. "So, what do you think about my computer-club idea, Abel?" He took a chair across from me.

Mrs. Limone took the picture back and dusted it some more before gently replacing it. "Looking for a way to get in my good graces, are you?" she said, showing a slight annoyed shift compared to the happy temperament she'd exhibited so far.

"Dear, it's just an added bonus. You'll see, computers have many purposes."

"Let's hope it fills our coffers back up and not just become a reason for a new club then. Please excuse us, Abel, how rude we're being." She maneuvered next to me, and the dogs trotted out of her way. The couch was quite springy, and I fell toward her when she sat down, accidentally spilling the tea down my pants leg.

"Whoops, up you go." She helped me right myself. "Oh, dear. Oh, dear, Solly, quick, a towel."

Dr. Limone ran out and came back with a dishtowel. Mrs. Limone took it from him and dabbed at my pants leg.

"I, uh, don't think they have computers at our school," I said while she dabbed.

"What's tha—oh, yes, no, they're not up to speed with my new one, but they've got them. I don't think they'd tell you about it as they only give seniors access, but I could arrange it so you could use them, too. Hey, let's go back down, and you can show me what you know about DOS."

"I, uh, should, uh, get home before sunset."

Dr. Limone looked over at Mrs. Limone, who had just finished drying my pants leg. She gave him a stern look, and I could tell something upset her.

"Well, um, you're right. We should be going. We can discuss computer club on the way back. Sorry, I thought you'd enjoy—"

The cups and saucers were quickly gathered as Mrs. Limone whispered something to Dr. Limone when they went into the kitchen. I petted the dogs for a few minutes and could hear them arguing about something in hushed tones. As Godiva started licking my pants where the tea spilled, Dr. Limone returned.

"Godiva, cut that out. Sorry, I'm sorry about all this. Goodness. Shall we go, then?"

Mrs. Limone took my hand at the doorway and thanked me. She turned my hand over and looked at my palm, then clung to it as if she'd never see me again. Feeling odd about her clinging to me, I said, "See you later," in hopes she'd release my hand. She told me to wait a second.

She returned with two cookies in a napkin. She was a sweet lady.

In the car, Dr. Limone rambled about how much he'd enjoy a computer club. I'd never joined a club nor really cared to, so I kept my mouth shut. I wanted to express how much I appreciated what he'd done for me, but I didn't want to lead him on. Instead of voicing my appreciation, thoughts filled my head of all the great books I'd have access to starting tomorrow. He explained about Mrs. Limone's concerns with money and how she didn't understand modern technology when we pulled up behind Shelly's Impala. Pigpie and Shelly's voices boomed out of the front windows.

"Shall I come in and explain how well the day went?"

"No, thanks." I quickly got out of the car. I bet the neighbors down the street could hear their yelling. Dr. Limone looked concerned, but I thanked him again and ran toward the back of the house. Mister Scratch couldn't get enough of Godiva and Fergus's scent when I sat down to wait for the yelling inside to stop.

"Seven months, get it! Seven months, and we're outta here!" Shelly yelled.

"Look at him. For the love of Christ, look at him. This is what you'll rely on? He can't even afford a decent jacket," Pigpie said.

A few seconds passed, and the front door slammed.

"Tommy, wait up! I hate you. Can't you see that? Tommy'll take care of me now!" The front door slammed again.

I waited enough time for Pigpie to find her seat in front of the TV again, and I entered the kitchen.

As I started past the TV room and began climbing the stairs to hide in my bedroom, Pigpie shouted, "You know damn well what night this is!"

I looked back at her in confusion.

"I don't see the cans out front. They're full to the top with trash, and I won't be waking you again so you can run them to the curb. Now, march!"

As I carried the first trash can out, I passed Mr. Sutkin standing on his front porch, watching Shelly and Tommy sitting in the car. They hadn't left, and she called me over. She wore glasses without any glass in the frames.

"I'm outta here. If you're so smart, you'd leave, too, right, Tommy?" She laid on the horn for no reason.

Tommy fiddled with something in the glove box and didn't look over at me. Tommy had one of those rolled-in-the-gutter looks, as if changing ones clothes or washing were too much work.

"What's so different about a Sunday night than a Friday or Saturday? She knows I'll still go to school tomorrow."

I shrugged.

"Bye, Abel. Stay away from her, far, far away. You have it, Tommy?" He wiggled the tape he'd found and pushed it in the player.

They pulled away, and I watched as the Impala turned the corner toward downtown. I finished with the cans, and Mr. Sutkin called out to me as I started back inside. "Tell your aunt I said there are other people that live in this neighborhood, would you?" I waved to him that I understood and kept walking.

Pigpie met me at the door when I came in. "What did he say to you? That stupid dog of his craps in our yard all the time. Who does he think he is? G! D! And what did Shelly want? If Shelly doesn't shape up . . ." *Slap.* "She better be back before *One Day at a Time* comes on if she knows what's good for her." She waved her Budweiser at the door, splashing some out of the top of the can.

I waited for her to dismiss me, but she walked over to the refrigerator and grabbed the plastic carry rings with two cans of Bud dangling.

"Fix yourself something. Cooking for two is a waste of time."

I went up to my room and lay down on my bed. I tuned out her occasional outbursts at the TV by trying to think of all the topics of interest I could research at Firestone.

CHAPTER THIRTEEN

An Erection of the Mind

7.3.9.18.12.20-7.18.12-8.50.3.51.64

There's a Chinese-food restaurant named Fu Kim's Garden a block from the St. Louis Public Library in Baden, Missouri. Uncle Evert never took us there, but he loved Chinese food, and when we first moved in with him, he had a huge order delivered to impress us with the success of his business. Mom chose the spicy Kung Pao pork, ate the whole pint herself, and spent the rest of the night running back and forth to the bathroom. On one of those sprints to the bathroom, she ruined her favorite suede Bass shoes. Thereafter, her enmity for Chinese food was well known, though it didn't prevent her from waitressing at Fu Kim's until they sacked her for suspected drug use. After her expulsion, she always called it Fuck Him's. I only heard her say it twice in jest before the pink slip. Two days later, she'd gained employment at Zep's Diner, a block in the other direction, and still within walking distance of the public library.

  Near the entrance to the library was a wall with decorative portals that worked perfectly for hiding and spying. We'd wait for the librarian to get the return carts from the back, which she did on average at 8:09 a.m. every weekday and 9:07 a.m. on weekends, then Mom would stash me in the audio room. As Hank might say, the librarians were so old, they had autographed copies of the Bible. They were so old, you had to shout at them, and anything or anybody existing below their waists went unnoticed.

The library had five main rooms and a few deserted peripheral ones. The audio room was one of those. I'd sit in there for most of the eight hours each day, listening to the language tapes or occasionally sneaking out to acquire books from the shelves I could reach.

My daily predicament might elicit comments of "How Horrible" or "She should be jailed for child abuse!" from mothers on *Donahue*, but I couldn't envision a better way to spend a day. Just think of the alternative: Mom waitresses until her bunions bleed and wastes her money paying for me to hang out with other babbling three or four year olds fumbling with shoelaces and picking their noses. Dante would flick a Hell like that from his cuff, but I certainly couldn't bear the thought.

Mom mastered the use of the word *brilliant* when I'd come out to meet her at the end of her shift. She'd poetically say things like, "You're my most brilliant rubber boy" or "How could such a brilliant boy come bouncing out of me?" This was always the best part of my day.

As time went on, she became terribly nervous, constantly fearing they'd discover us. She'd use her anxiety sometimes as an excuse to get high, but then again, she had every kind of excuse for that. I later learned there was no law about leaving me unattended in the library. She could've said she expected the librarians to attend to any of my needs. On the few occasions a librarian talked with me, any garden-variety three-syllable word worked well enough to scare them off or convince them I was older than I looked. I was two months shy of five when Mom came twice in one week to retrieve me because I was engrossed and forgot the time. The librarians finally figured out what we'd been doing, but by then Mom's ticket had already been punched—or pricked, if you will—for her first ride in meth rehab.

Now libraries are more like home than any other place I've lived. I can walk into any one, and once I find an author I've read, my hat is hung in Elysium—as the new saying I coined goes.

The forty-one individual fingerprints smudged on the glass entrance doors quickly blurred in my vision as I rushed to get inside Firestone. The exhaust fumes in the poorly ventilated bus made my impatience to get here worse, but I never felt worried I might get dizzy as I inevitably did when I snuffed the overwhelming aroma of books inside the entrance lobby. It is doubtful meth has anything on this kind of high, and even more doubtful that meth could ever give me such an erection of the mind. The woman who checked my pass tried to chat, but I acted as if I didn't hear her. Firestone Library fittingly welcomed me with Archimedes—his name, anyway, if not exactly a book authored by him. Its title, *Archimedes: The Lost Path to Calculus*, sounded exceedingly interesting, so in honor of Mom, knowing the book hadn't been checked back in yet, I stole it from the return cart to read, not to actually leave with.

The library is six stories tall, with three below ground and three above. I consulted the directory and found the card catalog. The pattern of the drawer handles dotting the island made me giddy. I started in the two hundreds to find religious books authored by Richard Pierson. I considered that maybe Dr. Langdeer wouldn't know all of Pierson's work. Unfortunately, he was correct. I found zilch, but two flights of stairs and some card flipping later, I located four titles on astronomy in the natural-sciences section.

Not so very coincidentally, four is the number of laws that Descartes created that I always use when addressing a new topic for research. First, don't believe anything until you know it's true; avoid hasty judgment and prejudice. I discarded thoughts that Pierson was a religious nutjob prone to hypergraphia. Second, chop up whatever you want to know into as many parts as is necessary to understand. I didn't know enough to chop it up much yet, but starting with his bio: male, rich, liked atypical architecture, liked painting flowers, liked writing lots of numbers, potentially married or involved with a woman with a child, religious, liked TV dinners, and learned of astronomy. Third, take the smallest or easiest parts to understand, follow or combine them with the harder parts until you get to the last law, which is to make sure you're as thorough as possible and to not skimp or take shortcuts. Pierson's books were my best next step at this point.

Stars in History sat on the top of my short stack. The book jacket had illustrations of constellations shoved into a calendar grid. It turned out the book was about the astronomical origins of various cultures' calendars. The book-jacket flap had a customary biographical blurb. After a few basic facts, I read, *an accomplished professor of astronomy at Princeton University, New Jersey.* That'd be why Dr. Langdeer recognized Pierson's name. I was surprised he didn't comment on Pierson being a previous professor of astronomy here.

Star Signs—Bound for Earth, the Mysterious Forces among Us, copyright 1952, was a book of questionable merit if one went by the title and the book-jacket image. I thought perhaps the human-made-of-electricity picture on the cover tried to warn of an alien invasion or that they're already here, but as it turned out, he'd merely created a 1950s-style titling ruse to mask a lackluster study of the astronomical effects on meteorology. I made it through but just barely.

Thankfully, a voice interrupted me halfway into the last book, one equally tedious—the book, not the voice—but detailed on the calculation of deep-sky objects accessible to amateur astronomers.

"There it is," a canorous voice like that of a bobwhite said.

I looked up to find a young woman in a man's light-blue dress shirt with the sleeves rolled up and holding a stack of five books in her arms. Her soothing tone didn't exactly match her looks, but one might describe her as cute. She stood next to a lanky, angry-looking young man, and I returned my gaze to the desktop when their concern became evident.

"Do you know we've been trying to locate this book for almost an hour now? I returned it. See, I told you I did." The man pointed at the Archimedes book.

I pushed the book toward the friendlier-seeming woman.

"I didn't know they let children browse here. Are you the son of a faculty member or something?" She put her stack down.

"Nope."

"Are you a student like us, or just a book thief, then?" the man asked.

I felt compelled to explain that I no longer went to public school and my presence was just as valid as his, but instead pulled out my library pass and held it up.

"My mother told me not to speak to strangers, either. My name's Bergit Henrik, and this is Jon Lenchner."

"*Jag heter Abel.*" She responded with a confused look, so I figured her accent wasn't Swedish as I thought. "Abel Velasco," I repeated.

The knit on Jon's brow told me his anger wasn't completely serious, but he wasn't giving the same friendly vibes as Bergit. "Abel Velasco. Sounds like a real jazzy wunderkind type of name." He examined the books. "Are you studying to become an astronaut or watching out for aliens?"

"Or is it math?" Bergit said, taking the Archimedes book from me and trying to soften Jon's attack.

"I'm—I like mathematics."

"Oh, good. We really do, too." Jon took a seat too close to me.

"Do you mind?" Bergit asked as she reluctantly followed Jon's lead and sat across from me.

"So, let's see. I'd peg you for a Gauss fan, although I should say Archimedes, shouldn't I?" Jon waved at the book Berit flipped through as she searched for something.

"Mm, yes, but, uh, no. Ruh-René Descartes," I said, looking at the calendar on the cover of *Stars in History*.

They both had shocked looks on their faces.

"Descartes? Over Gauss? Really? Why? Descartes was brilliant, certainly, but nowhere near a Gauss. Just my opinion, mind you."

"Jon, that's rude. Maybe he doesn't know Gauss," Bergit said, looking up from the book.

I rolled my gaze into my upper eyelids and tilted my head toward the ceiling, searching for a particular passage.

"Hey, kid, you all right? Crap, my aunt used to have these." Jon moved back from me. "Quick, grab his tongue so he doesn't swallow it."

I found the passage I needed from Bell's *Men of Mathematics*. Keeping my gaze toward the ceiling, I quoted: "Gauss had an illustrious career that made advances in math, physics, and astronomy. He is best described as a pure and applied mathematician. In his lifetime, he found no fellow mathematical collaborators and lived mainly for pure academics. In his *Disquisitiones Arithmetucae*, Gauss summarized previous work in a systematic way, deciphered some of the most-difficult questions, and formulated concepts and questions that set the pattern of research that is still in effect today. He is known as the Prince of Mathematics."

"Exactly. Impressive—" Jon started.

I tilted my head down and adjusted my glasses. "Descartes is known as the father of philosophy. His polymath qualities are of greater interest and intensity. He was a known gambler, defended and hired prostitutes, traveled extensively, and even fought in wars."

Jon chuckled. "I guess I'm a polymath then, too. I can brush my teeth, tie my shoes, and chew gum at the same time."

"As to math, he was the first of the modern school of mathematics. He created analytical geometry, and the universal mathematics that Descartes described has since been applied to optics, astronomy, meteorology, acoustics, physics, engineering, chemistry, architecture, accounting, and warfare, all of which Descartes foresaw. Plus electronics, microbiology, genetics, economics, and even politics, which he didn't. Descartes chose not to sit around like Gauss. Also, it takes—it takes two hands to tie a shoe."

Bergit started clapping and laughing as quietly as she could, but the woman three tables away still shushed her. Jon snuffed but couldn't repress his growing smile.

"God, you must be a little polymath yourself," Bergit said.

"We'll have to find you a war to fight in," Jon added.

I felt ready for them to leave.

"Now, if only you'd prove me wrong, my day will be complete," Jon said to Bergit.

"Let's see." Bergit turned the page and started reading again. I watched her pull on her earlobe while we waited. "Get ready for a really bad day." She traced along the words with her finger. "As I told you. Right here, it says between folios two and three."

Jon examined the page. "By a woman and a midget. Fine, now you both one-upped me. I see the corner. Who's got the dunce cap?"

"Jonnie, we're only teasing, but it was you who told me the lost pages went between folio three and four."

"I still swear that's what Dr. Kohn said."

While putting my library pass back in my satchel, my journal fell out.

"What's this?" Jon snatched my journal and started flipping through the pages playfully.

I thought about grabbing my property, but he leaned his chair back from me, preventing me from doing so. He stopped on a page and put it down in front of him. I reached for it.

"Not so fast, my little secret Gödel. Does this look to you like it does to me?" He handed the marked page to Bergit.

She took it cautiously. "I don't think this is something Abel wants to share." She started to hand back the journal.

"Sorry, kid. Just look at it, Bergit." Jon took it back and held up the journal for us to see. It wasn't one of my dialog transcriptions. I'd completed some work on one of the theorems I found in that *Monkey on your Back Math* book they'd accused me of stealing at Rutgers.

"What is this?" she said after looking more closely at it. "This looks like elliptical curve studies."

Jon nodded his head up and down, mute with excitement.

"I-I don't know much Field theory, so the Riemann Hypothesis has to wait. I'm trying out modular forms and this instead," I said.

Jon and Bergit looked at each other with repressed laughter.

"Please, let me know first when you solve that Riemann problem."

Bergit sobered. "He doesn't even know what he just said, Jon. Abel, this stuff has been worked on by some of the best minds in math. We don't mean to make you feel stupid, but it's just hard for us to fathom someone would even think of approaching problems like that. Let alone someone your age. Riemann is the most difficult problem, maybe in history—"

"We need to show this to someone, Gunning or maybe Kohn. They'd know what to think of it."

Bergit stared at me again. "We should apologize. I'm sure we've completely interrupted your studies." She handed back my journal.

"Have you been published? Damn, he's probably someone we should know." Jon picked up Bergit's books.

"Hold on, Jon." Bergit took my hand with her cold one. "Do you know Dr. Kohn or Dr. Gunning?"

I shook my head and pulled my hand away.

"Would you mind coming with us, then?" she asked in a casual bonhomie fashion.

"This is, uh, this is my first day."

"Oh, Bergit, look at the time. The tea is just starting, too perfect. We'll take him and show everyone at once."

I could feel my pulse in my collarbone.

"Abel, it's up to you, but would you please come with us? They'll be cookies and hot tea or other refreshments you might like."

Tea offered two days in a row. The heat in my face could probably warm a kettle all on its own. I acquiesced with a fear-filled, "OK."

"Oh, good, because we could take you another day if you're not up to it now."

"What Bergit means is that it's not a big deal, don't worry." He piled up my books and carried them to the return island.

"Professor Gunning's never at teas on Tuesdays. Maybe we should call him and let him know," Jon said as we checked out Bergit's books.

"Hsiang and Kohn will. They'll roust Gunning for this. What'll we say when we get there?"

"Miss, this book hasn't been returned properly. I'll need to check it back in before you check it out."

"We were just looking for this one. Remember, I explained I returned it, and you told me it couldn't have been?" Jon said.

"Yes, dear, but I'll still need to check it in."

"That's fine, we'll wait," Bergit said, giving us a look of mild exasperation.

The books in Bergit's arms looked like they'd topple as she finally added the Archimedes book to her pile. We started walking away from the library.

Jon took two from her. "I'll do the talking when we get there, OK?"

I felt a little nauseous. I hadn't gotten permission to go anywhere else on campus. They continued excitedly about what they knew of the Riemann Hypothesis, but their voices faded as we entered a swarm of people. Small crowds of students washed against me, staring down but more often oblivious to my existence as they passed. We took shortcuts through some buildings, and my stomach relaxed some when I saw the Washington Road sign. My bus stop ran the other direction on Washington Road.

"This is Fine Hall, Abel. Some of the best physics and mathematical minds in the world have spent time here," Jon explained.

It looked like an apartment building to me.

I stepped off the elevator on the fourth floor, and my stomach did a flip. My mild nausea became a full-blown puke threat. The framed photos and newspaper clippings hanging in the hallway started to close in on me. We turned into a long open room where a few people sat in chairs. Most were at the far end, huddled around a table with plates of cookies. There was a dramatic quality to all the bowties and sweater vests, like a backstage gathering of that BBC show *University Challenge*. We passed a chalkboard where someone had written out forms of differential equations. Jon stepped up to the table. I stood behind him and Bergit behind me. One of the older-looking men addressed the small crowd.

"To say the Chinese were a conservative bunch in '76. Who could blame them for a practical outlook? They were correct about no standards existing for beauty, and for me, the Chinese encapsulated their view perfectly with the classic quote from Newton, 'The basis of any theory is social practice.' How could any culture with a political structure such as theirs see the beauty in mathematics? Everything is about being utilitarian." He smoothed the strands of hair at the very top of his head.

"I'm sorry, Dr. Kohn, but I don't get it. Does that mean you think mathematics is discovered or is created?" a tubby student looking out of place in his shorts and tube socks asked.

Jon passed me a cup of tea and a chocolate-chip cookie. I tried sipping it to push the puke down my throat.

"In the West, the old debate about whether mathematical reality was made by mathematicians or, existing independently, was merely discovered by them is an easy pill to swallow for those who understand beauty. Mathematics was discovered. In the East, in China, it's different. That's all I'm saying. You should know my view by now, Bruce. If you grab a pencil for a shovel and start digging, you'll unearth in short order the tools God used. Communism blocks minds from seeing the world in this fashion."

"Now, now, professor Kohn, you simplify it too much. Communism and our Republic may buy us all a big pile of atomic bombs or an arms race where the end is really *The End*, and so there is reason to frown upon its political manifestations in various countries. But Communism is not a stop sign for beauty in culture. It's not truly East verses West any more than any philosophy is bound by geography," another older gentleman wearing black suspenders said.

"Ladies and gentlemen, the often laconic Gilbert Hunt is unusually verbose today. Thanks, Gilbert, but if you want me to start lecturing, I'll clarify; otherwise, tea time is for simplification of ideas, is it not?" Dr. Kohn added.

Gilbert tipped his invisible hat and started talking with two students standing next to him.

Bergit leaned down to me. "Are you OK? You look a little green."

I could tell by the conversation that I stood among people of interest. I just hoped they all didn't take much interest in me.

The crowd broke into smaller groups, and some started leaving when Jon tapped Dr. Kohn's back. "Excuse me, professor, but I have someone you must meet." Bergit's hand touched my shoulder, guiding me forward.

"Hello, there, Bergit. Who've we got visiting us today? A relative?"

"You don't know him?" Jon asked with too much accusation.

Dr. Kohn glanced at Jon over the rim of his glasses and then returned his focus back to me.

"This is a new friend of ours. We've only just met over at Firestone, but we think you may be interested in his work. Maybe you've heard his name? Abel Velasco."

They certainly were no Russell, but it was nice hearing Bergit refer to us as friends.

"Hello there, Abel, how are you?" Dr. Kohn stuck out his hand and looked down at the floor.

"Dr. Joseph Kohn born in Prague in 1932, emigrated to Ecuador in 1939 and to the US at the age of thirteen in 1945. Received his doctorate from Princeton University in 1956. Taught at Brandeis University from 1958 until 1968 and at Princeton from 1968 until now. The article in *Popular Science* did not have your full birthdate under your picture, but you approximately will be eligible for retirement in 1997."

Bergit started to laugh.

"I, well, good. I'm not quite ready for retirement yet." He looked at Jon, who looked at Bergit. Dr. Kohn seemed confused but then composed himself.

"You wouldn't by any chance be a fan of the game Go, would you?" Dr. Kohn asked me and glanced at Bergit. He leaned down too close to me, looking for an answer.

"This is my first day. They may-may-could be looking for me at the library." I started toward the door.

"Hold on, Abel." Dr. Kohn talked quietly with Bergit for a moment. "Maybe I could call someone? Who would be looking after you at the library, Abel?"

I stopped and studied the differential equations on the chalkboard.

"I would have to say it would be Dr. Langdeer, but I haven't seen him today. Today is my first day," I said to the chalkboard.

"Good, I know Dr. Langdeer well. A very fine bibliophile. Would you all follow me please?" Dr. Kohn walked past me, and I followed behind Bergit and Jon to the elevator. We boarded, and I turned my back to them to watch the yellow numbers glow as we ascended.

"So, you don't play Go, Abel?" Dr. Kohn asked in the elevator.

I shook my head, keeping my eyes on the numbers.

"Mm, well, it's something you should look into. Very fond of it myself. Really fascinating game."

We arrived at the ninth floor, exited the elevator, and walked a short distance to a door.

"Jon, see if you can borrow a chair from another room. Bergit, please tell me again where you met Abel." He led us into his office, and we took a seat around his desk. Books and filing cabinets cramped the room. A dry-erase board filled one wall, and on it were expanded versions of the same differential equations I'd seen on the chalkboard in the tearoom.

"There's not much to tell really. Jon and I'd been arguing about which folio the Archimedes palimpsest you'd discussed with us in class would have fitted into. We couldn't find the book. This book." Bergit took it from her stack that she'd set on his desk. "We'd given up when we passed Abel and saw it with him."

He examined the book jacket. "What were you doing with this?"

I couldn't bring myself to look at him, fearing he'd treat me the same way the men at Rutgers Library did. I tried to compose a lie about my intention to check it out or how someone else left it on the table, something that wouldn't make me culpable for its theft. Instead, I said nothing.

"Do you lack a tongue, or are you thinking about lunch already?" Dr. Kohn asked with a mirthful demeanor. "What a day I've had with this. That discussion of beauty in mathematics at tea was brought on by this very topic. I had a phone meeting before tea with a friend, Nigel Wilson, who bragged to me about a new palimpsest page he recently acquired from the estate of Tischendorf."

Jon returned with a chair. "I had to go over to Webster's study to get it." He bumped the chair into place and sat down.

I must've looked confused, and to a degree, I was.

"Sorry about the rambling. You probably know nothing of palimpsests. Jon and Bergit are familiar with my mild obsession on this topic. Sometimes I wonder how my students learn anything of use from me."

I struggled to get my mouth working. "*Palimpsest*, from the Latin *palimpsestus* and the Greek *palimpsEstos*, means writing material, as a parchment or tablet, used one or more times after earlier writing has been erased. Like this." I pointed to the dry-erase board.

"See why we brought it to tea?" Jon said.

"Him. I believe you meant brought him to tea, Mr. Lenchner." He turned to me again. "There you are. Just takes a bit to get that tongue warmed up, is that it? I'm sorry, of course you know what I'm talking about. You had the book so you must've read it already?"

"*Archimedes: the Lost Path to Calculus*. I have not read it yet."

"Hm. OK, then. Let's see, the lost path in the book's title refers to a book Archimedes wrote about his discovery of calculus-like mathematics in a treatise called *Method of Mechanical Theorems*. Stop me if I'll ruin this for you somehow, OK." He tapped on the book. "About eight hundred years ago, there lived a medieval monk who ran out of paper. He was writing a prayer book and took pages out of the Archimedes calculus book, turned them sideways, washed and scraped away the surface layer of ink, and wrote over them. Now some nine hundred years later, a team of scientists is teasing the two texts apart—oh, I almost forgot." Dr. Kohn picked up the phone and dialed.

"Dr. Langdeer, please." Dr. Kohn sandwiched the phone between his shoulder and ear, flipped to a page of the Archimedes book, and handed it to me, tapping on an image. "Dr. Langdeer, this is Dr. Kohn. Yes, yes, and how are you? I'm sure you are very b—well, I've got a special guest in my office that should make that easier on you. I'm speaking of a young man named Abel . . . he can't be blamed. Two of my students abducted him. Yes, he's been sharing those talents with us just now. OK, I'll return him immediately. Indeed. And good to speak with you. We'll have to talk Chaucer soon. OK. Bye now. Well, you've got Langdeer and a number of librarians in a twist, but he seemed greatly relieved you were with me."

He tilted the book so he could see it, too. "That's what we've been talking about, Abel. Archimedes' discovery was scraped to make room for words of religious fealty. What irony, I tell you. All along to be masking true mathematical beauty, true language from the creator. Think of how this is the only Greek source showing that Archimedes understood that by comparing two infinitely large sets, you'd find they have the same amount of members, and they said that the Greeks hated dealing with infinity. Where would mathematics be if this text was discovered at the time it was written? Foolish monks."

Dr. Kohn took the book back and stood up, signaling our departure.

"Wait, Abel, show him your work before we go. You have to see this, Dr. Kohn," John insisted.

I reluctantly brought out my journal and turned past the area where I'd written about the Pierson house design. The Archimedes book in Dr. Kohn's hands hung by my head, and a number storm started buzzing TV-static formulae in my eyes. Richard Pierson didn't have hypergraphia. He wasn't insane writing one number after the next in his Hebrew Bible. It was a formula written on top of the words, sort of a reverse of what happened on the palimpsests. Instead of the scraping away, I'd bet all my trading cards the numbers over the text were a cryptogram, Richard Pierson's personal journal. It was so obvious to me now.

"Abel? I think he's a little shy about sharing his work."

I clicked back to action, excited by the new idea formed with the help of Dr. Kohn's palimpsest work. I turned to the modular forms section that Jon and Bergit had examined, and handed it to Dr. Kohn, who started reading and stood up.

"You should see how sloppy my writing was at his age," Bergit said, defending my work. I thought I was quite neat, actually.

Dr. Kohn turned his back to us and muttered a few hmm's. "I'll need more time with this. It looks like work on

Taniyama-Shimura conjecture. I'm familiar but in no way an expert. I know it when I see it just like any first-year grad student would." He smiled at Bergit and started down the hall. "I know someone who could tell if you were on the right track. Can I keep this?" he asked as we followed.

"No," I answered as we stepped into the elevator. Dr. Kohn looked at Bergit, who shrugged back at him.

"I'm sorry. I should've thought you'd be using it. Would you make a copy for me? I'd say we'll need to meet regularly or, oh, you probably already have a mentor here?"

"No," I answered, thinking I wasn't sure I wanted a mentor.

"Good. I'll talk more with Dr. Langdeer and arrange it all for you."

Dr. Kohn directed Bergit and Jon to return me to Firestone. Jon delegated the job to Bergit, who dropped me at the entrance, giving me her telephone number and a heartfelt, if not somewhat awkward, good-bye.

I was relieved she didn't follow me in. Explaining to her why I needed a Hebrew Bible would've taken too long, and I couldn't be sure I was correct yet. Dr. Langdeer stood at the front desk with two harried-looking librarians. I received several minutes of tsk-tsk-ings and a mini-lecture on procedures for reporting my activities from here on out. Then he pulled out a sheet with required reading and told me he wanted a report on each book by the end of the term. He'd created a shockingly long list with the short time he must've waited for me, but I didn't mind as it appeared to have many interesting titles.

I asked where I might find the Bible I needed. The question had them shifting gears, and soon I sat alone again with my work cut out for me. It pleased me tremendously when I noticed they had the same version as the one I'd found in Richard Pierson's house, a Textus Receptus. I decided to proceed with Descartes's four steps and began by transcribing from memory the numbers written throughout the first few pages of the book before the body of the text. By writing them out in the way that Pierson had, I could start an examination of the patterns and try to ascertain what he'd encrypted. I used my journal but soon learned that in order to fit all the numbers on the same line, I had to write nearly as tiny as he had.

After an hour of work, I'd only completed a couple lines of one page when I had to run to catch my bus. Nothing was revealing itself, and I knew the process wouldn't be short. I tried factoring the time it'd take to complete the transcription into my journal while en route to the bus stop. With all my other responsibilities, including my new required-reading list, I could probably have it done by December. December seemed an eternity away, but that was my only option, and I wanted to know what he said. It'd be nice to know that Russell didn't get hospitalized for nothing. Maybe I could surprise him with a real treasure.

CHAPTER FOURTEEN

Feaguing For a Good Ride

6.8.9.10-23.9.6.2.13-103.6.2.4.5.22.1

If you were an old nag in the early days of horse exhibition, the smell of ginger might enrage you. The reason is feaguing. Horse breeders commonly feagued a sluggish horse at showtime. A suppository of raw ginger would be placed in the horse's rectum. The burning sensations made them very lively and forced them to carry their tails well. Now, let's say you're a tubby, lethargic nag they're desperately trying to unload. Instead of ginger, they'd feague you by placing a live eel into your fundament. Compassion obviously wasn't part of the thought process. I think of pointing out the items on sale at the Shop-N-Stop, like Hostess brand baked goods, as an effective feaguing of my own personal flabby nag, Pigpie. Unfortunately, I have to wait for the right circular to arrive, like the ones that occasionally come in Pigpie's Sunday newspaper, so I haven't been able to use it often. Yesterday's circular was stuffed with items—a sure bet. The Pringles coupons alone would've worked, but the addition of the fluffy Hostess Pink Snowballs for twenty-two cents a pack were a real live eel.

    Shelly and I had no school today as it is October 12, a day to celebrate the genocide and conquest of the American Indians that increased when Christopher Columbus arrived in America four hundred ninety years ago. Pigpie maltreated Shelly almost as terribly as the Spanish did the Indians ever since Shelly returned from her two-day runaway jaunt. She woke Shelly at 11:17 a.m. with a reminder that a vacation day did not mean she could waste it in bed. She repeated a list of chores with an inordinate amount of nagging details. While Pigpie alarm-clocked Shelly, I snuck downstairs to set my feague trap so I could avoid some of the same treatment.

Pigpie arrived, and I drank OJ, pretending to read the circular.

"There you are. Don't make any plans. I've got stuff for you."

"You, uh, you like snowballs, right?" I pushed the perfectly folded circular toward her with the eye-popping pink snowballs at the top.

"Whaa, hey," she said, lifting her tail. "Twenty-two cents? That's unheard of! And Pringles coupons?" *Slam.* The eel wiggled in, and she trotted off to get her keys. Shelly came down just after Pigpie's Buick left the driveway.

"Where's she off to in such a rush?"

I pushed the circular toward Shelly.

"Figures. What'd you get stuck with? I've got her bed sheets and blanket to wash. Her bed stinks like rotten Cheerios. Ugh."

I started smearing some peanut butter on a slice of toasted bread and watched Shelly pull down box after box of cereal. She chose Kix, dumped a half-eaten carton of Cracker Jacks on top, and mixed in eleven grapes. Eleven semideflated grapes that I wouldn't have eaten on their own, let alone doused with milk.

"Those grapes aren't good."

"I don't care. I missed breakfast, and I'm starving. She better pick up other stuff besides those snowballs."

I doubted she really starved by the heft of her arms. She hadn't packed on the same bulk as Pigpie, but she looked like she could go a few days without eating. She'd been putting on weight since school started, and she'd taken to wearing her glassless eyeglasses full time. She slurped down her cereal concoction, and the sound sickened me, so I went out back to see if Mister Scratch was around. He barked hello as he ran out from behind the trash cans and did a few loops around my legs. The crisp air gave him extra spunk. I decided to rake the backyard so Pigpie wouldn't yell at me for not doing any chores. Mister Scratch couldn't get enough of the scents and kept rolling in the piles. I considered touring him along Lexington Avenue for the messages from other dogs at the telephone poles and hydrants, but the desire to go bike riding besieged me, and I really didn't want to ask Mr. Sutkin if Mister Scratch would be allowed.

    The trees were in full fall bloom, and the light breeze made the walk to Russell's house feel like a vibrant dream. Mrs. Ghety's car was in the driveway with a rake resting next to it. I worried when their house, usually better manicured, had a shoddy appearance. Trash bags were piled by the garage with uncollected, melting newspapers bonded to the blacktop at the front of the driveway. Their yard had only one small patch of raking around Russell's bike. The bike rested in the same spot I left it. Small patches of rust started to show. Russell would be furious at its condition, so I decided I'd tune it up and return it to our hiding spot for safekeeping. I'd have to ask permission, which meant knocking. I braced myself for the possibility of prying info about Russell's health out of Mrs. Ghety.

    It took three rounds of knocking before she answered.

    "What is it?" She barely opened the door.

    "It's me, Abel."

    She looked down at me, opened the door wide now, and stepped forward as stale air wafted out of the house. Her oddly creased terry-cloth outfit looked slept in and had a dark stain from where she'd spilled something down the front.

"Russell isn't here, hon." She pushed her hair back out of her face.

"OK." I turned to the driveway. "His bike was always kept out of the rain."

She looked over my shoulder at the bike. "I told Pat to bring it in the garage. He doesn't listen."

I looked inside the house and could see they'd allowed a bull to run loose. I worried this was how they were taking care of Russell.

"Hey, how's-hey, how's Russell?"

"Oh, sweetie, he's getting better, we hope. I'll tell him you were by." She started to close the door.

Hon? Sweetie? Maybe she'd forgotten who I was.

"Hey-hey, can I borrow his bike? Chains rust when they don't get used."

"What do I care?" she said with a tired smile and closed the door.

I lingered there uncertain if that meant she didn't care if the chain rusts or she didn't care if I borrowed it. I decided I'd go with the latter.

Probably due to rain, the radio was dead when I tried the switch. It'd only been a few weeks but felt like a long time since I'd ridden. I traveled down to the train path and pedaled along it toward Howe's field. The plants had quit their photosynthesis for the year, and the brittle gold and gray of the remaining tall weeds broke away as I pushed through. I put my foot out and kicked some milkweed pods, sending tufts of fuzzy wishes into the air.

I knew the absence of light in the garage meant Will and Hank weren't around. Luckily, the hidden key remained under the brick, so I could get the oilcan. Walking in the garage felt creepy without the lights. I grabbed a rag but couldn't find any steel wool for the rust. Russell's bike wasn't in terrible shape, so it took me only a couple minutes to get it looking good again. When I went to put the oilcan back, the light from Hank's vending machine reminded me of the new arcade, so I made this my first destination.

    The new sign beaconed from the top of the hill. I'd passed it in the car with Pigpie one night when we returned from a cigarette run to the 7-Eleven. The arcade wasn't nearly as attractive during the day without the lit neon. I started to put the kickstand down when Russell's bike glimmered in the reflection of the window. Suddenly, I didn't feel like going in so much without Russell. It felt disrespectful, as if I'd be going against an unspoken pact. Russell acted equally, if not more, excited to visit the arcade, and by now we'd be scrounging for quarters.

    As I peered inside, kids manned every machine or anxiously lined their quarters along the screens, marking off their next turns. Jerry Hampton stood at the Centipede machine. He spun the trackball hard and pounded the console in exasperation just before he viewed me through the pane. He didn't like my witnessing his loss, but he turned away and plugged another quarter in. I felt less nervous because the Kevins weren't with him. I hadn't seen any of them since the day at the house. Two girls stood at the Ms. Pac-Man machine. One turned to make crossed eyes at me. While it made her look cute, I knew it was a taunt and time to move along.

    I rode out toward the shopping center like an idiot. I'd forgotten I sent Pigpie for snowballs, and she drove straight toward me, so I turned down Clay Street, feeling certain she spotted me. Luckily, after a few nervous glances, I knew she hadn't bothered to follow. Dumb luck. I reviewed the possible road options and realized I pedaled in the general direction of Kate's apartment.

    Hank talked plenty of how great the junkyard was over on Mays Street in Milltown, but there's a big difference between hearing about a place and riding a bike on your own to it. I felt daring as I crossed the waterway, the link between Westons Mill pond and Farrington Lake.

They called it a pond, but Westons Mill spanned a greater distance than Farrington. The houses built along the shore should've been condemned by the looks of them. Their condition was almost equivalent to the albino village. I followed along the lake until I discovered the old mill and turned down Tices Lane. Milltown's founders weren't from poetic stock, at least not if you went by their pathetic aptitude for naming. It was an old mill town, a small one that looked as if it lost its industry years ago. They had fourteen streets in all, including one cul-de-sac.

I reached Kate's apartment building on Broad Street in under an hour, but unfortunately, I hadn't formulated a plan by the time I found it. I could say hello and tell her more about people with her Chinese zodiac sign or even ask about her family's birthdates. It'd be so great. I rode around the parking lot before I worked up the nerve to go in. Reading the 2B on her door was as far as I got, if only someone could foist a bit of ginger or eel on me. I couldn't raise my fist to knock, so I quickly returned to my bike. I rode around for a while again and decided the best thing to do was to wait to see if she'd show up. It was a long shot, but I figured nothing could top it if I managed to see her.

A grubby store called Gary's Subs was located next door. I went in, purchased myself a Mountain Dew, and perused the boxes of trading cards. The always plentiful baseball cards: Topps and Donruss; *E.T., the Extra Terrestrial*; and some ancient *Charlie's Angels* cards. I completely lucked out locating an old pack of *Six Million Dollar Man* trading cards in a box of *Raiders of the Lost Ark*. The gum in the pack was even more crispy and stale than usual.

After browsing the cards, I parked myself on the bench outside where I could view her apartment doors. Only one hippie-looking bearded guy exited in the first half hour. I felt less nervous when Kate finally emerged sixty-eight minutes later. She yawned ever so sweetly as her amazingly gorgeous hair glimmered from the sunshine. I hid behind a post, but it didn't matter because she didn't look my way. I gave her a minute to get ahead, but that must've been thirty seconds too long. The bike pedals wouldn't straighten out quickly enough when I started after her. Kate had already arrived at the front of the Speedway Tavern when she came into view again.

Several women greeted her from their seats on the front porch. Every bar I'd seen looked similar, but the Pabst Blue Ribbon sign in the window proved it a reputable place. The handlebar brakes caught jerkily as I paused across the street to watch. A single car passed. I felt stranded and exposed as obvious as five into two, although no one turned my way. Just in case someone should, I put up my hood and tied it tight to my head.

The rising wind battled me for a hundred yards or so up the street, but I used its strength to fly back down, passing past the tavern twice before I decided to check the front office of the defunct gas station across from the bar. My spy instincts told me it'd be a great place for observation. I felt sly like James Bond as I guided the bike behind stacks of tires and glancing about with a daring squint. I crept quickly to the door using the breeze for cover and grabbed for the handle. So much for being a savvy spy—if only my instincts told me I'd need a blowtorch for the deadbolt. Hiding with the bike behind the stacks of tires would have to do.

Kate moved some hair from her lips to behind her ear. I almost couldn't watch, it was so great. I ripped up bunches of scallions and tried floating them on the wind, one blade at a time through the center of the tires. Green blades arced on the breeze, and I mentally completed the ellipses they began, using them to calculate the space from me to her. If four in a row made it through without touching the tire rim, she'd want me to go over. One, two, three, four . . . Kate rose, and I felt exhilarated, knowing I'd somehow caused her to get up. I started throwing the rest of the blades through the tire to keep her in motion but must've calculated wrong because she went inside instead of to me.

Sexy scallion fumes coated my fingers and brought back our first introduction. If only I could be close enough to smell her onion-infused breath now. I yanked up another handful, plucked little hollow green rings, and minced them between my thumb and index fingers to pass the time until she came out. A nice, emerald skin tint developed after about a half hour. A woman's skin must have a similar chemistry to that found in plants. Why else would so many poets relate a woman's skin to flower petals? Why else would Gaia and other goddesses be Earth mothers, green and warm?

Walter McCrone was a scientist who could recognize thirty thousand things by merely looking at them under a microscope. The report in the December 1980 *Scientific American* told of his talents and how he proved the shroud of Turin, one of Christianity's most controversial artifacts, was in fact nothing but an old painted piece of linen. I wondered what Walter would do in these circumstances. Certainly, he'd find no evidence denying my passion. I could ride to the 7-Eleven, call the tavern, and request that Kate, that Kate, leave the premises at once. But for what reason?

I didn't have to figure that out because just as I placed myself into Walter's reasoning shoes, she emerged again. Oh, God, her hair was so utterly gorgeous. The wind swept it up and flicked it at her cheeks. If I only had a camera to document such beauty.

The daylight cut the air at peculiar angles as clouds began taking over the sky. In the past hour, I'd noticed one particular guy in a brown leather jacket dodging the patches of light on his way back and forth from the grungy three-storied building next to the Speedway parking lot. On two of those occasions, he escorted one of the ladies sitting with Kate. I guessed he was trying to gather friends for a party but didn't want to invite the whole bar and accumulate all the guests at one time. Perhaps he worked for a secret evil spy syndicate who brainwashed women into caring for the rest of the spies in the private lodgings. Perhaps not.

He joined Kate and Sylvia, and I could tell he was a real creep. Kate stiffened when he leaned on her chair and fake laughed at whatever he said. He was not privy to the authentic, lighthearted laugh I'd experienced. Maybe she liked men with mustaches, or she really wanted to go to a party. Those were the only reasons I could think for why she'd leave Sylvia and follow him to his place. When the door closed behind them, I rode over to see if I could hear anything. Twenty-seven cigarette butts on the front step but no discernible party noise from inside.

Two kids a few years older than me jumped back when I pedaled past the tree stump into the rear yard area. The kids had been facing and leaning against the building. I couldn't figure it out and felt as if I'd stumbled into some odd dream with the dark clouds and the wild wind. It appeared as if the building suddenly repelled them. They darted through a tall hedge as if I might chase after them. I paused to listen for party music, but I couldn't hear anything with the wind blowing. Tissues and trash whipped along the ground, and the swaying hedge directed my vision to the sky. If I started now, I might make it home before the storm hit, but I'd have to pedal hard. The wind followed, pushing me, and I lucked out until I got to Lexington when I felt the first drops.

My sweat jacket couldn't have held any more water by the time I got home. I put the bike against the side near the trash cans where it might not be noticed and took refuge on the back porch. Even if I waited all night for my clothes to dry they wouldn't. Facing Pigpie was my only option. To my surprise, on the table I found a sandwich and a single pink snowball with my name scrawled next to it on the cardboard where the other once rested.

"Abel, is that you? Your dinner's on the counter!" Pigpie shouted from the couch.

I poured myself a glass of OJ and waited for her to come and ream me out. I thought I'd given her a fair time frame, but she didn't budge from her seat. She didn't even look my way when I crept by or when I creaked up the stairs. I took the plate to my room and ate the snowball before I stripped out of my wet clothes. It was hard to work on the Bible numbers with the image of Kate's windblown hair dominating my thoughts, but I spent the rest of the night writing the numbers out. After each completed line, I tried again to figure what they might stand for, but nothing surfaced. There were no patterns. Later that night, when I took a break to get a glass of milk, I feared I'd ruin my day of beauty with a Pigpie recrimination, but she didn't even ask me what I was doing in the kitchen. God bless that curpin Columbus. I could only attribute my luck to his celebration.

CHAPTER FIFTEEN

Drink Budweiser Beer = 666

49.90-5.25.26.1.5.29-66.1.26-25.49.4.84

I spent the next two weeks dreaming of Kate, working on the Bible numbers at night, and reading in the library trying to decipher James Joyce's *Ulysses,* which meant reading Homer's *Odyssey,* too. *Ulysses*—what a hunk of Swiss-Irish cheese. The convoluted holes were far more difficult, and to me less interesting or worthwhile, than the one Carroll's rabbit led you down. Plenty of examples of algebra, irrational numbers, calculus, and other higher-mathematical constructions were imbedded in language and structure, but mainly *Ulysses* was just a brilliant use of vernacular allusions with no overreaching decipherable theorem.

Take, for example, the aside in the chapter "Cyclops," in which Joyce wrote of the man hung by Rumbold:

> . . . *he, with an abnegation rare in these our times, rose nobly to the occasion and expressed the dying wish (immediately acceded to) that the meal should be divided in aliquot parts among the members of the sick and indigent roomkeepers' association as a token of his regard and esteem.*

The aliquot parts of a number are all the whole numbers that can be divided into that number. For example, the aliquot parts for 20 would be 1, 2, 4, 5, and 10. This is like that crap you find in Matthew 14:14-20, the verse about the Jesus miracle where he feeds a crowd of thousands with five loaves of bread and two fish. Other than that kind of mythological hooey and a desire to show his mathematical grit, Joyce doesn't map it with any other examples, even in the math-laden chapter "Ithaca." If you're going to go to all that trouble to use and direct your readers to think about mathematics, there should be a final proof.

  The math of the book forced me into second and third review, but that wasn't what slowed me down. Chapter three, "Proteus," took me on a special tangent. During it, Stephen, the main character, is walking along Sandymount Strand, an oceanfront southeast of Dublin. He falls into a reverie, which consists of several smallish episodes, but his internal debate about a trip to his Uncle Richie's gave me pause. I found myself on my own little nostalgic trip to my uncle's house—an incident both real and imagined. I thought there might be something to it, so I took the time to write it down.

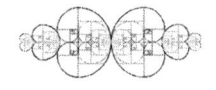

1:05 a.m.
  Through the knothole, I saw it all.
  Uncle Evert asked, "What's left?"
  "Don't know, check the shelf," Mick Washington said, thumbing through a crate of albums.
  Static-tainted reggae wafted from a radio. Uncle Evert's hand moved toward the Avon pheasant decanter but veered and turned up Bob Marley singing a live version of "Three Little Birds." He knocked some empties over, setting the pheasant free as he grabbed an unopened can. Pull tabs continually gave him trouble. He pushed too hard and popped every other ring off, making the can a

temporary tomb of beer. Uncle Evert grabbed for the Bic pen sticking out from the couch he shared with Tom Dooler. The Bic punctured the Budweiser logo as my uncle stretched a hole in the aluminum. The spray slowed and let him tilt the top of the can against his glasses. He guzzled about half, belched raw thunder, and wiped the bubbles from his wispy black mustache just below the words *Do It To It* on his t-shirt. Mick and Tom gave no response. His gaze settled on the maple-leaf patch sewn to the left knee of Tom's pants.

"Fuckin' Canadians. When we first got there, you know, seemed like every guy I met was a goddamn inspector. I remember this one had a bee in his asshole, and I says, 'Hell, no, I don't know any of the provinces' names.'" Uncle Evert gathered the cards resting on the steamer trunk. "And then the guy was trying to act as if he's not anti-American, and he says, 'I'm not so much anti-American as I am pro-Canadian.' Do you think I didn't pop him in the chops?" He pumped his fist at an imaginary nose.

Tom tucked the soft pack of Camels back into the blue bandana on his forehead. "You didn't pop nobody in no chops, ya hippie, Velasco. You can't even remember what Belushi just did on the boob tube. No way you remember something from eight years ago in Toronto." He slid a fresh cigarette between his lips and searched for matches.

Uncle Evert opened his lighter and lit it for him. "Fuck hippies. Try seven years, asshole. I led you and the boys from Shrewsbury to Canada when I was nineteen in sixty-nine. I think I can remember what I can fuckin' remember."

Mick sat forward on his recliner. He muffled a small burp and flipped a rope of hair from his eye. "So d'you know any ah the provinces, Dool? We lived there for six years, and I only know one." He began to spin Thin Lizzy's *Jailbreak* album cover on his index finger with practiced skill until it seemed it might float into the air.

"You probably don't even know that many, Monkey, which is why we won't let you in on our business," Tom said. "There's something, like, ten provinces, and then there's the territories, but who cares? I know there's fifty United States. As if Canada was all that great. I'm so glad we got the hell outta there." He leaned over, pretending he might put out his cigarette but toppled the album from Mick's finger instead. Mick ignored Tom, picked it up, and started again.

Stories I'd heard of their time together made Tom's statement about Canada not being that great seem untrue. The bus-driving job Mick landed after returning from Canada kept him away from Tom and Uncle Evert's drug sales. On several of my night-spying missions, I'd overheard them cajoling Mick for missing out on the money they were raking in. Only two times had I heard Mick retort with why he wouldn't join. The first time was when he mentioned disapproving of them selling cocaine, and the second when they bragged about widening the clientele to include high-school kids.

"Hey, hey, don't wurra 'bout a ting." Uncle Evert raised his beer for a toast, letting a small stream pour out of the punctured can, and brought the can sloppily to his lips to finish off what remained.

Tom stubbed his cigarette out with the others on the yellowing, burn-dappled floor. He grabbed the Bic and the last can of Bud from the shelf and swiveled his pack of Camels to the back of his head. He gave my uncle and Mick a "Look out!" face before shouting, "Shotgun!" Tom smashed the Bic into the side of the can, stuck his mouth over the jagged hole, lifted the tab at the top, and drank it straight down. His Adam's apple bobbed with each gulp. "Now that's what I call impressive," he said through belch breath.

"Top him, Ev. Don't let him beat you down," Mick goaded as he spun the album up by his shoulder.

"Beat down? I did that two seconds ago. I ain't gotta top anybody. You both know that was shit for nothing. We need more if you want to get real serious with this serious stuff." Uncle Evert waved his hands at the cans on the floor and shelf. The gesture seemed to tire him.

"Oh, I'd get 'em, but I'm busted." Mick clapped the album to a stop. "Joe's is probably closed, anyway."

"Joe's is open 'til three, Monkey, and this's on me this time." Uncle Evert pushed himself up off the couch. The rubber soles of his black Converse All-Stars sticking to the basement floor helped him balance as he made his way to the stairs.

Tom threw my uncle's jacket at him. "You'll freeze your ass off." The painted black peace signs flattened into view on the back as Uncle Evert slid his army jacket on. A navy knit hat popped out of his sleeve where it'd been stuffed, and he snugged it down to his eyelids.

"You coming, Monkey?" Tom asked, as he was already walking out the door.

Mick pulled his other glove from between the couch cushions and hustled after them.

1:23 a.m.

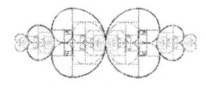

It's the nature of memory to twist into full view those things that once lived on the periphery of your vision. Memory, like dream, often invents life—or in this case, the vision of its ending.

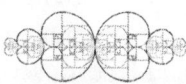

By the time Mick caught up, Tom had a cigarette lit. He blew a thick plume, creating a silhouette of a dark ghost against the streetlight. Salt trucks and plows had been clearing Arsenal Avenue all day. The three drunken friends waiting for green watched the multicolored Christmas lights add to the lively street palette. The lights held promise of continued revelry as they twinkled from every home and business including the windows of Joe's Wild Oats beer store two blocks away.

Uncle Evert stood a few yards from the crosswalk when he loudly slurred, "Last one there owes me a Slim Jim," and started running across the street before the light changed.

"Hey, Ev, watch..." Tom put his arm out to hold Mick back as if he were Evert, but Uncle Evert only heard street and wind in his ears. He still followed the "don't step on a crack" superstition he'd developed as a child as he leaped over the two slush tire tracks. He was focusing on the next two tracks when he glimpsed the car and heard the horn. His dark clothes acted as camouflage until the headlights reflected off his snowflake-speckled glasses. The horn made Tom and Mick flinch. Uncle Evert jumped to the division island at the center of the street, just as the fishtailing Ford barely missed him. The concrete lip stopped his foot from sliding farther, and my uncle stood with his legs spread apart, trying to balance.

He grinned back at them and started flipping off the passing cars. Mick and Tom heard his straight-flush laugh as he continued running and leaping to the other side. A slush track he'd landed directly on caused his final slide. The streetlight turned, cars came to a stop with warm heater air blowing against the occupants inside, and Tom and Mick started across when they witnessed the accident. Evert Miguel Velasco slipped and flew headfirst into an icy metal drain. He died with a winning smile migrating from his face and that accursed Budweiser on his breath.

"Before they left for more beer" is a historical fact I witnessed. "After" is an addition to the many scenarios I've created for how my uncle died in the street based on small truths about weather, location, and minor probabilities I know about the night. I'd never been told what really happened. Tom woke me the following morning, fed me a bowl of Frosted Flakes, and a day later I sat in the backseat of the Dersteins' station wagon. The Dersteins told me they were my new foster parents, and as soon as my mother was better, I could live with her again. What they didn't know but I had a better understanding of was she'd lost the battle one too many times already. Per the AMA, long-term effects include malnutrition, psychosis, kidney and other tissue damage, memory loss, anxiety, auditory hallucinations, and cardiac and neurological damage. Before he died, Uncle Evert explained that the barbiturates her doctor prescribed before my birth were what got her started.

 Reviewing the math in *Ulysses* and writing out Uncle Evert's episode inspired more Richard Pierson research. I wasn't making any headway with the numbers. If only I could know his history, know what he'd have been interested in, I might be able to find the necessary key to unlock this mystery.

 Luck came my way after I thanked Langdeer for letting me work with Dr. Kohn. On Friday morning, Dr. Langdeer walked me to the microfiche room, gave me a brief lesson on the mechanics of the machines, and told me I could review what I liked when I liked. The indexes housed forty-one articles with Pierson, Richard. I decided to plow through them chronologically, and after twenty-nine uninformative slides, my stomach gurgled for lunch. I'd packed two PB and J sandwiches.

 Most of the articles were condensed versions of information I'd read in his books, or brief articles about his departure from Princeton, which were all very formal and complimentary. Then I found something strange in the *Daily Princetonian*. The headline read, "Religious Leaders

Question Fuel Line as Cause." On June 6, 1966, a plane leaving Newark, bound for Chicago, exploded, killing all passengers due to a carbon blockage in the fuel line. A brief passage about Christian fanatics attributing the accident to Lucifer's will because of the date it occurred. While dates like that are of interest to me, I saw no reason to point fingers at Satan over a calendrical oddity. If that were true, then I'd have to say they elected President Ronald Wilson Reagan because Satan signs all his work. Reagan's first, second, and third names each have six letters in them. When he lived in Bel-Air, California, his address was 666, and if you add up the letters in the commonly found phrase: "Ronald Reagan, president and chief executive of the United States of America," it amounts to 666. Even with all that evidence, I wouldn't correlate Reagan with Satan.

I thought newspapers like the *Princetonian* were supposed to uphold integrity against such hokum. Maybe not in 1966. The article, a piece of sensational journalism better suited to the *Weekly World News*, pointed to signs that Satan lived among us—namely, the war in Vietnam. The author interviewed a Pastor Withers, who expressed sympathy for the great religious scholar Richard Pierson of Princeton University, explaining how he'd lost his wife and daughter in the crash. Three items surprised me about the interview. One, they didn't call Richard Pierson a professor. Two, he was considered a "religious scholar" when his only published works were on astronomy. Three, he'd lost a wife and daughter, which explained the picture at the house.

I felt itchy now and wanted to catch a bus to get to the bike right then. Another trip past the albino village would be necessary, although I didn't know what frightened me more: the village or the house. I decided to ignore the itch and finish what I started, since there weren't many articles left. Only one of the remaining articles caught my attention. A man named Rips in an annual report from the International Congress of Mathematicians wrote it. In it, Pierson is quoted, saying, "Time is transparent with mathematics. God speaks in arithmetical clarity for those with the sight." Here was a possible allusion to why Pierson would adorn a Bible with the numbers.

On the bus, I devised my plan. It gets dark early now, and I wouldn't have the time to accomplish it all tonight, so I'd set my alarm to wake me by five tomorrow. That should give me plenty of hours before Pigpie wakes to get there and back for whatever chores she has for me. It seemed simple enough, and the obese sloth rarely got out of bed on the weekend before 10:00 a.m.

Shelly and Pigpie were in the middle of something ugly when I walked in the door. A white garbage bag overflowing with clothes sat in the middle of the kitchen.

"None of it was yours!" Shelly screamed, pounding on the back of the couch in the TV room.

"Everything you own is mine! He's eighteen. His parents were right."

"He could stay with us until—"

"I won't have you slutting it up in my house."

Shelly stomped toward me into the kitchen. "We'll get married eventually."

"I'd rather you killed yourself. Then your life would be more over than it already is."

Pigpie came in, and I lost my chance to slip by to my room. I tried reviewing Descartes's *Meditation* in my mind and nonchalantly opened a cabinet. Bad move.

"Get out of there. You'll wreck your appetite." Pigpie pushed me away and slammed the cupboard door.

I moved behind the table. Shelly shoved the clothes back in the bag, which became too full to tie. She kept stuffing, but the bag started to rip, and the volume of her tears increased.

"Take it right back upstairs!" Pigpie shouted.

"They're mine. Mine!"

"It's not yours, it's mine." Pigpie pulled the bag until it ripped, and Shelly's bras and dungarees were suddenly strewn all over the floor.

"I hate you! I don't need that shit, anyway." Shelly moved toward the back door, but Pigpie grabbed her hair and yanked her to the floor. Shelly managed to right herself and kneeled in the clothes in front of Pigpie. "You're just jealous, and I'll sue you. If my baby dies, I'll sue you." Shelly sprayed spit as she yelled, and a long string of drool hung from her chin. It's ridiculous the things that come into your mind at these moments, but the shock of discovering Shelly's pregnancy caused me to imagine the spit string vibrating, and I could hear, "Baa, baa, black sheep. Yes, sir, yes, sir. three baaags full."

"Yeah, you'll sue me. Yeah, sure, you will."

"They'll take you and lock you up and give me everything you own. They'll give me all Daddy's money. It's mine, for Chrissake."

"Oh, for Chrissake. Oh, for Chrissake, your father never did a GD thing for you. Did I go and get myself killed? Did I take—"

Shelly jumped up and ran out the back door toward the front of the house. Pigpie kicked through the clothes and shuffled down the hall to the front door.

"That car is mine, too!" Pigpie barked at the windowpane, but Shelly had already started backing down the driveway.

Pigpie returned to the kitchen. Tears rested unnaturally in the corners of her eyes.

"What the hell are you doing in here? Take this shit back up to her room." She wiped her face on her sleeve and slammed open the refrigerator. A carton of milk fell to the floor as she pulled out a can of Budweiser. It flowed onto a bra and a KISS T-shirt. "Who is she kidding? She'll need me to help her raise it. She can't do this on her own. And I'm so nice, I'd even help . . . stupid kid. Shitty stupid.

Clean this up. You want dinner? Clean this all up and . . . and don't you think for one minute I'll forget about your school trouble. Your teacher, Dr. Limone, called for you, and I know teachers only call when you've done something wrong, even though he wouldn't tell me what it was that you'd done wrong, but I know it. I know it—and clean this shit up, and keep it cleaned!" Pigpie cracked the can of Bud open, letting the foam drip to the floor, and stomped out of the room.

    I wrapped the wet bras and the rest in the ripped bag and lugged it upstairs. How can it be that justice gives Shelly a ride to freedom and lands me in the clink, home alone with Pigpie? I worked on the number transcription for most of the night and ignored my hunger pangs. Pigpie never called me for dinner, and I felt too afraid to leave my room with her in that state.

    By 1:14 a.m., my stomach writhed in knots. Although I could still hear sound from the TV, I chanced sneaking downstairs. The lights were all out except for the TV. I avoided the floorboard that creaks and followed the low light coming from the kitchen. I found Pigpie sitting in a chair, eating a block of Velveeta. The bright moonlight twinkled through the kitchen window and reflected off the silver of the cheese wrapper. She whimpered a little at one point and started repeatedly moaning, "Carl, oh, Carl." Pigpie painted the memory of her husband with a toilet brush whenever she mentioned him. No hint of longing or mournful commentary ever slipped from her tongue. I stood still trying to determine if her mental state was an inconsolable anguish or might she be pacified by a hungry visitor. Could I get a piece of that cheese? Doubtful. I might, however, gain access to the cupboards where we kept the bread and peanut butter if I used some sympathy.

    I watched the kitchen clock tick off minutes. I couldn't see myself waking at 5:00 a.m. now, especially if I couldn't acquire some food. My eyelids struggled with gravity, and waiting this close to the food only added to their descent. I leaned against the wall, making a slight ugh noise. She didn't stir except to finish the cheese. She finally got up to blow her nose and slugged back to the TV room. I waited, and as she eased into the couch, I opened the cupboard door. Unfortunately, like an idiot, I opened the door where the canned goods were stored. I grabbed the first one my fingers touched, the opener from the drawer, and quickly crept back to my room. The hallway light revealed canned corn. Jesus H. Christ, canned corn.

CHAPTER SIXTEEN

Cheeseburger Babel

10.18.20-4.6-20.4.18.4.2.64

"Get up." Pigpie knocked me awake with the Green Giant can ho-ho-hoing at my forehead. "You wanna tell me why you have a empty can o' corn in your room?"

I blinked at her and rubbed my head where she knocked it.

"Jesus, you're a freak. Get up, we're going out."

Only the sandhill crane whose diet is 80 percent corn could come close to comprehending the terrible wonder of waking with the taste of stale canned corn in your mouth. I dressed and brushed my teeth. She was eating when I arrived downstairs, so I poured myself a huge bowl of Alpha-Bits.

"Hey, hey, hey, save some of that for Shelly. It's gotta last, you know."

I poured a little back in the box and took it out to the back step to eat with Mister Scratch. He ran from Mr. Sutkin's porch through the bad weather just to keep me company. The rain helped the earth give off those great fall scents that I could still smell over the effluvium of Mister Scratch. It's never easy to eat around a dog. He licked my face so much, I had a hard time raising my spoon to my mouth. I imagined I was eating breakfast with Queen Christina of Sweden because his stink made the Alpha-Bits smell a little like Welsh rarebit, a dish famous among royalty and also often made by my foster parent, Mrs. Derstein.

"What's he doing on my porch?" Pigpie shouted out at me through the storm-door screen. "Finish that up, we're leaving."

I didn't like all the sediments much, anyway, so I left the remaining Alpha-Bits for Mister Scratch and went inside.

She wore a plastic headscarf but still made me hold the umbrella above her head until we got to the car. While driving, Pigpie finished two cigarettes. I'd counted three hundred and six wipes by the windshield blades before I figured out what we were doing. She didn't mention the store or destination, but I should have known by the way she kept beaking her head left and right, seeking Shelly.

The address on Tommy's parents' mailbox clued me in to whose house we were at before Pigpie explained, "That's his house there, but where's her car? Jesus, if she makes me drive around all day, she'll be black and blue."

We checked every row of the mall parking lot for Shelly's car. Twice. We drove through Kent's trailer park, which was a return to one of the spots Pigpie used to make money from my talents. We drove around the high school and to all of Shelly's friends' homes Pigpie could remember. I knew the addresses of anyone listed in town, of course. At lunch, Pigpie even asked the guy at the Burger King drive-thru if he saw a car that looked like Shelly's. No dice. We drove past Russell's street on the way back through town, and it gave me an idea.

"Hey, can I- Hey—"

"Jesus, don't just start up like that. Give me some notice when you're going to speak."

"Hey, can I stay at Russell's tonight?" I asked, masking my true plans.

"Do you think I've got shit for brains?" Long pause where I could've composed a symphony of yes. "I know what tonight and tomorrow night are, and this is exactly what Shelly has planned. She's trying to piss me off just so she can stay out and cause trouble on Hell Night tonight." She grabbed my jacket with her free hand. "I won't have two of you out causing police to be knocking at my door."

"But I don't—" I started expanding on the lie about how Russell's parents wouldn't let us out but never got to finish.

She lit another cigarette. "If the cops catch you, you have them take you back to his house. I don't want to talk to nobody, and you might as well get dressed up for Halloween at his house tomorrow, too, because I'm turning the lights out by five." She'd bought four bags of candy that I couldn't touch because they were for trick-or-treaters. In reality, she probably wanted to gorge herself alone.

We stopped at McDonalds before heading home. I wasn't hungry yet, so I stashed the cheeseburger she ordered for me in my satchel. On the walk from the car to the house, she stopped and looked down the street one last time for any sign of Shelly. Fuming, she used the railing to help her stomp up the steps to the door.

I felt incredibly pleased I'd gotten the OK to go to Russell's because it'd be nothing but torture in the house with her mood.

"Bye!" I shouted into the TV room after I'd gathered the necessities. She waved her Budweiser can at me as she stuffed another neon-orange doodle in her mouth with the same hand that held a cigarette.

Small and somewhat sleepy, poor Mister Scratch lay on Mr. Sutkin's porch with his head on his paws as the rain dripped a few inches from his head. The tiny splashes didn't bother him as he watched me wheel the bike out from the side of the house. Mr. Sutkin saw me see him at his front window as I pushed the bike past, but he didn't bother waving and neither did I.

I slid onto the seat, forgetting to wipe it off first. Nothing like a wet ass to start a bike ride off wrong, but my yellow rain poncho had a wonderful hood that buttoned at the chin, so the chilly drizzle could offend only my hands and face. Satan must've organized Hell Night's ambience. It was certainly gloomy, cold, and dark early. At least the rain stopped by the time I started on the back roads. The ones Will introduced me to weren't as easy to navigate in the gray, end-of-day lighting, but I reached the house without any serious trouble. As I wheeled the bike to the central-pillar area, I briefly considered traipsing through the field to locate the Bible Schmill dismantled, but even if I could find it, I couldn't imagine it surviving the weeks of weathering.

I stood by the pillars and took in the dark silhouette of the house. The end of my Snoopy flashlight had banged into my ribs the whole ride, but now I felt happy to find the batteries strong and the light more powerful than I remembered.

I hopped across the grass partition in the double doorway and didn't know whether to be pleased or more frightened when the light switch illuminated the front hall again. The shadows were definitely larger than on my last visit. I stood still for a moment and swore that I felt the house sway as if on the deck of a large ship. To make sure I wasn't crazy, I pushed on the wall to test its strength. Although the structure had existed for decades, this weather made me question its resilience. When I flipped the second switch at the end of the hall, a distinct metal clunk came from the pantry area. Under such circumstances, I had to assume that the sudden light disturbed a squirrel or possibly a friendly raccoon. I stepped on several of my previous footprints as I crossed to where the desk hulked amid its draped webs.

Nothing stirred by the time I reached the desk and pulled the lamp chain for more light. I waited a minute to be sure. The desk faced the pantry, and I avoided looking toward it by reviewing the desktop contents again. The stacks of folders and books were still in place. I picked up the picture of his wife and daughter and tried to imagine them living. I thought of Richard Pierson working here with their memory frozen, smiling at him, and wished I owned a picture of my mother. Their happy faces reminded me time was fleeting. If I had months, I could go through all the stacks. But I had one night, possibly two if I rode to the 7-Eleven tomorrow to call Pigpie and tell her I'd taken her advice about dressing up with Russell.

All the desk drawers were empty except for one containing a pencil and another with a small cardboard box of thumbtacks. As I sat back in the chair to start organizing the folders, I noticed my disgustingly dirty hands. My poncho was also coated with dust sludge. I didn't want to muck up anything I found, so I removed the poncho and accidentally knocked the picture frame over. A few seconds later, another clunk came from the kitchen area, only this time it was clearer. The choice of a cold cheeseburger for defense might seem odd to some, but I couldn't think of anything else from my satchel to throw. A cheeseburger could blind or at least distract.

I started waving the yellow-paper-wrapped burger at my side to give warning. The path from the desk to the pantry had three sets of footprints. I stood and waited for something to emerge. But the only thing that moved was the swirling integers of the number clouds. Hoping I would find an animal and not something worse, it took all I had to get up off the chair. I would accomplish nothing if I didn't find out what made the noise because it might merely be the wind blowing through a window. The Snoopy flashlight beam cut into the pantry area and into the kitchen. I steered clear of the stacks of tin TV-dinner trays cocooned delicately in webs. The beam moved along a shelf of old crockery and a wide expanse of hanging pots and pans, none of it touched in decades, none of it moving.

As I turned the corner, I sensed someone else in the room the way I can sometimes sense when a formula is correct before I've finished. Snoopy's nose tilted toward the floor first and revealed a definite lack of other quadrupeds. A food-prep island stood in the middle of the room, and as I moved the light beam up one of its silver legs, I ended on a hovering white torso covered in rags. It must have been the ghost that pulled the beam higher, since consuming fear more than curiosity existed in me at that point. A white face with a silver beard and golden hair, glowing with the cool antilife that only the numinous exhibit, said, "Boo" and put his hand up to block the light from his eyes.

    He could have said, "Dada" or with prescience, "Where's the beef?" or anything else ridiculous, and I'd have reacted in the same way. I threw the cheeseburger at him, the yellow wrapper floating to the side, and with supernatural luck hit him right in the forehead. I swore I heard him spout an incantation of "ocean, stars, grass" to confuse me as I started scrambling away. His tactic worked because I forgot to point the flashlight ahead of me and ran right into the stack of TV-dinner trays. Number clouds moved into view, and I watched the desk lamp as I fell.

    Snoopy stared up at me from where he rested on my satchel and cleaned poncho, which sat on the little table next to my recliner. A skinny woman draped in a multicolored crocheted shawl touched my chin and examined my face. She adjusted the sling on my arm, which accounted for the pain in my elbow.

    Smoke from a skinny cigar rose in feathery ripples out of her mouth. "Don't worry, child. You'll be OK. Nothing's broken." The shells of her necklace clinked together as she sat back and clapped twice. "Come now, turn that off and get over here."

    A black-and-white dog, the one from the albino village, lifted its head from where it slept near the TV after she clapped.

"You know, I've got to get back to it soon. I need my rest," The man snapped at her and shifted in his seat.

"I don't care. Quit your gapin' at that Ginger woman."

"You quit it—"

She snapped her fingers at him, and he closed his mouth. *Gilligan's Island* played on a small black-and-white TV with huge rabbit-ear antennae. It crackled with static when he turned it off. His tall form strode on spindly legs across the room. The woman moved out of his way and picked up a basket of clothes.

"Do you think me gay, child?" His face still held the ghostly white I'd witnessed in the kitchen, only now his curious coloring looked solid and real.

You'd think with all the experience I've had passing out under unusual circumstances and waking to strangers' questioning faces, I'd be used to this. I blinked at him.

"Speak up, boy. Do you think me a gay man from New York City?"

"I, uh, I, uh, I don't know."

The dog growled after I said this and lifted his nose in my direction, smelling the air.

The man furrowed his brow. "Well, if not, why you wanna throw your meat at me, then?"

The woman laughed through the cigar clenched in her teeth. She hung a skirt on the line stretched across the room next to a large black-metal boiler that I imagined was what gave the room its toasty warmth. We were obviously subterranean, as I could find no windows and the walls were rough-hewn like the type you'd find in a cellar. He leaned close to stare into my face. The body's only palindrome may also be the window to the soul, but his were difficult to peer into. Dark gray, they looked like a mini-earthquake rocked inside his head as they vibrated from side to side.

"Look at this mus-tard streakin' on me." He pointed at his rags. "Waste of a perfectly good burger, and were you aiming to blind me with that flashlight of yours?"

I worried for a moment I'd been the one that caused his eyes to twitch. I shook my head.

"Hm, you don't look stupid, but you must be. Why else would you come stompin' around another man's house without being invited?"

He stood straight again and smoothed back his yellow-orange hair.

"Well? What are you starin' at? Haven't you ever met a white black man before? I'm the descendant of an albino king. Give respect." He stared intently at me.

"Are you John?" I asked, recalling the warning from the tunnel's entrance. The dog growled some more and continued staring at me.

"So, at least you can read. John was my . . . relative. I am the new king, King Allen, and this is Queen Bino."

"Quit it, would you? Yah don't mess with a sick boy. You know there ain't no John."

"Ah. all right." He paced away from me and then turned back. "Name's Allen Foster, and that exquisite Jamaican blossom is my wife, Heedy."

"If it weren't for his good looks and all that sugar, I'd dump the man out with my dirty bathwater," Heedy said, handling a pair of men's white underwear.

"You're lucky you have clean water for bathing." He leaned closer to me. "I build this beautiful mansion, and look at the appreciation."

"Appreciation? You worked for one week before that man stopped construction. You hammered in two nails if any at all."

"Hear that, boy? The donkey got a hold of some bad beans and is letting loose." He cupped his ear and raised a wiggling finger in the air with his eyes wide.

"Clear it up now, Mister Foul Mouth, and get going. Before you know it, we'll have a whole group of kids for me to nurse or setting the place on fire."

He grimaced at her and grabbed a shredded, dirty white shirt from the table. "See here, I don't know what you had in mind coming 'round, but I'm going to show you some trust. Will you not cause any trouble?"

I nodded.

"Good. Give me your hand." He pulled me to my feet, inciting the dog to give a small bark and stand up.

"Quiet down, Daggoo," Heedy commanded. Daggoo sat back.

"Now let's see." He lifted my sweat-jacket hood over my head and pulled the strings tight, tying them under my chin. He shook his head.

"Won't frighten anyone. You'll just have to try to stay out of sight. Follow me."

He had a small camping lantern that cast harsh shadows once we left the glow of the electric bulbs. I followed him into a labyrinth of passageways and rooms, all of which were beneath the house and all appeared to be lived in. We ascended stairs and emerged in a room that looked like the ceiling could crash down.

"This one still bugs me." He gestured upward. "But I've propped it enough. It's been this way since seventy-four, so don't worry, but imagine the trouble if I wasn't around to keep people from it." In a corner, he picked up a lumpy, black trash bag and slung it over his shoulder with a squishy thud.

The kerosene light made his beard transparent and thin. I could see his chin through the hairs and thought his beard made him look ancient. We wove through the poles he'd used to prop up the ceiling. I had to touch each pole after my flashlight beam hit it, an action that caused Allen to slap my good arm.

"Keep your hands to yourself around here, and turn that off."

I pulled my arm in close after that and worried my satchel wasn't with me. We passed through a final room, empty except for a nondescript magazine on the floor and the ubiquitous webbing, and out to a porch at the back of the house. He dropped his bag, turned out the lantern, and we stood in the dark. My eyes adjusted after a moment, but he waited for something, so I asked, "When's your birthday?"

He stepped closer to the railing, peered, and whispered, "You're some kind of kook, right?"

"Nope."

"Shush, we've got to be quiet, and I don't have a birthday."

I needed his date. I whispered, "Every-everybody's got one."

"Rude boy, you give me your name."

"Abel."

"Abel, tssss. A decent man, one who's not ashamed of who he is, always gives his full name. Allen Whitney Foster, that's me."

He waited for me to respond.

"Abel Velasco, that's me," I said.

"Much better. Here's our plan, Abel Velasco. First, entrance prep, then one trip 'round and up to the roost. Got it?"

I nodded. I had no clue but figured I'd follow and do what he said.

He searched the porch and the back step. "Ah, great, I left the bucket. Stick close now and hurry." He turned the lantern on, and we went back to the drooping propped room and through a doorway next to the one that led to the basement. He stopped quickly at a short stairway leading up, causing me to bump into his back.

"Watch your step in here. Do what I do." He held the lantern up for a moment as we entered a room with high walls like an auditorium. It was easily half a football field in size and with a broken-ceiling view to the sky. We climbed a rubble pile, stopping on a good-size chunk.

"Wait here on this; it'll be easier for me alone."

Allan deftly scuttled down the debris, and I worried about the enveloping shadows as the light from his lantern submerged beneath waves of water-slicked beam and slab. I wished again for my satchel as I wiped water from my glasses, repeatedly worked the flashlight's power switch, and generally distracted myself from my concerns for a time. Air whistled past dried mucous in my nostrils as I tapped my foot and splashed water over the ragged edge of the platform. Moonlight sliced through the clouds every so often, tempting me to leave my flashlight on and explore the rubble, but I didn't.

Allen finally came huffing back and handed me a bucket as he climbed the last ledge. The contents of the bucket discharged a briny stench and splashed darkly onto the platform. I waited for his lantern to illuminate the puddles and was somewhat surprised when it turned out to be blood, but what surprised me more was the crack it settled into.

"Please. Hold up the light, please."

"What?" He lifted the bucket.

"Hold up the light, please," I repeated.

"No time, we're already behind." But he obeyed, and as it rose, I could see now that I stood on the ground floor of where the roof had caved in. Below my feet the cracks were Hebrew letters filling with watery blood. I only had time for a quick glance around, but some of the pieces lay faceup and turned enough for me to see. I pushed Allen back from the puddle so I could read the rest of the slab on which we stood. It translated to "came upon a plain in the land of Shinar." Having spent weeks with the Bible, I was surprised I didn't initially recognize Genesis 11, a portion from The Tower of Babel, carved here. I continued to translate the slabs closest to me.

"It's just butcher's blood on that slab; nothing to worry about." He lifted the bucket and started back toward the propped room.

When we reached the back porch, he put down the bucket and retrieved the trash bag. He fished out some thin rope and kept pulling it until a limp, dead chicken popped out. Now I knew where the other stink came from.

"A waste of food, but it'll do," he muttered, dangling the chicken in front of my face. Allen splashed it into the blood and took the dripping mess to the steps. A tree stood next to the building, and one of the limbs grew above the porch doorway. With ease, he threw the rope over it and pulled the chicken halfway up, its feathers now bloody spikes poking out from its neck and wings. One would have to push it aside to get by, and I wished he'd had us exit first. Allen took the bucket and splashed around the doorframe and on the porch. I jumped to get out of the way, but it splashed onto my shoes. Wiping the blood only managed to spread it around and make my hand a stinking horror.

"Watch out your hands don't swell up like balloons. That blood's been cursed by a witch." He chuckled.

I thought of the Richard Pryor story about the voodoo woman who healed swollen feet with her piss. I imagined having to clean my hands the same way.

"OK, prep work done. 'Round we go."

I could tell this was fun for him.

He took the trash bag with us, much to my dismay. Something else weighed it down.

Allen turned the lantern off again, and we walked around the house in silence, stopping at various points to hide and observe. The streetlight from the road gave the landscape in the front of the house a visible pattern rather than the blurred, dark-blue-and-black vegetative forms we hustled by at the side and back. He made a ridiculous show of waving his arms up and down as we marched in the open field to the four pillars.

"This your bike?" he asked when we found it.

"Yup."

"Someone going to steal it tonight." He took the handlebars and pushed it hard into the field where the weeds camouflaged it.

We hid for a brief time, watching for other trespassers and breathing heavily, before walking around the rest of the house to the front door. I wondered why he didn't string a chicken up at the front, as it seemed the obvious place for others to enter, but I didn't ask. He stopped between the two doors. Instead of going into the foyer, we turned to follow a narrow grassy passageway ending at steps. The old, bent planks of wood dipped with each footfall but held for a climb of at least two stories. We exited onto a shiny, metal-rimmed platform that bordered the perimeter of the house. The metal rim must've been where the light that flickered through the windows on my first visit reflected off. The surroundings appeared to be a staging area for construction with old sawhorses and a stack of plywood. I walked over to view the collapsed room I'd seen before from the hallway and from below.

"You're gonna step back right now, and you're going to listen up."

The plank I stood on was snapped and probably looked precarious from Allen's vantage point. It felt sturdy, but the fear in Allen's voice was sharp.

"Come over by me, and I'll tell you one last time, stick close."

When I got to him, he put his arm around my shoulder in a protective way. I managed to get from under his arm as we walked to a covered area out of the rain and sat on two sawhorses, facing the roofs of the albino village.

"He was trying to make his house larger, as you can see, but some of these planks is trouble, so." He looked around, thinking. "Over there's the lake. You can see the surface, see. See now. The moon pokes through, and you can see the water." He turned to the road that came from the side of the house. "The road here's too easy, and most folks looking to cause mischief won't take the road, so they come the path you must've, past the old homes."

"I took the road."

"Well, good for you. Who asked you?"

"No—"

"Nobody did, but that's fine. OK, so what we do is sit and wait. If you see someone coming, grab a tomato or an egg, and give it a hurl." He opened the bag and pulled out an egg. After about a half an hour of watching, I started to find the decaying scent from the trash bag almost comforting. The clouds thickened, and the rain came harder.

"What day were you born on?" I asked again.

"I told you already, I don't have one. My brothers and I went to separate orphanages. Nobody needed birthdays. If you'd ever lived in one, you'd understand not to ask such a question."

"I lived in foster homes."

"Every home I lived in was a foster home," he said with no humor to reveal his pun. "How come you didn't bring your friends with you?" He stood up. "Your friends aren't here already, are they?"

"I came alone."

"Probably would've heard them by now, and what about your parents? You'll have to take their punishment tomorrow. No use tryin' to get home in this."

"My aunt thinks—she thinks I'm at Russell's."

"Russell's? Who? Not Russell Ghety?"

"Yes," I said, surprised he knew him.

"How is the boy? Gave Heedy a shock that day, washed up on the side of the road, lookin' like he'd been through a blender."

"I don't know."

"You don't know what? Russell?"

"I do, but-but don't know how he is, not since September twenty-fifth."

"Kooky child, who can understand your words when you scatter them about the way you do?"

He made me think of another part of the Genesis 11 chapter on the building of the Tower of Babel, and without thinking, I said, "And let us make a name for ourselves; otherwise we shall be scattered abroad upon the face of the whole earth."

He lifted the lantern to my face and furrowed his brow at me without comment, examining me. "Are you tryin' to scare me now? Don't be quotin' scripture at me, gimpy. Do you know who I am? I know those words. I've read those words many times. Why did you say those? Have you been in my room?" He started pacing.

Glue made of fear formed on the edges of my lips. I stared back at him and worried about what to make of the calculation my brain created for his anxiety and sentence structure.

"You're a creepy boy, Abel Velasco. Why would you be quotin' that to me today, tonight of all nights? You're tryin' to frighten me?"

He stopped pacing and peered down from the corners of his eyes, as if he were afraid to look straight at me. "Fair is fair, I scared you, but you know I helped your friend, and he told you about me, and you've been spyin' on me, haven't you?" He walked in the rain to the edge and looked down into the collapsed area. He spoke toward it like a preacher. "Little weasel creepin' about. God will smite you, OK? You need to know that God will smite you, and He'll smite me and these words . . . if you knew what I knew, you'd know these words are not to be trifled with."

I'd obviously shaken him up and didn't know how to stop it.

"I read it on the slab." I pointed down into the room.

"I-I didn't spy—"

He rushed back to me. "Lying! You are a liar."

A number cloud covered his face.

"It's Hebrew. I read it on the slab," I said, trying to dispel the cloud.

"Can you read it? Hold on now. You can read it?" He examined the sky after asking.

I started quoting as fast as I could. "Now the entire earth had one language and the same words. And as they migrated from the east, they came upon a plain in the land of Shinar and settled there. And they said to one another, 'Come, we will make bricks, and burn them thoroughly.' And they had brick for stone, and bitumen for mortar. Then they said, 'Let us build ourselves a city, and a tower with its top in the heavens, and let us make a name for ourselves; otherwise, we shall be scattered abroad upon the face of the whole earth.' The Lord came down to see the city and the tower, which mortals had built. And the Lord said, 'Look, they are one people, and they have all one language; and this is only the beginning of what they will do; nothing that they propose to do will now be impossible for them. Come, let us go down, and confuse their language there, so that they will not understand one another's speech.' So the Lord scattered them abroad from there over the face of all the earth, and—"

Allen took over. "And they left off buildin' the city. Therefore, it was called Babel, because there the Lord confused the language of all the earth; and from there, the Lord scattered them abroad over the face of all the earth." He backed away from me and turned on the lantern. "You couldn't blame me. You can read it, and so, you know, you can see. Anyone would be curious if they knew, and I was the only one who knew what he was up to. I was the only one who could understand his grief when it collapsed, because I know Genesis since I was younger than you, but it's too much for me. I'm not a professor. He was a professor. I do it in praise. Yahweh knows. I deserve a blessin'. He could smite, but I deserve a blessin'."

I started walking in the other direction around the house because the calculations were adding up to either an attack or anger. My bowels and bladder felt gravity's pull.

"Hold on now." He moved toward me. "Don't go 'round that way. Hold—"

I picked up my pace and tried to pull my flashlight out, but I fumbled and it bounced over the side of the house. Allen's lantern gave enough for me to maneuver around the piles, but he moved quickly, and in no time his hand had a hold of my hood, yanking me to a halt.

"You walk that way without knowin' your step, you'll end up worm food."

"Don't-don't hurt me," I managed as I put my glasses on straight.

"Who's hurtin' anybody? If I was hurtin' you, I'd let you go off on your own." He released my hood, and we faced each other until he relaxed. "Couldn't be, who are you?" His eyes held me until he turned and sneered down at the side lawn. "Nobody's comin' 'round here tonight, and if they do, they'll get a bloody bird in their face. Come on." He started off without me.

CHAPTER SEVENTEEN

Phi and a Scoop of Long Division

282.5.18.457.26-11.4.4-298.11.17.5.18.53.39

We climbed back down the stairs into the house. He stopped to lay open his trash bag on the grass between the doors. I thought of Mister Scratch briefly and hoped he lay comfortably out of the rain.

We hurried back through the kitchen to a stairway leading to the basement area again but through a different section. We paused at a closed door.

"Hold this." He shoved the lantern into my hand and began twisting a lock until it pulled free. He took the lantern back and worked his way through the room. I waited, assessing the odd shadows thrown from the room's mounding contents until lights came on, allowing me the full view. I estimated my location to be a storage area, although one might also think it a kind of disarmingly chaotic study. Heaps of cardboard boxes, folders, newspapers, old lamps, chairs, and two walls of books packed the room. Allen manipulated a lamp so it'd shine on items tacked to a wall and those that were spread out on a long folding table. More watercolors of flowers, several of them incomplete, some brushes and a dried-out watercolor paint palette, photographs of architecture, star charts, and a single sunflower bookend—the exact same as the ones I'd taken from the desk drawer, if not the actual one that pelted Russell. A picture of a man with the name *Marcus Mosiah Garvey* printed on it hung just above the bookend. A fake flower with scarlet, green, and yellow petals pinned where the date *8/17/1887* was printed.

I pointed at the picture and quoted, "Marcus Mosiah Garvey, born August seventeenth, 1887. Died June tenth, 1940. An influential black leader who started the back-to-Africa movement for Americans of African descent. Born and raised in Jamaica, Marcus Garvey traveled in Central and South America, then moved to England to continue his education. In 1914, he started the Universal Negro Improvement Association and advocated worldwide black unity and an end to colonialism. In 1916, he moved to the United States and—"

"Praise God. I knew it. Heedy won't let me be a Rasta. Says it's a man's religion and she won't be married to a man who represses her, but if she hears you talkin', she'll tell me to start prayin' to Selassie I or Jah or Jesus or whoever it is that's speakin' through you."

"The *Encyclopaedia Britannica*, volume seven, page 491."

"See, you reacted to my Marcus Garvey picture, my only contribution to all this. Well, that bookend's from when we helped your friend out, too, but either you've been watchin' my every move, or somethin' is speakin' through you to me." His ebullience was frightening, but I'd ruled out the possibility of him harming me. He scanned the wall collection, running his fingers in the air along the pages.

"Well, look here. This here is how the roof was going to be. He knew you gotta make the words big for God to know you mean business."

The largest of the pictures on the wall were diagrams of the external support or the shell added to the house and how the roof slabs were to be laid out. The plans for the marble slab's text were written in lines on a grid separated into six sections. In Hebrew on the first and second sections were Genesis 11 and a portion from the Book of Job, but the other four sections contained a series of numbers, which made my heart leap, even though the numbers were in sets and not long strings, as I'd been writing out.

"Here's where I knew what you were sayin'." He held up a page with translated English versions of the Tower of Babel and the Job text, next to the Hebrew version. The numbers were still numbers on the translated page. "That was right here and hasn't moved. I've left everything in the area it belongs." He slapped it back down on the desk. "How would you know that? And see this, Mr. Pierson used the story of Job to say he understood that God tested him the way God had the Devil torture Job, to test his faith, and them numbers is like the pictures of beauty." Allen pointed to various watercolors with numbers written along their tops and bottoms.

"Mr. Pierson knew that even if God had taken his wife and child, he'd left him with the beauty. I know this, see. And here are the ways others have talked to God through architecture. See, the old Greek and Egyptian gods. You can tell I've been figuring these things out, can't you?" He pointed at the photographs of the Parthenon and Great Pyramid of Cheops.

A white cat jumped up on the table and started rubbing its face on Allen's shirt. "Hey, when did you arrive? Well, just in time, friend. We've got ourselves some help now. Meet Abel. Abel, this is the great albino greyhound." Allen laughed, gave the cat a quick pet, and put him on the floor.

"He keeps mice from nibblin' the papers. Powerful mouser." Allen grabbed a small pipe from the center rest of a wide-dish ashtray. He dug inside the pipe's bowl with his pinky finger. When he withdrew it, his finger was coated in black ash. The pipe tapped a quick rhythm on the ashtray edge. He eyed me with suspicion as he pinched tobacco from a blue pouch, stuffed it in the bowl, and lit it, sending the sweet smoke scent throughout the room. The cat jumped up on the other end of the table and curled up next to the sunflower bookend.

Taking the pipe from his mouth and puffing smoke in spurts, he said, "So, who are you? You see this, and you know I know about it. Now, I want to know who you are and what you know." He tried to appear brave, but I could see his face still exhibited slight fear.

I picked up the paper with the translated text, trying to give the impression I was reviewing what he'd said. Pierson used onionskin-typing paper, thin and semitransparent. The information in English was typewritten while the Hebrew was written by hand. I recognized Dr. Pierson's tiny script immediately, and as I scanned it, I found ink had bled through from the back. I flipped the page over and discovered a numbering system. Each Hebrew letter had a number written next to it like the Gematria. I'd thought to try the Gematria as a code breaker when I began working on the number strings from the Bible. The letters of the Hebrew Bible could signify a code, but it didn't work. The numbers in Dr. Pierson's Bible didn't match the Gematria in any way. I placed the page down with the numbers facing up.

"Here is the Gematria," I said because I didn't have anything else to say.

"Ooh." Allen moved the page closer to him.

"The Gematria, see, uh, in the Hebrew alefbet, numbers go with each, ah, with each letter. The letter Aleph aleph is equal to one. The letter *bais* is equal to two. This first number right here on the page is a one, as you can see, so it could mean aleph. This number is a four, so it could be a *daled*. Switch out each number for a letter, you could read it." I pointed at the roof diagram where the numbers were.

"So, it says somethin'? You can read it. Read it to me, quickly." He tapped on the wall layout of the roof.

I thought about trying to explain I'd been working with Pierson's numbers, and it was unlikely the Gematria would work on the roof numbers for translation, but I knew I'd just confuse him since I explained already how the Gematrias work, but I followed his directions and tried to translate.

I stared at it and became certain the Gematrias wasn't in play but didn't know what to say next since he expected me to translate.

"It, uh, doesn't work. These numbers don't work."

He stared at me and at the onionskin paper, trying to figure something out.

"What is the . . . are you tryin—what are you tryin' to do here? Oh, wait, wait. If those numbers don't work, hold on, hold on." He moved swiftly to a barrel and began unrolling tubes of paper, looking for something.

"This one, here, these are the same thing, right?" He stretched and tacked it over the top of everything else. The same Gematria was written in one line along the top of the page. Allen probably didn't understand that only one Gematria existed, and if it didn't work with the first, it wouldn't with any other. Regardless, the rest of the newly tacked paper he brought out was curious.

A series of diagrams was printed in precise details, as if Pierson wanted his writing to be properly interpreted. The details focused mainly on the use of the ratio of Phi to create an algorithm. I began devising how I'd explain it all to Allen, but I couldn't help myself from pulling up an image of Pigpie. The only thing my aunt had in common with daisies, pretty spiral shells, and the sex life of rabbits was her body's relation to the divine proportion, Phi. The great Euclid of Alexandria first defined Phi, If you divide line AB by point C, and the ratio of the length of AC to that of CB is the same as the ratio of AB to AC, then the line has been cut in extreme and mean ratio, the Golden Ratio. The famous spiral of Fibonacci, the glorious never-ending number: 1.6180339887 . . .

A WHOLE LOT

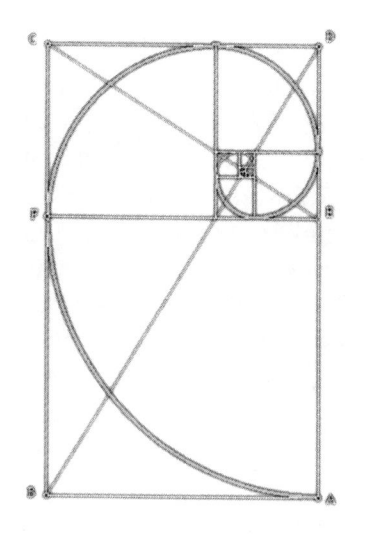

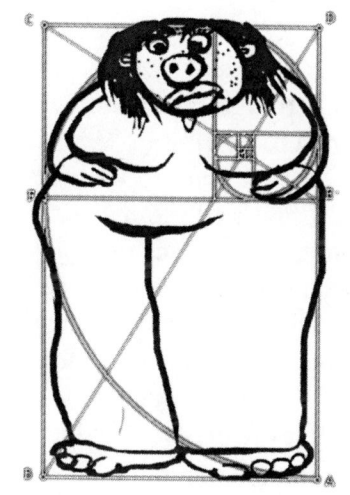

Dr. Pierson used an algorithm related to pi to generate a key to his Gematria. While he wrote the Hebrew letters along the bottom in the normal fashion, he also wrote the new Phi- related numbers directly below them—a key to the code. Here it was. In my head, I started applying it to the beginning sequence of the Pierson Bible numbers I'd been working on. It read, "I have begun this documentation on August 17th, 1968." I wanted to leave at that point and get to my satchel, but instead I started taking down the paper Allen had tacked up. Allen helped when he saw my excitement.

"This one works." I started applying the key. I pointed at the roof numbers. "Uh, right here, at first, it says, 'Sing unto God, sing praises to His name; extol Him that rideth upon the skies, whose name is the LORD; and exult ye before Him.' Then the area here . . ." I tried applying it to the others, but it didn't work for them. "Is there-are there other papers with these types of numbers?" I asked, pointing to the scroll where I'd learned the helpful code. I'd hoped there'd be another key someplace else. What if the new key didn't work for the whole Pierson Bible?

"Lots of places, lots of them. The man was a prophet, a real genius. There's so much. Look, look at this." He grabbed another piece of onionskin paper and started reviewing it. "This one, uh, no numbers on this, but Heedy was goin' to write to Dear Abby about it to see what she'd say. Tell me, what do you think?" He started reading from the paper, his eyes growing wider with each sentence. "Abraham Lincoln, elected president 1860. John Kennedy, elected 1960. Both slain with wives next to them. Both shot in the head. Both succeeded by men named Johnson. Both assassins killed before trial. Lincoln and Kennedy both have seven letters. Andrew Johnson and Lyndon Johnson both have thirteen letters."

I thought about what he read for a moment, recalled reading something similar in a magazine called *The Tall Target*, a magazine devoted to GOP congressional-committee issues, very boring. The information didn't appear to be related to any of the scripture items. The facts he read certainly could be considered odd, but at this moment I didn't care, since my bladder felt gravity's effects now. He handed me the page to read, which I promptly placed on the table.

"Do you have a toilet?" I asked, considering the pleasure of removing the remaining dried blood from my hand.

"Yes, but—"

I began walking toward the door, thinking about how much I could learn in this study and how connected I felt to Allen, even though he came across as being somewhat crazy. He reminded me a little of my uncle but more intelligent. He caught up and led me through the basement back to the room with Heedy.

Daggoo announced our arrival with some barking, but Heedy quieted him quickly.

"You catch any more trouble?" Heedy asked.

A WHOLE LOT

Relief washed over me as I spied my satchel and poncho, both unmoved.

"Nothin' to worry about." Allen pointed toward a door on the other side of the room. "It's through there."

I finished my long division and came out of the toilet closet to find Heedy standing with her hands on her hips. She sniffed at me, looked at the wall, sharply then back at me.

"Prove it." She marched up close to me.

I evaluated the new pinkish-brown stain on my wet sneakers while I waited for her to sit down again. She didn't retreat and instead took a long draw on her cigar and blew it toward my feet. The light flickered a little, and we all paused to listen to muffled thunder.

"How's God's mouthpiece goin' to hurt his elbow like that?" She relaxed and took the sling from my hand. I'd removed it from my arm to get my pants down and up. She squatted and unzipped my jacket to examine my elbow. "Your bruise is going to be a terrible yellow and purple tomorrow." The cigar on her breath smelled like the toilet room, but her hands were warm, and I almost didn't mind them touching me. She kissed my elbow and tucked my arm back.

"He's got some notion about you being God's mouthpiece. Please, tell him it's not true. Too much. Already he's diggin' through junk instead of getting a second job."

"When's your birthday?" I asked.

"See there?" Allen clapped his hands. "See, that's what he wanted to know from me before it all began. Go ahead, tell him."

Her dangling hands and lowered brow indicated her acquiescing to my question. "Sonny boy, I was born in May of 1951 on the twenty-fifth—"

"May twenty-fifth, 1951. You are 429 months old, or 12,942 days old or 310,628 hours old. You can retire with full government Social Security benefits in 2013." She looked at me with increased interest and a small grin. "It is a fact, and you are a Gemini, the twins. You bring out the best in others but can become deflated if you are out of the limelight for too long. Your sharp wit and keen powers of observation make you a good raconteur, although you have a tendency to exaggerate, which can cause trouble with your relationships. You share your birthdate with jazz musician Miles Davis, the boxer Gene Tunney, the tap dancer 'Mr. Bojangles' Bill Robinson, and the woman often seen trading quips with Paul Lynde on *Hollywood Squares*, Karen Valentine." I stopped when she backed up, thinking her retreating grin signaled she was done with my evaluation. I was right but continued, anyway. "In the Chinese-Chinese zodiac, you are a rabbit. Rabbits have a tendency to get too sentimental and to be superficial, to avoid conflict and emotional involvement. Being cautious and conservative, they usually take no risks. Their best life partners are Sheep or Pigs." I could see in her eyes I'd gone too far, so I added, "Porky Puh-puh-puhpig has a severe stutter and made his first appearance on March second of 1935 in '*I Haven't Got a Hat.*'"

"I'll tell you a fact. You're a . . . a turtle with a bird's head, and I want you out." She cocked her hip and slapped it like Pigpie might have done, causing Daggoo to rise to his feet. The house vibrated with another powerful crack of thunder as she moved to get my satchel and poncho from the table. Her cigar flipped downward and sparked on the floor where she stepped on its glowing cherry with precision.

"Wait, Heedy, don't worry. He's a good boy," Allen said, rising from his chair.

"What night is this night? What color is his shirt? The Devil's beatin' eardrum songs, and you're dancin' along, fool."

"But he figured out the numbers—"

Daggoo barked twice as Heedy shoved my items toward me and snapped her halt-all-action fingers at Allen. Women frighten me in several ways, from the beaconing false promises of their eyes, lips, and chests to the contradictory nature of their never-ending search for the fashionable and unique. Most of all what frightens me is their number. Their number is nine, and with Heedy, nine dug its base in the earth and called forth lava to square itself. I slung my satchel over my shoulder and pulled the poncho on, hoping that covering the blood color of my sweat jacket might ease matters.

"Get out of my house, devil boy," she demanded with both hands on her hips. I quickly took the stairs to the kitchen, looking back to see Heedy blocking Allen and holding Daggoo from following me. Allen shouted something, but I couldn't make it out. With no flashlight to inform me of webs or dangling bloody chickens, the climb was more frightening than my first visit when I walked around in darkness, wondering if someone might be behind me. Light came on in the main room, which I attributed to Allen helping with a switch he had access to instead of some hungry spirit, but it still startled me. I spied the folder of watercolors on the desk, and out of spite, I grabbed it and tucked it into my jacket. Serves them right—what had I done, anyway? Where would I go now? My focus should've been on my present circumstances because as I walked through the front door, I stepped down into Allen's bag of rotten eggs and vegetables. His trap sprung. I bet they'd have a good laugh about it later.

The rain pounded me like nails seeking vengeance on a hammer. I wore both my sweat jacket and my poncho hood, but they failed to keep the water off my glasses. I figured most everything was a dark blur now, anyway, so I put them in my pocket. Trudging through the high weeds looking for my bike helped soak the bottoms of my pants, making my lower extremities chill. In this downpour, the only option was to walk my bike. My luck would have me riding into a ditch otherwise.

    Severins Road had plenty of traffic, and after four cars rushed by, I thought of Hank and the garage and how they'd take me in if I asked. Mi would prepare something warm to eat, and we'd laugh while listening to soft, calming jazz, something like Miles Davis's 1959 release *Kind of Blue*, one of Hank's favorites. I tried listing Beatles albums chronologically by their UK release dates as I hiked. *Please Please Me, With the Beatles, A Hard Day's Night, Beatles for Sale, Help!* . . .

    When I knocked, Hank yelled out, "I ain't got no more candy!" After the third time, he opened the door with his fist raised.

    "I, uh, I, uh—"

    "Jukebox! What, swimming's for the summertime. Don't you know nothin'? Get in here."

    The apartment smelled lightly of pickled fish and cigarettes.

    "I was at the house, and—"

    With sincere concern, Hank interrupted, "Here, let me take your jack—"

    "Ah-bel, oh, my God, what happen to you?" Mi came in wearing pastel-green flannel pajamas.

    "Get the boy a towel, would you, Mi? He's dripping all over the floor. Come on in here, Juke." He ushered me into the kitchen and pulled my poncho from me. Rain soaked my sweat jacket down the front. Mi returned with a towel, T-shirt, and sweatpants that must have been Hank's.

    "Come on here, you change in the bathroom." She gave me the clothes and started wiping my face and neck with the towel.

    The clothes were much too big for me, but they weren't wet, so I didn't care. When I came out, she handed me a mug of tea with a sprig of mint in it.

"Drink that. Come in here, we're watching HBO movie."

"Have you seen this?" Hank asked from his recliner. "It's called *The Shining*. I saw it in the theater a couple years ago, and it scared the hell out of me."

"Here, sit by me." Mi took my mug, placing it on the coffee table, and curled her arm around me. "Will out boxing, so you keep me warm, OK?" She wrapped a blanket over both of us and clung close.

"We need to call your aunt. We'll call her after the movie, OK?"

"She, uh, she thinks I'm at Russell's tonight."

"You had a fight with Russell, huh?"

"No."

"How come you're not there, then?"

"He's not home."

When Jack Nicholson started yelling at Shelley Duvall about leaving him alone, our conversation stopped. I watched the movie with them but didn't really follow it. I kept thinking about the numbers, the codes, and how I might get back into the house. The last thing I recalled before falling asleep was watching a burgundy elevator door opening and blood pouring forth into the hotel hallway in a threatening wave.

CHAPTER EIGHTEEN

Six-Million-Dollar-Men

41.12.27.2-2.32.4-85.32.4.55.41-12.8.23.6.1

The following afternoon, Mi, Will, and I rode out to an Asian strip mall in northern New Jersey to buy groceries. Will had won his bout the night before and was treating Mi to one of her favorite places, but Mi still harbored anger for him coming home so late. Apparently, arms full of grocery bags can induce amnesia in her. Mi began to lose her memory of Will's late-night entrance while roaming the dried-vegetables aisle and started kissing him next to a bin with a sign that said *dried asparagus*, though it looked more to me like black Q-tips. I loved the store—all the edible yet inedible-appearing items and the dazzling Day-Glo Halloween decorations. They bought me little salty-sweet candies in the shape of bats. It came in a big bag that would probably last me until the following Halloween, considering my second piece lasted me twenty-seven minutes and since they tasted a little like soap. We had an outstanding day, complete with another Pabst Blue Ribbon given to me by Hank when we got back to the garage. I felt most pleased to be busy and not to have to go home to deal with Pigpie's blather until late afternoon.

    Dr. Limone called that night, asking if I'd like to come to his computer club. He apologized for not contacting me sooner and asked why I hadn't returned his last call. Before I could answer, he moved onto an obviously rehearsed pitch. He said he had a "small quorum of interested futurists" and was sure I could help him "propel the excitement for binary bits and bytes." He said it all with a Count-from-*Sesame-Street* accent and laughed ah-ah-ah after he said *bytes*. I wanted to say no to his offer but thought the computer could be helpful with the code resolution.

The numbers of the Bible appeared clearly in my mind without having to write them all out. I felt almost guilty for reviewing Dr. Pierson's words of grief and sorrow. I'd have felt worse if it wasn't obviously written for "those that are capable of understanding my encrypted" words about God's interaction with the world, which all was ultimately a guide directing you to the main text of the Bible. It mentioned a "special formula" but didn't provide a new key. I tried applying both of the keys I'd discovered at the house, to no avail, and while it thrilled me to make it through the first section, I still wanted the answers to it all. I had an idea to resolve what I saw as the dependent variable of the number problem. If I could use the school's computer to run a program that would run tests on a variety of functions, I'd save weeks of work. Mostly, I needed to rule out the possibility that my dependent variable wasn't a logical fallacy I was enforcing on the equations. I wanted to be certain I wasn't fooling myself the numbers were a code when they could just as easily be Pierson counting seconds using random numbers—at this point, that was improbable but not impossible.

I biked through the high-school parking lot just as school let out on Monday afternoon. A couple students gave me the judgmental there-he-is eyes and a few "alien kid" comments. As I experienced the horn honking and paper-ball throwing, I realized I didn't miss this place. The typical high-school scent hit me upon entering: a combination of body odor, pencil erasers, and floor cleaner. The hallways buzzed with painted banners for the pep rally as I passed the soccer team walking the halls sock-footed and carrying their cleats, and climbed the stairs to Dr. Limone's room.

He sat at his desk, reading from a piece of paper.

"Abel, how nice to see you. Um, wasn't expecting you until tomorrow, though."

I stood there, uncertain what to say.

"Are you still planning on coming to the meeting tomorrow?" he asked.

"You said, you said the meeting was today, now."

"Did I? Oh, dear, I'm so sorry. Well, no, unfortunately, I must have made a mistake. Meeting is tomorrow, but that's fine. That's fine, and this will give us a chance to catch up."

I felt a little relief, actually. I wouldn't have to worry about who else might attend the meeting and if there would be time to discuss my needs with Dr. Limone.

"Well, it's nice to see you. Really nice. Why don't you have a seat?"

I sat down, placing my satchel on the desk.

"I could use, use a computer today if you have one I can use," I said.

"Oh, well, you see, I didn't schedule any time for students until tomorrow. The lab is probably in use already. Was there something specific you were looking to do?"

I took my journal out and flipped to the numbers I'd already transcribed.

"These need a dependent-variable program."

"May I?" Dr. Limone walked to me with his hand outstretched in request of my journal. I handed it over uncomfortably. "Mm, this is odd, isn't it? No calculation to be found here?"

I shook my head and took the journal back. "I found the number string. I need to run the program to find out what the string is related to."

"Mn, sounds complicated. I'd love to be of help. Oh, and speaking of help, I've not heard back about a tutor for you yet, but I plan on putting another call in this week. Thought I'd run it by you first, make certain you are still interested. How are things going at Princeton?"

"Fine."

"What've you been keeping busy with?"

I dug out my list of reading that Dr. Langdeer gave me.

"Yes, this looks thorough, doesn't it? And how about your maths, then?"

"I've met with Dr. Kohn two times."

"Dr. Kohn? I think I know that name." Dr. Limone looked over at his desk.

"He's a professor. He's interested in working with me."

"Ah, so you already have a tutor, then? Good, good." Dr. Limone glanced again at his desk, but this time I was sure it was at the stack of papers. "Listen, um, would you like to use my personal computer? No doubt the missus would love to see you again, and it'd raise my marks with her about the purchase if I said you'd had a real reason to work on it. The thing is, I've got to tend to a bit of paperwork, but then we'd be off. Shouldn't take me long." He looked at the clock on the wall. "I'd say about fifteen, twenty minutes should cover it. Shall we meet up outside by the steps?"

This was better than I could've imagined. I would avoid the club and see Godiva and Fergus again. I nodded and walked toward the door.

"OK, then, see you soon," he called after me.

As I started for the stairwell, I noticed Phillip Macklehorn anxiously writing something in his Trapper Keeper. Another kid, whose back was toward me, told him something to which Phillip nodded in agreement and wrote something down. I really didn't want to deal with Phillip and decided to stand a few lockers away to see if he'd leave. Two chattering girls by an open locker worked as my shield, but they turned out to be a poor choice because I disturbed them when I leaned against the lockers. They closed theirs up and walked away, leaving me directly in Phillip's view. I turned, but he noticed me, said something to the other kid, who looked over at me. I immediately recognized him as Jerry Hampton. I froze. Jerry clapped Phillip on the arm, and Phillip fished his wallet out. Jerry prodded him to hurry and snatched some bills from Phillip's reluctant hands. Phillip walked briskly away.

An altercation brewed, and I started calculating my options. Clouds appeared and buzzed, nearly obscuring my view this time. I could run out of the school or back into Dr. Limone's room. The percentages were not on my side in either scenario. Jerry came at me with his eyebrows cutting into his eyelids. My feet itched to walk, but before I could, Jerry put his arm out to the side. He made a fist with his extended hand, whacked me in the chest as he passed, and ran down the other stairwell. The humiliating part was I could probably have moved out of his range. The pain was less bothersome than the tall girl's eyes that met mine as he struck. I could just make her out through the clouds as she flinched with me and worked a sympathy frown onto her face. Other students began laughing, so I ignored my obscured vision and hustled down the stairs.

I waited outside for a minute, but with every passing student, I worried the next would be Jerry. The percentage was too high that it would be him and not Dr. Limone, so I decided it was better to stand up Dr. Limone.

The bike lock couldn't release fast enough. I pedaled hard, steering through gaps in the parked cars, the most direct route off the school property. The candy bats in my pocket filled my palm, and I thought of them as Japanese stars, weapons of the ninja, as I tossed them toward trees at the side of the road, envisioning a half dozen slicing into Jerry's back. A stick caught in my bike frame, and I road on, seething with anger as it clicked away in the spokes and picked up its steady rhythm. My chest felt tight. I wanted to go back and find Jerry and tell him to fuck off. Phillip Mackelhorn must really be an idiot to do business with that Jerry. I didn't even really want to go to that computer club. I rode past Chaims Street, and the ratio of pedal revolutions per minute with the stick clicks gave me an idea that Jerry's day wasn't looking so good. The numbers were on my side. The stick had to be detached before it passed the two thousandth click, so that his odds couldn't be improved. I paused on the side of the road and snapped it out of the frame. A rusting, orange VW Rabbit drove by playing Smokey Robinson's "Being With You," and I recalled that Hank mentioned going to the dump today.

Like a turbulent ocean, soapy, colorful paint streaks swirled around one-half of the arcade window as if someone had begun cleaning the paint but got distracted halfway through the job. The Frankenstein, Wolfman and Vampire Pac-Men were alive, but I could tell by the tip of the hat the witch was gone. I slowed to a stop and caught a few bars of midi music as three boys exited. I did a double take realizing Will was at the Joust machine. He wasn't the only adult in the place, either. I thought he might look my way, but he didn't. I decided to stick to my personal pact with Russell. Will would probably pay for a few rounds, but no matter, because it wouldn't be long before Russell contacted me. I dragged my feet on the way down the hill in case Will came out and I could ride down with him. He didn't emerge, so I skidded to a stop and parked the bike near the empty oil bottles.

"Ooh, you are not wet today?" Mi kidded me as she walked out of the office and lifted my satchel to inspect my sweat jacket. "What a plea-sure to see you again." She pronounced everything slowly. It was so tremendous to be with someone I liked and that liked me. I used her shirt cuff to gently lift her hand up in the air.

"It is a fact: This has twenty-seven bones. Eight are in your wrist." I waved it around so she could feel them under her skin. She paused the wiggling, put her warm palm against my face, and kissed me on my forehead.

"Stay this way forever. Don't get adult. It not such a party as your age is. Hey, you come with me. Hurry." She dashed into the front office and hovered around her fishbowl that had a new scarlet occupant with a long flowing tail.

"After we drop you off, Will took me to buy her. You can't have two—they fight if two—but isn't she so pretty?"

"*Betta splendens*," I said and tapped on the bowl.

"Will love me. He get me new fish, and I call her Rose because it like he gave me a red rose." She said *red rose* with so many *l*'s, I tried to translate it from *led lohse* before I realized her accent masked actual English.

We watched Rose zigzag across her bowl until Hank showed up. He leaned against the vending machine. "You here to give me a hand or just looking for free grub from Mi? She's got our bookwork to finish up. Right, Mi?"

"Quiet, old man. I finish tonight." She tugged on his sleeve.

"Hey, hey, you know, you know, you are 588,863 hours old, Hank. Did you know that?" I said, happy to be here and not at the high school.

"Hey, hey, you, you, get offa my cloud," Hank sang at me and danced away from the vending machine. "I could use a dump. You busy?" He laughed hard after he said this.

"Nope."

"Mi, you're welcome to join us if you like."

"Oh, no. I have bookwork, right? I can't go to trash dump with all my booookwork. You go, and I have good food when you come back. You stay for dinner, Ah-bel?"

I shook my head.

"No? It's OK. Lunch next time, OK?"

"Tell Will when he gets back from goofing off not to forget about Mr. Schmidt's tail pipe. Tell him it's gotta be done by five-thirty, all right?"

"I tell him, but Will goofing for long time."

"If he's not here by five, call Mr. Schmidt and tell him it'll be ready tomorrow. His telephone number's in the—"

"I know where number's at. You go now." She waved us out of the garage.

Hank was almost as proud of owning his Lincoln as he was of the garage. He kept it shiny and bright like his vending machine. I'd only seen it with the top down once and wondered why have a convertible if you spent the summers with the top up, but he didn't trust the weather, calling Mother Nature a "fickle bitch." I didn't see the harm in leaving it out in a storm maybe once, if only to wash some of the yellow off the plastic and blow away the cigarette butts overflowing from the tray. He put my bike in the trunk. The trunk was so big, you could've put two more bikes in there with it.

I loved riding with Hank because he loved driving me around, acting as my tour guide. He pushed the *Best of the Four Tops* eight-track in, and the *oohs* of "Baby, I Need Your Loving" started. His Chiclets box clacked in his pocket, calling to him until he dumped a few in his mouth. He handed the box over to me. Fruit-flavored.

As we were crossing the bridge into Milltown, Kate came rushing into my mind with her sunlit hair softly hovering and glossy lips slightly ajar. I should have been back to visit her before now. I bet she'd love it if I knocked on her apartment door.

"Did I ever tell you about the big stir over that Milltown bridge?" He thumbed toward the back. "When I was growing up, nobody wanted it. People from North Brunswick used to think people from Milltown were trash because, well, because they always had the fastest cars. Racing used to be big in these parts. Brunswick folks only ever went into Milltown for the races. I used to be quite a dancer in Milltown, you know." He laughed.

I'd only heard the part about the racing before, nothing about his dancing, but it smelled like a Whopper with cheese already.

"The North Brunswick folks knocked the first bridge down right as it was almost finished. They was afraid the black folks who worked at the mill were gonna sleep with their daughters. Many of the girls liked to come dance at the Speedway, you see, which was where the workers always had a good time. Used to take those girls over an hour to get to there; with the bridge, it'd be 'bout fifteen minutes. I was seventeen first time I went to the tavern, and I danced my ass off. I could really dance, I ain't kiddin'. If the MTV was around back then, they'd put me on it." He waved his arm in the air to the beat of "Shake Me, Wake Me."

The Lincoln slowed as we turned down the street where the Speedway tavern Kate hung out at was located. To my surprise, Jerry and Phillip stood with their bikes across the street in the parking lot of the same abandoned gas station where I'd watched Kate from.

"There it is. Man, I have some great memories from that place. These days it's nothing but whores. See that guy?" He pointed at a guy wearing a leather flat cap and sunglasses. "Pimp if I ever saw one." I might have been angry with Hank calling Kate a whore, but I knew he didn't know her like I did. He slowed again and suddenly turned into the Speedway parking lot. I thought he tried to hit the guy he called a pimp. I held tightly to the armrest as he parked.

"Wait here a minute. I'm gonna run in an' get something for Tig."

I slunk down a bit more in my seat and turned to see if Jerry and Phillip noticed me, but they were in the middle of a conversation. I wondered what they were up to in such a place. It looked like Jerry was angry with Phillip. Jerry kept talking sternly to him, and Phillip kept adjusting the brake on his handlebars. Phillip crossed his arms at one point, and Jerry took hold of his jacket, pushing him toward me, which almost knocked Phillip off his bike. Jerry started my way, cranking his pedals and waving his bike from side to side, but he angled more toward the back of the building where Kate went to attend the party. I ducked but looked out again as he disappeared around the corner. Phillip stayed put for a minute and, with a pout, followed Jerry. I ducked again as he passed. Hank frightened me terribly as he opened his door.

"What you hidin' from?"

I sat up in the seat. "Nothing."

"Didn't look like nothin'. Those kids givin' you trouble?"

I denied it with a head shake as he put the car in reverse. We pulled out and started back down the road. I tried to locate Jerry and Phillip on the other streets we passed, but I didn't see them.

"They don't even have any good music in there anymore. I tell you, this area's gone to the dogs."

We turned onto Mays Street, which had a metal fence running along it, behind which you could see a landscape of exciting junk. "But it's still got this place. Look at it," he said with enthusiasm and wonder, as if it was the first time he'd ever been here.

Hubcaps decorated the entrance, as did a *Welcome to Tig's Salvage Yard* sign with a picture of a roaring tiger. Anyone with a taste for nostalgia from the recent past would relish the heterogeneous view. The place consisted of a row of VW Beetle husks, pyramid stacks of the door-delivered Charles Chips cans, a barrel of wigs in gray and brown, and on and on. I opened my door and immediately spotted a Six Million Dollar Man doll with his bionic arm and head still attached but no other appendages. To find him in that shape seemed like a disservice to his inspiring technological wonder.

Mr. Tig slouched on his recliner outside the front door of the office. He had a little kerosene heater lit with a pan of water steaming on top. A German shepherd sleeping next to him jumped up to check us out. He licked my palm and buried his nose in my crotch. Mr. Tig was so hunched, wrinkled, and gray, he looked like he could crumble into the earth at any minute. I petted the dog, waiting for Mr. Tig to say something while Hank took four of the nut-and-bolt boxes from the backseat and placed them beside others outside the office. He pulled a pen from his pocket and wrote *$1.00* on the top of each box.

We joined Mr. Tig at his chair.

"Tig! Hey, Tig, what's up?" Hank shouted very loud near his ear.

"What's that? Who's there?" Like a robot, he came to life and tilted his head revealing cloudy eyes.

"It's me, Tig. Hank, and I'd like you to meet my friend, Abel. I told you about him, remember?"

"Hank?" A big toothless grin filled Mr. Tig's face. "I thought I smelled something bad." His chuckling turned quickly into a bout of coughing, which I thought might shake him apart. Hank took the crooked, vein-bulging hand Mr. Tig held out for help and held it until Mr. Tig's cough subsided.

"Quit showin' off. Nothing different-smelling about me you don't smell every Tuesday." Hank lit a Pall Mall.

"You tryin' to kill me again?" His gravel-coated voice and the dingy bucket by the door half full of butts suggested he'd smoked many of them himself, but he waved the smoke away slightly as if offended. Hank held the cigarette over to the side, away from him.

"Hey, Tig, I was just telling Abel about the old Speedway. Why don't you tell him about how it started your business?"

"From the Speedway, don't need 'em. Park 'em over there, and I won't charge you anything," he said, as if still keen on the ways of bartering. He gestured to an area where the VW husks were rusting.

"Tig used to take all the wrecks from the races, and mechanics came from miles away to sort through them for decent used parts. This place was a gold mine. Gave me my first job taking them apart, didn't you, Tig?"

"Hank Flynn, gotta be the laziest kid in town and smelled, too. Who else gonna hire a stinky kid like that?" Mr. Tig began chuckle-coughing again.

"Don't start."

"Tried to blame it on a skunk. No skunk gonna spray you every day of the week."

"One time, only one time I showed up to work smelling like that dead animal. Wasn't even a skunk, and it wasn't even me. It was my car tire giving off the scent. Man can't remember what he had for breakfast, but he can remember that."

"Says you. I remember. I remember that one day you was playin' in the sandbox. You stank so bad, my cat Chunky came along and buried you."

We had to laugh at that one.

"Keep it up, old man, and see if I bring you another one of these." Hank pulled a small square bottle of liquor from his pocket.

"Sweeeeet Mary." Mr. Tig found new energy as he grabbed the bottle and held it near his head. "Better than a wife. Keeps me company all week long." He tried twisting the cap off but couldn't, so Hank took it back and got it started for him.

"We're gonna get some more nuts and bolts from your pile, OK?"

"Same price. Penny apiece."

"You drive a hard bargain," Hank mostly said to himself as he went into the office and left me standing by the heater.

I put my hands out to warm them in the steam and looked closely at the blank gaze of Mr. Tig's eyes. He turned his head toward me as if he could see. "What're you staring at?"

I started to ask him for his birthdate but instead answered, "Uh, you."

"You got a camera?"

"No."

"Take a look around. If you find one, bring it back here and take my picture, and then stare at that instead of me. Here, Chester, sit." Chester sniffed my crotch again. "Chester, what's wrong with you?"

"It is a fact: Dogs can smell forty-four times better than humans. Humans have five million olfactory receptors in their noses while dogs have over 220 million in theirs."

Hank returned pulling a wagon with a stack of empty boxes piled in it.

"Dog factory? You talkin' like a fruitcake."

Hank interrupted. "All righty, we'll be back in a while."

"Hunky-dory." Mr. Tig removed the cap from his bottle, took a satisfied breath and a swig to match.

We hiked out to the back of the gated area. During the first ten minutes as we navigated through forgotten debris, the melody of *Sanford and Son* ran through my mind. Hank loved the show because he loved its star, Redd Foxx. I started reviewing the episode I saw when I lived with the Chungs and placed Mr. Tig in the Redd Foxx role and Hank as his son, Lamont. Wasn't sure where I'd fit, but I cast myself as the Grady character. Too bad I'm not a woman because I'd love to play Aunt Ester. She had the best menacing sneers. I'd read in the 1975 September issue of *TV Guide* that the show was based on a British TV show called *Steptoe and Son*, which had the same premise of a love-hate relationship between father and son who ran a "rag-and-bone" business.

"Didn't get into no trouble staying with us the other night, did you?"

"Nope."

"'Cause if you want, I'll make something up to clear you with your aunt."

"S'okay. It's—I stayed at Russell's," I explained, and Hank winked knowingly.

The wagon caught a wheel between two hunks of metal sticking out of the ground, and we paused to free it.

"You let me know then. You need me to, I don't mind." I could tell Hank fished for information about her, probably worried why I didn't want to go home that night. I hadn't given him much of a reason.

Finally, we located several large mounds of nuts and bolts. I couldn't imagine anyone would ever find these if Hank didn't, hidden as they were behind a row of refrigerators. He pulled two quarts of oil from one of the boxes and handed me one.

"That pile over there looks like it's getting a little orange. Sprinkle that real good until that bottle is empty." Hank spread his oil on another mound, and I did as directed.

He took a small shovel and started filling up the boxes in the wagon. "Don't get me wrong, I'm glad for your company as always, Juke, but you usually space your visits out, and this is day three. Something going on I should know about?"

I was glad he was looking at my back. "Nope," I said as casually as I could. No clear reason for it, but I felt the furnace kick on in my neck and cheeks. He'd have been a good one to share all the latest happenings with even if he didn't understand, but I felt ashamed I hadn't fought back. I thought about explaining how Jerry had punched me, or about giving him a history of Dr. Pierson's house and numbered Bible, or about how Shelly was pregnant, but the figures didn't align properly.

"See, that's what I always like about you. No complaints, nothing but stories like Carver inventing peanut butter and a positive attitude toward work. You'll keep some woman smiling, that's for sure."

I laughed to myself when he started humming the *Sanford and Son* theme song. He did a little soft-shoe dance, too, to exhibit the skills he boasted about. I thought of Kate again and wondered where Phillip and Jerry went after they rode behind that building. The guy Kate went to the party with could be selling drugs. Maybe Jerry's moving into my uncle's old business instead of his typical gum and candy. It could be that Jerry was going to use Phillip as his accountant. If my uncle had one, he probably wouldn't have blown through his money so often.

It didn't take us much time to fill the new boxes and head back to the car. Before we left, Hank handed Mr. Tig a twenty and a five for them. From my estimation, he only owed $16.60.

When the doors on the Lincoln closed and I knew Mr. Tig couldn't hear, I said, "You-you paid too much."

"Did you want him to count them out or something?"

"N-no."

"I know. Seems funny to bring back the boxes sorted and counted for him to sell after I paid, right?"

I nodded.

"Tig and his Gerty raised me as much as my own parents did. Like I said, he gave me a job, pretty much gave me my career with the loan he made me to start my garage. Now that's interest-free, too. Here, you start saving this. Maybe one day you can buy me a drink when I'm Tig's age." He dropped a five in my lap.

We were passing the bar again, but Phillip and Jerry were nowhere in sight. I turned around to see if I could observe them dealing behind the house when Hank got ruffled.

"Stay the hell away from that place, hear me? Boys your age getting little peckerwood every morning, I know the drill. Don't go looking to start jumpin' before you're sixteen at least."

"Just say no to drugs," I quoted Nancy Reagan. He gave me a curious look and laughed.

"You got it, Jukebox. Women's the most po-tent narcotic around. Nothin' shoves you down a well like trying to give one up you still want."

Maybe I was addicted to Kate, but if so, I wasn't ready to acknowledge it. I vowed to return this coming weekend. It felt as if I'd waited too long, but I figured I could ask her to lunch.

Hank pulled up in front of my house and got out to take my bike from the trunk.

"You mind if I come in to use the facilities?"

It made me nervous not knowing how Pigpie might react, but I had no reason to deny him. I called out hello once we came in the front door. I rarely use the front door and never say hello, so this aroused Pigpie immediately. She came out with a Budweiser looking bleary-eyed and belligerent. Shelly hadn't come home yet, and this consumed her.

"This-this is Hank. He's from Flynn's Garage."

"I know who this man is," she informed me abruptly and tried a lame attempt to put on her guest veneer, though she clearly had trouble focusing her eyes. "How do you do, Mr. Flynn. What brings you to visit?"

"Just here to use the facilities, Ms. Stacks. If you don't mind, that is. Young Abel was kind enough to allow me in," Hank said, assuming her formal patter.

She gave a long pause and finally said, "Yesh, well, uh, please, go right ahead. It's right through here." She led him to the first-floor bathroom and gave me an evil look, draining the can of Bud while we waited. When he came out, Pigpie stood by the front door to make his welcome clear.

"If you don't mind me, and I can't see why you would, since it's my house. Why my house? Is your car broke down?"

Hank looked at me and I at the ground, afraid he'd tell her he'd given me a job like Mr. Tig had for him. I knew our relationship was something he took pride in, so I waited for the high-percentage answer.

"No bother, Ms. Stacks no bother. I found Juk— Abel on the side of the road, trying to work out them pesky bike chains, and figured I'd give him a hand. I replaced plenty of them when my son was his age. Since you lived so close, I decided it'd be easy to drop him off. Abel said it'd be OK if I got rid of the chain grease." Hank showed his clean hands. "Thank you very much for letting me clean them off so I didn't get my steering wheel dirty." He put his hand out for her to shake. I worried his lie appeared obviously illogical. Why would he drive me home if he fixed my chain? Wouldn't he have already gotten his steering wheel dirty? The deception flew in the stratosphere miles over her head.

"As you may know, I take my car to Jenkins for service," she stated as she raised her can, shaking the remaining contents into her open mouth.

"Jenkins does good work. I don't blame you."

The can tilted empty as she took the last sip and swayed when she put it down on the side table.

"Do you? You wouldn't happen to know my daughter, Michelle, Shelly Stacks, would you?"

"Yes, ma'am, I've seen her around town."

"You have? When? I've been looking all over for her." She looked like she wanted to bolt out the door, which in her state would have been fun to watch.

"I'm sorry, ma'am, not recently. I meant in the past."

Pigpie's eyes narrowed. "Why'd you wanna lie to me? My poor daughter's pregnants and out there on her own, and I let you foul my toilet and you mistreat me—"

"No, no, I'm sorry, didn't mean to mislead you. I'll keep an eye out for her for you. She's a pretty girl, very pretty." Hank moved toward the door.

"Tha's right, she's my daughter." Pigpie smoothed back her oily hair, pushing the door open. Her voice changed back to the guest voice. "Thank you so much for stopping by, Mr. Flynn."

Hank and I nodded at each other as she let the screen door close behind him. I moved toward the stairs, knowing I hadn't yet received the wrath indicated from her evil-eye moment.

"Where do you think you're going? For the luff uf Christ, what were you thinking? Don't chew effer bring a stranger in my house." She slapped the back of my head.

"Excuse me, ma'am." Hank's voice came from outside the screen door.

Pigpie turned around, ready to strike.

"I was just wondering, I could use an extra hand at my shop, and Abel is just the type of boy I'm looking for. You think he might come help me out a couple days a week?"

Pigpie looked back at me as I rubbed to reduce the sting. She looked even angrier as if this were my plan.

"No, he will not be available. He's got far too much to do around here. Besides, what would they say at that hoity-toity college of his if they heard he was working at a gas station?"

When she finished, I felt my gut boiling. Her incorrect terminology was maddening. I nearly punched the wall, not only because she'd continued the misuse of the term *hoity-toity*, for the word stems from *hoit*, a verb from the sixteenth century whose meaning is "to play the fool" or "to indulge in riotous and noisy mirth." *Hoity-toity* once described those who engaged in thoughtlessly silly or frivolous behavior compared to its contemporary usage, where it's wrongfully a synonym for *pretentious*, which is how she meant it. Also, she'd called Hank's garage a gas station, a known insult to Hank and Will. They didn't sell gas, and Will could go on for hours after a customer called them a gas station. "Do you see any gas pumps out front?" But I held myself in check because the numbers started rolling. I hadn't told her about Princeton, and I was certain she'd make a big stink. She must still be thinking of Rutgers.

"No problem, ma'am. Thought he might like a little extra cash is all."

"If he wants cash, I'll take him to Atlantic Cities, so good-bye and no, thank you." She closed the main door, and the curtains blocked Hank from view. She turned to me and jutted her lower jaw out oddly.

"Are you still here? Get your assss upstairsss, and don't think I don't know you put him up to that, asking me about that. I know your sneaking ways. Don't let me catchew anywhere near that station."

I pushed my satchel to cover my back and climbed quickly. I only hope she didn't know my sneaking ways because I'd be putting them to use later on to obtain some sustenance. With the amount of Budweiser she'd already consumed, she'd be asleep shortly, and I could finally address my hunger pangs.

CHAPTER NINTEEN

Ivan Nikolayevitsh Panin Wasted 50 Years

14.26.19-33.4.3.3-27.6.74.6.11-11.6.8.13.25.11.6

My life's first great disappointment was the day I found out my mom's meth habit would have her assigned to a long-term treatment program. The second would be the day I learned I wasn't the first to figure out the relation of the Fibonacci sequence to the golden ratio. Euler discovered the golden ratio in 300 BC for Chrissake—as if I had a chance. I guess it doesn't matter because since then, along with all the other figures I swim through, one of the guiding lights of my life is the mystery of the golden ratio, Phi, and the way the divine exhibits itself in the universe through it. It's fun to think that way, to believe God is working through the mystery of numbers, even if it's baloney.

I spend what could easily be described as a prodigious amount of time relating form to formula, and so it aggrieved me to no end to know that I didn't recognize Dr. Pierson's love of Phi and Fibonacci before Allen revealed it to me. There I was, staring at the folder of the flowers on my first visit, and smacking me so hard I should've passed out were the lily, buttercup, and marigold paintings. He'd illustrated specific flowers with Fibonacci-related numbers. The sequence works as follows: 1, 2, 3, 5, 8, 13 . . . add the first two numbers to get the third, the second two to get the fourth, and so on. Lilies have three petals, and he painted three lilies in the picture. Marigolds have thirteen petals, and he painted thirteen marigolds. It couldn't have been more obvious.

I'd spread them out in front of me in proper numerical order at the library when Bergit happened by.

"Hey, stranger, where've you been hiding? Wow, those are pretty."

"H-Hello."

"Did you paint these yourself? They're very well done."

"Nope."

She stared at them a little longer.

"That's funny. I'd think they were done by you since they're all Fibonacci flowers."

Just as if she'd smacked me without knowing.

"Rich-Richard Pierson painted them." I decided to navigate us away from my humiliation. "I need- Could I use a computer, do you think?"

She tilted her head, and her sweet birdsong voice said, "I don't know. Can you use a computer?"

"Yes, I can." I started packing up the pictures.

Bergit examined her slim watch and pushed her hair back. "Hold on, Speedy Gonzales. I've got some books to gather, but if you can get the OK from Kohn or what's-his-name head librarian, I'll meet you at the Fine Hall library at, say, one p.m."

Dr. Langdeer had no problem letting me join Bergit once he'd called and OK'd it with Dr. Kohn. I ate my lunch on a bench outside Fine Hall and read some of Maugham's *Of Human Bondage,* an item from Dr. Langdeer's required-reading list. A miserable story with no math but it's a helpful one, seasoned with examples of how to deal with women. Mainly, how to avoid all horrible ones.

Bergit found me at the bench.

"I-I talked with Dr. Langdeer."

"I know. I ran into him. He gave me an earful about how I should've escorted you to the library, as if you aren't capable of walking without me or something."

"I can walk," I said as we went inside.

She directed us to the elevator. The doors closed, and I suddenly felt self-conscious alone with her.

"So, in order for me to let you use a computer, Langdeer said I had to find out why you wanted one. He said you couldn't just play with one, as if people play with these things."

We dropped one floor, and the doors opened. She took me to a room with rows of computers, most of them glowing with green or amber text and a few with multiple colors. Three solitary individuals typed at keyboards and didn't respond to our presence. We sat down in front of one of the green-text ones. I had to fill Bergit in on my hunt, but she started talking first.

"Now, hold onto your hat. This is a sixteen-bit, 134,000-transistor processor capable of addressing up to sixteen megabytes of RAM. In addition to the increased physical-memory support, its chip is able to work with virtual memory, thereby allowing much room for expandability." She sounded like an ad for IBM.

"Wow," I said, knowing that's the reaction she wanted but mainly surprised she knew anything about computers.

"So, tell me what you are looking to do."

Images of the Hebrew text started flowing through my mind.

"I found a Bible that Richard Pierson wrote in. He-he wrote many small numbers, a string in the beginning. He wrote about his dead wife and daughter. He, uh, he loved God. There's more numbers above the printed text, but the cipher for the beginning doesn't work for decrypting the numbers above the printed text—"

She looked at me for a moment and said, "I'm not exactly certain what you just said, but it sounds interesting. Can I see this Bible you found?"

"Nope."

"I can't help you if I don't know what we're working with."

When she said, *we're*, it was as I'd feared. She'd already started thinking she was working with me.

"And I can say, I don't need help. The numbers are in here," I explained, pointing at my brain. "I certainly do need computer help for an optimal-variation program."

"Uh, OK. Codes can be very hard, and I happen to know some people very good at working with them, but..." She put her hand on the monitor. "Sounds like you're not going to smash it up or anything, I guess. I've got some studying to do. You go ahead, and I'll check back with you in an hour."

She left the room, and I took out my journal with some of the programs I'd written out. I typed for maybe twenty minutes when she came rushing back in.

"Does the name Ivan Nikolayevitsh Panin mean anything to you?"

No image of him or his name came to mind. "Nope."

She dropped a book on the desk, and the three other guys turned their heads our way, annoyed at the disturbance.

"This is a book on Panin and the Torah Code," she said, as if I couldn't have read it on the cover. "It looks like he worked on what you're trying to do. I have to run because now I'm really behind where I thought I'd be. Hope it helps." She rushed out again.

Half an hour later, I'd finished the book and knew that what Panin had discovered and whatever it was that Pierson explored were different. It was almost as sad a story as *Of Human Bondage*. Ivan Panin was born in 1855. A supposedly brilliant mathematician, born in Russia, exiled for plotting against the Czar, he studied in Germany before heading to the United States, where he got a degree from Harvard and then spent the next fifty years learning the mathematical secrets of the Hebrew Torah and Greek New Testament. Unfortunately from what I've read of the math he used, he created a lot of the "underlying pattern" himself. Fifty years wasted as far as I could tell, but it seemed he never knew that. He wrote about the heptadic structure of the Old Testament, aka the Torah, and the New Testament. Heptadic structure is a fancy way of saying the number seven, or how multiples of seven reoccur throughout the Bible. The seven seals, Sabbath on the seventh day, seven years of famine in Egypt, the seven trumpets of Jericho, and so on. He wrote of the potential for God to be talking through numbers, but Panin didn't provide us with anything new—other than maybe the number seven is a number God really, really liked. Even if it's true, it's like the math in Joyce's *Ulysses*—pointless. I went back to my program and completed a healthy portion before Bergit returned.

"Hey, I've got to go, which I think means you have to go, too."

"OK, OK. I need a floppy disk."

She went over to the main desk and took a fresh one from the box.

"Did you look at the book?"

"Yup," I said, starting to save my file.

"Well?"

"It is a fact: Panin does not prove anything."

"You're a mathematician, right?"

I smiled at her compliment.

"So, you know we know a lot more than we've actually proved."

I didn't follow.

"I think-I think your syllogism doesn't work." I looked at the fluorescent lighting in the ceiling. "We know a lot more than we've proved. Panin says he knows, but doesn't prove, that there are approximately 48,000 signs from God in the Hebrew and Greek texts of the Bible. Therefore, God must be showing he exists through the number seven?"

"That simplifies it a bit, but, yes, that's right."

"Did you, uh, did you know I like strawberry jelly? Did you know I'm a male? Therefore, it must be a proven fact, all males like strawberry jelly."

"Oh, I see. You don't believe in God."

"Uh, yes, I do."

She appeared frustrated.

"Look, I'm just saying that there are things in the world that we haven't proved are true but might be, like with math, and if you want to read more about these kinds of codes, I'll show you the shelf I found the Panin book on. Something else there might help with what you're trying to do, but I've got to get going."

She walked me over to a section with some titles on code breaking and pointed out the row where she'd found the Panin book. I thanked her before she left and briefly reviewed the titles, but nothing interested me. It gave me an idea, though. Consulting an expert on the Torah, someone who's also a mathematician might be helpful. I asked the man behind the help desk.

"Interesting. Well, I can tell you that only about two percent of Americans are Jewish."

I nodded, knowing this fact to be true.

"But there are many, many Jews that are also mathematicians. Georg Cantor, John Von Neumann, Paul Erdös, Norbert Wiener. But you want one you could contact, well, Paul Erdös is still alive. You could try contacting him, or—oh, I just shelved someone. Hold on."

He walked me to an aisle and retrieved a book.

"Here it is." He started reading the back flap. "Yes, it says he's mostly known for his expertise in group theory. Da, da, da. Let's see." He turned to the index. "Right, it says he got his PhD from Hebrew University and teaches there now. Mm, nothing about him being Jewish, actually, but I bet he knows something about the Torah if he studied there. Eliyahu Rips is his name. Want me to write it down?"

I looked at the book and shook my head.

Eliyahu Rips sounded familiar. At least, it gave me a place to start. I started back to Firestone Hall to use the microfiche library.

The index listed an article with Eliyahu Rips that I'd read when searching for biographical information about Dr. Pierson. I recalled it now. The International Congress of Mathematicians annual report is where Dr. Rips said of Pierson, "Time is transparent with mathematics. God speaks in arithmetical clarity for those with the sight." They must've known each other at some point. Contacting Dr. Rips would be a great idea, and I ditched the microfiche to compose a letter. I introduced myself, asked him of his knowledge of Dr. Pierson, and how I'd found the Bible Pierson worked on. I even wrote out the computer program I'd started, figuring he might be impressed to see computer code and therefore take me seriously. The Hebrew University's address was easy to locate, and on my way out of the library to catch the bus, I stopped for assistance from the white-haired librarian, Ms. Farber. She retrieved an envelope, and so excited about sending something to Israel, she offered to post it for me, too.

CHAPTER TWENTY

Hamburglars

5.27.3.13.38.35.20.158-13.38.6-20.5.2-2.13.17.20.5

I gave my letter a week to get to Dr. Rips in Israel and another week for him to send a response. The following two weeks after those first two, I left the library early, rushing home every day in the hope of finding a response before Pigpie did. I took the 12:20 p.m. bus, knowing from last summer that mail delivery always occurred between 1:00 p.m. and 1:37 p.m. I didn't know what she would think if she read a letter containing the information I hoped for, but I couldn't chance she'd be in a snit that day and drop it in the trash without my knowledge.

During those weeks, I also begged Bergit regularly to help me obtain more computer time. She always had an excuse and Dr. Kohn was always too busy after his lectures with other matters to accompany or arrange it for me. Nothing went my way. Every day I planned to visit Kate, it rained. Russell still hadn't contacted me, and no sign of him surfaced the few times I went past his house. Not to mention living with Pigpie alone was what I'd imagine sleeping with fire ants would be like. She exhausted me with her tireless verbal pinching. Every room of the house shone with my elbow grease except for the couch area, where Pigpie spread plenty of grease of her own. All of Shelly's chores became mine and, according to Pigpie, I never did them as well. Coming home early each day to appease Pigpie only extended my lists of things to do. By the time she let me go to my room to study or read, I often felt too tired to accomplish much of anything.

I arrived home on the day before Thanksgiving to find Pigpie sitting at the kitchen table eating cranberry sauce from a can. I deposited the mail on the counter in its proper location and started to go visit with Mister Scratch when Pigpie cleared her throat.

"You don't know how to say hello when you walk in a room? I know your upbringing was pathetic, but if I teach you anything around here, it'll be manners." She was blind to the incongruity of her statement as she slopped more cranberry sauce out of the can. A portion of it made it to her mouth, but the dollop that didn't joined a few others on the floor.

"Get the mop. I haven't seen you clean the kitchen this week." She took the cranberry sauce and returned to her nest on the couch.

On my way to the basement stairs for the bottle of Mop'N'Glow, the phone started ringing.

"Get that!" Pigpie screamed from the other room.

"Hello?"

"This is Officer Chapman. Is your mother home?"

"My aunt."

"Sorry?"

"Aunt Cecelia, Officer Chapman." I held out the phone.

Pigpie hastened to the kitchen, leaving one of her gray-pink slippers in the other room. She looked at me questioningly with condemnation, angry that the officer was calling about something I'd done, I guessed.

"Yes?" Pigpie said into the receiver, wiping her mouth on her robe as she listened. "You did? When? Well, why wasn't I called? It's been a month. No, no, that's OK. I'll come right ov—yes, that's our address. Fine. Yes. Thank you, officer." She hung up the phone and looked around the kitchen, slapping her bare foot against the linoleum. "We might have fifteen minutes. Get your ass moving. I want this place sparkling." She turned and went as fast as her legs could carry her up the stairs.

I continued cleaning the kitchen. I did a rush job, but I knew her couch sty would need more focus. I shoved as much as I could under the couch and was fluffing pillows when Pigpie came down the stairs and stopped to examine her face in the front hall mirror. She had a compact and was smearing makeup over some moles when the lights from the police car flickered through the front window. Pigpie put her finger to her mouth to hush me and waved me out of the TV room. I went to the end of the hall by the kitchen to watch.

Pigpie started wailing when Shelly came through the doorway wearing her glassless glasses. "Oh, my sweetness. Oh, my sweetness," she wept and tried to hug Shelly. Shelly's pregnant belly looked obvious now, and I feared for the baby as Pigpie's girth bumped up against her.

"Thank you, officer, thank you." She released Shelly and went to shake the officer's hand and didn't let go for a painfully long time. "Can-can we have the lights turned off on the car?"

"It's police regulations, Mrs. Stacks, sorry. May I speak to you alone for a minute?"

They moved into the TV room, and Shelly came toward me and into the kitchen.

"Hey, cuz, what's going on?" She seemed so unaffected by it all, as if she hadn't been gone for a month.

"Hi, Shelly. You missed—your birthday was on the twelfth. It is a fact: You are eight hundred and eighty-eight weeks old this week." Her chin and neck looked thicker than they did before.

"Ew, you make me sound ancient. I only turned seventeen. Shhh, I want to listen." She pushed her hair over her ears.

We moved behind the wall to where we could hear them but they couldn't see us.

"And you all know how many times I've called looking for her. Why would I kick her out and then look for her?"

"I'm very sorry, Mrs. Stacks, but that's what was reported. I can see you're upset and happy to have her home, but the social worker will still need to visit next Tuesday. They'll call to arrange the exact time."

"I don't need anyone messing into our personal affairs. Can't you see we've been through enough?"

"Sorry, ma'am, I'm not the one in charge. I'm just here to return Shelly into your care and inform you of what's been arranged."

"OK, but if I'm not fine, then I'll have to get some legal ramifications started. And I won't pay for a lawyer. If it comes down to it, your station will be paying for it. I've seen my rights on TV."

"That's OK, Mrs. Stacks, I understand. Can I see Shelly and your son before I leave?"

"You mean my nephew. You can see Shelly. Shelly! Come in here."

I walked in the room behind Shelly, and Pigpie gave me her squinty evil eye.

"The officer wants to see you and then he's leaving." Pigpie folded her arms and packed a fierce pout onto her lips.

"Shelly, you know what we discussed. You can call whenever you like. It's Adam, right?" the officer said, looking down at me. A gun resting in a holster on his hip prevented my lips from moving.

"His name's Abel," Shelly offered.

"Sorry, Abel. Shelly has my number, and if you want to call me, you just get her to help you with the phone, OK?"

I nodded my head, wondering why he thought I couldn't work the phone on my own. He said his good-byes and once the car pulled away, Shelly went into the kitchen. I followed behind Pigpie.

"Where's the turkey at? StopNShops probably sold out by now. I can't believe we won't be having a turkey. Tomorrow's Thanksgiving, for Chrissake." Shelly slammed the freezer door shut.

Pigpie's face briefly wore a confused look before her anger puffed out as if she were a corn kernel in the high heat of the air popper. Her little finger quivered at her hip. Then —*bang!*

"How about..." *Slap. Quiver.* "... starting with where the hell you've been? How about starting with how sorry you are, or what the hell..." *Slap. Quiver.* "... you've told the police? I've been worried sick..." *Slap. Quiver.* "... just sick. I could barely sleep or eat, and I'm probably going to have to see a doctor."

"Oh, give me a break." Shelly opened the Wonder Bread bag. "Nothing stops you from eating. Maybe if you bought a goddamn Jane Fonda tape, slapping me around wouldn't have been your only exercise."

Pigpie flinched when Shelly said *goddamn* and started toward her.

"Just keep your ass away from me. I'm pregnant and the police know it, and you have to take care of me, even though I'm not going back to school. And if you don't, my social worker will put your ass in jail. I told you. I told you I would, so you better listen to me." Shelly slammed the mayonnaise lid on the counter and started spreading generous amounts of it on her bread.

Pigpie could barely control herself. She paced over to the table and smashed the bowl with the last two bananas in it against the back door. Mister Scratch started barking from next door.

"Don't push me!" *Slap. Quiver.* "Because if you push me too far, you'll find yourself very GD sorry." *Slap. Quiver.*

Shelly shoved the mayonnaise sandwich in her mouth, smiling at Pigpie with her mouth open full of white goo.

"I raised you better than that. I deserve better. Every night I sit here, worried sick, and if you want to eat mayo sandwiches until you're fat and ugly, you go right ahead. But I won't be taking care of that thing inside you. You better believe that right now."

"Yes, you will."

"No, I will not. You want to talk to social workers? Well, I can, too, and I know they have homes for young mothers, and you better GD believe that you'll be living with them, not me."

Shelly tried to seem unconcerned while Pigpie ranted, but I could see she was worried. Shelly looked at the clock.

"I'm watching *Gilligan's Island*, and . . . because my baby and I need to be comforted and calm after all this." She grabbed a Pepsi from the refrigerator and sat on the chair next to the couch, leaving Pigpie and me alone in the kitchen.

"Clean that up!" She pointed at Shelly's mayo jar and dirtied knife. "And you didn't clean this floor like I wanted. You think the officer didn't notice? He thinks you're a pig. Nobody cares about pigs, so get to it and then get upstairs." She pinched my arm as hard as she could, walked into the living room, changed the channel, and slammed her body into the couch. As I rubbed my arm, Laverne De Fazio groused at Squiggy with her New York City accent on the TV. Pigpie and Shelly started fighting about the merits of *Laverne & Shirley* versus *Gilligan's Island*. I made myself a PB and J sandwich before I put the bread away and finished recleaning the kitchen.

The only thing I felt thankful for on Thanksgiving Day was that no one spoke to anyone, except for the brief time Pigpie gave me chores. Well, Shelly actually said, "Happy Thanksgiving" when she handed me a triple rectangle of the Ellio's pizza she'd baked us for dinner.

The following morning I was working on another computer program when Shelly bounced into my room.

"You're coming shopping with me. It's Black Friday, and we have to go to the mall." She had on a framing outfit to show off her condition: black tights, a T-shirt that barely fit over her belly, and an unbuttoned red-and-black flannel shirt with the sleeves rolled up.

I grabbed my winter vest and my satchel, excited by the thought of getting out of the house before Pigpie could give me something to do. Shelly took the keys to Pigpie's car rather than her own. I knew this wasn't a good idea but also that there wasn't much I could say to stop her. Until we moved beyond that first stop sign, I kept expecting Pigpie to come rushing out to tell us to get out of her car. Shelly turned the radio on, laughed at what she found, and sang along to the Carpenter's "Sittin' on Top of the World." As we passed a bar, I noticed the neon signs lit.

"Did you—did you know that it is a fact in 1977, James Colburn was paid five hundred thousand dollars for saying two words in a commercial for Schlitz Light? Two hundred fifty thousand dollars for saying *Schlitz*, and two hundred fifty thousand dollars for saying *Light*."

"You got any money?" Shelly asked, apparently unimpressed.

"Yup. Two dollars and seventy-three cents."

"Good. You can buy us something to eat when we get there. I'll pay you back, don't worry."

We sat in the mall parking lot for a few minutes, waiting for the doors to open at 10:00 a.m. As it was Black Friday, we weren't the only ones.

While we waited to add my $2.73 to the retailers' GNP, I thought of Pigpie waking to an empty house and to her car missing. I thought of the possibility we'd arrive home to the police waiting for us. When the doors opened, I thought for sure Shelly would trot inside, but she sat in the car and watched the others rush toward the entrance.

"We'll give them fifteen minutes," she said, not explaining who "them" were exactly. I couldn't believe it after twenty minutes had passed, she still hadn't directed us out of the car.

Three coats of lip gloss and several hair flips later, she huffed and we got out. We headed straight to the McDonald's counter where Shelly started wading through her huge purse, pretending to the greasy-cheeked guy at the register that she'd pay, but then she turned to me. I reviewed her order and knew my cash wasn't enough for both of us to eat, so I handed over what I had. She asked for a receipt in a flirtatious manner, but the cashier simply pointed to the slip on her tray. She snatched it up with a bit of pomposity and shoved it in her purse.

Even though the fried-food smells entreated loud gurgling from my stomach, I wasn't hungry yet, so it didn't bother me to wait while she slowly ate her Egg McMuffin. Her eyes danced behind the black rims, spying—I imagined for "them" or anyone she might know. I watched a little boy who wore a black baseball cap on backward spin his french fries before he ate them. He spun each one, and I wondered if it was to cool them off or just something he liked to do. Three fries spun, one bite of cheeseburger; two fries spun, two bites of cheeseburger. I followed the pattern, but it was random. The kid had no plan, and just as Shelly finished, I wondered how it was he got the fries at all. A quick glance at my watch revealed they'd have started serving lunch seven minutes ago. Ronald's cardboard cutout, topped festively with a Santa's hat, induced Shelly to bump into him as he waved good-bye with his ridiculous maniacal grin. He fell flat, and we commenced with our store-to-store trek.

    The walkways of the mall were packed with wild-eyed shoppers eager to purchase their loved ones holiday gifts. We made our first stop at Jake's Jewels. Shelly held an unnatural look on her face. It looked something like the nurses used before they took blood. At the second store, I had a better idea of Shelly's no-money-in-her-purse weird-face plan. She smiled at the jar of body butter she held in the air with her left hand and placed another from the shelf into her open purse with her right as the clerk rounded the corner and happily asked if we needed any help. She gruffly said no and marched past him as if he'd offended her by asking. Every store from then on out, she'd relocate something so masterfully I began totaling her bounty. After one complete round of the top level, the items I could price came to $283.12, not including sales tax. If it were me, I'd be rejoicing at my haul, but she grew more belligerent with each store, commenting on how there was nothing worthwhile in any of them or how "shoddy" the holiday décor looked. While we descended the escalator, Shelly's demeanor shifted as she quickly flipped her flannel shirt open wide with a proud grin on her face.

    "Hi, Maryanne!" she squealed at a girl riding up with her mother. Maryanne's face didn't register that she knew Shelly, but she smiled when she passed. "Bitch, she could've at least said happy holidays to me. We had, like, two classes together."

    After we'd visited nearly every store, Shelly took me back to Jake's Jewels. I grew extremely restless as we stood outside the store while Shelly rifled through her purse, looking for something. Just as I opened my mouth to say I'd meet her later at the Dream Machine arcade, she said, "Don't open your mouth unless I ask you a specific question. Got it?" We waited in line and finally got to the counter, where I stood beside her.

"Hi. I'd like to, um, return this. I bought it here last week." She took a boxed necklace from her purse and placed it by the register.

"I'll need a receipt, miss." said a gentleman with a nametag that read, *Ask me for help: Mark.*

Shelly started going through her purse. "Oh, no problem. It's in here somewhere." A line of people developed behind us, and Mark gave me a "come on already" look. The heat in my cheeks raised a few degrees.

"Miss, if you'd step aside, maybe I could help some other customers while you locate it."

"Hold on a minute. I came in earlier, but it was too busy then, too. Just . . . it's here." Shelly kept digging, and after another painful thirty seconds, she pulled a crumbled ball of paper out. "Here you go. Sorry about that."

Mark unwrinkled the ball. "This is for McDonald's, miss." He shoved it back at her.

Shelly lifted up the box. "Well, look, right here it says your store's name and that it costed $27.99." She turned to rub and hold her pregnant belly. "Ooh, it's moving. He must be hungry."

Mark looked at her stomach and then at the price tag and finally at the crowd behind her. He started tapping on the register. I almost couldn't believe it when he pulled the cash out and handed it to her. She smiled at him with a warmth that made me almost believe she'd purchased it there and felt sad she had to take the money back. She topped off her thank you with an overly enthused, "Happy Holidays."

Shelly said nothing to me except to remind me to keep quiet, as the Jake's Jewels routine replayed in other minor variations at every store we'd been to. It even worked for the $3.49 body butter at Spencer's. She'd skip stores that looked too empty, and some of them would only give her a store credit. With four hundred and twenty-one dollars and eighteen cents weighing down her purse, Shelly was full of holiday spirit as we returned to McDonald's. After ordering herself a Big Mac, large fries, large chocolate shake, and an apple pie, she said, "Go ahead, get anything you like. I told you I'd pay you back."

While I ate my cheeseburger, I imagined myself dressed in black-and-white prison stripes as the Hamburgler.

"Here." She handed me a twenty-dollar bill. Only once before had I been given that much money. My second foster family, the Jeffersons, gave it to me on my tenth birthday. Two days later, they told me I'd be living with a new family. The Chungs lived closer to the library, anyway.

I wasn't sure what caused my upset stomach: the cheeseburger I'd wolfed down or the guilty twenty in my pocket.

"Don't say a word to anyone," she commanded with narrowed eyes as we left.

We stopped at the Hallmark store on the way out and bought three boxes of chocolates, then at the For Eyes store to buy a pair of fancy designer reading glasses. In the car, Shelly said the chocolates would shut Pigpie up for "like, a week" and directed me to pop the lenses out of the new frames. The old ones came off her face and hit the shoulder of the road as we sped home.

CHAPTER TWENTY-ONE

A Breath of Fresh Air

1.19-17.2.12.1-7.1-17.12.9-33.3.56.19.35.3

The genius Isaac Newton was so small at birth, he could have easily fit inside a cereal bowl. He was born to a family of farmers on December 25, 1642, Christmas Day. Due to the date of his premature arrival, some saw Newton as the second coming of Christ. Secularists who commemorate his birth instead of Jesus's call this date Newtonmas Day, which they celebrate by decorating an apple tree and giving gifts of knowledge. To be fair to those who champion the Gregorian calendar (which we all do, for the most part), Newton's birthdate could be considered January 4, 1642, but why quibble about the use of the Julian calendar they consulted? Jesus's birthdate cannot accurately be established, either.

    I've considered celebrating Newtonmas instead of Jesus's birth. Jesus left only speculation on his actual words until four others wrote their versions of his truth in the gospels, forty years after his death. Forty years of desert-sand-filled ears playing whisper down the lane might have smoothed out the rough edges of his preaching and life's story. His rough edges may be similar to the one Newton confessed to: threatening to burn his mother and stepfather alive in their house. Pyromania and matricidal tendencies aside, Newton left us with plenty to know him by, and although he was a bit kooky about some things, he left two written works that make him especially worthy of worship. The first is one of the greatest scientific books ever written, *the Philosophiae Naturalis Principia Mathematica,* or *Principia* for short. It became the first book to describe the Laws of Motion, the Laws of Universal Gravitation, and the Motions of the Planets. *Optiks* is Newton's second major work. It didn't bring light as God is claimed to have done, or Jesus professed to be, but instead delivered to mankind an understanding of the nature of light. Light is one of the basic necessities of life. Because of Newton, we also know why there are rainbows, which are one of my favorite things.

I bring up Isaac Newton not only because his biography was on my required-reading list from Dr. Langdeer, not only to point out his supernatural genius, and definitely not because I wanted to remain a virgin as Jesus and Newton supposedly did, but to praise him for spending twenty years developing notions about celestial motion, gravity, and light. If he could focus that long to put out two books on the scientific nature of God's creations, why couldn't I spend six months working on a computer program to figure out the nature of the algorithm of Pierson's Bible numbers? Unfortunately, I'm no Newton and am limited by my brief one-hour-a-week access to a computer. By the middle of March, I felt no closer to knowing what the Pierson numbers meant than I had since the Hell Night revelations. I still felt focused, but truth be told, I was growing a little bored with it all.

I can't blame Pigpie, either, unfortunately. Since her meeting with the social worker after Thanksgiving, Pigpie had become oddly robotic and less of a roadblock in my life. The past couple of months had been the most peaceful around the house since I first moved in. During February, I overheard Pigpie coolly whispering on the phone with Father Mullens three times. I waited for the announcement of my next money-generating performance, but it never came. She went about her days with very little yelling, less torturing, but increasing my allotment of chores as Shelly's expanding belly gave her an excuse to opt out. Shelly mostly ruled the house now, and Pigpie toed the line.

"Who watches that dog from next door?" Shelly asked accusatorily during breakfast. "I'd never have my baby around such a smelly dog. I think we should put up a fence."

Pigpie diverted Shelly's attention away from the fight Shelly sought.

"I'm having Father Mullens over today. Would you like to join us for his visit, or did you have some shopping you'd like to do?"

"How much?"

We paused, waiting for more from Shelly.

"How much what?" Pigpie finally asked.

"Don't act dumb. How much are you going to give me to shop with? It's freezing out, so I may need more for cocoa or something."

"Don't worry now. You let me know what you want to buy and I'll give you enough, but I'm not made of money, you know."

Pigpie again diverted the tension and turned to me. "Are you still interested in working at the garage on Livingston?"

I didn't know how to react. A trap felt like it was closing on me. I found it hard to believe she remembered Hank's offer.

"It'd be good for you to learn a trade so you don't turn into some kind of criminal. Be nice if you could help pay for things around here, too."

Instead of getting a job with Hank, why not arrange for more exhibitions of my talents? Maybe she wanted the funds from both.

"Run down there today and talk to them about it. Remind that man Hank that he already offered."

I nodded in agreement but felt nervous, a combination of Pigpie's potential trap and the worry you feel when you haven't seen friends for a while and wonder if you're still friends. Months had passed since I'd last visited Hank, Mi, and Will. I tried procrastinating by filling in the conversation formulae in my journal and checking the Rosens' yard for piles Biggs had recently deposited. Lucky for me, Biggs's deliveries were wet and bountiful. The long way around to the garage gave me time to enjoy the scent and for it to wear off my soles so Hank wouldn't be upset about "stinkin' up his joint."

At the top of Hermann Road, I watched for brown remnants stuck from my Bobos in the small piles of melting snow I left footprints in and took note of the gradual sloping of the land toward the lake. One year ago today—March 26, 1982—was the day I found that mother carp with the tiny mound of what I first thought were a strange collection of bubbles but turned out to be eggs. With the weather so perfect today, I bet I'd find another. I hiked to the lake, and all of nature welcomed me back. Who could question the day's perfection when I not only made four frogs jump in, disturbed a family of mallards—the six ducklings waddled *plunk, plunk, plunk* into the lake—but also saw a rather large water moccasin slither under a fallen cedar?

I found Russell's bike dumped on the ground at the trees that marked the beginning of Mank's creek. It showed no rusting or damage, which I was happy about, as part of me felt responsible for it, but the radio that always adorned the back was no longer attached. Its absence made the bike a little less exciting. I set it against a trunk in plain sight and started along the stone path. There were more minnows than I'd ever seen on one visit. Spastically, they'd dart away from the sides of each rock I landed on. I'd counted thirty-two by the time I reached the shortcut to view the tree fort. From the creek, I could see blackened limbs where the fort should be. I decided on a closer inspection and was shocked when I discovered the scorched remains.

A burned husk of the tree stood empty with fallen black limbs stabbed into the earth around it. I walked about the wreckage envisioning what the scene may have looked like as it took place. A tipped-over can of lighter fluid resting on top of one of the old paint cans gave proof of foul play. I'd have loved to witness the Kevins finding it in ashes.

When I returned to the creek, I noticed a figure crouched with a long stick near the wide patch of pebbles where, if you stayed on the creek's rock path, was a good place to rest without fear of falling in. I recognized him immediately. Russell's black disheveled hair and my earlier bike discovery made it easy. He looked at me and started waving in a friendly fashion.

"Hey, Apple! Hey! Hurry up. Here's turtles! Shhh!"

Here Russell was, acting as if nothing had happened, as if he hadn't been away from me for months, but something appeared odd about him. His eyes were just slightly mismatched. It couldn't be strabismus and must have been residual from the fight. Russell used a stick, trying to pull in three baby turtles that swam in the deeper part of the creek.

"Hey-hey Russell. You found four painted turtles."

"Yeah. Now, shhh and go get a stick and help me."

I found a long stick in the weeds that had a rake-like end. With it, I easily pulled one of the little guys in.

"Ooh, that's it. It's mine, you know," he said as I brought it within reach.

"It is a fact: Turtles can breathe through their anus," I said, trying to bring back some of the old fun. I'd told him last year, but I figured he'd have forgotten. My comment elicited no response as he was busy poking the turtle to coax it from its shell.

"It is also a fact: Dragonfly nymphs can breathe through their anus, but you-but you rarely see them."

After a bit more poking at the turtle and a short delay, Russell started laughing hysterically. I couldn't be certain he laughed at anything I'd said. He kept laughing and placed the wiggling turtle away from the water to watch it scramble to join its siblings again.

"What's so funny?" I finally asked.

He stuck out his hand. "Money talks. Bullshit walks."

I didn't understand him exactly, but I pulled out a dollar from my satchel and handed it over. I figured it was the least I could give, seeing as I'd used his bike so much. When the dollar was in his pocket, he put his fingers to his temples and squinted at me. I had no clue and so just shrugged my shoulders. He finally said with mild exasperation, "I was trying to tell you, wonder what his breath smells like when he yawns." He started laughing again, picked up the turtle, and threw it up in the air, almost dropping it. "Hey, get another so we can both have one."

I'd have laughed at his turtle-breath comment if it hadn't surprised me to hear something creative come from his mouth. A real shocker. I started trying to catch another with the branch, but they were too far over on the other bank now. The trees from that side prevented me from gaining access. I'd gone to get a stone to perch on to extend my reach when Russell began shouting.

"No, no, no, no, no!" he howled with his face crumbling, as if he'd start crying.

I looked at his hands. In one were the broken remains of the shell, and in the other the head of the baby turtle.

"I wanted to see if you were right." He looked at me as if I could fix it, and when he saw my horror, he smashed it down on the rocks, wiped his hands on his pants, and laughed another weird laugh. "Come on, let's hike up to the stew-of-poo."

I hesitated a moment before I stepped over the turtle carcass and followed him. He'd smashed crayfish before, but he blamed his violence on their pinching him. Plus, crayfish were like smashing insects, so it only mildly bothered me. I loved turtles, though, and began wishing I went straight to the garage.

About three-quarters of the way to the sewage plant, I noticed Russell's hair only somewhat growing over a long scar that traveled from his neck toward the top of his skull.

"You-you're out of the hospital?" I asked as he jumped a few rocks ahead of me.

"Hospital? I haven't been in the hospital since months ago. I go to a new school now. I stay there and sleep there. I'm going back in, uh, pretty soon. After Easter."

"Oh!" was all I managed.

"Didja hear what I did to the Kevins' fort? Bet they all had a big shitfit. Man, that day was crazy, huh? I remember waitin'!"—Russell suddenly shouted, then returned to a normal speaking voice—"for you at the house and them all chasing me, but not much else besides going home from the hospital. Did you get any cool scars like me?"

He stretched his shirt's collar to reveal another one, a bright-fuchsia line tracing along his shoulder. He turned to draw back more hair to show the one I'd already seen. "We burned it up when I came home at Christmas. Man, it was so great. With the snow so deep, you could jump off the platform and not even get hurt. Tim and I screamed at the flames, but you know, we had to run because of how high they went. Tim said it was the best revenge I could get, but Tim's kind of retarded, really, because kicking their asses would be better."

Russell expounded excessively about the revenge until I finally tuned him out as we came to the widest and deepest section of the creek. I imagined I was walking over liquid copper as the light hit the surface and danced on the orange-brown sediments at the bottom. We climbed to the large boulders and stood in the middle as we'd done so many times before. The melted snow and recent rains brought the water all the way up to the grassy borders of the creek, but the level of the land must've had the proper equilibrium to slow the water down because the small sticks we threw floated incredibly slowly toward us along with the wisps of oil slick. I was pleased when my stick tapped along the thin, green ring of algae on my boulder instead of Russell's.

An odd shadowy mass shifted in the water over on the other side where the smaller boulders made an arc. At first, I'd hoped for a giant snapping turtle, but when I arrived at the end of the arc, I found something better, a tadpole swarm the size of a schoolroom globe. They hypnotized me. I tried to count them, but their motion would only allow a good estimation. I figured between seventy-nine and eighty-six. Something in their undulations made me think about the program I'd been working on for the Pierson Bible. I'd devised a loop grid, but its uniformity kept diverting me from the randomness I needed to address. They folded back on one another and swarmed in the way you sometimes see swallows fly in synchronized motion.

"What'cha find?" Russell asked as he joined me on my smallish boulder. "Wow. Lookit them all." He modulated his voice oddly again, almost sounding angry this time.

Complex computations are like fireworks if I close my eyes and focus on the light and form numbers take during my brain's toiling. If I focus too closely on the fireworks and then open my eyes, time feels as if it's slowing to an incalculable velocity, nearly stopping. There wasn't enough room for us both on the boulder, and as Russell tried to use me for balance, I began to lose my own. I hovered above the tadpole cloud; the instant slowed in the same manner as focusing on number fireworks. The tadpoles turned glacial, a gathering of commas. I tallied eighty-one and fell face-first into them. My mouth opened as I reached the water and the foul creek flowed in. Little tails wiggled in my throat as I swallowed and came up for air, coughing and splashing.

I couldn't see since my glasses had water drops all over them, but a warped Russell jumped to a larger rock and extended his hand to help. I waded over and slid out of the freezing water and onto the rock. "Hey, Apple. You. Are. Craaazy. Did you catch any? I almost fell in with you," he said with sincerity and blame.

The wiggling continued in my stomach, but as I coughed up water, nothing swam out. I didn't know if he'd pushed me in exactly. I didn't feel a push, only an arm around my back. I wanted to yell at him, anyway.

"We better start back to my bike now." Russell nervously eyed my dripping sweat jacket and watched as I wiped my glasses and wrung out my sleeves.

Somewhat angry, I hung back and checked to see if the contents of my satchel were dry; gladly, they were. Even when Russell was seven yards distant, I knew he'd thought we were still hanging out. It was no surprise I found him waiting for me by his bike. I did feel rather miserable, so I accepted the ride he offered, figuring it could be his reparation. The air chilled me more, and I couldn't believe how much warmer I felt just by stopping at an intersection to wait for traffic.

"Hey, have you been to the Soap-N-Spin yet? Oh, my God, I almost got my initials on Joust yesterday. We could play doubles. Wanna go?"

I couldn't believe it.

"No," I said, wanting to punch him in the back. I wasn't sure what angered me more: the turtle torturing, not hearing from him for months, not knowing if he'd purposefully soaked me, or that I'd kept away from the arcade for nothing.

"No? Yeah, I don't have any money, either."

Liar, I just gave him a dollar. The hill slopped down

toward the bridge to Milltown or up toward the center of North Brunswick. It pleased me to see our intended path to the center would force him to go more slowly.

"Hey, Apple, this is great, right? Like olden days."

"I'm w-wet."

"Yeah, I know, but how about we head this way? It's perfect weather for a ride."

CHAPTER TWENTY-TWO

The Price of Babylonian Blood

36.23-53.5.3.2.70-12.3.14.10.12.47-34.9.3.2-7.47-9.36.12.17.1

Russell started down the hill toward Milltown. I knew he also chose this detour because he could coast down instead of pedaling up and would probably ask me to ride us back. If we hadn't already picked up too much speed, I would've jumped off.

He sang *Billie Jean* loudly and so off-key, birds flew from nearby trees. "I called Tim, and I told him he had to hear it. I put the phone right up to the radio. Man, I love that song. Tim said 'Rock With You' is better, but cooome on, but he thinks Martha Quinn's so hot. So what does he know? You think Nina's hotter than Martha, right?"

He sounded like Mom when she'd come home stoned, rambling on about nothing anyone cared about. I tried to ignore him by counting my drips as they created a dotted line behind us.

"Hey, turn, turn here," I said when we came to Broad Street.

"Here?" He didn't listen to me and kept going straight. "Nothing looked good down that one."

He didn't know about Kate yet.

"Here, how 'bout here?" he said, turning toward the Speedway tavern and Tig's junkyard.

Even in my state, I was excited to be back. I held on until he slowed near the abandoned gas station, where I hopped off.

"Waait, what're you doing?" he shouted nervously from a few yards ahead while braking.

I walked behind the piled tires and peered over at the tavern, trying to forget about Russell. Huddling up close to the tires for warmth didn't help with my chill. Russell rode over. I would watch for Kate, and if she didn't show in a short time, I would go in the tavern and call Hank. He parked the bike and joined me.

"Hey, cool, we could make a great fort outta this place." He went over and tried the locked door of the station while I located some fresh scallion greens to smell. She'd probably forgotten me by now.

"We could break the lock—hey, what're you starin' at?" He joined me again and looked through at the tavern.

I didn't know how to express that I wanted him to leave. He leaned too hard on the tires, so I backed up in case they toppled. Two guys about our age rode their bikes behind the building where Kate went to the party with that guy. The sum rose to nine bikes when they dumped theirs with the others on the side of the building.

"I see. Wow, something's going on, huh?" Russell wiped his mouth on his sleeve. "What're we hiding out here for? Come on, maybe they found puppies!"

Admittedly, I was curious, but I knew I should go into the Speedway or hike over to Gary's Subs and call Hank. Russell mounted his bike and waited for me to climb on. I tried recalling what initially made me want to be friends with him.

"Come on already," Russell insisted.

I got on.

No one guarded the bikes parked next to the side of the building, but we left Russell's with them, anyway. As we turned the corner, we discovered a small crowd of eight guys clustered behind a juniper hedge and staring at two others that stood close to the back of the building. The two peered into what must've been holes. We heard a little whistle, and one of the guys waved us over behind the hedge. The whistler met us as we squeezed through. They all looked older, around fifteen maybe.

"Two bucks each," he said, holding a roll of bills in his hand.

He had hair starting to grow on his upper lip and chin and a cigarette box bulging from his front pocket. His face was also tremendously flat, as if someone hit him with a shovel.

"Two bucks for what?" Russell asked.

"You pay me, I pay them for you to watch for five minutes. No guarantees, though."

"Hey, Abel," a voice called from the front of the line. Phillip Macklehorn. "I'm still after him," he told the guy behind him and came over to us.

"Geez, I wouldn't have thought Jerry would've sold it to you. He seemed real pissed and said I wasn't allow to tell anyone about this place, right, Alfie?" Although somewhat incredulous, Phillip appeared glad to see me.

"You know these kids?" Alfie asked, annoyed and obviously not on friendly terms with Phillip.

"Uh, yeah, sort of. I know him, anyway."

"Can they be trusted, or should I get rid of 'em?"

"I don't know. He's like a genius or something, but I don't buy it. They say he goes to Princeton. Geez, look at him, though. Kid's not even smart enough to wear dry clothes."

"He is too a genius," Russell said, coming to my defense. "Show 'em, Abel. He can practically *read* minds."

Numbers buzzed at my peripheral vision. My stomach felt queasy, and I wasn't sure if it was their stares or something else. Each of the eighteen eyes, including Russell's two, was trained on me now. Many of them familiar faces I'd known from the high school. The temperature of my neck and chin rose, and when it hit my cheeks, I looked down at the state of my sneakers—not a bit of brown left on the sides.

"You gotta ask him something," Russell explained nervously, a small glob of his mouth spittle bubbled up in a drippy clump.

They kept staring at me, mute and irritated, until one of the guys at the wall slunk away from his five minutes and ran around to the bikes. Gouged into the side of the building, the hole looked like one of the cuts coated with engine oil I'd seen on Will's war-pocked arm.

"All right, go. You're next," he said to the kid with a *Disco Sucks* T-shirt. Disco Sucks kept looking at me and finally asked, "What's infinity divided by infinity?"

I felt woozy and put my hands on my hips to steady myself. Oversized pink erasers rubbed and dusted away their heads while tails flicked at the walls of my stomach.

"Come on, Apple, tell him," Russell urged.

The earth and sky were blending, tilting toward an unnatural point until I found my mouth forming a Newtonmas gift for them. "What's, uh, anus divided by air? It's not a number," I said with great futility, knowing they wouldn't comprehend any present of wisdom. Infinity isn't a number, so asking what you'd get if you divided it by itself is as ridiculous as asking what you'd get if you divided anus by air.

"Hey, yeah, he just told me all about how turtles can breathe out their asses. That's genius, right? Bet you didn't know that," Russell said to Disco Sucks, but DS shook his head in disgust and went to take his turn.

"You got the cash or not?" Alfie asked, smacking the green wad in his palm.

Russell pressed me with his squinting eyes to do something else, but I resisted.

"I don't get it. What do we get to see?" he asked, giving up on me.

"Who sent you?" Alfie asked, obviously aggravated.

"Nobody. We just came over to see what was going on, so what is it?" Russell made a big show of pulling a cigarette out of a soft pack he retrieved from his jacket pocket. He stuck one behind his ear and put the pack away.

"Maybe nothing, but maybe you get to see a woman getting sex. Sometimes they take off their clothes before they turn the light out. Sometimes they leave the light on. But hey, two bucks, and you take a chance. If it's dark for the five minutes, there's no refunds." He looked at his watch and shouted, "Crap! Hey, kid, you've got two minutes left with the blonde, and you, yeah, you're done." The kid took a last peek and rejoined the line. Alfie turned and swatted Phillip's arm. "You're next."

"But I was waiting for the blonde," Phillip said, rubbing his arm.

"Go or lose your turn," Alfie said.

Phillip turned to me with anger. "If Jerry finds out you were here, you better not mention my name. I never said anything, anyway." Phillip squeezed through the hedge and ran quickly to the open hole.

"What about the door? Looks like someone could catch us from that door," Russell asked.

A dirty white door was closed about three yards from the holes.

"Nobody's comin' to catch anybody," Alfie said with irritation.

Russell looked at me for some kind of help.

"OK, but, when are we allowed to come? I can get some money, but I only have a dollar now," Russell said, making a show of fingering the cigarette at his ear.

"Someone's usually here, but if not, all I can say is you better watch out because the owners don't like giving freebies." He pointed up at a window on the top floor.

"Plus, it sounds like Jerry don't want you here, but that's not my problem."

We stood for a minute, watching them peering through the hedge and the hole. Alfie shouted, "Time!" and Russell tugged me to follow him as Phillip began his turn.

Russell finally lit his cigarette. "So, if we ride fast and get some cash, do you think we could make it back today?"

I didn't respond, feeling a little sick to my stomach, and mostly wanting to get out of the wet clothes.

"Don't tell me you're going to chicken out. Oh, come on." We'd arrived at the bikes. Russell picked his up and swung his leg over the bar between the seat and the handlebar. He took a long drag on his cigarette and blew it out his nose. It looked painful, not cool as I knew he intended. "Fine, don't. I'll just get Tim to go with me when he comes." He threw his barely smoked cigarette toward the bike pile and stood there gaping at me. After a short wait, he finally asked, "Are you getting on or not?"

I looked at his pinched face, at those massive eyebrows, and felt no fondness for this individual any longer. I started walking toward the Speedway to call Hank.

"Oh, my gosh, you are the biggest chicken. You're not going in there. I know you're not." Russell rode his bike to the front of the tavern and waited for me.

"Chicken! Bawk, bawk. You are the biggest chicken, Apple. If you don't come with me now, you can forget it."

I stood on the front porch of the tavern and looked down at him.

"Bawk! Bawk! Bawk! Go ahead, go in there if you're going."

My nerves were tight, but I opened the door, and a weird bearded guy came walking out. He appeared as startled as I felt. I looked over at Russell, and he pedaled quickly away.

"Why, thank you, sir," the bearded guy said to me in a slurred voice.

He started fumbling in his pocket, and Russell's bawking started up as soon as he was at a safe distance. The bearded guy pulled his pocket inside out, emptying some change and trash onto the ground. "There's a tip for you," he said and climbed down the stairs and away. It looked like nothing, but I saw a crumpled dollar bill, forty-six cents in change, plus a matchbook wrapper and possibly a tissue or napkin balled up tightly. I let the door close and looked for Russell, who was out of sight now. The bearded guy was a good distance down the sidewalk, but I waited until he turned a corner before retrieving his tip. With excitement, I unrolled what I assumed was a dollar. It turned out to be a five.

I wanted to wave the bounty in Russell's face. I was no chicken, and now I was rich. He could go with Tim to the arcade all he wanted. I kept hearing his bawking even though he was long gone, and I decided I'd be first. I'd be the first to look through the peephole, and I'd tell him so next time I saw him.

I marched right back over to flat-faced Alfie and without saying anything handed him my five. He laughed through his nose. "You sure you want to?"

I nodded, and he gave me back three dollars.

"You get five minutes. Tell anyone, and your ass is grass, got it?"

I nodded and stood in line. Phillip had already left, but there were still four other guys in line ahead of me. Disco Sucks lurked at the front of the line, and he glowered back at me a couple of times before he ran for another peep. I waited nervously with Alfie standing behind me, and since no one returned to the line, I was the last to go.

Alfie called the time on the final two and turned to me. "OK, genius, looks like you get a choice. Brown's on the left. Blonde's on the right."

I pushed through the hedge, briefly smelling the juniper, and walked swiftly to the holes. The impending thrill infused me with power, but mostly, I didn't care and wanted it over with. I'd seen it in magazines and probably better. The hole on the left was closest. I glanced back at the hedge for Alfie, put my hands against the wall, and leaned in.

Surprisingly, the room inside was bright and quite small. Two people occupied it. A skinny, hairy man sat naked at the edge of a single bed only a few yards from the hole, and a naked woman lay next to him with her back to me. I almost left as soon as I saw them because of the overwhelming exposed sensation. They must've been able to see me, or at least that someone was at the hole. I stared at the woman's feet, feeling embarrassed, but as soon as I was certain they hadn't noticed, examined the rest of her. She was all legs, butt cheeks, and back from my view. The man leaned over to tap his cigarette and offered her the ashtray. Resting his in the tray, he stood up, exposing his shaggy, dangling parts and whisked them inside a pair of white underwear. I heard muffled conversation and a little laughter as he grabbed his pants from a chair. The woman climbed to sit beside the man, and I still couldn't see much of her because his body blocked my view, but as he bent over to pull up his pants, she became fully exposed. It was my Kate. All my fears and suspicions proved correct. I looked away from the hole at the ground and became conscious of my wet clothes again. I looked in once more and without doubt knew. Definitely her profile but the direction her eyes pointed was indiscernible. Even so, a beauty like that couldn't be forgotten. The man finished buttoning his pants, and she put her face into his crotch. He

A WHOLE LOT

laughed, and she pulled back, laughing. My Kate was a peep girl.

I withdrew from the hole, swung my satchel to my side, and walked to the Speedway, trying not to get sick. I wished I'd never run into Russell today, wished I'd never been his friend. Two men exited a truck when I got close to the entrance. I stumbled over a concrete parking block and heard one chuckle. They grew closer and climbed the steps close behind me. One of them opened the entrance door, and I looked up at him, but he just waited for me to go in. No asking what I was doing there, no telling me I was too young to go in. I entered, and they moved around me into the dimly lit bar. An older man on a stool looked at them, but no one seemed to notice me as I scouted out a phone. The smell of cigarettes and mild sour beer hit the back of my throat. Two feet to my right, a pay phone hung beside a cigarette machine. I wasted no time getting the coins from my pocket and spinning the garage number on the dial.

"Flynn's," Will answered.

"Hi, uh, hi."

"Yes, how can I help you?"

"Will, uh, can Hank pick me up?" I said with lowered voice.

"OK, now, who is this? Mrs. Schwartz?"

"No, uh, Will, it's me. Abel Velasco."

"Abel? Oh, Juke, yeah. Hey Jukebox, what's spinnin'?"

"I, uh, I need a ride home."

"You do? Well, where you at? I thought you were Mrs. Schwartz looking for someone to give her another free taxi ride. Don't know what she thinks we're running here. Drop your car off, and get a ride to pick it up like everybody else on the planet."

"The Speedway Tavern."

"You're at the Speedway?"

"Yeah, uh, I need a ride home."

"I got you, Juke but—hell, Hank's on his way back, but I hate that place. But, no, no. Hey, for you, no problem. Be out front, though. I'll be there in about ten or fifteen. I'll leave right away. OK?"

"OK, bye." I hung up but was a little afraid to turn around and face anyone. I felt a little wobbly as I stood by the phone for a moment, staring at the receiver. I heard a pinball machine ringing behind me, and it felt like the whole bar suddenly started laughing. My heart raced as I grabbed the door handle. I thought I heard a "hey" but walked out and down the steps. I sat directly in the road and didn't turn around to look at the tavern, even when I heard the door open and close.

The minutes dragged, but Will and Mi arrived in eleven minutes thirty-one seconds. Mi jumped out as they pulled to the curb.

"You in the street. Come here, Ah-bel. You know you should stand on side, not sit in street. Hey, you wet, all wet." She patted down my sides and legs as she helped me up.

"Hank said—my aunt said I could work at the garage. Hank could write a note." I felt a sneeze coming on, but a wave of nausea replaced it.

"Hold on, honey, you no look so good. We going to take you home. You all wet."

Will revved the gas, causing the hairs on my head to vibrate, and we got in.

Will had *The World Is a Ghetto* by War playing loud, and Mi leaned over the seat to talk. Will lowered the volume as he pulled away.

"Can't be walking around in wet clothes, Juke. What you doin' this far out? He lives over on Bergey road, right? Who walks this far?" he said, more to Mi than to me.

"I'm-I'm-Babylonian blood runs through me," I blurted out.

"You do, huh? Yeah, yeah, you do. It's called Southern-fried Babylonian blood, but don't worry, Juke. Plenty of good fighters come from Mexico. We'll get you back into fighting shape soon."

I ignored the numbers darting at me and focused instead on the backseat ashtray. An old butt stuck out. I shoved it in so that it could close completely and thought of how I wasn't Mexican.

Will kept the music lowered and continued to check on us in the rearview mirror. We crossed the bridge and came to a stop. "Did I tell you? So, I have a fight in LA at the end of April and not only that but a manager, too. He says I have the 'it.' Man, I says, I've had the 'it' since I was born, but yeah, can you believe it?" He revved the gas some more. "Cal-i-fornia. Gives us enough time to drive out and set ourselves up so I can get the vibe before I get in the ring. Bet that cheers you up."

Mi put her arm around my shoulder. I wanted to ask Will if he'd mind turning the heat on, but the number clouds were increasing, and it took all my concentration to hold them back. The tadpoles flicked their tails against the tide, lost and confused in my belly—a Melville reversal. Mi leaned close and held my head up, looking into my eyes. She unintentionally breathed a little garlic-fish air up my nose, moving my stomach like a whip until it unleashed its *crack* onto the backseat floor. Will skidded to the side of the road and hopped out of the front seat so fast, you'd think I stuck a pin in him. He pulled me out and dumped me in the wet grass near the sidewalk.

"Aw, Jesus, Juke, look at that. Damn it, what'd you eat today? Shit's all creamy purple." I fell forward near Will's legs. "Get back, dammit. Mi, hold him back." He shoved me back lightly.

Will took an old white t-shirt he had tucked under the seat and started wiping it up.

"Hey, he sick. you can't yell." Mi leaned down and helped me to my feet. Once standing, I dropped immediately to my knees and heaved some more. I searched my vomit for the tadpoles, but they must've stayed inside because it was all fluid, no chunks.

"Get him in the car. We gotta get something before that stink is permanent."

The car revved high while he sped toward my house. I sank in abstract calculation when he pulled behind Pigpie's Buick and suddenly felt incredibly tired. The windowpane brushed cool moisture against my forehead as I slipped toward the lock. Everything had a nightmarish quality, and I felt as if I was waking up when the door beside me opened. Will carried me to the house, and I worried how living in my colon were more bacteria than the total number of humans that ever lived. My bowels began rebelling. I caught a brief glimpse of Mi behind us before my eyelids became too heavy, and I let the shadows win.

CHAPTER TWENTY-THREE

The Milk Duds Defense

11.21.12-114.3.9.9.17.55.75.43-17.1-17.9-16.11.17.21-1.3-1.7.17.21.52-14.8-51.3.29.75.12

Two of the shadow-visions that haunted me during my time stuck in bed make me hate Immanuel Kant. He's obviously at fault for them not evaporating away with my fever. The first vision that continues to turn my stomach is of Pigpie spooning dinner into my mouth one night. I thought Milk Duds were dropping off her face into my soup. I can clearly recall the caramel-chocolate chewy goodness. Imagine my revulsion when I became lucid and realized the truth and how relieved I felt after a frantic count to find each mole still intact.

In the second, I had a visit from Cragnus, the billion-eyed frog god of the East. Dazzling with his eyes made of diamond and an allover sheen of golden slime, he croaked about how I was doomed to a life like Erwin Nyiregyhazi. Erwin was a brilliant musical prodigy who at the age of four could play anything he heard once on the piano. Unfortunately, by eighteen, Erwin still couldn't tie his own shoes, feed, or dress himself. Cragnus finished his condemnation and bellowed mucus-coated laughter before disappearing.

Immanuel Kant said we couldn't know if the world exists like the sensory pictures of our mind because to know whether these pictures show the external world as it really is, we'd have to be able to compare the inner pictures with the outer ones, but we can't. We can only know the world through the inner pictures our brains create. How am

I to disprove completely the falsity of Pigpie Milk Duds and Cragnus if that is the case? This difficulty confirmed Immanuel as a curpin of regal stature. Furthermore, Immanuel pilfered the idea from Descartes like a contemptible thief. I'll look past Descartes's role in this matter, as his birthday is coming up on March 31.

My journal lay open on the desk. I could see the lines of Bible numbers and thought it a good idea to write out the formulae for Cragnus and Milk Duds so I could be done with them. I swung my legs over the side of the bed and sat up. Whoa, obviously the medicine Pigpie had been spooning into me hadn't killed the tadpoles. I stood to get my underwear from the drawer. Someone must've heard my stirring because commotion rumbled in the hallway. Small storm clouds hovered at the doorknob before Pigpie suddenly came through with Dr. Limone in tow.

"Abel," she barked. "Abel, get under the covers. I'm terribly sorry, and you've come all this way to bring him schoolwork." She brushed the pile of tissues from the blanket.

I sat back down and covered my lap with the blanket.

"He was sweating like a pig. It's my cold sponge baths that kept us from paying for a hospital stay, I can tell you that."

"Don't fret, Mrs. Stacks. Same equipment I was born with." He smiled cordially and dug inside a large paper bag, withdrawing a manila folder. "I've actually brought some information about his medical history you might be interested in reviewing with Abel and me. I located a very helpful individual at the Missouri State Representative's office who obtained copies of Abel's education records also."

Pigpie's face wriggled from bemusement into determination. She abruptly snatched the manila folder from Dr. Limone's hand. "Oh, I'll take that. We can review it together when he's feeling better," she said with false sincerity.

"Um, well, I thought maybe... yes, well, that should work." Dr. Limone looked apprehensive. He glanced awkwardly about the room, pausing on my open journal before addressing Pigpie again. "OK, then, are you interested in joining us for a little mathematics?"

Pigpie emitted a befuddled huff. "No, I'll leave you to the teacher stuff. If you need me, I'll be in the TV room." She gave me an angry look and swiftly left with the folder dangling from her hand.

More relaxed now, Dr. Limone looked around my room again. "Your aesthetic is, ah, a bit minimalist." He grinned down at me. "I'd ask how you're feeling, but it's rather obvious." He took the paper bag from under his arm. "You might listen to your aunt in this instance. Wouldn't want to help the nasties attacking your body." He removed his overcoat and pulled the chair from my desk next to the bed.

I pulled the covers up to my waist. Dr. Limone dropped the bag on the bed next to me and pulled several items from it. He set a Hershey bar on my bedside table first.

"Mum always brought me chocolate when I wasn't feeling well. I couldn't acquire the Cadbury bars she'd bring, but Hershey's seems popular and Madeline hides their kisses throughout the house." He winked at me and added, "I'd wait until after dinner, though."

I worked my head up and down mechanically, nodding in appreciation.

He assessed the pile of borrowed literature near my lamp. "Yes, and on to business. First, please accept my apology for not having come 'round sooner. Meant to check on you after you failed to return for the computer club. Sorry, again, for that date mix-up. Yes, so, I received a call from Dr. Kohn yesterday when you didn't make it to your appointment. Apparently, you've made quite an impression on him and Dr. Langdeer. I wondered why your aunt hadn't called for you, but don't worry. After I spoke with your aunt, I informed them of your health difficulties. They said to wish you well and a speedy return."

I hopped back farther on the bed. Part of my scrotum was tucked under my leg, and I had to adjust it so as not to crush its contents. Dr. Limone's face had a wide-eyed look signifying he waited for a response to what he'd just said. I quickly searched for something to say. "It is a fact: Descartes wrote in 1641, 'How many times have I dreamed in the night that I was right here, dressed, next to the fire, although I was totally nude in bed.' Descartes slept in the nude."

Dr. Limone chuckled. "Yes, well, bravo, Abel. No doubt many famous men in history have." He pulled the rest of the contents out and folded the paper bag, placing it on the floor. Multicolored striped paper covered one of the items he had. He pulled a pocket calendar from his bag, flipped a few pages, and tapped on the thirty-first. "Picked this up at the bank for you. According to what I've discovered, tomorrow is a special day, is it not?"

I nodded some more.

He placed the calendar on my side table and held the striped package up. "Mm, so, this one is for you to open tomorrow. Maddy said you're not to open it 'til then, and we must always follow what Maddy says." He smiled and placed the present beside my bed.

"March thirty-first is Thursday, but I was born on a March thirty-first that was a Tuesday."

"Mm, yes, it doesn't say anything about that in the folder I received, but it does mention a few other items I think may be of interest. You'll remember to remind your aunt to share the information when you're better, won't you?"

I heard his request, but my mind was stuck on tomorrow's date. Since the age of four, I'd generated a litany of events occurring on the thirty-first.

"It is a fact: Descartes was born in the Easter cycle on the Sunday of the Passion. In 1596, the year of his birth, the juxtaposition of the moon and the sun was exactly like that of the year when Christ was born. Every 532, years this celestial event occurs. It occurred in the years 1, 532, 1064, 1596, and will again in 2128. His name comes from Saint René due to the extraordinary significance of the year of his birth. *Rene* in French means second birth."

"You've become quite a Descartes scholar, haven't you? So, am I to deduce from this that you see Descartes as, ah, the second coming?"

Dr. Limone looked at the cross Pigpie had hung to impress Father Mullens above my desk and then back at me. I shrugged. It was the only item to look at, as my walls were otherwise bare.

He waited a few moments to see if I'd add anything.

"All right, and these are a few magazines Maddy thought you'd enjoy and some books on computing I found interesting. I'd still like it if you happened by our computer group sometime. It continues to meet every Monday after school."

He stood up and readied himself to leave. "I can't imagine your bed rest would persist much after the Easter holiday, but please, if it should, contact me. I'd be most happy to make a trip to Princeton for you." He waited for a response. My nose started to tickle, prompting a quick sneeze. "Gesundheit. You'll be needing a refill, I'd say." He picked up the empty bottle of Robitussin. "I'll let your aunt know. Well, early happy birthday to you. Try and enjoy your day tomorrow." With that, he placed the bottle on the table, smiled and walked out of my room.

Pigpie returned again and again to spoon a new bottle of Robitussin into me over the next several days. It tastes like crap, and I blame it for why I mostly slept through my birthday. At the end of another week in the house, during which I mostly felt fine but Pigpie wouldn't let me out, I woke feeling light and healthy and decided I'd see if she would. My brain rolled with activity, and upon checking the time, I found I still could make the bus to Princeton if I hurried.

When I got to the kitchen, Pigpie noticed the bowtie and white dress shirt Dr. Limone and Maddy had purchased for my birthday.

"What're you doing with that on?"

"Today is a school day," I said.

She sat thinking and finally asked, "Isn't this still Easter vacation?"

I shook my head no.

She thought some more. "Well, don't dawdle after school. You've got plenty of chores to make up for around here."

In the kitchen, I took some bread and slathered jam on it. Shelly ate the peanut butter from the jar, so I didn't bother asking for any. Her belly had grown to an enormous size and stuck out grotesquely below her breasts. I averted my eyes from the combination of the belly and her spooning peanut butter to prevent my queasiness from returning.

"Don't you know better? You don't get well on a Friday and go back to school. You wait until Monday at least," Shelly said as I wrapped my sandwich in a paper towel and stuffed it in my satchel. "What, I do your chores for, like, the past month while I carry around this bowling ball, and you can't even look at me?"

I looked at her face, and she rolled her eyes.

"I want you to clean up that crap out back when you get home. No one's scooped it, and you practically have to wear a clothespin on your nose to hang stuff. I don't care if you were sick or not. Shoulda called the police on Mr.

Sutkin, but you're the reason that mutt comes over here to go. If my child is deformed because I had to breathe that stuff in, you won't even want to know what'll happen." She tapped her spoon on the tabletop once, waiting for me to say something.

I ignored her and searched the kitchen for fruit. It was a rarity that Pigpie bought any, but I hoped something changed. Shelly eased herself up out of the chair and, spoon in mouth, took her human zeppelin to the TV room. I couldn't find any fruit, but two odd-looking stamps—one with a peach on it; the other a portrait in red—stuck out of a large pile of junk mail on the counter near the back door. Upon closer inspection, the stamps obviously were foreign.

I checked the TV room, relieved to see Pigpie and Shelly in their usual mesmerized positions, and slid the thick letter from the pile. *Mr. Abel Velasco* was handwritten along with my address on the front. There was no return address, but it had *AIRMAIL ISRAEL* stamped on it in blue, and fortunately, the letter remained sealed. I exited the back door as fast as I could and flattened two decaying piles, one for each shoe, as I jogged toward the bus stop. I ripped the envelope open while I waited but feared that a wind would suddenly whip up and take the pages from my hand, so I didn't remove the contents until I got on. The scent of the paper filled me with excitement as I held it to my face. When the bus arrived, I slid my change into the slot and shambled toward the back where I found two empty seats. I used one for my satchel and one for me. Even the paper felt different as I pulled it out. I read it repeatedly until I got to Princeton.

February 10, 1983

Dear Abel,

Greetings, dear Abel. I can't express enough how sincerely pleased I am you contacted me. If you'll please excuse my honesty and candor, your letter arrived like a beam of light from God. Your research and the accompanying computer program appear to have a cosmic resonance, which I'm sure you'll agree with once you review our alterations to your programming code.

Richard Pierson and I did indeed know each other. We communicated for a time. He was very interested in the work of Rabbi Chaim Michael Dov Weissmandl, who also had an interest in hidden codes of the Torah, but contact between Richard and I ceased for several years after his dire loss. I learned of his passing only a few years ago. I was sincerely grieved to hear it.

I've shared your findings with Doron Witztum, a physicist friend of mine, and Yoav Rosenberg, who knows computer programming. Dr. Rosenberg was able to clarify your start. I think you'll agree that the convergent findings of our Equidistant Letter Sequences (ELS) are of historic significance. We would like to include you in the rest of our research. I feared a floppy disk might not weather a trip to the States. Instead, I had Dr. Rosenberg print out the program code for you, along with a sample of interesting items we've located in the first five books of Moses. We would appreciate it if you contacted us at your earliest convenience. 07-941-19-10039 * Please see attached.

Sincerely,

Eliyahu Rips
Jerusalem, Israel

Following the printout of the program code were sections of Genesis showing the numbering system Richard Pierson created with yellow highlighter emphasizing certain Hebrew characters. I found written in blue ink at the top: *The names we found were taken from the Encyclopedia of Great Men in Israel. If you are not familiar with them, you might refer to that source. The list of conceptually related words was of our own creation.* —ER

On the final page were names and birthdates clearly taken from that encyclopedia. Then a list of related words like *Auschwitz* and the other death camps of the Holocaust.

I arrived at Firestone and thought of avoiding the administrators completely but feared I'd be found. After a tiring review of what Dr. Langdeer expected of me during my remaining time this semester, he allowed me to return to the computers at Fine Hall. He said it was mandatory for me to consult with Dr. Kohn, but he didn't specify when that had to take place.

I worried the whole jog to Fine Hall that the computer room would be full and I'd have to wait. Luck was on my side, however. The four students in the lab did their usual staring but left me alone with my work. It felt as if glue coated my fingers. I was so excited, I could barely type two commands or a short string of numbers without making mistakes. The afternoon bumped along with my struggle to input the program code into the computer. I only accomplished a small portion before I saved it to a floppy and had to leave to catch the bus. Dr. Kohn could wait another day.

I returned home and found Shelly really giving it to Pigpie. Shelly looked like a ragged comet with her hair in an odd, short ponytail that jutted straight back and her mouth flaming every possible curse word. Pigpie sat and took it. I watched from the hallway in astonishment. Who was this cowed woman? Robotic no longer fit as a description of Pigpie. Even a robot would have had to react to the heat of Shelly's ire. Pigpie's view from the couch appeared threatened by Shelly's belly, which almost hit her in the face.

"There's no way you remember what it was like. Look at me. Look at these pits." Shelly lifted her arms to show the sweat marks. "You don't get pits like this if it's cool enough. I'm soaked because we got one shitty air conditioner. I need one here and in my goddamn room. Why can't anybody understand how hot I am?"

"I understand you're hot. Every GD person in the neighborhood understands it," Pigpie raised her voice to Shelly for the first time in months, but then added, "Oh, darling, don't worry. We're almost at the finishing line."

The temperature of the house wasn't anywhere near hot, and an air conditioner running in April seemed excessive. I tried walking past them to my room, but Shelly noticed me.

"It's about time. It's about goddamn time."

I looked at Pigpie to see her response, and she looked back with an eerie calm. The hint of a smile even tugged at the corners of her mouth.

"If I go outside and find one stinking nugget, you're dead. I can't even eat in the kitchen anymore. I tried to eat lunch in there, and I know that crap is getting in here. One goddamn piece, and you'll be eating it for dinner."

She was a madwoman; so frightening I backed hurriedly into the kitchen and out the door to the porch. I retrieved the cutout-bleach-bottle scoop and the wooden paddle from beneath the steps. A few day-old piles smeared as I maneuvered them into the bottle, just enough to break their hardened outer coating and free the scent.

I wished I'd had enough out here to keep me occupied all night since Shelly continued yelling inside. Mister Scratch joined me from next door after I'd finished my first review of the yard. His fur felt a little stiff, as if he'd rolled in dirt earlier and it dried. Licking my hand and gazing at me with his always-happy-to-see-me face calmed the number clouds. Shelly could really love Mister Scratch if she'd come see his eyes. She wouldn't like the stink, but you can't deny his love-filled eyes.

I scanned the entire backyard for the second time to make certain every pile was gathered. I checked the sides of the house, too, even though Mister Scratch had never relieved himself there. A pile of grass clippings out on the slopes to the tracks served as a burial location for the collection but not before I fortified myself with a final unhurried sniff. Shelly waited for me in the kitchen. She was probably watching the whole time.

"Don't touch anything. Take your filthy shoes off and use this." She plunked a bottle of Ajax cleanser next to the sink.

I followed her command while she leaned against the kitchen doorway, making sure I obeyed. Pigpie came in from the TV room to remove some boiling pasta from the stove. She noisily placed the steaming pot on the adjacent burner and grabbed a colander from the cupboard. I made newsprint balls to help dry the sneakers and set them stuffed by the door. Shelly continued watching while Pigpie wiped the sudsy Ajax water from the counter and put the colander in the sink.

"What the hell are you doing?" Shelly yelled.

I moved the sneakers farther to the side of the door, thinking she meant me.

"Do you think I'll eat that after his dog crap was in the sink? Don't you have a brain?"

Pigpie glued a fake smile to her face, kept the colander in place, and strained the pasta in it.

I started toward the hallway to escape.

"Don't go anywhere. Dinner will be ready in a few minutes," Pigpie barked my way. Shelly finally calmed herself and joined me in the TV room. *Rockford Files* was ending, and she flipped the dial to another that showed the credits for *CHiPs*.

"For Chrissake, can't anything go right for me? Now I missed *CHiPs*."

Shelly kept it up like that for the rest of the night. After dinner, which only Pigpie and I ate, I went upstairs to take off my bowtie, reread my letter from Dr. Rips, and escape Shelly's ranting, but the walls weren't thick enough. I transcribed the formulae from the night's conversations into my journal and worried about what the formulae suggested. Life at the Stacks residence wasn't going to get better anytime soon. Factoring a baby into the equations left me uneasy. I lay in bed with the letter until my eyelids grew too heavy to keep open.

CHAPTER TWENTY-FOUR

You're Number Two

56.127.47.47.115-99.5.7.52.2.3.18.3.42.22-19.18.3-3.42.19.25.2.3-127.42.25.24.3.2.30.3.129

One would think I'd have been prepared for the next day by the preceding night. I should have recognized the warning when a number storm pounded me awake. It was a dream of liquid abstraction. There was nothing concrete to hold onto, no obvious narrative to share besides glowing numbers pelting a darkened, flat landscape. Numbers smacked the ground, joining a watery cacophony before sinking into a rising tide.

    The dream imagery continued while I showered, but it drained away when Shelly arrived. She banged on the bathroom door and grumbled about my being a bathroom hog as I exited. Back in my room, the letter from Dr. Rips lay beside the bed and I stared at it with pride, recalling its contents as I pulled up my dungarees. I chided myself for not concealing it the night before in case Pigpie or Shelly found it. As I shoved the letter into my satchel, I recalled the package Pigpie took from Dr. Limone. Dr. Limone found the information for me, and if I didn't retrieve what was rightfully mine, I'd never see it. Pigpie clanged about in the kitchen, and Shelly continued showering. Now was the perfect time to look for it.

    I slipped past the bathroom as quietly as I could and crept into the sty haven of my aunt. Entering Pigpie's bedroom was foolhardy at best, and if caught I'd be subjected to unknown tortures, but this was the only place Pigpie thinks private. Clothes were strewn everywhere, along with a large dresser littered with powder canisters, bottled lotions, and a multitude of hair-grooming items. A great mystery surrounded what she actually did with all this stuff. Besides her bed, Pigpie's room had one large dresser, one side table, and a walk-in closet. Why Shelly or I had not been forced to wash the mounds of clothes on the floor is a mystery. Maybe Pigpie didn't see the need for clean clothes since she always wore that grimy robe. I stepped quickly to the bedside table and slid the drawer out. A framed picture lay over a collection of empty Luden's cherry-flavored cough drop boxes and a jar of Vaseline. *Cecelia & Carl* written in loopy gold lettering at the bottom of the frame clued me into who it portrayed. Hard to believe the attractive, grinning, slim woman could actually be Pigpie. She was very young in the photo and, judging by the red-and-white checkered suitcases at their feet, about to leave on a trip. The telltale mole pattern I knew so well gave final proof.

  Only a fingernail clipper and comb remained in the back of the drawer, no folder. A small door click sounded in the hallway, increasing the rhythm of my heartbeat pulsing in my head. I closed the drawer quickly and waited until I heard Shelly's door shut before moving again.

  On tiptoe, I could peer in the top dresser drawer, which had a large collection of Smurf figurines that must have belonged to Shelly at some point and other various items, but no papers or folders. The next, a few skeevy undergarments, but she used the second to last drawer as a filing cabinet. Old bills and ripped envelopes filled it. Sneaky exhilaration filled my chest after removing a Bell telephone statement to find the folder with Dr. Limone's handwriting. I pulled the folder too hastily and some pages slid to the floor.

  The letterhead of the top page came from the New City School. Dr. Limone must've finally obtained the reports from when I attended. I began shuffling the papers together when I noticed *corpus callosum* typed on one. It's a term you don't see all that often, but I knew it as the segment of the brain that connects the left half with the right half. I started reading further. *Contusion to the left— no affect on corpus callosum... resulting only in left-hemisphere damage to his brain... documented epileptic seizures first two years of life... last seizure August '72... M. Velasco admitted to "kind of dropping him," followed by unusual language-acquisition skills – uncertain if related to "dropping"... M. Velasco rehab: St. Louis Brightlife for Women (6/69, 8/71)... M. Velasco/A. Velasco scheduled observations.*

Another clicky-click sounded in the hall. I managed to get all the papers back and the folder almost in my satchel when Shelly burst through the door in her bathrobe.

"What are you doing? You know we aren't supposed to be in here."

My brain raced as I glanced about the room. "Did you, did you ever see the picture in her drawer?" I asked as I folded the cover over my satchel.

She moved up close to me. "What picture? We're not supposed to be in here."

Shelly followed me to the other side of the bed as I retrieved and held it up for her. Her eyes grew wide.

"I remember this. I haven't seen it since I was little." She rested the frame on her belly shelf and stared. "Look at my dad. He was so good-looking—wow, it's like Mom is a completely different person. She's actually pretty here. I mean, if you scraped some of those moles off, she'd be a real looker, right?"

She moved past me and examined the rest of the drawer's contents.

"Hey, this is mine," she said, pulling the comb from the drawer and putting it in her back pocket. She held the picture up again and gazed at it, clutched her belly, and glanced at the doorway. "I'm getting out of here, and you've got chores." She stated this nervously, put the picture back, and left. I closed the bottom dresser drawer to cover my tracks and joined Pigpie in the kitchen.

I was eating a bowl of Super Sugar Crisp and considering the implausible revelation of having once been dropped by my mother when the phone rang. Shelly, wearing another stomach-revealing outfit, had just waddled in and answered the phone before Pigpie could put down her newspaper.

"Hello? Oh, hello, Father. You're sweet. Well, it can't happen soon enough, but they say any day now. A relief isn't even close. It'll be more like Heaven. Yeah, she is, hold on. It's Father Mullens," she said, leaving the phone on the counter.

Pigpie picked it up. "Hello, Father. Yes, she's still here. OK. No, that's good news. I'll wait until you arrive with the papers. One o'clock's fine. OK, then, buh-bye." She hung up the phone, and something about her changed.

"Shelly, dear, Father Mullens said he'd be by around one today. You might get yourself fixed up for him. You, too, Abel. He's been good to our family, so we really should show him respect."

Shelly must've smelled Pigpie's curdle as I did.

"What's he coming for? Why don't we just see him at church tomorrow? I mean, I'd go because we have to be nice, I guess, if we're going to have him christen the baby."

"Yes, yes, that's what I was thinking. We'll have him over so he'll be more familiar with you and make the christening really, really wonderful. He'd probably be too busy after church, don't you think?" Pigpie said with a pathetically disguised irritation.

"Uh, not really. Honestly, tomorrow at church would be better."

"Oh, I don't know, Shelly. What if you go into labor tonight and don't get a chance to talk with him?"

"Then I'll talk with him afterward. He'll do it, anyway. He has to. It's his job."

"He doesn't have to, and he's coming today, so it doesn't really matter, does it?" Pigpie said, letting her irritation take control.

"No, it doesn't because you can talk with him on your own. I'll be in my room."

"You'll be in your room packing."

"For wh—no, I won't."

"Yes, you will." Pigpie's sudden commanding animation startled me, but Shelly's bravado deafened her to it.

"No. I. Won't. I'm going out for a drive." Shelly strode to the front door, and Pigpie took the shortcut through the TV room to block her escape.

"Get out of my way, Mother."

"I'm sorry, dear, but I don't think you're legally allowed to drive in your condition." She tried to recover her counterfeit affection, but it was analogous to her stopping at a single bite from a cheese block.

"I'm not going to say it again." Shelly said, edging toward the front door. "Where the hell are my car keys?"

"I've put them away because you won't be needing them."

"What?" Shelly took a second to process Pigpie's statement. "Um, what?! Sc-screw your fat ass." She wedged past and out the front door.

Pigpie trotted after her. "You stupid shit!" *Slap.* "Where do you think you'll get to? You're about to give birth for Christ sakes." *Slap.* "Get in here." *Slap.* It'd been months since I'd seen her body quiver from one of her emphasis slaps. It appeared almost awkward coming from her now.

I followed and watched their muffled silent-movie arguing from behind the front-door window. Pigpie and Shelly's mouths flapped open and closed, wide with anger as they stepped on and off the walkway and the grass. Pigpie trembled, shot through with gamma rays, rage greening forth her inner Hulk. She started shoving Shelly toward the door with her pointer finger. I opened the door because it frightened me to see pregnant Shelly shoved. Neither were backing down.

"Mullens guaranteed me the service would pay a lot for that child, and it's not like you can afford it. So you either get us paid and finish high school, or go live with shelter women who got themselves knocked up."

"I fucking will not. This is my baby." Shelly's face quivered with fury and fear as she began crying.

"Your baby? Who do you think will feed either of you after it's born? I can tell you who it won't be." She pressed closer to shove Shelly again, using her whole hand this time.

Tears streamed down Shelly's face, and her breathing huffed like a runner who'd just ended a race. "You filthy—you're so foul. Who could love a peazoshet luh-ike you. This is my baby! My baby couldn't ever love y—I've never loved you. You didn't pay for shit."

"I paid for everything." Pigpie pushed her again, and Shelly shuffled back a few more steps.

"My father paid. You pig, you cunt." Shelly wobbled but wasn't relenting.

"Get your ass in the house, and get packed."

"Fuck you! Are you deaf, you cunt? Are you deaf?"

Either the number clouds pushed closer from the edges of my vision, mottling my view, or Pigpie's face truly contorted and wrinkled in a horrid way faces shouldn't. A long-pent wrath infused the final shove, and Shelly sought balance but lost it as she turned and tangled her legs. The pregnant belly emitted a monstrous, glutinous thud as Shelly bashed onto the concrete steps, cracking her forehead painfully near my feet. I waited for Shelly to get up, but she rolled and sat back, dazed, with thick, wheezy gasps as she sought more air. Neither Pigpie nor I moved. Shelly's bulging stomach hung oddly to the side. Mister Scratch barked loudly, and Pigpie glared toward the backyard.

"Didn't you hear me? Get your lazy ass inside and pack."

Pigpie's rage sent tremors over her body. Her face continued to scrunch unnaturally. I thought if I didn't stop her now, she'd kick Shelly, maybe even in the stomach. A small trickle of blood drew a dark line from Shelly's hairline down the side of her ear. The number clouds shot lightning.

I bolted out of the house and hammered Pigpie with tightly clenched fists. I continued until I didn't feel anything, until the raining numbers throbbed in my ears and water choked my vision. I wanted to shout at her that I knew it. I knew she wasn't just being nice to Shelly. I knew she was just waiting to strike. Connecting with bone and flab and hair, my fists pounded. My hard-soled Bobos connected again and again.

"You're number two! You're number two! You're number two!" I repeated until my vision cleared and I found Pigpie kneeling on the ground, covering her head, shrieking in fear. Shelly gave out a deep, painful moan that made me want to start hitting her, too. I only wanted the moaning to stop. My journal and an eraser had come out of my satchel and lay at Pigpie's bleeding ankle. I started to retrieve them, but Shelly moaned again so I glanced at her stomach. Her sweatpants were soaked as if she'd pissed herself. It was a lot of piss. People shouldn't piss that much. She was staring at blood on her hand, moaning at it as if it might reply.

I ran. I ran into the backyard, nearly tripping over the loops of clothesline, and startled Mister Scratch. He continued to bark excitedly as I flew past. I grabbed the mulberry branch at the yard's edge to swing down onto the train path. The branch smacked me in the head as I dropped, knocking my glasses off my face. They caught on my satchel, and I held onto them, running half-blind until I got to the wooden plank steps of the old sycamore tree and could put my glasses back in place. My forehead ached terribly where I'd been hit. Shadows grinned from the fir trees. Now that I was here, I realized I couldn't climb up. I'd be seen.

I ran back toward the train path and stopped where it crossed over a concrete bridge. The creek was only about seven or eight feet below. I considered jumping but instead slid fast down the thirty-degree concrete slope, causing horrible brush burns on my forearms, and landed on the muddy banks. The tunnel under the bridge was narrow, and I could see the other side. I thought about standing inside, but the thin ledge would be too difficult to balance on for long and I didn't want to stand in the water. My arms ached dreadfully; my head pulsed.

The shaggy shrubs lining the tracks would provide cover. Anyone searching would have to climb down the bridge and peer over to find me. It could happen, but I couldn't keep going; my body hurt too much. Scallions grew in huge hairy clumps like pillows, and their scent drew me in as I lay back into them. I tried pushing away the numbers and chanted to the beat of the throbbing: Mom-Mom-Mom-Mom-Mom-Mom-Mom-Mom-Mom-Mom-Mom-Mom . . .

I woke later to an ambulance siren whirring in the distance. It had to be for Shelly and Pigpie. If they hadn't already, it wouldn't be long until they sent the police dogs into the woods for me. I rose painfully and trudged a good distance up the creek in the water to throw off my scent as I knew one should do. The creek would take me to Remsen Avenue, which had too much traffic, so I climbed the banks through spiny branches, scraping my arms again, to Beech Street. I realized once on Beech there really was no place to go that I wouldn't run into more people or more traffic. I was trapped, plus I'd left my journal. How could I have left it? Beech Street was a mere two hundred yards or so from my house. Only trees and the train path separated us. Was that a helicopter? I rushed up the Beech Street sidewalk past house after house to the path that led to the Arkens' backyard. Before I got to their dog Charley's chain-link cage, I could make out people near our back porch through the trees. Charley barked at me until I was past his cage, but I don't think anyone else saw me.

    I climbed down to the train tracks again and moved along behind the trees slowly as to not draw attention, worrying less about the men and more about Mister Scratch seeing me. Two officers stood in front of the clothesline pole. Mr. Sutkin and Father Mullens stood with them. I crept to where I knew the trees and shrubs were thick enough to hide. Gray, dried needles of two blue-spruce trees pressed into my hands as I climbed the slope and hid under the limbs.

    Descartes practiced vivisection on rabbits and dogs. It's what first came to mind when one of the officers stepped aside and Mr. Sutkin bent over to unwind clothesline from him.

        From Descartes's Description of the Human Body:

> If you cut off the end of the heart of a living dog, and through the incision put your finger into one of the concavities, you will clearly feel that every time the heart shortens, it presses your finger, and it stops pressing it every time it lengthens.

    Hanging limply against the pole and clearly dead was my friend, Mister Scratch. Mister Scratch! I could only imagine Pigpie running to halt his barking and kicking him as she might have done to Shelly had I not stopped her. One of the officers held my journal open, examining the pages. I hope they didn't think I killed Mister Scratch. It had to be Pigpie. It had to be.

She'd tell them I went crazy. Father Mullens would back her up. He'd be pissed about the money he'd lose. He'd probably make money off Shelly's baby, so he'd back up Pigpie. It'd be them against me. And the officer wouldn't know how to read my formulae to see how evil Pigpie was. She'd tell them I'd been sick, and it must've gone to my head. *For chrissake, he's an animal! He beat me and Shelly and then that Sutkin's dog.*

I eased back down the slope, sliding along the needles and dirt, and started along the tracks as the knowledge of what actually happened seeped in. When I noticed one of Mister Scratch's tennis balls resting in the weeds on the path, I began running. Hot tears rolled to my ears as I rushed toward Lexington Avenue with Mister Scratch's happy eyes haunting me and obscuring my way. I picked up speed, barely pausing to rip a branch of blackberry prickers from my sleeve. I continued running until I got to the pavement and needed to catch my breath but started up again all the way to Howe's field. I could see the garage now and wanted to call out to Hank or Mi, but knowing they'd never hear. I became a pinball rolling down the bike path toward the flippers almost near the exit as I arrived at the garage. Game over.

CHAPTER TWENTY-FIVE

It's All Right – I Think We're Gonna Make It

42.15.21-21.2.6.21-66.47.3.28.4.125.21-62.3.6.4-1.3-28.2.47.15.20.12-28.21.47.58

When I arrived, a U-Haul trailer sat in the garage bay closest to the apartment door. For the minute I waited for someone to show, I questioned why they'd fix a trailer that doesn't have an engine in it. I thought maybe they were changing a tire until Will came down the stairs followed by Mi with cardboard boxes in her arms.

"Hey," Mi said, grinning and rushing past Will.

"Hey, Juke." Will raised his guitar case up for a hello, and both of them ducked into the trailer to deposit their cargo.

Hank popped his head around the corner from the supplies closet and came out with a bottle of orange liquid soap in his hands. "Whattaya say? Hey, look who's here."

Mi and Hank walked toward me, and I watched their gazes shift and expressions change as they saw the state of my face.

"Didn't I tell you he wasn't safe with that barnacle-faced woman?" Hank said. "I knew it. They should've taken you to a hospital so it was documented."

Mi looked surprised at Hank. "So, she get him sick, and when he better, she beat him?" Hank nodded as if he knew what happened. "Ugly woman, rude woman," Mi said lightly, touching my ear.

Will came out from the trailer and hustled over to see what happened.

"What now?" He started shaking his head side to side. "Mm, look at that. You start training without my help?" He came closer to look at the bump on my forehead. He seemed unsure of what to say. "Damn, Juke, your face looks like mine." I could see the concern in his eyes as he joked. "Ma man, we're practically twins."

"Get me warm towel and put water on stove," Mi said to Will, pulling on his sleeve. "He need tea."

"Hey, go finish up your boxes and start that tea. I'll talk with the boy." Hank waved them away and took me into the office.

He placed the soap on the counter and seated me in the chair. I caught a glimpse of my messy hair and puffy vein-filled eyes in the mirror atop the vending machine. With my bump, I frightened even myself. I swiveled the chair away from the reflection and faced the counter.

"Serious business. Seems like real serious stuff." Hank paced the room, running fingers through his graying hair. He scratched the back of his head for a few moments and leaned on his forearms so he'd be at my level. "Let's talk now, Juke. Tell ol' Hank what happened. Someone do this to you or, ah, did you get in a fight with some other kid?" He kept looking at my bump. "Looks like the Devil jumped up and bit you."

I avoided his eyes, trying not to cry, and stared at my knees. The heat grew so strong in my face, my ears prickled. He came back around the counter and tilted my head back, examining my bump.

"You hurt anywhere besides that?"

I lifted my arms, and he rolled up my sleeve, shaking his head at the slightly bloody chafing. "What's gone on here?" He turned both my arms up to face him. "You get it anywhere else?"

I shook my head.

"Listen, son, you don't gotta be ashamed with me. We're like family, aren't we? I think we are. Haven't seen you in a while, but the kids told me about dropping you off, and I know how your aunt . . ." He put his hand on my shoulder, and that started my tears going. He let me sit there for a moment as the numbers flew in my mind and the words wanted out.

"I beat, she pissed, and I ran-I can't-I can't swing right, and I-I hit my . . ." I pointed to my forehead. "He's dead. She killed him, and he's-he's dead." That was all I managed. Hank pulled me to his chest. He smelled like cinnamon and engine oil. My glasses pressed into something hard in his pocket.

"It'll be OK, don't you worry now." He patted my back firmly. "We'll get this all straightened out, you'll see. Don't you worry now."

Mi came into the office with a towel, and Hank backed up.

"Oh, what's wrong? Oh, here, here, Ah-bel," She took my glasses and started roughly wiping my face and nose, then folded the towel and gently put it on my forehead. "We send Will over, and she will never forget who she did." Mi kept smoothing the towel onto my head and looking into my face. She started to well up. "What did she do? You tell Mi. It OK."

Will came in carrying a tray with teacups that spilled over their rims and set the tray on the counter.

"You tell me you think she a terrible woman and racist after we left. Right? Right? So now, you right. What kind of woman yell at sick boy, remember?" She took a cup and emptied the saucer before replacing it underneath and handing them to me.

"Hold on," Hank said. "Let's all calm down here. Let him drink your tea. If we need to call the law, we will." Hank looked at Will and waved him away.

"Let's finish up, Mi. Dad's got this. Sorry, Juke, but we gotta get on the road soon." He pulled Mi with him, and she wiped at her eyes and reluctantly left.

"Whooie, this day's one for the books. Kids are making for California, and now you. I guess it's like April use to say, God only fills what your bag can hold." He smiled at me. "Woman probably listened to too much o' my Jimmy Brown albums. Finish that up, and we'll see what's what."

I sipped Mi's tea slowly. Hank lit a cigarette and took a seat at the patron's bench. After a few sips, he started asking questions. I gave answers and soon explained more thorough details of what took place. He gave me the second cup of tea, which he hadn't touched, and told me to drink it while he went and talked with Will.

A calendar lay open on the desk. Because of the circled and crossed-out numbers, I slid it closer. A black number one was circled on today's date. Someone had been counting down the days for the past two months. Hank had nine cars lined up for service the following week, but the following days had big *x's* drawn through them. I wondered how he'd deal with the work on his own. I took a last sip from my cup before I gave up on the tea. Seven minutes later, Hank returned with Will, both wearing stern faces.

"Look here, Juke, we've got an idea." He wrung his hands together. "The choice is yours. Now, now, we could call the police, but where would you be—"

Will moved a cup so he could rest his arm on the counter. "You're coming with us. We're pulling out soon. I wanna be on the road before it gets dark. It's better this way, you know. Mi's real upset about that dog, and any woman who'd do such a thing to a dog, you know, could do worse, right? I mean, your cousin could be dead, and say the police take your aunt's side—no good. Hey, it's up to you, but we're almost done, so . . ."

Will knocked on the counter with a let-me-know face. I looked at both of them and felt afraid. What option did I have? I nodded my head to let them know I heard.

"Come on upstairs," Hank said.

Hank led the way, and we climbed to their apartment. I sat with Hank watching the local news and eating the Lebanon-baloney-and-Swiss-cheese-with-mustard sandwich he made while Mi and Will transferred the remaining boxes to the trailer. Mi did a couple of passes, checking cupboards and drawers for items she might have missed, asking Hank if he wanted this or that, and glancing at me nervously. I could tell she'd been crying.

They finished faster than I expected, and as Mi put on her yellow windbreaker, Will came for my answer.

"You coming?"

I reluctantly nodded yes. Mi smiled at me and then at Will.

"Well, all right." Will grinned wide. "Let's get going then." He hustled ahead of Mi and me. Mi looped her arm through mine and guided me down the stairs.

Will backed his car up and attached the trailer while we stood transfixed as if it was a TV show. Hank stuffed two boxes of peppermint Chiclets in my pocket and looked me in the eyes. "I told you I'm heading over to the home, right? Got me a fine view of the pond out back and can keep an eye on the new owner, make sure he runs this place the way it should be. You need to talk, I'll be here until the end of the month. Then you just call over there, and we can talk anytime. OK? Plus, I'll be coming out, probably 'round Christmastime. Be nice to get away from the snow."

I nodded.

He gripped my hand firmly and shook it up and down. It barely bothered me.

"You take good care now."

I nodded again and climbed in the backseat.

He turned to Mi, and they hugged for a long time. Mi cried in his shoulder, and I looked at the floor because it felt wrong to keep watching. I lifted my head as she settled into the front seat. Hank and Will stood facing each other for a moment. Will broke in, making promises to call along the way, and jumped in the driver's seat. He gave Hank a long handshake through the car window before he got out and gave him a proper hug. Hank didn't fare as well as Will and kept wiping his eyes while we pulled out of the lot. My ducts were dry by then. I didn't cry, but my chest swelled with grief and sustained fear as I watched Hank through the rear window. Will kept saying, "All right then," taking deep breaths as Mi cried into her sleeve until we got to 287 North.

    I knew the routes we could take that might get us there at a better rate and others that would be less obvious to the police, but Will said he wanted whatever was easiest. An almost straight shot across Route 80 West fit that description. Several hours later in Snow Shoe, Pennsylvania, a little west of the middle of the state, they started talking to me about how great life would be, how they'd buy me new clothes to hold me over until we got to Los Angeles, how Mi would get a job at a grocery store so they'd get a discount and maybe some free food, but mostly about Will's strategy for breaking into the boxing scene. He would make big bucks, not like what he'd get if he tried to make it in the New York circuit. It sounded like he'd thought of every angle.

    We drove listening to whatever radio stations we could tune in. Mi offered me some of the beef jerky and Pepsi she'd packed. I didn't accept. My stomach felt queasy, worrying me that the virus had returned. Each green-and-white reflective sign that announced the next exit or how far from the next town we were squeezed more anxiety into my belly. How quickly do the police start manhunts? Would they think to question Hank? I'd never return to Princeton now, never talk with Dr. Limone again. I'd never see Shelly or Pigpie or Mister Scratch, never see Mister Scratch again. I rested against the door and attempted sleeping to avoid the thick number clouds and the passing signs, but I wasn't tired and instead watched the oncoming cars' headlights comb along the ceiling.

We stopped for the night at a small town in Ohio called Hudson. Mi and Will fought over whether they should continue until Toledo, but Mi won out by using the "He needs a good night's sleep after all he's been through" defense. She was right. I wanted out of the car. Eight hours in the cramped backseat with only one pit stop was beyond my endurance.

"Welcome to the Nite-Nite motel!" Will announced happily as he ushered us into our room.

It could only be described as shabby. Will's enthusiasm was a bit much for our two double beds with pale-yellow nubby comforters, a lamp, and a TV. Except for my mother, I'd never shared a room with adults before. I decided I could get away with removing my sneakers and climbing in bed with my clothes on. The sheets had a mild mildew scent, but I didn't care. My body agreed with the rest of me about wanting the day to end.

They took turns in the bathroom with the door closed. Mi donned a robe, but Will came out practically nude in his white BVD underwear. His scarred body, colossal and muscular, was startling. I'd seen the arm and hand scars but not the marks that washed up and down the right half of his torso. Will was too big for the bed, and the covers almost completely came off Mi once he'd settled, but she snuggled up closer to him, and they whispered to each other for a while. I thought I'd gotten used to it in the car but, mixed with the room's other odors, his cigarette smoke was making me sick. My eyes felt itchy as well, but it could've been due to exhaustion. I couldn't make out what they said over the PBS poultry documentary on the TV Will wanted left on, but it didn't matter because I fell asleep.

Will's deep voice commanded me awake in the morning. The static from the TV blended with remnants from another number-storm dream. Mi brought a wet washcloth over to my bedside and wiped my face gently around the bump. She held my chin and said, "Today a good day, OK? OK." She eased me to a seated position and helped me to my feet.

Mi forced Will to buy us breakfast at the International House of Pancakes before we started back on Route 80. When I came out of the bathroom in the motel, they suddenly clammed up and Mi's lips held tight with anger. I figured Will let us eat at the House of Pancakes because of a fight they'd had. But when Mi told me to try to use the bathroom after we finished breakfast and they clammed up again after I returned, I worried their fighting was related to me. Mi walked ahead of us and slammed her car door as she got inside. She quickly hopped out and got in back, slamming the door again.

"Hey, looks like you get to ride shotgun for a while, Juke. Maybe give me a little Pryor or some Redd Foxx. Whattaya say?"

When he closed his door, I thought he might stick a dollar in my pocket and make a request, but he didn't. He looked at Mi in the rearview mirror and turned the volume up. I knew something must have been wrong because he left on Christopher Cross singing "All Right." Just yesterday, he'd said, "Can't believe they play this crap" before he changed the channel. We weren't heading back to the highway, and I didn't ask why nor why we pulled into a Kmart parking lot.

Will handed me a twenty-dollar bill. "Here, I want you to go in there and buy yourself a pack of underwear and a pack of T-shirts." I looked back at Mi, and she smiled.

"You want me go with?" she asked.

I nodded.

"I go with him. You can't send boy like this to buy underwear on his own." She got out without waiting for a reply from Will.

In the store, she ripped open a pack of white underwear and held a pair up to me. It looked too small, so she took a pack from the next size up. She grabbed a pack of navy-blue Fruit of the Loom T-shirts and tucked them under her arm. We paid but instead of leaving, she took me to the restroom and instructed me to change. She smiled broadly at me when I came out. She hugged me tightly, released me and hugged me again.

"You look good. You good boy, aren't you? I think you be OK."

It was all a bit confusing, but I did think I looked better with the new shirt on.

By noon, we'd passed several signs telling us Chicago was close. Will surprised me when he took the downtown exit, which navigated off Route 80. Mi didn't comment, and I guessed we might be getting lunch. St. Louis had a good-size downtown, but it didn't compare to Chicago. The heights and amount of the buildings were breathtaking. At 1,450 feet tall, the Sears Tower, the tallest building in the world, loomed like a titan, like a god. I couldn't believe I was this close. I doubted I would get to go inside and wondered if Will decided on some sightseeing when we reached the downtown. He was tight-lipped, still not speaking with Mi, but he seemed to have an idea, so I just waited.

He pulled into a train-station parking lot in an area that appeared as general as the other areas we'd been driving through. I got excited about seeing some long city trains and considered we might be at a city mall where there'd be restaurants with windows to watch. We walked to the station instead of the adjoining building. I honestly didn't suspect anything until we were heading toward the ticket booths. Mi followed us, and her muffled crying worried me, but it still never dawned on me the tears were connected to my impending departure, even when she sat at a bench while we continued on.

"Look, Abel." Will used my real name for the first time since he gave me my nickname. "Mi doesn't agree, but she don't have the same stakes I do. It all just happened too quick, you know?" He looked over at her glaring from the bench. He put his hands on my shoulders and apprehensively removed them. "It was my idea, so I'm gonna buy you a ticket and what you do is, see, you take a train back to North Brunswick. Dad'll come pick you up. You call him before you leave. I would call but, you know, we gotta get going. If the cops come after us, we could be in big trouble, and I have my career to think of." He looked over at Mi again. "Tell Dad to take you to the police and say he found you. You'll be better off if an adult tells your story, and Dad could check in with you to make sure everything's all right, right?"

It sounded reasonable, but I became frightened by the sudden factoring. Variables showed great potential for the plan failing. Pigpie was a big variable. I didn't want to go back to her now.

"OK," was all I could respond. I didn't have a choice.

When we got in line, I turned to check on Mi, but she'd gone. Will bought me a ticket leaving at 2:11 p.m. from Union Station. I looked it over as he tried to apologize some more. I'd arrive in Pittsburgh at 12:17 a.m. and then in North Brunswick the following day at 7:30 a.m. I figured by the time Hank picked me up, it'd be around 8:00 or 8:30 a.m. I could easily be back with Pigpie by lunch tomorrow. This wasn't good.

He went over the details with how it'd all work, where I would go, and what I should do if I got confused. He glanced about, looking for Mi, who'd left her bench. I interrupted him when he started to say good-bye.

A WHOLE LOT

"Can we find Mi first?"

"She's probably waiting at the car, Juke." He looked at the bench again. "Like I said, she didn't want you to go, and I can't see her following me if I went and tried to get her. How 'bout I tell her you said good-bye, OK?"

I nodded and pulled my satchel to my chest. I couldn't believe Mi knew and didn't say good-bye. He stuffed the train tickets in my satchel for me, took out his wallet, and handed me a twenty.

"That's if you get hungry or something. We'll call you when we get to California, OK? You're OK, right? I know you're real smart. You'll be OK. You take care of my dad, all right?" He put his hand out for me to shake but took it back, remembering I didn't like to and gave a big smile. Before I could say anything more, he turned and walked away. People swerved around me. I watched him walk toward the parking lot as he craned his neck, searching for Mi.

CHAPTER TWENTY-SIX

Human Faucet Sonata

4.7-4.24-8.4.6.13-43.8.34.11.35.11.28.19.6-
8.485.20.34.4.24.4.7.11.28.24.1

Having a plan and tickets in hand gave me focus. I followed Will's directions and went to the platform for the Union Station train. My disappointment over being deserted by Mi and Will was somewhat lessened by thoughts of train travel. I'd get to ride on at least three, and that would be something worthwhile. Trains left from this gate to Union every ten minutes, and I had to get there to catch my train to Pittsburgh. Happily, the outside platform allowed me to see other train activity. I pulled my hood up and found an empty metal bench in the middle, but as soon as I sat down a man smoking a cigarette sat next to me. The unpleasant mentholated tobacco kept wafting into my eyes. As if I were nonexistent, he reached across my chest and took one of the free pamphlets on my side of the bench. His rudeness bothered me, but then I noticed the pamphlets said *Transit Schedule* on the cover. Reviewing the train and bus schedules gave brief pleasure until my train arrived. The wind from the train crashed against my glasses as the cars slowed to a stop. Others on the benches stood to board, and I followed suit.

    I'm certain people found ways to keep themselves happy every minute of the day all over the planet. Undoubtedly, it wasn't a task beyond my means. Descartes ran off when he was seventeen. He left books behind to gamble in Paris and try soldiering in Holland and Bavaria.

It's been reported Descartes even spent time with prostitutes during those years. I tried to convince myself I'd be fine and could even enjoy this. A window seat toward the back was open, so I sat down and focused on my sneaker laces as we pulled away from the station. I tried to remain calm, but all it took to startle me was the clearing of a throat. The presence of someone next to me wasn't evident before that moment. A small man, only slightly larger than me, with frizzy, long, dark hair and a bulky nose glanced about and stopped at my eyes.

"Zis train is to Union, no?" he asked meekly.

"Si," I said using the proper form of yes for answering a negative question in French, my small clue that I understood the language well.

"I could not find a sign to confirm what I'd been told, thank you. Chicago is a great city, isn't it?" he continued in fluent French.

"Don't know. I just got here."

The woman in front of us looked back between the seats at me with curiosity.

"While in Rome, do as the Romans do, you know," he said loud enough for the woman who was eavesdropping.

I kept looking forward as I tried to concentrate on what he just said and smiled politely in response.

"And you must have an agenda. Otherwise, you'll miss out on something good. Always explore, always keep questing for new experience."

I forced myself to look at him this time and nodded.

"You aren't keeping a journal of your travels?"

"I, uh, lost my journal."

The woman glanced back again, and I flushed.

"One must always keep a journal when traveling. How would you recall all the brilliant things you think of and learn along the way if not? So, where did you live in France?"

"No, I never—uh, I lived in Missouri and New Jersey, United States of America."

"Someday then, you must get there, and Holland is worthy also. I've lived in both."

I nodded, feeling the woman's eyes on me. I decided to check my satchel to throw her off, make her think the man and my little tête-à-tête had ended. My journal still wasn't there. I'd hoped somehow it would return—all my weeks of writing out the tiny numbers gone. Every page was still in my head, but the loss of the physical work concerned me. The letter from Dr. Rips with the programming code and also the folder from Dr. Limone remained. I pulled out my tickets, knowing the Frenchman might be watching.

"Where are you going? Home?"

I didn't want to say yes because I didn't believe it true. Home certainly wasn't with Pigpie.

I finally nodded so as not to be rude.

Just as the train's brakes were engaged, the woman in front of us commented to her traveling companion about how it was "dangerous for children traveling alone" and thumbed behind her, in my direction. The train eased to a stop, and simultaneously everyone stood. Mass confusion ensued while I secured my ticket again, and when I turned to tell the Frenchman I'd be sure to get a journal again soon, he'd already left. The train was too crowded for him to slip away so quickly, and I couldn't see how he'd have squeezed by me without my noticing, but somehow he had.

Once I exited, I looked for the Frenchman at the station, but he must've disappeared into the throngs of people. The frenzy of motion made me dizzy. I joined along with the moving crowds, but the contact with others became a bit much, and I ducked into a store to get out of the fray. I browsed magazines briefly. Among the pens and tape for sale I found two stacks of spiral-ring notebooks with the option of flowers or a unicorn on the cover. Using part of Will's twenty, I bought the one with the unicorn. The saleswoman looked nearly identical to the robot-wife character Tina Louise played in the movie *The Stepford Wives* I saw on TV. She creeped me out a little as she tucked my receipt into the cover and plunked a free pen in the bag with a condescending smile. I tried to think of her as the character Ginger from *Gilligan's Island* that Tina Louise also played, but she was closer to the *Stepford Wives* version.

A food vendor next to the bookseller had a long line, but the grilled food confirmed my hunger and told my stomach it'd be worth the wait. The choices were disappointingly meager when I got to the front. Portability should be key at such locations. The food was mostly sit-down and cut up, but they had two sandwich choices. Written on the sandwiches in masking tape were *Tuna* (I hate the smell) or *Bacon and egg*. Bacon and egg was my purchase, along with a pint of milk to go with it.

I located the gate for my Pittsburgh train and situated myself on another metal bench. With an hour to kill, I thought it wise to pace eating the sandwich. The tinfoil looked reused, which worried me some when the interior contained no other wax paper or wrapping. The evil aura of the sandwich compounded my concern. They'd burned the toast a little, and the sliced, hard-boiled egg's yoke was slightly uncooked. One should probably avoid examining one's food when you buy it at a train-station stand. I dreamed of a PB and J, closed my eyes, and took a bite. A whole slice of fatty bacon flapped against my chin as my mouth came away from the sandwich edge. When I opened my eyes, they met those of a narrow man standing next to me who looked at the bacon dangling and made a disgusted face. After that, I felt compelled to finish quickly, using my milk to wash down each bite.

Exploring the station wasn't of interest, far too crowded, but I heard the Frenchmen goading me to see the sights. Still, I stayed put and pulled out my new notebook. The calculations for the Frenchman and my interactions with saleswoman robot gave me a great idea for future research.

I've come across several references to Descartes's interest in automatons or robots. He thought of all animals as such, that is, without soul or capability of feeling, and there are those that believe he pursued the technical interest to an extreme. Descartes lost his daughter, Francine, when she died at the age of five in 1640. Largely due to his being so grief-stricken over Francine's death, he eventually created a perfect robot replica of her. The article I read in *OMNI Magazine* briefly explained how Descartes brought robot Francine with him everywhere. One night on a ship while Descartes was out of his room, the ship's captain searched it to see if the rumor that Descartes was traveling with a corpse was true. When he found the inactive Francine, he threw her overboard for fear of a curse following the ship. Due to her lifelike qualities, it is highly likely she had enough substance to float rather than sink. Possibly she has been found since that 1978 article, so my first search could be to see if that is so, and if not, I could then start a search for where the ship was and what the tide calculations would be to see where she may have drifted.

Just as I began detailing how I might go about it, twenty-two minutes after eating the sandwich, my intestines started laughing a shadowy, malevolent laugh, giving me clues to their boundaries and twists. I burped sour milk and eggs into the back of my throat and thought I might need to begin exploring soon. How could I have been so stupid? An average of one six-second cramp every ninety seconds started. I continued counting the cramps, stiffly maintaining a state of denial rather than getting myself to safety. After the sixth, I rose with alarm at my lower intestine's liquid slip.

A WHOLE LOT

By the time I found the sign directing me to the bathroom, I was already clutching my cheeks together for temporary defense like a pinky in a dam. I banged into the men's room door without even noticing the *Out of order* sign, and without care, U-turned and pushed my way into the ladies'. I moved so quickly, I doubt the woman at the mirrors had time to notice my gender.

Hard to estimate which was greater, the solace I found by making it to the bowl or the discomfort that followed. My gut became an accordion, testing the bathroom's acoustics and my endurance for pain. Plumbers' ears perked up around the state when hearing my human faucet sonata. It flowed far longer than I imagined the small sandwich's volume should've generated, and I realized my pancake breakfast must've buckled under its spell also.

I'd never done so in the past, not even as a child, but I began crying over it. The stench, the pain, the humiliation of the location. I could see Will shaking his head and telling me to cut it out, to be a man. I heard Pigpie slapping her thigh and demanding that I stop it that instant. But I didn't, I couldn't. I clutched my stomach, thinking pressure might ease the pain. I held my breath for the same reason. Nothing worked. My watch explained that my train had arrived and left. The fear it generated forced my stomach to propel in the other direction, and my shame overwhelmed me as I shot liquid out both ends. I caught most of the cupful from my mouth in my hands and poured it between my legs with the rest.

When the action subsided, I wondered what I'd do now. I didn't have money for another ticket and couldn't be sure they'd let me use the one I had for a later time. A little deus ex machina reaching into my life story and my gut—taking out the disruptive microbes—might be nice at this point. I pounded the stall weakly, and a metal box attached to the wall bounced its lid making a small clink-clink.

Inscribed on the top was *Ladies Receptacle*. The term repeated in my mind until the waves finally subsided.

Nineteen minutes and a quarter roll of toilet paper later, I finally felt comfortable pulling my pants up. I didn't leave the stall yet. Better to be warm and comfortable than exposed and running for cover again. Next to the ladies receptacle were little pink plastic bags. They were pretty and had a floral scent, making me feel better. I lifted the metal cover to see what it contained. They looked like little packages. It seemed so civilized to be given a gift. Pink baggies to take your gift in—how pleasant. Unwrapping one soon told of my mistake. I found a maroon-soaked pad, the kind Shelly or Pigpie might toss in the wastebasket next to the bathroom sink. The *receptacle* half of the term seemed so obvious now. A little of the maroon remained on my finger, and I took a quick sniff just to see. Mostly, it smelled like any blood with a bit of the floral scent mixed in. I rubbed my hands on my pants and stood.

It was now or never, so I exited the stall, keeping my head lowered, and washed my hands and face at the sink. The two women at either side of me might have been sticking their tongues out for all I knew because I didn't look at their faces.

The next train to North Brunswick left at six-thirty. I had no idea what I'd do for four hours. I certainly didn't want to spend it sitting on hard metal benches. I went to the ticket counter to look for literature that might give alternatives. Explaining why I'd missed my train would be difficult, so I didn't ask for help. C-class Tickets: Nontransferable. Nonrefundable. I located those terms in the pamphlet with fare information. Nothing about "if you miss your train, just catch the next one," or "C-class tickets for missed trains can be refunded," or anything close to what I hoped I'd find. I only had sixteen of the hundred and fifty-seven dollars I'd need. I felt defeated in so many ways.

The great cavernous hall induced an atomic feeling. I swirled about as an electron without a nucleus, free roaming and unimportant. I took a seat and watched two policemen walk through the station. They looked around, but I couldn't fathom it'd be for me as I hadn't been gone long and the probability of Will explaining where I was located was highly doubtful. I pulled out my unicorn notebook and started listing options in code:

1. Contact police and tell them story—might endanger Will and Mi.
2. Find ticket seller who'd fall for fake tears—figure out how to fake tears.
3. Generate enough money to buy new ticket.

Three is a magic number, as anyone who watches Saturday-morning cartoons will attest, so I circled it. Why not? I'd made plenty with Pigpie. She'd always handled the details, found us a stand and whatnot, but I could probably work that out as easily as Pigpie would. A busy street corner in a city like Chicago shouldn't take me more than a few hours.

The sign at the station's exit I used said *Adams Street* in brass letters. When I stepped out on the sidewalk, up the street to the left were mammoth gray buildings. I was pleased for once that the streets were crowded, each person a potential sale. I flipped my journal open to the middle and wrote *MIRACLE BOY* in big letters and *Ask a Question* in smaller letters. A woman with a small brown dog on a leash stood beside me, waiting to cross the street. I bent over to pat the dog, but it growled at me, so I refrained. I moved away from where people were crossing but close enough that they'd all get a good view of me and sat Indian-style next to a trash can. I propped my sign up beside me.

An hour passed, and then another, and no one said one word to me. It must've been my bruised face. Number clouds started buzzing heavily in my periphery, and my legs grew itchy, so I rose to find another location that might attract more attention.

As I lifted my notebook, the receipt fell from the front cover. I picked it up and immediately knew I owed Shelly a thank you. Shelly's "return an item with a different receipt" trick that worked so amazingly for her would be a far-better solution.

I went back into the station, but none of the stores had what I needed. I'd have to try each one of them to earn enough, and it would up the percentages that someone would catch on. I only wanted to do this once. I needed a mall or a large shopping center and went back out on the street to see if I could find one. A taxi pulled behind another parked taxi in front of me, and a man with a big colorful winter hat like a mushroom cap stuck his head out of the driver's-side window. I looked at him and he back at me.

"Yah need a taxi, Mr. Shortie?" he shouted with a thick Jamaican accent.

I looked behind me to see if it was someone else he was talking to but pointed at myself, asking if he meant me.

"Yah, you rubbasheets. You need ah taxi?" His grin spread wide and bright.

I momentarily debated whether I should trust him but asked, "How much to get to the mall?"

"Mall?" He rubbed his chin. "I could take yah tah Marshall Fields for about tree dollah, kid. How's dat?" He smiled, holding up three fingers.

I nodded and got in the back. As he pulled away from the curb, I felt exhilarated and nervous. This would work. He clicked a black box, and I watched as the digital number next to the dollar sign started to climb by ten cents.

"My names Charles. Yeh like reggae?" he asked but didn't wait for my response. He turned up the volume and started bobbing his head. "Dis here's the great albino, Yellowman. If yah nevar heerd da man, yeer in for a treet."

I couldn't imagine there were that many albinos that lived in Jamaica and wondered how he might be related to Allen Foster's family.

My stomach started to slip a bit, and I worried more action was on its way. I put my face into the breeze from Charles's open window. Luckily, the trip was over before the second song ended.

"Tree dollah, like ah say. Right on da nose."

I pulled three from my satchel and laid them on the seat.

His spindly fingers claimed the bills. "Hold on, kid. No presha, but lil tips is kind."

I didn't understand but got out of the taxi and thanked him again.

"OK, den, best to yah," he called from the window and pulled away.

Marshall Field & Company turned out to be like Wanamaker's or Sears. Perfect. My gut rolled a little again, so I stopped to use the men's room, with urinals this time but no doors on the stalls. I hoped this was my last visit today.

The bathroom wasn't far from the men's department. I found the cologne and accessories and spent no less than two minutes selecting a digital watch with a sticker on the box that said $249.99. At the closest cash register, two salesmen were in the middle of conversation. I shuffled the rest of the watches on the island as if inspecting them but really I spread them out.

The men looked too savvy, but the register on the other side of the department had a tall woman who appeared to be in her forties. Any female wearing pigtails at her age deserved to be swindled. I walked up and plopped the box on the counter.

"Good afternoon, young man. Would you like to purchase this?" she said with a smile that told me, "I'm as easy as high-school math."

"Uh, no, no, ma'am. I'd like to return. It's from my- from my aunt Cece."

"A gift? Your big tenth birthday, I bet?"

"Uh, no, I already have one. See?" I showed her my Casio.

"Yes, but dear, this one's brand-new." She eyed the box, making me nervous. "And for a big boy like you are now. It's Polo. Are you sure you want to return it?"

I nodded.

"OK, then, no problem. I'll just need a receipt. Did your aunt give you one, honey?"

"No, ma'am, she gave me the receipt." I answered feeling the heat rising in my face as I realized what she asked and what I responded. I dug around in my satchel and played the same "can't find it" game as Shelly would. I took note of the few items I had stashed: the rolled-up T-shirts and underwear Mi bought me, the condom Russell had given me in the fort, two pens, trading cards, my remaining funds, the unicorn notebook, and its receipt.

"I'm sorry, honey. Did you say you have the receipt?"

I nodded my head and kept rooting, trying to increase her impatience. A woman got in line behind me.

"Maybe I could help this next customer while you find it?" she offered.

"N-no, here it is." I handed her the diary receipt, wishing I could drum up the contempt Shelly expertly delivered.

She looked it over. "I'm sorry honey, this isn't it." She handed it back.

I paused, looking at her and to the watch. "It's-uh, it says the price, doesn't it?"

She turned the box over. "Yes, it does, but I need the receipt."

"I, uh, that's what my aunt gave me."

"Well, I'm sorry, but you'll have to get the right one from her and come back another time. Here, I'll put it in a bag for you." She placed the watch and receipt in the bag and handed it back, trying to move me along so she could get to the next customer.

"Sorry," I said and stood at the register for an extra moment in case she changed her mind.

Another store might work better, but I felt certain this would do. I walked past where I'd picked the watch up from and saw one of the remaining men at the register there. I walked up to him and placed the bag on the counter.

"She, uh, she said you could return this for me. I don't- I don't have a receipt, but it has the price on the box. I could just take the money." My audacity had the hairs bristling on my neck.

He put down a *Vogue* magazine. "Hello to you, too, partner." The man stunk of heavy cologne and had his shirt collar turned up. He yawned as he opened the bag and took the watch out.

"Pawning her work off on me again, is she? Tah!" He looked closely at the watch face. "Sure, sure, I'll help you. You have a card you want to charge this back to?"

I shook my head no.

"Cash it is, then." He looked at the box and hit a few buttons on his register. The register tape started printing, and the drawer opened. My heart began beating wildly.

"With tax, you get $264.98. You don't have two pennies on you, do you?"

I dug into my pocket and pulled out three. A drop of sweat rolled down the side of my body from my armpit as I waited for him to count out the cash.

"Thanks you."

"No partner, *thanks* you," he responded mockingly and handed me the money with a wink.

I shoved it into my satchel and walked as calmly as I could to the nearest exit. Two hundred sixty-five dollars! Holy shit, I did it. A young couple passed me as I pushed through the exit. The man gave a short snuff as our eyes met, but I suffered no fear and felt like stopping him to boast about my masterful chicanery. The late-afternoon air hit me, goading my feet to move quickly.

I didn't look back. I jogged right past an empty taxi and kept going. I felt grown up and could almost see through Shelly's empty frames now. No more worrying about how to survive alone. It'd be easy.

I didn't stop until I arrived at the corner of Adams and South Lower Wacker Drive. I wanted a good look at the Sears Tower across the street. Three hundred and sixty-two times my height. I wondered if birds flew to the top to roost. I would if I had wings. My stomach felt better, and I thought about filling it with a hot dog from the cart on the corner. They smelled good, but I didn't chance it. The light changed, so I followed the crowd across the bridge and looked at the river. Rivers had noticeable banks. Rivers were nothing like oceans or starry skies or large grassy lawns. Their songs were only a chorus more than creeks. I whistled at the river and patted my satchel with a reggae beat. Maybe I could handle lawns now.

Nameless people seemed reducibly frightening when one had cash in their pockets. I placed the money needed through the glass slot at the ticket counter and asked for the six-thirty train. Hank would be there for me. He always was. I'd call him when I got to Pittsburgh.

"I'm sorry, sir, but that train has been cancelled. We've been told maintenance was needed in Waterloo. The next to North Brunswick . . ." He checked his chart. ". . . is five fory-five or ten thirty-five tomorrow morning."

The man behind me practically breathed on my hair, so I asked for my money back and moved to the side. I went over by a trash can to think things over. I didn't want to stay at the station all night. I probably didn't have enough for a hotel room and the train. Shelly's trick would work again, but I didn't have another performance in me today.

A small woman bent over digging in the trash beside me wagged her head. It looked like it might topple off her shoulders. She was grimy with blackened fingernails and three layers of shirt. She squinted up at me, keeping one shadowy eye closed, looking a little like an Asian cousin of Pigpie.

"You're a scaaaab. Your mother's a scaaaaab," she moaned in Korean, making me want to slap her. She lived an impoverished life but that didn't mean a thing. Rude is rude, and my patience drained away with lunch. I really would have slapped her if she hadn't started digging again immediately, as if she'd said nothing. I started breathing normally again, watching her a moment more and left. I passed a man holding a woman against a wall. I couldn't tell if it was fun for her or not and didn't stop to find out.

A poster of a very adventurous looking black man climbing a mountain faced me on the wall ahead. It said *Yosemite* in large letters across the top. Yosemite National Park is in California. Southern Miwok and Mono Paiutes, the native residents, lived in the vicinity of Yosemite for some eight thousand years. The pattern of oaks and grassland noted by early explorers to the Yosemite Valley is probably a direct consequence of the intentional burning of underbrush practiced by native people. I had to go to California. California was the destination of many adventurous Americans. In California, I'd find Mi and Will. They'd have to take me in, and if the police confronted them, they could say I'd just shown up at their door. They couldn't be faulted. We'd be a family, and I know Mi could convince Will it'd be OK. I'd offer to do anything he needed to help with his boxing career. I'd work at the grocery store as a bag boy.

I went to the counter again, a different clerk this time. "How much for a train to Los Angeles?"

He checked his book. "Two hundred thirty-three dollars. Next one leaves Gate Nine at seven forty-three tonight, arriving in Denver tomorrow morning at five a.m. Connecting train from Denver arrives in LA tomorrow night at eight fifteen."

Wouldn't leave me with much for once I got there, but I could figure that out then.

"Or you could catch the six fifty to San Francisco for a hundred ninety-seven. Looks like you could stay aboard in Denver, since that train arrives at the Transbay Terminal tomorrow at nine forty-two. You'd take the ten p.m. to LA from Transbay for another thirteen dollars, which would take longer but cost less. You'd arrive in LA at twelve forty-five. Different pricing if you want a sleeper car."

"Through San Francisco, please."

"Sleeper car?"

I shook my head.

"Two hundred and ten dollars. It's already boarding, Gate Fourteen."

I pushed the money through the glass slot, and he pushed my tickets back.

CHAPTER TWENTY-SEVEN

Ponce De Leon Never Beat Up a Fat Woman

67.4.6-9.13.18-174.8.4.53.18.103

Insomuch as a train seat can be considered so, mine seemed a small slice of creamy leather and comfortably padded paradise. Today's lesson: A con man can enjoy respite on a stolen seat in Heaven. The car felt new, actually, or maybe it was just that it wasn't a commuter train and all traveling cars had an aura of this sort. Didn't matter, really, as I was so excited about riding long-distance on a train that everything was a thrill. A heavyset balding conductor with a neatly trimmed mustache asked for my tickets and welcomed me. He inspected each one, looked me over somewhat suspiciously, and asked, "Traveling alone?"

I nodded.

"All the way to California? Well, don't worry, I'll be traveling on from Denver with you. If you need anything, don't be afraid to ask. Name's Mick."

I nodded as he handed back my tickets. Something seemed familiar about him, but I figured I'd seen him in a crowd at the station at some point. He didn't leave as I thought he would.

"From California originally, are you?"

"Yes," I lied and looked out the window, wanting him to go away.

"Mm, well, enjoy your ride."

He moved on to another passenger toward the front of the car. I'd only ever known of one Mick personally, Uncle Evert's friend, and knew of few others, like Mick

Jagger of the Rolling Stones. None were bald, heavyset, or had mustaches. I watched out the window for an hour or so, and as it'd been a long day, I pulled my satchel into my lap and closed my eyes.

I woke at 8:32:43 p.m. Only the sound of the wheels on the track clued me into our speed. We were moving fast. The darkness outside turned my window into a dull mirror, and I stared at myself in the reflection. The double pane blurred me, but I looked older. I felt older, older and famished. The *Welcome Aboard* magazine mapped the dining and lounge car toward the middle of the train, so I decided to visit. I didn't enjoy the eyes on me as I traversed the other passenger cars but loved the feeling of motion that jostled me as I went.

The dining car had white Formica tables and hosts at both ends to usher customers to their tables. There were plenty of empty tables at this hour, but they put me immediately next to a couple who appeared to be in their twenties. I didn't complain. None of us introduced ourselves even though only salt-and-pepper shakers separated our tables. They lowered their voices for a few minutes when I sat but resumed a normal level once the waiter arrived.

The waiter repeated my choices of a number eight—fruit-cup appetizer—and a number thirty-two—PB and J, annoying me and causing the couple to giggle. My selections seemed perfectly normal to me, but she clearly said "fruit cup" and giggled. How immature. Revenge couldn't be gotten by giggling when the waiter brought their bland chicken-and-rice dinners six minutes later because they'd moved into deep conversation by then. It's hard to laugh at chicken, anyway.

"It is a fact: There are about four and a half billion chickens on the planet, one for every human alive," I quoted from the PBS documentary I'd fallen asleep to at the motel, because it came into my mind and immediately out of my mouth.

Their eyes blinked; their forks froze. Her mouth stayed ajar, readying for a bite, but it didn't respond. Her chin was pathetically small, as wide as her lips. I almost felt bad for her. Imagine if she fell on it. It'd crack like a fortune cookie.

"Fascinating," she finally responded, rolling her eyes, and they continued their conversation.

Glaring crossing lights flicked by the window on the other side of the train, erasing the distractions. I flipped my paper placemat over to work on an idea I had. My food arrived, and as the first squish of jam and peanut butter filled the roof of my mouth, I decided from here on out my life would be lived with little concern for what others wanted of me. I'd finish the unresolved *Monkey on Your Back Math* problems I'd started after Rutgers, and if I chose, share the results with the worldwide mathematical community. They could pay me to visit with them. I'd be the new Paul Erdös, a well-known, respected, and prolific mathematician who travels around staying with other mathematicians for free by swapping my math expertise. I should hope to be as prolific at seventy; most mathematicians peter out by thirty, they say.

The Millennium problems—as Hilbert titled them in 1900, the top twenty-three most-difficult mathematical problems—didn't take people all that long to resolve. Most of them are proven, and a century hasn't even passed, so why should this new *Monkey* top ten be so daunting. Whenever I think of the list and start running one problem or another, I wonder why the list exists at all, except maybe people are too lazy to work them through. I certainly wasn't going to be that lazy. Dr. Kohn had me working on those abelian varieties for his elliptical integrals studies, so tackling the Birch and Swinnerton-Dyer conjecture might be a good place to start. On my placemat, I drew a big torus, its doughnut shape briefly raising my curiosity as to whether some pastries might be available for dessert, and began a few preparatory notations.

I'd nearly finished my dinner when Mick came down the aisle toward me. He slowed as he got to my table but didn't stop to talk, only nodded hello. The waiter brought my bill soon after, and I quickly paid before Mick could return and ingratiate himself as I imagined he might. The Mick I remembered would have bounced around me like a dog begging for a treat. He also would've been stoned or drunk, and this guy appeared more respectable. There was, however, a certain familiarity in his face.

I grabbed a handful of paper placemats from the unmanned silverware area on my way out. Back at my normal seat, I worked on the conjecture on my tilt-down tray. Mick came through at about 10:30 p.m., leaned over to look at what I was doing, and left a small blanket for me from the stack he handed out.

"In case you get a chill."

I nodded my thank you and kept working.

Everyone had their overhead lights out by eleven. I wished I'd bought myself a snack. Sneaking chips or pretzels to my room was a common occurrence at Pigpie's. She stocked the house well. I can generate a powerful snack craving if I'm up late and become slowed by something difficult. Fritos with a good sour-cream-and-onion dip would be super. Since they weren't in the cards, I couldn't focus or complete anything worthwhile. I copied the important formula work into my journal and balled up the mats before I turned out the light.

The next morning, I woke with a ridiculous boner in my pants and mountains out the window. I couldn't shake the dreaming sensation, mainly related to the vision out the window. These mountains were such a thrill, so monumental, almost as if I were at the top of the sycamore tree. So dreamy, I waited for a sharp turn and a space-alien landscape exhibit to appear or the backdrop to snap up suddenly like a wild window shade. Hard to believe I'd slept past 11:00 a.m. and missed out on so many train vistas.

A cart drifted toward me. The porter announced his final run to a woman who opened her eyes so wide, you'd think he'd shouted her breasts were flat as pancakes, which they were. She might have been a man. The cart stopped in front of me with beverages, fruit, bagels, and of all things, egg-and-bacon sandwiches. I held my breath as I bought juice and a bagel. Even with the thick coffee vapors, a tiny whiff of the egg would be all I could handle.

I stayed glued to my seat through the rest of Colorado, on through Utah, and most of Nevada. Mick visited once as we were leaving Colorado, clearing his throat before he reminded people on board about the time change and once in Utah where he gathered my balled-up placemats and the accumulated wrappings from my lunch and dinner. I nodded. He nodded. I almost asked him his full name after our nods, but he left too quickly.

I was busy with another series of tori drawings when I noticed a man standing next to me, holding an unraveled placemat

"Is this your doing?" he asked, smoothing out the placemat some more on the armrest. Along with the calculations, I'd drawn three tori on it and thought they looked decent considering how fast I'd drawn them and that I didn't use a compass.

I nodded and pointed to my most-recent placemat calculations.

"Do you mind if I ask who you are?"

I shook my head.

"So?" He looked excited.

"Abel Velasco," I said, remembering what Allen Foster told me about always giving one's full name.

He looked to the ceiling in thought. His dark hair and protruding nose reminded me of an older version of that guy Mike Damone from *Fast Times at Ridgemont High*.

"I'm sorry, but I don't recognize your name. Mine's Ken, Ken Ribet. I teach at UC Berkeley." I looked at the hand he extended but didn't take it. "Mind if I sit down?"

I didn't find him threatening but wasn't crazy about being interrupted, so I shrugged at him to say, "If you want to, but don't expect me to be thrilled."

"That's quite a bruise you have there." He pointed at my head as he plopped into the seat next to me.

I shrugged again.

"So, this is pretty heavy-duty stuff you got here."

I shrugged once more.

"Who are you studying with?"

"Nobody." Which at this point I considered true, because I was done with Dr. Kohn and Princeton—and the whole East Coast, for that matter.

"Far out." He nodded and tried arching his neck to look at what I worked on.

A few moments of awkward silence passed before he continued.

"Do you mind?" He didn't wait for my response and pulled the placemats from under my hand.

He shuffled through the pages. "This is the Swinnerton-Dyer conjecture, right? I wasn't sure, but do you know what you're working on? I'm sorry, how stupid of me." He flipped back and forth between the placemats, "Maybe ten, twelve years old?" he said to himself. He looked at me briefly. I looked back, and he kept reviewing my work.

Mick came through the door toward us carrying an armload of pillows. Ken stood to block the aisle.

"You were right," Ken declared, waving the crumpled placemat at Mick like some damsel in distress.

"Thought maybe," Mick said, scooting past him. "Looked like the same stuff. Don't come across too many folks traveling and making drawings like you two, but sorry, m'on duty." He nodded at me and left.

"Funny, I was just now working on congruence between modular forms of different level." He shook his head with a smile like the commercial with that guy who won the state lottery and couldn't believe it. "The conductor must've seen my protractor. Can't see how he'd understand the similarities between what we are working on. If you wanted to come take a look at my . . ."

I pulled the placemats back onto the pull-down tray.

"Oh, I'm sorry. You're busy, and I'm interrupting. Maybe if you come to a pause, you'll join me for something to drink or eat? You've probably already had dinner, but I'm in seat thirteen B, car twenty-one."

I nodded, and he kept looking down at my notes.

"Hard to believe. So, you're going home to California? You don't live in San Francisco by any chance, do you? Oh, gosh, I'm sorry. There I go. Please join me later."

I nodded again, and he got up and started to leave.

"Train arrives in about an hour and a half," he added finally, nodded twice, and left.

The sweat from the side of my fist created an elephant-trunk mark on my paper. I added ears and an eye and watched the trunk disappear. Ken Ribet was in an article I'd read last month on PhD scholars from Harvard who made thoroughfares in analysis and algebraic geometry. His appearance gave hope that life on the road would be easy, that I'd find plenty of other mathematicians and places to stay. I couldn't see how I'd avoid explaining my predicament or whether he could be trusted, so visiting with him didn't make sense. I had much I wanted to accomplish before the train arrived at Transbay station, in any case.

Not surprisingly, when we were disembarking from the train, I found Ken waiting for me.

"Sorry to bother you again. A shame we didn't get a chance, but hey, if you ever wanted to talk or had an interest in comparing notes, you might come visit me at Berkeley. Here's my contact information." He handed me a business card. "I wrote my home information on the back if you wanted to write me there." I read it over and handed it back to him.

"Don't you want it?" he asked, somewhat upset.

"I have it." I pointed to my head while looking at the papers sticking out of his briefcase.

"Oh, splendid. OK, then. Nice to have met you, Abel Velasco. I'll be keeping an eye out for you." He waved at me again before he wobbled off, taking the closest stairwell with his briefcase around his shoulder and his suitcase in hand.

Our train from Denver had arrived a little early in San Francisco, so I had about a half hour to find my gate and wait for the connecting train to Los Angeles. The terminal was smallish, which made it easy to find where I needed to go. I started on my way there when I realized I didn't have their Los Angeles address or telephone number. The panic hit me again, and I looked at the clock and thought compass, I need a compass. It's doubtful that Ponce De Leon would have left home without a compass, but Ponce never beat up a fat woman and went on the lam—at least, not that I know of—and if he did, he might have forgotten his compass and more. I never owned a compass, unfortunately. As I was passing a soft-pretzel vendor, I noticed the pay phones that lined the wall next to the mustard-application and napkin area.

"Flynn's Garage."

"Hello, today."

"Heeey, Juke, that you? How's it going?"

"Hello, Hank, and I am in San Francisco."

"Wow, San Francisco! What do you know, but now, that's a little north of the mark, ain't it?"

"I took a—I took some trains."

"Trains? Must've had car trouble, huh? Hey, let me speak to Will. I need to tell him something."

"He's not here." I held back the sudden rush of tears as best I could.

"Go get him, then."

"He's-he's in Los Angeles."

"Los Angeles? Without you? I don't understand why the hell you aren't with him?"

"I was supposed to go back to you. He said-he said to call and to take the train to you, but I'm going to live with him. I'm on my way, but that's why I'm calling. Do . . . do you have his address there?"

"Will's? No. No, no, he said he'd call when he got there, but listen, I want you to—"

A recorded voice interrupted us. "For an additional one minute, please deposit another seventy-five cents."

I rooted through my satchel but only had a nickel. I shoved it through the slot.

"Juke, Juke, the police were here earlier. You should go to them there. They talked about your aunt and the death of—"

A click followed by a dial tone cut him off. Shelly is dead. I knew it. No more change. I should call someone; someone needed to help me. I didn't kill Shelly. I needed more change and wished Hank had an 800 number like a hospital, like a hospital. People at hospitals help you if you are hurt, but not if you are in special situations. I am hurt. My head has a bruise.

"St. Mary's, how may I direct your call?" said a stale receptionist.

"Marie Velasco, puh-please."

"Is she a patient or an employee?"

"Puh-puh—"

"One moment." The second movement of Barber's *String Quartet No. 1* played. Panic filled me as I tried to think straight. Shelly is dead. I didn't have Will's address. "I'll transfer you to her location, one moment please."

The pretzel vendor looked my way, so I turned to the phone's change return. *Bell system made by Western Electric. Push for coin.*

"St. Mary's, how can I help you?" said another stale voice.

"Ma-Marie Velasco, please."

"Who may I ask is calling?"

"This-This is her son, Abel Velasco."

"Hold, please." The adagio for strings again, this time until its ending, then silence. Did I get cut off? The police are looking for me.

A new, more-cheerful female voice finally said, "Abel, sweetheart, your mother can't come to the phone."

"Why not?"

"Oh, honey, she's not capable of something like that. Is an adult around that I might speak with?"

"Marie Velasco, please."

"I'm really sorry, honey, but she doesn't use the phone. Maybe you could discuss this with your guardian?"

I hung up. It was pointless, but to hear her voice, just once, just now, would've been nice. I studied the rotary dial and spun it just to hear the sound. I pushed the coin return in. Empty. The pretzel man had a patron, and I thought of getting more change to call Hank back, but as I waited for him to finish, it sunk in even more—Hank couldn't help me. The information board flipped my train's status from *on time* to *now boarding*. What would I do in Los Angeles without a way to contact them?

My feet stopped at a large movie-poster advertisement. Across the top, it read, *Something Wicked This Way Comes* with two boys running toward a giant man in shadow wearing a top hat. Near the giant's outstretched hands in smaller type was written, *What would you give a man who could make your deepest dreams come true?*

All my options sucked. Returning to North Brunswick sucked. I'm the only one who saw what happened to Shelly, and Pigpie's an adult who's friends with Father McMullen. I had nothing to give to any man who could make my deepest dreams come true, but if I did, I'd ask him to fix my predicament, to take me to my mother, to make her brain all right again, to teleport me there now.

In the poster, the two boys weren't merely running toward a shadow man. They were running toward his offer of a sparkling night at a fair—an obvious false oasis, a paradise mirage of dazzling light where kids could ride on rides while the shadows secretly consumed them. Flipping numbers on the train-schedule board drew my attention from the poster. The number two kept flashing, telling me to be as firm and resolute in my actions as I could. It said to be decisive, to follow even the most-doubtful option once decided upon until its end, so as to not end up like one in a forest heading this way and that. On the timetable for local trains, I found a listing for Berkeley and knew that Ken Ribet was my option. He did appear exceedingly excited about me and could be the start to my Paul Erdös lifestyle. This was my start.

Thirteen dollars down the drain for LA, but it only cost me four to catch the ride to Berkeley, and the woman at the booth said I'd be there in fifteen minutes.

CHAPTER TWENTY-EIGHT

How To Kill a Shadow

75.37.79.21-13.37.6-50.3-13.50.65.4-50.28

No reggae in the taxi, but it took me to the 1010 Alvarado Road address Ken wrote on his business card in sixteen minutes. Cost me another six dollars, lowering my remainder to forty-one—definitely not enough for a motel room if this didn't work.

Lights were still on upstairs and down. He must be awake. I stood on the walkway, trying to figure out what I'd say if he answered. My heart raced at the thought that this wasn't his house. That I hadn't seen correctly or that he wrote it down wrong. I trotted up to the door to get it over with. The bell chimed a bit louder than I expected. Movement and approaching steps—it looked like a man's form—and the door opened. Ken's questioning face came into the porch light.

"Hello?" he said, looking straight at me.

I choked, unable to form words.

"Abel Velasco? That's you, right? Are you OK? Come on in here." He ushered me into the foyer. We stood awkwardly before moving into the better lighting of the kitchen.

"So, what do I owe the pleasure of your visit?" He shifted the apple he had in his hand from his right to his left to his right again. I didn't know what to say.

"Hey, why don't you have a seat?"

I held onto my bag and sat down.

"I could- help you- with your modular-form congruencies," I mumbled at him, fearing he'd say no thanks.

He looked at me like a difficult formula, rubbing his cheek and chin.

Cautiously, he began, "How about we start with if you're OK?"

I nodded, opened my bag, and took out my journal so he'd know I'd come prepared to work.

"Abel, is there someone I can call? Your mom or dad, maybe? They must be wondering where you are at ten o'clock on a Monday night."

A thin, pretty woman with thick glasses and hair pulled back came into the room. They exchanged odd glances.

"Laura, this is Abel. Abel, this is my wife."

She put out her hand, but I waved at her instead of taking it. Her smile reminded me of melting butter on an English muffin. The warmth filled every cranny of her face as the grin widened.

"We met on the train. He might not look it, but he's a brilliant mathematician."

"Same could be said of you, good lookin'." Laura looped her arm through his.

Both gazed at me. I waited for my face to spontaneously combust from the heat I felt it producing. Luckily, I had my unicorn journal to flip through.

"Maybe you should leave us alone for a while," Ken whispered.

"Can I get you boys anything to drink or eat before I head off to bed?" Laura asked.

"Nothing for me. Abel?"

I shook my head.

"OK, then. Good night." Laura kissed Ken.

"Good night," he said, kissing her again softly and raised his eyebrows with a weird smile.

She left, and Ken took a knife and a cutting board from the counter. He joined me at the table and started slowly peeling the apple, keeping the peel in one long, thin piece.

"I don't have family," I finally responded.

Ken thought about what I said for a moment, "Mm, OK. No one at all I can contact? How about one of your teachers? Can't you tell me the name of one of your teachers?"

I didn't say anything.

"I'm kind of at a loss here, Abel. Your offer is generous, but I don't really think that's why you're here, is it?"

I nodded.

"You met me for two minutes on a train, and you decided I needed immediate help, huh? Is it that obvious?" He smiled at me.

I shrugged.

We sat quietly, listening to the footsteps of his wife above our heads. He continued peeling until he finished without breaking the strand.

"Well, I'm afraid you're going to have to start talking, Abel. You've got quite a bruise on your forehead, and I'm worried about you. Please tell me what's going on with you, or you could give me a telephone number for someone who might." He cut the apple into eight equal slices and pushed them on the tray into the middle of the table.

He took one from the tray, but I didn't. I began writing in my normal short-symbol-and-numerical notation about what I figured I could convey to Ken for what had taken place.

"That looks like pi, but it's not, is it?" he asked, pointing to my altered mathematical symbol for pi.

"That does look like pi, but it is Pigpie. Pigphi would be better but my cousin liked pie," I explained as I finished the notes. "I-I'm living-I lived with my aunt. She's fat, and

Shelly and I called her Pigpie but not to her face, which is full of moles."

Ken tried to squeeze back a smile. "She sounds terrible."

I nodded.

"I'd move away from her, too," he said, humoring me.

I couldn't help myself, being at the end of my patience reserves. I couldn't take the humoring and pounded on the table, making the apple slices jump.

"Oh, my," Ken said.

I rubbed the edge of my hand.

"No, that's fine." Ken picked up the apple peel timidly. "So, where did you live with your aunt?"

"She's from Washington and from New Jersey," I said.

He started rolling up the peel and waited for me to continue.

"We lived in New Jersey."

He finished rolling the peel into a tire.

"Many fine math teachers live in New Jersey. It's on the other side of the country. That's a long way." He flung and unraveled the peel across the table toward the slices, seemingly to emphasize what he meant by long way. It came off a bit ridiculous, and he yawned to cover up.

"Two thousand nine hundred and nine miles, depending on the route taken."

"Right, and so it'd take a lot to get here on your own."

"Can I stay here tonight?"

He looked at me and down at my notes. Apprehensive, he spun my journal so he could inspect them better.

"You can, if you tell me what this is."

"It's my . . . notes for what I said," I answered, feeling he continued to humor me.

"A code, then. I thought so. Well, it's late and I'm dreadfully tired, and I don't think we're going to resolve things tonight. A night shouldn't make much difference to anyone, but I want to be clear. If there is someone out there looking for you, and I'm sure there is, they are worried about you, and you should be calling them. But I can't force you to." He paused to see how I might respond, but I kept quiet. He shook his head a little. "I've got some blankets. Will the couch be OK?"

I nodded.

He paused in thought. "You don't even know me, Abel. I'll make proper introductions tomorrow, but this isn't a good way to go about things. You can't always trust strangers like me—"

"Ken Ribet studied at Brown University. Received his PhD in 1973 from Harvard, where his advisor was John Tate. Three years teaching at Princeton and two years of research in Paris. Ribet joined the Berkeley faculty in 1978. Approaches strangers on trains."

"Mm, got me. Where did you—"

"It is a fact: You were in the *Daily Princetonian*, March fourteenth, 1981. I shall go to France one day, too."

He thought for another moment. "You should. Best bread in the world. All right." Ken kept shaking his head with disbelief and stood up. He paused at the telephone and studied it for a moment but then escorted me to the couch. He sniffed in the air a couple times.

"I don't mean to offend, but I think you need to shower before bed."

He showed me the bathroom.

"Towels are in the cabinet. I'll leave a blanket and pillow out for you. If you need anything else, we're at the end of the hall, OK?"

I nodded, and he left me to clean off three days of dirt.

Laura came and gently shook me in what felt like only a few minutes of sleep but in reality was the following morning, albeit a very early morning.

"Ken's in the shower. He'll be ready shortly. Would you like something to eat, a banana or some cereal?"

I shook my head. She offered me a kind face and turned on a lamp before she went into the kitchen. My watch said 5:46:31 a.m. I smelled the back of my hand. Irish Spring soap lingered, but I still had a funk about me. I checked my pants to see if I'd gotten anything on them during my ladies' room episode. I could find no noteworthy stains.

Ken came down, chipper and animated, and took a mug of coffee to the table. He looked in at me and waved cheerily. I moved the covers and waved back as he began writing in a notebook. I started drifting back to sleep, but it wasn't long before he called over to me to get dressed as we would be leaving shortly.

The sunrise turned the sky an orange Creamsicle. It was the type of heavy-aired morning that promised a lovely late-spring day. I couldn't believe the number of cars on the road at this hour, each with their windows cracked open. The trees were different, more tropical. The air smelled different, too. Cleaner, brighter, more-oxygenated, maybe. Beach Boys music should've been playing on the radio instead of the news. Mom loved the Beach Boys.

Ken was preoccupied, wearing his concentration as others wear hats. I wanted to avoid all conversation about home and figured if I opened my mouth, it'd force him into asking about me. I stayed quiet until we arrived and knew it was a lucky day when I spotted a waning gibbous moon in the sky. In the university's parking lot, a woman with a neon green–and-pink shirt waited for her Pomeranian, who arched his back in the telltale position by a palm tree. Another bit adding to the good vibrations I'd been experiencing so far in California.

"I've got a few matters to attend to this morning, and my class isn't until four, so we've got plenty of time to figure things out," Ken told me as he walked me from the parking lot into one of the orange-shingled, white-stone buildings that populated the campus. Ken's office reminded me very much of Dr. Kohn's, only about a third larger with abundantly more chalkboards.

Ken started scooping ground coffee into a filter at the small table behind his desk. "Take a look around. There's plenty of reading material."

The room filled with the smell of his strong coffee, and we left each other alone. I inspected the chalkboards to see what he'd been working. Besides a few boards obviously devoted to teaching, most of them were nonmodular elliptic curves. One board appeared noticeably different, being neither for teaching nor of the same focus as the others. I stood in front of it trying to figure what separated it, made it unique.

Ken looked up from his desk at the board.

"Interesting, isn't it? That's by Gerhard Frey. Do you know him?"

"Gerhard Frey, German mathematician, known for his accomplishments in number theory. Graduated in 1967 from the University of Tubingen. Postgraduate studies in Heidelberg, where he received the Ph.D. degree in 1970. Professor at the University of Saarbrucken from 1975 until now."

"Guess I should just assume you know about everyone." Ken smiled.

I examined Gerhard Frey's work with a different perspective now and at one of the chalkboards where Ken started but had not finished. Spending a bit of time thinking about the two boards, items became clear, and I started bridging their work. Ken came over as I wrote out a few equations at the bottom.

"Interesting. I hadn't seen this." He pointed at what I thought obvious. "Hm, at the conference in Denver, I recently had a similar thought but didn't think of Frey at the time. Funny how something can be right in front of you."

He wrote *TS!* and circled it below what I had written. I could sense his excitement.

"I'll help you like Paul Erdös."

"Mm, we could collaborate, and I'll earn myself an Erdös number one instead of my three," he said, referring to the way mathematicians number themselves by the degree of separation of collaborating on papers with Erdös. A one is directly with him; a two would be working with someone who worked directly with him, and so on.

"Dare I ask who introduced you to the efforts of Gerhard Frey?"

"I don't... know it. I read about him when I read about Eliyahu Rips."

"Eliyahu Rips. I think I know him—"

"He is from the Hebrew University. He also won the Erdös prize in 1979."

"Oh, yes, I'm sure I've read something of his . . . group theory, right?"

"Uh, mmhm, I've been helping him, too."

Ken's face read of patronizing disbelief again.

"You sure get around, don't you? How is Jerusalem? I've never been there."

I opened my bag, pulled out the letter from Dr. Rips, and handed it over. Ken's face fell as he started reading it. He flipped the pages and reviewed the computer program's printout as well.

"This is interesting, Abel, very interesting. Do you have the envelope the letter came to you in?"

I didn't respond, and he continued to review it. "Have you run this?"

"Not yet."

He kept reading.

"This is—you came up with this first?" He looked at me and back at the letter again.

"It is, ah, came from Richard Pier—"

"I could have this typed into a computer for you if you want."

I nodded to begin a statement about how that would be nice and how I'd started already at Princeton, but he interrupted and went for the phone, stretched out the coiled cord and dialed a number. "Margaret, I'm so happy you're in already. Good, hey, listen, is there someone around that might do some typing for me, someone good with computers? Great. Oh, that'd be perfect. I'll be over shortly."

"I started it at Princeton," I said, pulling the floppy from my bag.

Ken took the floppy from me and handed it back. "I'm sorry. You don't mind if someone enters the rest into a system here, do you? Margaret's help are all brilliant and trustworthy. I work with them on occasion."

"S'okay, I don't mind," I answered, more excited that I'd get to see the results than annoyed at him for taking over.

"So, you were at Princeton? Did you go to school there?"

I nodded.

"Who'd you work with? I taught there, you know?"

"I know."

"That's right, that's right."

"I worked with Dr. Kohn. Sometimes Dr. Kohn helped with mine. Sometimes I helped with his, like with the ideas from Dr. Shimura before I drank tadpoles and became ill."

Ken's eyebrows were about to explode off the top of his forehead. "Dr. Kohn? Wait, how old are you, Abel?"

"Thirteen."

"It seems so impossible, but you are real." He poked me on the shoulder gently. "I know Kohn from when I was at Princeton. So, you were working on the Taniyama-Shimura conjecture with him?"

"Taniyama died in 1958." I wanted to be clear I only helped with Dr. Shimura's work, and not the bigger conjecture Taniyama and Shimura were famous for. "He committed suicide."

"So that's no, you weren't working on it, or—"

I shook my head no.

"Such a waste about Taniyama. He was only thirty-one."

"Until yesterday, I had no definite intention of killing myself. I don't quite understand it myself, but it is not the result of a particular incident, nor of a specific matter," I quoted Taniyama.

"Maybe we should sit down."

We sat at the two closest chairs.

"You're thinking of killing yourself? That's so sad. Think of what Taniyama could've done had he—"

"No, no, I'm not," I stopped him.

"What was all that intention of killing yourself, then?"

"Taniyama wrote that, in his suicide note. The-the shadows consumed him, but I don't think he knew it."

"The shadows consumed him?"

I studied the board with the Frey formulae briefly. "You know, like Descartes talked about."

"No. Why don't you explain?"

I wasn't sure where to begin and sat in the chair for a minute until it came to me. I drew the delirious-eight-on-its-side symbol for infinity on the chalkboard.

"This is—this would be where the shadows dwell." I tapped at the board. "It's, uh, everywhere and nowhere."

"The shadows dwell in infinity?" Ken cut in. I nodded and pounded my knee.

"Descartes said- he said, 'I think, therefore I am.' Descartes knew the shadows, and Descartes knew them well. Anyone who reads Descartes must learn of the demons controlling us. And Descartes used logic and math to figure out life."

Ken looked closely at the symbol for infinity. "You know, the reverse could be said. Life or the physical world could have forced human logic on Descartes, and his view was therefore consistent with what life offered. He may not have had a choice. Mathematics comes from logic. This is why mathematics is consistent with the physical world," Ken replied as if delivering part of a lecture.

"Um, uh, Newton proposed the theory of gravity," I replied, knowing he missed my point. Ken's constricted lips held back an "and so?" "His math model for it was exc- exceedingly accurate, far better than the existing measurements taken by astronomers at the time. The, uh, the math didn't come from the measurements. It wasn't forced on Newton's work."

He smiled at me, stood, and turned toward Frey's formulae.

"I guess when it comes to the math-was-discovered or was-created debate, I'm an agnostic. Sometimes I see it as the mathematics we have is a feature of the biological details of humans and how they perceive the cosmos. I'd say it could be that math exists only in our minds. A parrot or an orangutan wouldn't see the math. An alien with different eyes and senses may have completely different math. And I suppose, more broadly, it may be that math could be invented to describe anything in nature, but I don't have these answers for certain."

"That's the shadow demon, right there. You know, like the Parahã tribe."

"Are they aliens?" he joked.

"The Parahã tribe from the, uh, the Amazon can't learn to count. They have no words for colors. One plus two would stump any of them. That's the shadow. The shadow could, could make us see the world, any way it wants. Descartes said it. It could remote control our lives, making us think we understand life and math, and then one day it says, go kill yourself, and you do."

"Whoo, boy. This is tough." Ken looked at the blackboard. "You've glanced at the *Principia Mathematica* or at least some of Russell's work?"

For a moment, I wondered if he meant Russell Ghety, but he meant Bertrand Russell. I nodded.

"So, do you recall his famous paradox, then? His class of all those classes that are not members of themselves? The Barber paradox?"

I started to nod yes, but he kept going.

"In a village, the barber only shaves everyone who does not shave himself, no one else. The question that prompts the paradox is this: Who shaves the barber? If he doesn't shave himself, he must shave himself, but that can't be, because then he shaves himself—and he *only* shaves people who do not shave themselves. Heh, confusing to say out loud, but I'm sure you see. No, wait, wait, I have a better way to show you how logic can trap you."

Ken stood up and placed his hands on his hips.

"Walk with me to see Margaret, and I'll tell you what I mean." He started for the door. We walked down the hallway, past large corkboards of paper flyers, and headed up stairs. He stopped suddenly.

"In order for a person to get to Margaret's office, that person must first go halfway there, as is now the case with this stairway. In order to reach the halfway point, the person must first reach the midpoint between the start of the walk and the halfway point. And to reach halfway to the halfway point, the person must cross the halfway to the halfway to the halfway point. The philosopher Zeno argued that the process could be continued forever. The gist of the argument is that in order to reach Margaret, an infinite number of points must be crossed. And logic tells us that an infinite number of points cannot be crossed in a finite period of time. Therefore, logic says it's impossible to get to Margaret." We started walking again. "We've already begun to prove logic wrong, haven't we?"

I considered his points and followed him up the stairs.

"That Zeno paradox is an oldie, and I bet you've already read some form of it, but the lesson is that there are always mental ways to trap yourself and the way beyond those traps is to introduce new limits. Descartes taught us this, right? Much of science is based on describing the material world mathematically as an enormous machine whose parts work together according to uniform laws of motion. That's called being Cartesian, right?"

I nodded.

"Descartes launched that way of looking at life probably to dispel that shadow demon. Probably to say, 'I can't know if the shadow demon is real, just as you can't, and so it's better to shift your focus away from the unknowable; try to break it apart into pieces so you can know it eventually.'"

He had me thinking about the shadows differently. This was good.

Before I could respond, we reached an office door. A woman by a watercooler filled a paper cone and started toward us as we entered.

"Hi, Ken."

"Margaret, how are you? Margaret, this is Abel, a new friend of mine. He's got a program that needs typing into one of the systems next door."

Margaret was a simple and attractive woman who wore a powder-blue suit with her hair up in a clip.

"Rach," Margaret called to a student who came over to us. "Rach here volunteered to help. He's a whiz programmer."

"We just need someone to type it up. Abel says he started already."

I pulled out the floppy and the pages from Dr. Rips's letter and gave it to Rach.

"No problem. When do you want it?" Rach asked, sliding a pen behind his ear.

"As soon as you can."

"I'll start now. Maybe an hour, by the looks of it." Rach took it into the next room.

"Thanks, Margaret, we'll be back then."

CHAPTER TWENTY-NINE

Jesus, John Lennon and Norman Vincent Peale

38.24.40.4-5.96-4.43.14.13

Ken took me outside, and we walked to a little park where students were congregating on the grass.

"I've got work left to do for my class. Why don't you hang out here and meet me back at Margaret's around ten?"

I felt abandoned at first but realized that he hadn't pressed me on contacting anyone and without a doubt I'd impressed him, probably enough to let me stay and attend Berkeley. I was certain he'd be back with good news once he'd caught up.

The clouds bumped and rolled above me playfully. At ten-forty in the morning, one would think more students would be in class rather than cavorting in a park. A yellow Frisbee landed close to my legs.

"Hey, throw that here, man," demanded a student that reminded me of Hank if Hank were young and had hair.

I picked it up and tried to throw it, but it banged quickly to the ground and rolled in a semicircle between the two of us.

"Nice try," he said with sincerity but didn't throw it to me again. I was happy about that.

I continued to watch and imagined myself flying through the air, riding on the Frisbee, caught and returned with laughter and affection. Why didn't people play Frisbee in Princeton? I could see Ken throwing a Frisbee. He probably played with his wife. I tried to imagine Dr. Kohn playing. Working with him had been so formal, but here, already it felt better, more natural.

I pulled out the unicorn to make a fresh entry and transcribed some of the dialog formulae from conversation with Ken. I paid special attention to our talk about the shadow demon. The formulae from it were unusually elegant. Ken made sense, and he was a smart man. I flipped back to the notes I'd jotted the night before and roughly crossed out the symbol for Pigpie. It was an act of desire. I wanted her not to exist. Why couldn't I just stay here? This should have been my next foster home instead of the other coast. I'd learn Frisbee, maybe even learn to face the ocean. Pigpie called me a chickenshit in Atlantic City because of my troubles with looking at the ocean right after I'd earned her plenty of cash. Why should I ever have to face her again? She'd made enough off me. I could send an anonymous note explaining what she'd done. I looked up from my journal to find Ken walking toward me.

"Having a good time?" he asked, taping on his watch.

I nodded. "Hey, you know-you know I could be your Ramanujan, and you could be my Hardy."

"Oh, you'll accomplish more than Ramanujan." He helped me to my feet. Ken checked his watch four times on the way to Margaret's, and I began to feel guilty that I didn't meet him when he requested.

Back in Margaret's office, we found her and Rach in a frenzied state.

Rach came over to us. "I typed in *Newton* and *gravity*. You won't even believe it."

My ears perked up at the mention of Newton.

"I was just about to see what he's been going on about. Shall we?" Margaret waved toward the door.

Rach led the way, and we joined him at a computer.

"These computers new?" Ken asked Margaret, looking at Rach's monitor.

"Apparently, you can't even buy them yet, but the university is previewing them, I think. Rach could tell you. He works more closely with Professor Finks and these—"

"Forget the computers, look at this," Rach said as he scrolled through the Hebrew characters and reset the program. "I haven't really examined it since my bar mitzvah, but this is obviously the Pentateuch if you didn't recognize it, or if you like, it's the Torah or the first five books of the Bible in a string of 304,805 characters. So first, it took me longer to input because I had to access another archive through our new TCP/IP link, where the Pentateuch was available, because it's referenced in the code. But we obviously didn't have it in a format I could work with—digital, that is. Then I had to set up the monitor to properly display the results. But once I'd gotten that configured, it didn't take me long." He beamed proudly. "I tried the list at the end of the letter here with the concentration camps, and they showed up, but I thought maybe you designed the program for those, so I tried my name, *Rachamim Milton Drosnin*, and just *Rach Drosnin*, but they didn't get me anything. Guess I'm not historically significant, but then I typed in *Newton* and *gravity*."

A poster of Magritte's *La Grande Guerre*, or "The Great War," hung behind the computer. It depicted a man with a green apple hovering in front of his face. I started to feel part of that surreal world as I leaned forward to watch *Newton* and *gravity* scroll onto the screen with Rach's typing. He followed them with *<search>* and *PROCESSING* began flashing on the screen above the Hebrew characters. No one spoke while we stood, waiting with anticipation, staring at the blinking *PROCESSING* as the minutes passed. Then, like a crossword puzzle, we saw *Newton* highlighted in a descending diagonal row from top

A WHOLE LOT

right to bottom left, no letters skipped, and *gravity* crossing horizontally through *Newton*.

"What's it mean? Is it freaking you out like it is me?" he asked Margaret.

"I don't read Hebrew, Rach."

"Oh, sorry, this spells out *Newton* and this spells out *gravity*. Same page, the two are crossing each other. What are the odds?"

Margaret looked at Ken, but his eyes focused nervously on his watch.

"So, this is the full text of the Torah in order?" Margaret asked, and Rach continued to nod enthusiastically.

"I don't know, this is, what, maybe a sign that God exists, right? But this couldn't be legitimate?" Margaret asked.

"Oh, I checked to be sure it's the correct Torah referenced in the code. This is the real thing," Rach added.

Ken snapped as if just realizing something. "It's unbelievable. More tests are needed certainly, on the full text, not just Genesis. And there'll need to be others more-equipped to review it, but yes, Newton obviously wasn't around when these were written."

A newspaper headline flashed in my mind. *April 12, 1983: Abel Velasco Discovers Hidden Word of God.* I now understood Dr. Rips's excitement in his letter.

"Try something like *John Lennon*. He said he was more famous than Jesus, didn't he?" Margaret added.

Rach typed, we waited, and bing, bing, bing, *John Lennon* appeared diagonally. Rach and Margaret looked over at me.

"Where'd you get this?" Rach asked.

"He didn't appropriate this, Rach. He created it," Ken explained. "But I'm not sure finding John Lennon in the Bible means anything specifically, does it? Couldn't anything show up if you gave it a whole book to search through? The odds would become significantly more difficult if you had a string of words that were connected in subject matter. *Newton* and *gravity* are closer to proving something."

"What about *John Lennon* and *Mark Chapman*? Try that, Rach," Margaret directed. Rach started typing.

Again we waited, longer this time. I felt certain it would fail and could sense the heat in my cheeks starting. After a tense five minutes, where the rest of us found chairs to sit and watch, and they continued to discuss what Rach understood of the computer coding, the search successfully ended. I felt like yelping with delight and may have if it actually found a full statement like, *Mark Chapman killed John Lennon on December 8, 1980*. But finding them on the same page with the last *n* of *Chapman* sharing one of Lennon's, well, that was pretty great, too.

"My God!" Margaret exclaimed. "Where's the closest church? I think I have some catching up to do."

"Who should we tell? I told you the concentration camps showed when I entered them, right?" Rach asked with breathless excitement.

"Mm, yes, you did, but we better keep this under our hats, at least until I have a chance to review it more thoroughly—or at least contact Eliyahu Rips and the others who worked on it. Margaret, thank you so much for your help with this. I'll keep you informed of our findings. Rach, would you mind saving it to disk for us? And then please remove the program from this system."

Rach wasn't pleased. "What about him? Couldn't we just ask him? I thought you said he made this."

"He worked on it, but I think it more appropriate to discuss this with people more informed on such matters," Ken said.

I wanted to correct him and say it was mine, that they merely refined it, but more so I wanted to try other patterns, to see what else I could find out. Instead, I waited with Ken while Rach copied the program to three floppies and deleted it from the hard drive.

"Let's go back to my office and take a look at the program code together. Maybe you can explain some of what inspired you," Ken suggested as we started down the stairs.

He rushed along distracted by something other than the code. Surprisingly, he didn't talk about the program's results. It boggled my mind why he'd quit so soon before exploring the program more. I wanted additional time with it. We slowed upon arriving at his office. I couldn't be sure, but there definitely appeared a certain worried quality about his face. The floppy disks slipped from his fingers onto the desk beside me as we took the same seats from earlier.

"Look, Abel, here's the thing. Last night, today, is a bit out of control. I should've taken a day off or something. I'm concerned. You seem like an exceptional young man, but you also seem, well, troubled at the least, and I haven't even found out what you're doing here. I mean, after what I've just witnessed, I worry somehow I'm missing that you've been sent to me for a purpose, but it'd be irresponsible of me—"

His talking droned out as the numbers built up steam. They poured down, and the storm raged. It amounted to the same calculations as Will's good-bye speech all over again. I was losing my chance to stay with Ken, slipping away in the words, sinking beneath the numbers. I needed him to know who I was. Ken knew my work from the train and the program. Wasn't that enough? I slid my satchel to the floor and suddenly felt tired and angry. I stomped on the floor, which sent my satchel sliding a few inches toward Ken's feet.

"This is what I'm talking about, Abel. I'm just not capable of dealing with this. Our time together has me incredibly interested in you, and I hope we get a chance to work together more, but—"

I leaned down and pulled the file that Dr. Limone had given me from my satchel. As I sat up, I handed it to him.

"What's this?" he asked and started moving through the pages.

I placed my satchel on top of the floppy disks on the desk and moved my chair closer, wanting to see the old papers and report cards that I hadn't gotten around to reading yet.

"I've never heard of the New City School," he said when he found one of my first progress reports. "So this is your academic hist—" He stopped and laid the file on his lap. His finger started moving along a page I recognized but had forgotten. *Corpus callosum* flashed at me again as it did that day when Shelly interrupted. His eyes saw them now. Dr. Limone must've read it, too. The numbers flowed backward as my eyes rolled and trembled.

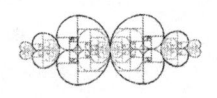

Mom was worried. She'd been out of it all weekend and kept saying I spoke like an alien. I must be sent away. She said I had to go to school—go to school, she said, to learn to talk like a human. She was scared, but I knew it was the drugs. I didn't know she'd be bothered by my saying a few things in Russian. She left me in the room with Melinda, the nurse. Melinda was very nice to me. A doctor came through the door. He came past Melinda, Melinda who was very nice to me. He rubbed up close to her as he came in, and she left quickly. She didn't like him rubbing up close to her. I could tell he was masquerading as a teacher the way he asked in Russian about where I'd learned Russian and told me he was a great teacher and would help me. I knew you don't tell a five year old what a great teacher he has or how Melinda understands it very well or put your hands in your pockets to adjust your thing as you tell it. He said my mother wasn't coming for me and that I had to answer him. He continued with questions in Russian and raised his voice when I didn't answer. His eyelids were too droopy and his ears had hair coming out of them.

I'd met him before, during the first tests. He had a gold ring on his finger then, and he hadn't spoken Russian. A white band of skin marked his ring finger where the gold ring used to sit. I thought of what Uncle Evert would say. I said, "I bet your wife liked you once but you're old. Melinda thinks you're old." The doctor pulled on my shirt, yanked me up off the chair, and smacked me.

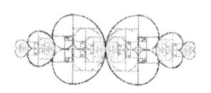

"And for a kid who was dropped on his head as a baby, you seem to have done pretty well for yourself. In seventy-six, you were, what, six when you wrote this: *The Rise of Rail Transportation—a Short History of Trains?*"

"Second paper I wrote for Mrs. Bird." I stood up.

"Have you seen doctors since this time frame?" He looked up at me.

I shook my head no.

"You should read this, here." He turned back a page and pointed to a paragraph that read: *Epilepsia arithmetices— seizure potential while performing arithmetic manipulations. Brain wave measurements show abnormalities in the inferior parietal cortex. His lesions may affect mathematical ability, writing, and spatial coordination.*

"Have you had any seizures lately? Any seizures while doing math? Is that how you got that bruise? Why don't you sit back down so we can finish our talk?"

I shook my head to all four.

"I'm not a doctor, but these look like you're a very special case. You've proven yourself the most-intelligent young man I've ever encountered, but you still require someone to nurture that, to watch over you, especially considering this history. It's time we gave that aunt of yours a call. I know you don't like her, but—"

"No, no, that—that's not a-that's not a possibility."

"Abel, come now, someone once said, 'Become a possibilitarian. No matter how dark things seem or actually are, raise your sights and see possibilities—they're always there.' You must think of the good things your aunt's done for you, and what she might still."

"Norman Vincent Peale said it."

"What? Oh, right. Well, guess I don't hate Norman Vincent Peale as much as I thought I did." He rubbed his temples.

I considered stomping again.

"Sorry, the quote just came to me. Sounded like my father there. He was always—"

A man in a blue suit and a woman in jeans and a white shirt knocked at the open office door and entered. I looked at Ken.

"I'm sorry. See, I didn't have your aunt's name—"

I took my file back from him, stuffed it in my satchel, and slid the floppy disks in with it while he looked toward the suits.

"Professor Ribet?" the man asked.

"Yes."

"Jim Swanton. We spoke on the phone," he said, holding his hand out. "This is Triana Matto."

I moved my satchel to cover my stomach.

"They're from social services. You don't have to be nervous." Ken put his hand on my shoulder, and I took a step back. They all appeared tense, waiting to see what I'd say. "Thanks for coming on such short notice. I'm certain

Abel will appreciate the help you'll be able to provide him with."

"Can we speak with you alone for a moment, professor?" Triana said.

Ken looked at me and around the room. "Abel, would you mind reviewing some of Gerhard Frey's work again?" He walked me to the board with Frey's work and returned to the officers. They whispered among one another for several minutes before calling me to join them.

"Abel, you must forgive me for not—" Ken said before I interrupted him.

I shifted back and forth on my feet. "Can I-I need to use the bathroom."

You feeling OK?" Ken asked.

I nodded and gestured at my groin.

"It's down the hall to the left, but hurry back," Ken said.

They all were watching as I glanced back before I exited the room.

We'd passed the bathrooms on our way to Margaret's. It was just beyond the halfway point. I quickly transgressed Zeno's paradox on my own—up the stairs and back toward Margaret's office. Past her office and down the stairs at the other end of the hall that I figured were toward the front of the building.

Florescent lights to bright daylight as I exited the building, cars and palm trees, maple trees, grass closely trimmed, and students with bicycles and motorcycles and stoplights. Twenty-two blocks of concrete matched with six-inch curbs and yellow paint chipped in fourteen places. Bus stop, bus stop, bus stop. Hands in my satchel. I've got money still, plenty of money still. Four steps up to the driver. Seventy cents to Oakland. One dollar and forty cents to downtown San Francisco. No transfer necessary. "Kid, kid, you on or off?" Two dollars, I give him two. Two quarters and a dime placed back in my hand. Put it in your satchel, Abel. Save it. Forty-two seats, two to a seat, eighty-four passengers minus seventeen empty seats plus the one I take. Sixty-eight, isn't prime. A boring sixty-eight, and away the bus goes. I'm moving, and they are in the room waiting.

A tubby teenager with huge boobs and a black-and-orange baseball cap. I could rest on her boobs, rest there for a few minutes and catch my breath. The storm is filling me up, and I'm tired. Too tired not to sleep, I'll just rest on these like falling asleep on Mom's. This teen has plenty of room and a hat for some shade.

"Hey, get off me," she says, but she's smiling. One front incisor darker than the other, she's smiling—four incisors, canines, premolars, molars, thirty-two teeth.

The seat metal is cold on my cheek, a polar opposite to her soft, wide body, but it won't reject me. Oakland, Emeryville, the Oakland Bay Bridge. Hadn't I gone over this last night? The taxi must've come across, there is no other way, but I don't remember crossing this high. I don't remember the water. Yerba Buena Island connecting the two suspension sections. The Bay Bridge opened for traffic on November 12, 1936, six months before San Francisco's other famous bridge. The Golden Gate Bridge, built in 1937, was the largest suspension bridge in the world when they finished. The numbers sliding across made my vision too difficult, so I closed my eyes. I'd know we were there when the bus stopped.

When I opened my eyes again, it's as if the world did a flip. The bus headed back across the bridge. I got up quickly. Hand to pole to pole to pole to driver.

"'Scuse me, I, I missed it."

"You missed it? OK. Where you going, kid?"

"Uh, downtown."

"Aw, nah, you're leaving downtown, kid. Where you from? Marin?"

"No, uh, North Brunswick."

"You could get off in Emeryville. Catch another back across the bridge, or you could stay on with me and we'll loop back in about an hour, but if you don't want to waste your time, just take Emeryville back. Take a seat, I'll tell you." His teeth had plenty of gaps, which to me meant he was kind. He looked like Bruce Lee from *Enter the Dragon*, the movie Russell and I watched on Saturday, July 31, last year.

The stop in Emeryville was also the train station, and as I'd spent so much time this week at train stations, there was a recognized comfort to the atmosphere.

My stomach twisted, wringing the bile because I didn't have much left to digest. When did I eat last? A PB and J would save me right now. There's another pretzel stand. I'd have a pretzel.

"One and a lemonade, please," I requested and paid.

Five women, two men, woman, man, child, child, woman. I took a seat at the end of the row and ate my pretzel. In between lemonade sips, I counted floor tiles, and Nike zips, and ankles until the night came. I bought three more pretzels and two more lemonades. When possible, time was spent collecting the scents of strangers. A tricky game I'd played only once while waiting in a crowd at the mall in St. Louis when I lived with the Jeffersons. It requires you to get uncomfortably close to people and take in their smell. The game would be much better if not for the proximity to others it necessitated. She comes from a world of spices, baked goods, and wooden cabinets. He's a musty, foam basement couch, Old Spice, and coffee. I could lay down a formula using oscillators based on their scents and calculate how long until they'd fall in love, how long until their hair would fall out, how long until their next dental appointment. Every face a new face, every life competing with the next to prove its complexity, and all of them coated with angles and lines, surface tension and anomalies that most would miss, but not me. I had their number. I had their life scents and maps. Given their birthdates, I could direct them to paradise or misdirect into shadow.

In the bathroom at the mirror, at the mirror with the black-marker graffiti that looked like it said *DREAM* on one corner, my reflection looked bluish from the fluorescent lighting. I turned the water on and breathed. My scent unraveled no mysteries except for my fondness for pretzel mustard, or the capability of the back of my hand to retain soap scents. I looked to the floor to try to steady myself. My blood-and-grass-and-shit-stained shoes revealed the greatest information about me—mainly that I didn't want to walk in Pigpie's backyard without the potential to step in Mister Scratch's piles. I didn't want to step anywhere near her. The pressure of tears for Mister Scratch pushed against the edges of my eyes, but I repressed them. Instead, as I stared into my own eyes, I barked, barked at my dirty reflection. Barked and barked until a white-haired man next to me shut off the water at my sink and told me that was "enough goofing around." I barked at him and pushed out of the room.

Walking the perimeter of the station grew tedious. I sat by the ticket counter, listening to where people were going. Portland, San Diego, Las Vegas, Hastings, El Paso. No one mentioned a city or town in New Jersey, and I took it as a sign. I'm not going back there. Anywhere else would be better.

"Hey, uh, hey, hello there!" a familiar voice came from in front of me.

I looked from the departure board to find the conductor, Mick.

"Short trip, or are you just touring train stations in the San Francisco area?" His mustache rose with his eyebrows.

I didn't respond.

"Reminds me of something your uncle would've done, or did, really. He didn't have a clue when he was taking us to Canada. Acted like he did, but we all knew he was just wingin' it. Name's Mick Washington. Monkey—they called me Monkey, remember?" Mick's eyes scanned the station as he spoke. "You're Marie's kid, Abel, right?"

I stared for a bit at him and nodded.

"I thought it might be you on the train with the math you were drawing. I didn't know, I wasn't sure what to say on the train. I mean, what could I say? Hi, you knew me when you were like four or something, remember? Your dead uncle's friend." Mick shifted on his feet, glanced to the left quickly, and then back at me. "I felt bad for not saying hi, though. I wanted to say hi plenty, but I mean, would you believe I work on trains now? From driving buses to trains. You'd be surprised. Working for Amtrak isn't the life of adventure everyone thinks, but I make a good living. So, you ended up in Chicago, huh? I figured Chicago, but it could be San Francisco, right? Someone adopted you, right?" Mick's words came fast and awkward. He appeared to want to leave after he spoke and kept looking around but not at me.

I was stuck on what he'd meant by drawing.

"I wasn't adopted," I finally said.

"Oh, yeah, they said you were in a foster home. That's what they told me about, about you, when I went to find out about you. I thought you'd be adopted then, but damn, it's so hard to believe nine years passed already since Ev was hit by that truck."

"Um, seven," I said, realizing he'd just explained one of my long-held mysteries: Uncle Evert died when he was hit by a truck, not tripping into a metal grate or any of the other scenarios I imagined.

"Jeez, I never could keep track. Seems longer. Long time, anyway. So, where you headed? Home?"

I looked at the board to check what might be departing soon but couldn't decide. The train to Los Angeles leaves in four hours, and I couldn't fathom how

I'd explain why I'd be here so early, so instead I asked, "Where are you going now?"

"'Nother long run across, but then I get a four-day break. It'll be nice to be back in my apartment and have a few at Tank's. Nice group of guys there. I live in Hoboken since I got this job. I thought about Chicago, too, but then I thought, Why not New York City? But then I ended up in Hoboken. St. Louis had too many of the same faces, you know?"

I nodded, thinking about his proximity to Mom in Hoboken.

"So, you? Back to Chicago by tomorrow, I guess?"

"No uh, I'm going to New Jersey, too," I said without thinking.

"No kidding? Whereabouts?"

Each of the major cities in New Jersey raced through my brain, but pathetically, I just continued with the truth. "North Brunswick." Hank's face came into my mind.

"Holy shit, a coupla Midwest boys living near the Big Apple. Who'd a thunk it, huh? So, you're on the eight-forty with me, then, right?"

I nodded.

"Well, come on then. You can board with me. I'll show you around."

He took me to the control room, toured me around behind the scenes, and said I could share his quarters if I didn't mind. He said his were much more comfortable than one of the seats.

"You get any of that sewer smell through the vents after we stopped in Denver?"

This made me chuckle. "Nope."

"Oh, lotsa people were complaining about it. Toilets backed up or something. I couldn't do anything; no word on why it was, but I had to take it from everyone. I've pretty much learned to shut up and do whatever people ask of me since I lost the bus job. OK, well, I gotta get to business. There's a Coke in my bag if you want it." He donned his cap and closed the door behind him. I lay down on his bed and let the numbers wash over me, lulling me to sleep.

During the three-day trip back, he treated me as I recalled my uncle doing. Talking to me as if I were his age and bringing me food and magazines. I counted threes in the *Sports Illustrated* he'd given me to make it look like I'd read it, but the *People* magazine was OK, nothing with any decent math or science. I just worked on my formulae most of the time.

On the second night, he was off by seven. He napped in our room for an hour and woke up starving. The dinners he brought back even came with salads. The armrests pulled up to become personal tables. Mick typically ate with his mouth open, but I ignored it as best I could. He asked about my visit to California, and I told him I'd met with professors at Berkeley, which was true. He asked what living in foster homes was like and said he'd been adopted when he was a baby, a fact I never knew. After an hour of mostly one-sided conversation during which he filled in details since "that bad night," he stopped and leaned closer to me, inspecting my face.

"You remember how you used to call your uncle 220 and me 284?"

Recalling the fact made me smile. Certain numbers are friends to the other. The friendship happens when each number is equal to the sum of the other's proper divisors—divisors other than the number itself. The proper divisors of 220 are 1, 2, 4, 5, 10, 11, 20, 22, 44, 55 and 110. They add up to 284. 284 = 1, 2, 4, 71, and 142, and they sum to 220, so 220 and 284 are friends.

"You were one weird kid." He gazed out the window. "You know, Tom Dooler and I used to fight all the time over who your mom liked better." He looked closely at me again. "You're the spitting image of your mom. I mean, you sorta look like Evert, too, not that he was your dad, but man alive, it's weird. So, she's in North Brunswick, too?"

"She's staying at St. Mary's, the hospital on 308 Willow Avenue, in Hoboken, New Jersey."

"You mean the Hoboken where I live now?"

I nodded.

"Well, why didn't you say so? Wow, can't believe she's that close. She's sick, huh?"

I nodded again.

"Man, we should go visit her when we get back. Wouldn't that be a kick? Oops, so, is it still drugs, or she didn't break a leg or something?"

"She'll be all right," I said.

"It'd be no problem. Heck, it'd be my pleasure, even. We could stop, and then I could give you lift back to North Brunswick. Really, I don't mind. I'd like to see Marie."

He was so enthusiastic, and I wanted so badly to see my mother at this point that I didn't bother with the full truth.

CHAPTER THIRTY

Miscalculated Certainty

140.4.77.11.7.75.7.14.24.11-20.2.140.43.13.49.11.2.1

Mick's work trip ended at Grand Central Station. He told me I could ride free with him instead of getting off at Trenton—all assumptions on his part, as was the idea that I'd ever had a ticket. He never asked. I hadn't been to New York City before and felt a rush of excitement and fear as we took a bus ride from the station to the Park 'N' Go lot in Hoboken.

"Where's this hospital again?" Mick asked once we got in his Dodge pickup.

"Three-oh-eight Willow Avenue."

"I live down by the reservoir on Prospect Street. Do you know if it's near that?"

I knew exactly where he lived. I'd sought out the map of Hoboken immediately after Pigpie told me where Mom was.

"Take the Observer highway, left on Clinton Street. You'll see it at Third Street."

"Damn, so weird how you know everything. We should go buy some lottery tickets." He was very serious, if not slightly sheepish about it. He turned up "Eye of the Tiger" on the radio. "Let's stop at my place first, so I can check on things, and then we'll go see Marie."

I couldn't believe it. I wanted to cry and hug Mick. He'd take me to see her, and I bet she'd see me, and maybe seeing me would even make her feel better, too. I was rising up like in the song, filling with hope and determination. I bet Mick would let me stay with him until Mom was all better, and maybe Mick would be her friend again and we could all stay together until Mom and I got our own place.

We stopped to get the mail that packed his little box in the side hall of the apartment lobby. The weather was chillier here than in California. He fumbled with keys for an uncomfortable span of time before he managed to let us in the front room, where I was pleased to find warmth. Unfortunately, my lungs filled with open-beer-bottle stale air as I took in my first breath. With a quick glance around, I counted twenty-three empties on the table next to his recliner, mostly Schlitz but also six Budweiser, which I didn't hold against him.

"Junk mail, junk mail. I gave the maid the week off," he said before he hit rewind on his answering machine and it started automatically. Three messages played from the same breathy-voiced woman wondering where he was and when he was coming over.

He directed me to relax and make myself at home, which without a window to crack for fresh air was a foul impossibility. He changed into a gray sweat suit with a wide orange stripe and matching Adidas sneakers.

"Just got these,. Nice, huh? You know what Adidas stands for, right? All day I dream about sex. My pal Gary told me that, so I went and got me a pair. Jeez, I need to dirty them up some, though. Hate it when sneaks look this new."

His sweat suit hung on him oddly. It may have been that I was used to seeing him in his work uniform, but his lack of an athletic physique didn't help.

The drive to the hospital took us seven minutes, happily within walking distance from Mick's.

"Do you know what room she's in?" Mick asked as we climbed the concrete steps toward the entrance.

"I, uh, I forget."

"You forget? Really?"

"I don't think they ever told me her room number. They just, uh, they just took me to her last time."

"Oh, gotcha. Yeah, we can ask."

The nurse at the front desk looked up my mother's name and picked up the phone. She kept watching me with each call she made.

"I'll need you both to sign in here, and you can take a seat. Someone will be right with you."

We signed our names and joined an older couple in a waiting room with two horrific floral paintings with eleven white roses and one white daisy in one and the same in yellow in the other. The old woman cried against the old man's shoulder. I felt bad for people waiting who were forced to look at these ugly pictures, but I began hating that crying woman. I wanted her to stop and preferably immediately. Why would you cry in a waiting room?

Finally, a large woman with a head draped in braided hair arrived, looking for us.

"Hi, I'm Dr. Kessie Baldwin. I'm told you want to see Marie Velasco?"

Looking at her feet, Mick said, "I'm an old friend, Mick Washington, and this is her son, Abel. It's still visiting hours, right?"

"Certainly, visiting hours are from eight a.m. to seven p.m., but I'm afraid that won't matter. It's dinnertime for most in her ward, and Marie would need a special clearance to have a visitor."

"Abel's her son, though. That should mean he can see her anytime, right?"

"Abel, it's nice to meet you." She leaned in close, and I could smell children and something that reminded me of celery. "I can see you have your mother's eyes."

Heat rose in my cheeks.

"Please follow me," Dr. Baldwin directed.

We walked down several corridors until we came to another waiting room.

Dr. Baldwin put her fingers on my shoulder. "Abel, it's an unlucky fluke. I usually remember to get magazines for this room. It's not used very often, I'm afraid. Would you mind waiting here while I talk with Mick for a minute?"

I shook my head, knowing she would fill him in on my mom's status without me. I slapped the couch when I sat down, mainly because Dr. Baldwin had used the term *unlucky fluke*. A fluke originally meant a lucky stroke in billiards, and it still means a fortunate chance event. There are lucky flukes, but no unlucky ones, and she's a doctor, for Christ sakes. You'd think she'd know what *fluke* meant. I grew antsy within a few minutes, so I got up to walk around.

The hallway was only partially lit by long, fluorescent ceiling lighting, and the polished tiled floors reflected light from the window at the end of the hall. I stopped at an observation window and found a view into a spacious room with a collection of aging patients. Many were in wheelchairs parked in front of a TV. There weren't any Shegechiyo Izumis—he's the oldest authenticated centenarian, lived to 115—but most of them looked pretty old, much older than Mom must be, at any rate. Numbers tugged at me; the calculations for what I saw were irregular at best. A woman stood by a window; she had long, white hair, and one would think she'd want to watch what was happening outside, but she stared at a fire extinguisher encased in glass. She twisted her hair around her finger and watched it for longer than anyone could find it interesting.

I'd visited Mom on three separate occasions in the rehab hospitals with Uncle Evert. There were plenty of asymmetrical people, many unpleasant smells, but not many old people, and none that stared at fire extinguishers.

"Here you are," Dr. Baldwin said as she and Mick joined me at the window several minutes later.

"You spooked us for a minute," Mick explained.

"Let's go back to the room I asked you to wait in, shall we?"

We walked back, and they sat opposite me.

"Abel, I've explained the situation to Mick. I must tell you, I'm not crazy how this visit has come about, and you should have contacted the hospital about it, but under the circumstances I've agreed to let you see her. Mick thinks you'll do fine, and I believe it might be a good experience and help you understand why this won't work in the future. That said, would you like to see her now?"

I nodded slowly, worried why it wouldn't work. Did she mean this couldn't happen again?

Mick put his arm around my shoulder, and we walked down the hall together. We stopped at the end of the corridor, Room 112. Through the window in the door, a woman in light-green pajamas who looked like she could be my mom sat on the edge of a bed.

Mick removed his arm from around my shoulder, and Dr. Baldwin turned to me.

"Mick seemed to think you'd visited with your mother here before, but we know that's not true, right?"

I nodded.

"You know your mother's been ill for a long time, right?"

I nodded again.

Dr. Baldwin turned to the door and watched Mom.

Mom sat staring like the fire-extinguisher woman, but her gaze rested on the heating vents.

Dr. Baldwin turned to me and put her hand on my shoulder, and I backed away. "She's OK, Abel, or at least she's physically very healthy. Her mind is just not what we'd like. And as you might know already, the damage she has done to herself is irreversible. She never shows discomfort or pain, but she'll never return to the way she once was."

"Don't worry, guy." Mick patted my back.

Dr. Baldwin led us into the room. I followed the pattern of the floor tiles until I could see my mother's legs and the edge of the bed blanket.

Dr. Baldwin put her hand on my shoulder again. "Abel, you can say hello if you like."

I looked up to see my mother. So close, so real. The last time I saw her, she had much shorter hair with more curl. Those were her eyes, but they didn't shine as they did in my mind.

Dr. Baldwin's voice broke the quiet after a minute. "Hello, Marie, good to see you today. I brought someone with me. This is your son, Abel."

Mom didn't stir. Her focus shifted to my arm. I stood motionless, watching her face until the urge overcame me, and I bent over to put my arms around her neck. Her hair smelled mildly of strawberry shampoo. I kept hugging her, hoping with everything I had she would hug me back. Her arms failed to move.

The tears started and kept coming until Dr. Baldwin gently took me from her shoulders and held me until I stopped. I wiped my eyes and nose on my sleeve. I looked to see my mother's reaction, but her face was pillowy and dull. If only the strain I exerted in every sinew and bone to urge her eyes to look up at mine would work, but it didn't. My calculations for this moment had proven wrong. After a few minutes, I felt Dr. Baldwin's arm around my shoulders, turning me.

We walked from the room, and Dr. Baldwin took my hand in hers. I took a final glance through the glass as an orderly wheeled covered dinners past us. I counted 379 tiles before we arrived at Dr. Baldwin's office.

"Please have a seat. I'll be right back." She left quickly.

A WHOLE LOT

I sat in a chair draped with brightly colored patterned cloth. Mick sat next to me.

"You OK?" Mick asked.

I looked at my knees.

"I guess we can just wait till the doctor gets back. Sorry, Abel. I didn't figure she was here 'cause of those drugs back when we were all still together. I thought your mom had a broken leg or something. It's—I just didn't know."

I kept quiet, and we waited a few more minutes before Dr. Baldwin returned.

"Quite an experience for you, I guess?" Dr. Baldwin asked handing me a can of 7 Up and one to Mick.

Mick looked at her until I nodded and opened his can. The 7-Up was too cold to keep holding, so I put it on her desk unopened and wiped the moisture from my fingertips.

"Abel, I have to ask you some questions now, OK?" She sat down behind her desk and picked up a pen. "I've spoken with one of the administrators that work here, and they've informed me about a call from you they had a few days ago and that the police were inquiring about you. Do you know that people are looking for you, Abel?"

I nodded and looked at the pictures of her children hanging behind her.

"Do you want to talk about what's going on now?"

I shook my head.

"Well, there are people you're going to have to talk with, and they might not listen the way I can. I can help you, Abel, but you'll have to let me."

She looked at Mick.

"Mick tells me you were in California, that he rode with you out and then brought you back here. Is that true?"

I nodded.

"But I didn't take him out with me. He was on his own," Mick added.

"I understand, don't worry."

"Abel, you were on your own on the train when you travelled to California, is that correct?"

I nodded.

Dr. Baldwin's questioning continued until she got most of the story from me. I told her about Pigpie being the one who pushed Shelly, about seeing Mister Scratch dead, and about my friends trying to help because they knew all about Pigpie. The calculations from her responses suggested Dr. Baldwin understood, and she gave me her word she'd tell the police and anyone that asked what I said and how she thought it was the truth. It all felt somewhat fixed by the end of talking with her, but I didn't know where or how I'd go from here. All I really wanted now was a peanut-butter-and-jelly sandwich and a library.

CHAPTER THIRTY-ONE

Paul Erdős's Shoes

7.1.39-1.17!

I stayed with Mick until my exoneration and Pigpie's culpability and confinement were established. It didn't take long since I received the wrong information from Hank. Shelly didn't die, although sadly her baby did. A lawyer came to take my statement, and apparently Shelly's testimony and my contesting to its truth proved the case. No one ever asked about my beating up Pigpie, well, except the therapists.

The group home they placed me with was crowded with other boys about my age and younger. I'd forgotten the nuances of these homes: the forced comradeship, everyone going through the same difficulties, seeking normalcy and their own space in the overcrowded conditions. I didn't hate it as much as living with Pigpie, but the thought of staying here until another foster home became available wasn't attractive. The interviews with the therapists and legal professionals about what happened with Pigpie and Shelly happily ended in a few weeks and everything slowed into a bland routine of psychologists, regimented meals, reading, and TV, with the occasional visit from the Limones.

For a brief time, I thought they might offer to take me in. There was a cautious tone in every conversation I had with them that suggested they were feeling things out. Maddy's greetings were always extremely warm and her good-byes were tearful, but I understood it wasn't to be when Dr. Limone talked of an impending romantic vacation and a planned trip back to England this coming summer. The reading materials he provided regularly left me enormously pleased, in any case. I especially enjoyed the many science magazines with good articles on all the recent computer developments. I'd love to have had access to a computer to run the Pierson code program again. I had many tests I'd wanted to process since Berkeley.

    I took Dr. Limone's advice and shared my health and education files with the therapists. Everyone was intensely concerned that my history and recent experiences might *create long term negative effects in my emotional state*. The visits were mild compared to some of my past sessions, but it felt an awful lot like I was stuck in an old nightmare full of clinical routines I wasn't interested in. Even though I gave plenty of evidence that working with Dr. Kohn would be a good idea, they hadn't arranged schooling at Princeton or elsewhere because of viewing me as being ill. It's difficult to change their minds about such things. During a review of my research on the Pierson code, they said I might be having difficulty understanding matters of faith due to my *prodigious savant syndrome*, which apparently is a bit related to autism, only not as disabling but "may skew my emotions and comprehension." I let them describe me however they liked since they were obviously not listening to me. I still brought up Dr. Kohn and Ken Ribet to help provoke thoughts of their involvement.

    Ten weeks of communal living passed with frustration and continued elbowing for space when the home director, Mr. Kimbels, asked me to visit his office.

    "Good afternoon, Abel, please come in."

    I took a seat in a chair that I had to move, since it was far too close to Mr. Kimbels.

    "It's been a pleasure to have you with us, but as you're probably aware, we are past our housing capacity at the moment. That being the case, we've decided to move you to a more-permanent living situation that doesn't entail waiting for a new foster home. From our conversations, you've enjoyed the homes they placed you in previous to your aunt's, but we think you need a bit more stability than any home might offer just now . . ."

The excited tone in his voice as he spoke about the new *opportunity* being a boon seemed exaggerated. The living situation he detailed meant my moving into the city.

"This great decision is based on all consulted parties, and we agree you will no doubt enjoy Brooklyn. It's where I grew up, so I should know."

I placed repeating fractions across his brow and divided the lower part of his face into equal parts, considered volumes for a few moments, and ignored as best I could the chatter about the many splendors of his favorite borough.

"Unlike placing you in another foster home, St. Vincent's will give you the potential to earn a little money and maybe even find you a family interested in adoption."

He continued to tout the St. Vincent's Home for Boys as a great institution, but I could only focus on how there would never be a couple who'd want to adopt me. I'd be stuck in a group setting until I was old enough to live on my own. I'd lived in several group homes in St. Louis, then with the Dersteins, with the Chungs, with the Melvilles, and finally in Hell with my aunt. Living at St. Vincent's would be extending my jail time by four or five years—I immediately began to make different plans.

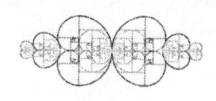

Two nights later, I thieved a few provisions including several canned goods (but not a can opener, unfortunately) and caught the ten-forty bus to the Port Authority bus terminal in New York City.

My spirits were lifted by the light, marching rhythm drummed on a bucket by a performer in a blue-knit cap as I exited the building. The beat helped calm me, gave me something to count as I walked to the first restaurant I saw. I used the last of my funds to purchase some egg rolls from Fu's all-night Chinese food restaurant. Mom's spirit was with me that first night, and I was dreaming of her when the waitress woke me the next morning and told me I must leave.

On the street, in the daylight, I knew my new life would be like soda bubbles, like cake icing, like pizza cheese. I'd skim the great surface and study everything worthwhile. Performers filled practically every street corner and park in New York City, and I had no problems earning enough for the train fares. That first week on my own was much easier than I'd imagined, even with the rain. During the day, I played Shelly's merchandise-return game at various stores instead of the outdoor fortune-telling that I'd planned and rode the subway to the public library. It took me no time to learn about life on the streets and the cheap hotels closest to libraries in any of the cities I visited. Loneliness was a minor struggle, but an occasional phone call to Hank helped quell it, and I've visited with him at the home now, twice. On both visits, he's tried to figure out where I'm staying. I haven't shared the full truth yet.

During my first visit, Hank told of Will's successes in California and that Mi asked about me. On both visits, he's also introduced me as his grandson to the new friends who live with him. I wore a baseball cap and my new sweat jacket so nobody in town would ever recognize me, plus I hadn't had my hair cut in months

Nebraska is very attractive. It was the eleventh state I visited once I slipped on Erdös's shoes and began my peripatetic lifestyle, sans the ability to visit other mathematicians for fear it would tip off authorities to my whereabouts. I knew when I turned eighteen, possibly seventeen even, all the real math collaborations could start, but until then I'd practice the travelling that Erdös must've been a master of and correspond anonymously by mail with mathematicians of interest. I love movies yet think that if given a choice I'd take the views from a train over any Academy winners. Nebraska is well deserved of being called the Flat Plains State and not at all as boring as one might imagine from that epithet. I'd known about the Bennett Martin Public Library in Lincoln because of its extensive science collection written about in *OMNI Magazine* from March 1980. Most of my choices of destinations are directed by such matters. There are great many collections to be explored. I wanted a long-term plan of study and couldn't craft it until I visited as many worthy American libraries as I could, to know exactly what is what and where.

At Bennett Martin's after continuing my search for Decartes's robot, Francine, and coming up empty, I found a fascinating biography on Leonard Euler. Euler was a man said to be able to calculate as well as others breathe—the most prolific Swiss scientist ever. He wasn't only extremely prolific in math but also with generating offspring. He fathered thirteen children. The biography included an account of the fictitious story of a quarrel with the philosopher Denis Diderot. The legend states that urged by Catherine the Great, Empress of Russia, to stop Diderot from spreading his atheism, Euler argued that God existed because $\frac{a+b^n}{n} = x$. The biography also contained other algebraic formulae Euler published to prove God's existence. None of them was satisfactory on its own to prove any transcendent notion, at least not in any apparent fashion.

Euler's formulae started me seriously considering the Pierson code again. I'd thought of it regularly since leaving California, but I hadn't had much luck locating a computer that could run the program like the one in Berkeley. I called Bergit to feel her out, but she immediately mentioned that Dr. Kohn and others had been looking for me, and I knew they'd turn me in so Bergit and Princeton were out. It wasn't until I met a computer salesman named Wayne Wenzlaff that I had access to an adequate system again. I read about Wayne in a Minneapolis front-page article titled *The Dawning of the Computer Age*, and his computer store was easy enough to get to.

    He was very helpful with my request but didn't know what to do when I ran the code for the first time, explaining what it could do. His numbers reminded me of Heedy's at the Pierson house when she told me to get out. He didn't kick me out, however.

    For fun, I typed in his name but found nothing. Then I tried my own name and it appeared in the fifth book, the book of Deuteronomy, in chapter thirteen. More shocking than that was the fact that the word *"codE"* connected to my name via the *e* of AbEl, and *transLator* connected diagonally via the *L* of VeLasco. I didn't tell Wayne about it when it quickly became obvious to me. He was too busy on the phone with someone to care, but the revelation of my action being foretold was a bit frightening at first. It could certainly be attributed to a main reason why I sought to apply Euler's formulae to the code. Something that could strengthen it and provide an even-greater clarity to what God might be conveying.

    No doubt Wayne was shocked when I deleted the program from his system and promptly left while he was still on the phone, his third call as I worked on the program. He yelled after me as I walked out, but I don't think he understood that I knew the last call was to a newspaper reporter.

    I reworked the code for nearly a month and finally got a chance to apply it to the program. I was thrilled to find the New York City Public Library recently equipped with a computer system powerful enough to test it out. I discovered faults in the code that neither Euler's nor any additional formulae could assist or repair.

After that, I started reading the Bible itself. I tried a few different versions to be sure, but there was no way in any of them that God was using math as a guide in it, even in the original Hebrew. You'd think He'd have taken the time to deliver more math-appropriate holy discussion. Where is the conversation about the golden mean phi and its appearance so often in nature? Where is the conversation about that accursed infinity as it approaches pi? In I Kings 7:23-26, it basically says pi equals three— three! Not even a foreshortened 3.14159! Pi's greatness is so easily a way to connect the majesty of a transcendent force to our lives, and the Old Testament, or Torah, gets it wrong. The final straw for me was when I read that the Torah's text has changed many times over the centuries and the one Richard Pierson used wasn't definitive.

I wrote Dr. Rips about what I discovered, beginning with the identification of my name along with code and translator, and ended the letter with a full explanation of the code's failings. Today, I received a letter back at my PO Box in NYC.

September 23, 1983

Dear Abel,

Greetings, dear Abel. It was a delight to receive further correspondence from you, and as requested, I shared your findings with Michael and Doron. We are all astounded by your improvements, some of us more than others, I'm afraid.

I believe Doron might continue correspondence with you on the matter. I'm certain you can expect a letter from him soon. He is a great believer in this research and thinks you should continue to work toward perfecting it.

As it stands, of our group, I'm the only one who is in full agreement with you on its capabilities, or insufficiency, I should say. I may side with the Pythagoreans that mathematics is god but have yet to be convinced it is clearly encoded in any of the great texts. Your work and what I know from our research confirm that all attempts to extract messages from Torah or Bible codes are futile and of no value beyond the math.

But thank you so very much for your help, and please do stay in touch.

Sincerely,

Eliyahu Rips
Jerusalem, Israel

After his letter, I pursued it a bit further. The final straw popped out of the whale spout when I found the code worked on any decent-size text. I have put it aside and pushed on, leaving whatever Richard Pierson was seeking, if it was more than what I'd accomplished, in the realm of the unknowable.

At Grand Central Station on Thursday, November 10, 1983, I spent St. Martin's Day Eve celebrating by watching how others spent theirs. I sat near the entrance to Gate One. A man in a white lab coat talked sternly with a teenage boy carrying a small suitcase but then hugged him tightly. I counted thirteen seconds pass until they let each other go. Who else might document these events if not for me? How many windows will be opened today that no one will look out? It's essential that I codify it all for future formulae; no doubt it will be of some use. On occasion, I saw people who I thought were someone I knew, and quite often it was a boy who'd remind me of Russell.

Just like this moment, right now, a boy who easily could have been Russell was walking toward me. He wouldn't look me in the eyes, no matter how hard I stared

at him. He makes the thirty-seventh Russell look-alike I've seen, but then there are a lot of skinny boys with messy black hair in cities everywhere. I wondered if Russell saw doctors regularly for his battered brain, if he'd ever fully recover, and what he would possibly dream of becoming in life. I placed my fingers at my temples and tried sending the boy who walked past me a mental hello, just for fun.

ABOUT THE AUTHOR:

Bradley worked as a toy designer for K'nex Industries, as an IT manager for Pearl S. Buck International, and is currently a Director of IT for a child-focused non-profit. He keeps bees, raises chickens and two lovely girls with his wife in Chester County, Pennsylvania. His short writings can be found in the compilation *Words to Music* and at the Year Zero collective.

Author's note:
Any resemblance to persons living or dead should be pretty obvious to those in the know, especially where I used their real names. All events and information described herein seem real to me but a good deal of them are just baloney I made up, except on occasion where they are not.
I'm incredibly pleased you have read my novel. Thank you! It's been a long road from start to getting your eyes on it. Please, if you enjoyed reading it, annoy a friend until they buy a copy, or even better leave a breathtaking review on Amazon.com.

I'd love to hear from you: bwind3@gmail.com

To read more or see some of my visual work, please visit: www.bradleywind.com